LOVE SONG

Sarah was seventeen; Farrel was thirty. Sarah was Jewish; Farrel was Protestant. She was a southerner; he was a northerner. But when they met and fell in love nothing seemed to matter. He was everything Sarah wanted in a husband—or so she thought. If only she would have taken him seriously when he told her that his work was the most important thing in his life . . .

TROLLEY SONG

Electric streetcars—or trolleys as some people called them—were Farrel's strongest passion, the pulse beat of his life. It was a whole new phase in the development of America and he had started it all. If only Sarah could share in his glory! He did love her, but what she wanted he was unable to give—and what he gave just wasn't enough . . .

HEART SONG

When George looked at Sarah he felt a special yearning and desire. She needed to be loved and cherished and he couldn't understand how Farrel could neglect her so. If only she belonged to me, he thought. But that was utter madness, a dream that could never be fulfilled. The one woman he longed for was another man's wife—a man who he could never betray . . .

BLAZING CIVIL WAR SAGAS!

NEW ORLEANS (826, $3.50)
by Miriam Pace
Three sisters, sharing the same passions and dreams, face very different fates—adultery, adventure, patriotism—with the onset of the civil war.

MEMPHIS (807, $2.95)
by Shana Clermont
When Southern belle Melanie Beresford met Yankee officer Blake Townsend, she never dreamed she'd fall in love with the enemy! While the Civil War rages, so does Melanie's passion—does she dare risk loyalty for love?

VICKSBURG (789, $2.95)
by John T. Foster
Palatial Lightfoot Landing burns to the ground, the nation erupts in a bitter war, homeless Nora Lightfoot flees to Vicksburg. In peacetime, she had known love and passion—and Nora is determined to survive the war and find true love again. . . .

RICHMOND #1: THE FLAME (654, $2.75)
by Elizabeth Fritch
Amidst the rage and confusion of the Civil War, Melissa Armstrong fights a personal battle for an ominous goal: to maintain loyalty to her family—without losing the one man she loves!

RICHMOND #2: THE FIRE (679, $2.75)
by Elizabeth Fritch
Now, in Richmond, Melissa knows a passionate love for a Cavalry lieutenant who helps her forget the only home she's known. If only she could forget that their destinies lie on opposite sides of the flag!

RICHMOND #3: THE EMBERS (716, $2.95)
by Elizabeth Fritch
If time could heal a nation stained with the death and blood of the Civil War, perhaps Melissa's heart would mend one day also. But she never really believes it—until she rediscovers love.

Available wherever paperbacks are sold, or order direct from the Publisher. Send cover price plus 50¢ per copy for mailing and handling to Zebra Books, 475 Park Avenue South, New York, N.Y. 10016. DO NOT SEND CASH.

TROLLEY SONG

BY SHEILA
RAESCHILD

ZEBRA BOOKS
KENSINGTON PUBLISHING CORP.

ZEBRA BOOKS

are published by

KENSINGTON PUBLISHING CORP.
475 Park Avenue South
New York, N.Y. 10016

Printed in the United States of America

FRANK JULIAN SPRAGUE (1857–1934)

Frank Julian Sprague, an innovator and electrical genius, was a pioneer in electric equipment. He built the motor which made streetcars a viable reality, beginning with the opening of the Richmond line in 1888. He developed the electric elevator motor which led to the modern world of skyscrapers. He transformed the elevated railways by discarding the limiting locomotive principle and designing an electrified multiple-unit control system.

Frank Julian Sprague's brilliant mind and his Richmond streetcar system provided the inspiration for Trolley Song which is, otherwise, purely fictional.

One

September 12, 1888

Mr. and Mrs. Farrel Hurstwood sat in silence listening to the clacking of the train along the track. They each heard different messages in the hypnotic sound. Less than two weeks after their wedding, Sarah and Farrel were already beginning to realize just how different those messages were.

The train rattled on into the dusk. Sarah smoothed the skirt of her fawn-colored traveling suit, fussed with the lacy bow of her white silk shirt. Her hands fluttered about as though they were butterflies. Sarah touched the brooch at her throat, a coral cameo with a woman's head etched on it surrounded by a row of seed pearls, a wedding present from her parents. Farrel shifted uneasily in his seat and Sarah realized that her fidgeting might be annoying him. Self-consciously, she folded her hands in her lap and stared out the

7

window at the unrolling world. She spotted a house like the one she'd grown up in, a long narrow house with a large Monticello window which dominated its front. It was hard for her to imagine that she wasn't going back to her parents' home. Instead she would be moving into a strange new house with a strange man—this stranger, her husband.

My husband, she repeated to herself. She closed her eyes and the feel of his hands moving under her night dress rushed back at her. Hot breath had blown at the wispy strawberry-blond curls on her neck, as Farrel had whispered through his full lips, their sensuality only slightly masked by his clipped mustache, "Relax, Sarah. Just try to relax, my dear."

He loomed above her, a shadowy shape in the shadowed room. She could just barely make out the intense look on his face, the two deep lines that formed so frequently between his heavy black eyebrows. She touched the hollow place beneath his high cheekbones; he was too thin really, she knew, but his angular lanky body excited her. Then she felt his weight on her; felt the shock as he entered her. He moved inside her in a rhythm not unlike the rhythm of a train. Her heart began to pound at the memory and she opened her eyes languorously. She could feel a slow flush rise in her cheeks, so she leaned her head against the cool glass of the train window.

It had been scary at first, she had to admit. The first few times it had even hurt her. But then she began to look forward to his frequent urging, to yearn for more of those new kisses and touches. She couldn't be so forward as to tell him so, but Sarah had begun to anticipate eagerly their time in bed. She held herself ready for his soft-voiced invitation: "Sarah?"

"Sarah," he said now from the seat beside her. "Yes." She felt as though he could read her thoughts. Perhaps he even felt the same way, had the same thoughts. They were in a private car, after all. Although she was shy being on a public train, if he wanted her she would say yes. It was her duty to her husband, she reminded herself. She leaned toward him eagerly and rested her hand softly on his arm.

"It's the accident!" he burst out. "I can't stop thinking about that damned accident! If those rails had been laid right as I had ordered, that train couldn't have derailed, I feel sure. It would have taken a mountain of dynamite even to harm the rails, in fact. Goddamn it all to hell!"

"Mr. Hurstwood!" Sarah felt assaulted by both his words and his violent anger. He had never used such foul language around her. Her father would most certainly never have done so. She said primly, "Father always told me, 'Cursing is a sign of an inadequate vocabulary.'"

"For Christ's sake, Sarah, that's not the point. Besides, you're not a child anymore, you're my wife. Who cares what your father says?"

Tears blurred her eyes. She turned blindly to the window, but the world outside appeared smudged like a watercolor left out in the rain. Abruptly, Farrel stood up. He turned his back on his

9

miserable wife huddled on the far side of the seat. Anchoring his hands on both sides of his waist, he stretched his back from side to side. His gold watch chain, fastened from one pocket to another of his gray serge vest, made a golden arc across his flat stomach. He slipped into his pin-striped jacket and buttoned it neatly. Still ignoring Sarah, he checked in the mirror to make sure that his oiled black hair remained neatly parted in the middle. He slicked it down again for good measure.

"I'm going for a smoke," he announced in a flat voice. He directed his words up at the lazily turning fan overhead. Sarah sniffled, but didn't answer. She made herself into a statue until she heard the compartment door click shut behind him. Then she let the tears flow. She threw herself across the length of the seat in luxurious anguish. He doesn't understand me, she sobbed, with the raw stab of pain that comes when that thought enters a woman's mind for the first time.

Maybe my parents were right, she thought with a pang. They'd warned her over and over that the differences were too many and too great. She listed them now in her mind. First of all, she was only seventeen, whereas Farrel was already a man of thirty. Second, she was a new American—her parents had escaped with her from Russia only seven years ago although she prided herself on not having an accent, on not seeming "foreign"; while Farrel's family, having come from England with the early settlers, traced their history in this country back several generations. The differences went on and on. They seemed to multiply as she allowed herself to think about them in her unhappiness. His family was much richer than hers, of course; that was a big one, though she didn't believe money was all that important. Maybe that was the reason Farrel's mother disapproved of the marriage, a marriage she probably felt was beneath her son's station in life.

Another big difference in Sarah's mind was that Farrel was a northerner, a Yankee. He'd lived his whole life above the Mason-Dixon line. She, on the other hand, delighted in being a southerner, part of that wonderful tradition, living in what had been the capital of the Confederacy during the war. Almost all the history she'd learned in school was about the Civil War and how glorious the southern cause had been. No dishonor in defeat, she quoted to herself, a motto from some old school text. The words sent a shiver straight through her. If they applied to her city, those words, to her beloved Richmond, Virginia, could they not also apply to her life, to her marriage?

She hadn't yet allowed herself to think about the biggest difference of all: the fact that her family had fled Russia because of the pogroms, because of the persecution of the Jews, because they were Jews. While Farrel was one of the others, the non-circumcised, the rulers of the world, the Christians. Sarah had the sinking feeling that her being Jewish was the real reason for his mother's disapproval of the marriage. Farrel was some sort of Protestant, though Sarah always forgot which kind. Oh, yes, she reminded herself, he was an Anglican. She remembered because it sounded

11

like angels and she liked to think of angels fluttering invisibly just above her head. Angels who would protect her from harm. Tears rose in her eyes again, but she knew they wouldn't last. She'd just about cried herself out. No use, she told herself, crying over spilled milk. Another motto. It seemed that was all her schooling had given her to help her deal with life's problems: a collection of mottoes.

Farrel sat in the club car swirling the ice in his Scotch. A blue trail of smoke coiled its way up from the cigar between his fingers. Sabotage, he thought, it must be sabotage. Could Rankin be involved? My foreman? My friend? No, I won't believe it. Farrel sipped at his drink. At least not without proof. But Rankin was solely in charge of those tracks. Every mile of track, every foot. Farrel dragged at his cigar, then blew the smoke into a hazy curtain in front of his face. Sabotage, damn it! He gulped the rest of his drink down in one fast motion and signaled for another. Damn it, he cursed again.

He made a conscious effort to put the accident out of his mind. No sense playing it over and over like a popular roll on a player piano. Think of something else, he commanded himself, and almost at once he drifted back to that day seven months ago when the first big streetcar line in America had started its operations. His line: the Richmond Electric Street Railway! The first in America, he thought proudly. He remembered that day so vividly that he could still see the

12

banners strung across the streets, the throngs of people lined up along the curbs to get their turn at a ride, the six streetcars which stood ready, polished, and gleaming. Twelve miles of track with some of it steeper than a ten-percent grade, by God. No one had believed it possible—not even Tom Edison, Farrel's old boss, who had scoffed at the idea of electric streetcars as nothing more than a mere novelty. That was why Farrel had left Edison. Farrel believed completely in every application of electricity. He'd found backers in Virginia and that had decided his location, his destiny. Finally, after more problems than he'd ever imagined—did one ever foresee them all?—on February 2, 1888 he'd set the first car in motion.

He himself played the part of the motorman during that first run. He could still feel the control in his hand. He pictured the open car with its wooden seats and benches, with its leather straps that hung down from overhead brass bars so people could stand when the seats were full and sway with the car's movements without falling. That first day saw those straps put to good use. Each car started off packed with townspeople trying out the new toy. There was no charge to the public, of course. Farrel knew that if people were going to accept these electric streetcars they would have to be comfortable with them. They couldn't feel awkward or afraid, and he'd figured a holiday of riding them for fun would be just the thing to win the folks over. He'd been right, too. In a matter of months, people were using the streetcars instead of their buggies, instead of the old horse-drawn cars, instead of their feet. Even to go short distances, they'd jump aboard the streetcars. Richmond's streetcar system quickly became a point of civic pride too. The Richmond community could show the rest of the world how advanced and modern the new South really was.

At the end of that most successful day in his life, Farrel had proposed to Sarah. They hadn't known each other long, but he'd always made rapid decisions. When he saw what he wanted, he went after it. So far he'd always gotten what he went after.

That day he'd taken Sarah for a private ride after the others had left. Halfway through the route, he'd stopped the car. The pale yellow lamp used to light the tracks ahead of the car also cast a kind of halo around the two riders as Farrel began his prepared speech. He was a rational man and proud of it. He couldn't imagine leaving anything as important as convincing Sarah to leave her family and marry him up to the whims of whatever words entered his mind at the moment.

"Sarah Seewald," he had said, "I wanted you to share this special day with me because it marks the true beginning of my commercial success in the same way that I believe meeting you marked the beginning of my personal happiness. Will you marry me so we can share our lives?"

How young and pure she was. He remembered how she'd blushed and stammered that he'd have to ask her father's permission, but her eyes had already given him the answer he'd wanted. Their pupils had widened until her eyes had become deep black pools in which he could have drowned. He'd leaned over then and pressed his lips to hers and she hadn't resisted. It was their first kiss.

Remembering that moment, Farrel felt remorse over the way he'd stormed out of the compartment leaving his weeping bride. He stood, stubbed out his cigar, and paid for his drinks.

As he rocked his way back down the aisle toward his wife, the train's motion began to calm him. He loved the feel of it under his feet, the jolt in his knees and hips, the rhythm which coursed through his body. Yes, he was a train man by nature, that was certain. He'd always been one, in fact. Every locomotive that traveled on tracks appealed to him, but especially streetcars, of course. Streetcars were the great love of his life. He slid the door open to join his new wife in their compartment. A composed Sarah gazed up at him with love in her gray-green eyes.

"Welcome back," she said. She patted the seat beside her in invitation.

Farrel sat down and took Sarah in his arms. He kissed her deeply, feeling the lovely fullness of her body pressed against him. As he embraced her, he realized that he must try once again to explain what troubled him so about the accident. She was his wife, after all, and she deserved an explanation. Moreover, if they were to share a life she would just have to understand his feelings about his streetcars.

"I'm sorry I got so upset, Sarah," he began, "but this accident business is driving me crazy. I can hardly think of anything else. I know how disappointed you must be to have our honeymoon end this way and I'm truly sorry." He paused a moment, then went on. "Last night I woke from a dream where I saw it all happen right before my eyes. The streetcar rounded Main Street. It was going too fast. There was a flash. Everything turned upside down and then there were people screaming and blood. Oh my God!"

Farrel let his head sink down to Sarah's shoulder. She brought her fingertips to his smooth black hair in an effort to ease his pain.

"It mightn't have been that way, Farrel dear. You don't know the details yet. You'll have to wait till we get back to find out the real story. Besides, in any case, none of it's your fault. I'm sure of that, darling."

He raised his head and his dark eyes flashed at her alarmingly. She hasn't understood any of it, he thought.

"People are hurt. Maybe dying. Because of *my* streetcar. Of course it's my fault!" He pulled away from her on the seat.

"Darling, please don't fret yourself so." He frightened her.

"You know, Sarah," he said trying to speak calmly, his teeth clenched against his anger, "you must understand this right now. Streetcars mean everything to me! They've been my life—up until I met you," he added, a bit too late to escape her notice. "And now this. An accident on my own streetcar line barely eight months after it begins operation. I feel responsible and I will be held responsible, make no mistake about that."

16

She looked at his hurt, bewildered face and put aside her own worries about the new house and her unknown life. She moved closer to him and leaned against his chest. He took her into his arms again. As the train rocked from side to side they remained locked together. Though Farrel felt vaguely comforted, he continued to stare straight ahead at nothing.

The scene began to form again in his mind's eye, the scene that had taken place days earlier and then had been reported to him in an urgent message: Car derailed. Cause undetermined. Two seriously injured. Come at once.

As they sat together now, night took the world into its fist and squeezed the light out of it. Farrel felt that the darkness reflected the condition of his soul. Sarah, who stared out the window, saw only an occasional patch of land dimly lit by a lantern outside a house they were rushing past. Mostly she watched the static portrait of herself which was reflected off the glass. Her features were just as they had been before her marriage, she thought, handsome in their way, but too plain, too obvious. She had hoped that marriage would soften them and add a note of mystery. Perhaps it was too soon to hope for such a change. She regarded her large wide-set eyes, her bold nose, and the lips which she had always considered a trifle too full. Behind her, she saw the shape of a man who cast his shadow over her. She was seventeen and newly married, but still she knew a sudden sorrow such as she had only felt when the first birds began to fly south in the fall. Something had ended for her, she realized.

Ended far too soon.

After a while, the porter came in to make up their beds, so Farrel and Sarah went to the dining car to eat a supper neither of them had any appetite for. They hardly spoke as they struggled to eat their roasted chicken with its mandatory accompaniment of corn-bread dressing and gravy. Sarah stabbed at a salad that looked as wilted as she felt. Both the Hurstwoods were grateful when the waiter finally came to clear their plates away.

"Coffee, folks?" he asked.

"Oh, yes, please," Sarah answered. Farrel simply made a brusque movement with his head which the waiter seemed to understand, since he returned only moments later with a silver coffee pot from which he poured them each a steaming cup of coffee. Then he placed the pot neatly between them. While doing this, he'd managed a most exquisite balancing act required of him by the fact that the train, just at the time he began to pour, made a huge horseshoe turn which produced quite a number of jolts and bumps.

When the waiter moved off down the aisle, Sarah remarked on his skill. Farrel smiled at her innocence. He'd almost forgotten that she'd never been on a train before their honeymoon journey.

"Yes, I suppose it is an art," he answered. "It's a feeling you get into your legs for the way the train is about to move. Almost as though you become a part of the train itself."

Sarah, who stumbled from side to side every time she tried to walk anywhere on the train, could understand what he was trying to say, but she

18

couldn't imagine ever coming to feel that much a part of any machine. Nonetheless, when they'd finished their coffee and were returning to their compartment, she tried to walk a straight middle path down the aisle and did feel she'd succeeded somewhat better than before.

The meal had done little to ease the tension that charged the air between the Hurstwoods. Sarah and Farrel took turns in the small bath where they changed into their night clothes. Then they went to their narrow individual beds and lay chastely apart in the dark as much to avoid the need for speech as out of any sense of tiredness. For the longest time, in fact, Sarah lay wide awake, staring into the dark, unable to escape into sleep. The occasional wail the train emitted sent shivers up and down her spine. This would not do, she told herself, as she resolutely turned her thoughts back in time to a happier day, to her wedding day. Even there she could not completely avoid the feelings of tension.

Her parents, who had reluctantly given their permission for the marriage, had felt strongly that without a Jewish ceremony their daughter would not be truly married. Farrel, on the other hand, felt that a large church wedding with a catered reception was absolutely necessary in order to improve his acceptance by the Richmond social order. It was political wisdom, he insisted. Sarah hadn't been completely easy with those terms in relation to her wedding. It now seemed to Sarah that the way they'd resolved the conflict would typify their lives: unhappily compromised, she labeled it.

Her parents had arranged for a small Jewish ceremony to take place in their backyard only an hour before the scheduled church wedding. The Seewalds explained the significance of each custom to Farrel and Sarah. They set up a *huppah,* the traditional marriage canopy held up by poles at the four corners, and explained that it was an ancient custom as was the tradition of marrying out of doors to make sure that "God should bless the union with as many children as there are stars in the heaven." The sky, however, covers everyone alike, so the *huppah's* purpose is to make a special little room just for the bride and groom.

Sarah's mother explained so much to her about getting married Jewishly that Sarah, for the first time since her babyhood in Russia, began to feel Jewish. It was ironic, she realized, that she should begin to feel Jewish just as she was about to marry a Christian. Rachel told Sarah that she should fast before her wedding to insure that God would forgive any past sins at the start of this new life. Sarah, too nervous to eat anything that day anyway, found it easy to follow the custom.

When Farrel and she had stood under the *huppah* together, the *hazzan,* or officiating minister, who was in this case Sarah's father because as her mother had explained a layman is as good as a rabbi as long as the intentions are honorable, recited a beautiful verse. It had stayed in Sarah's mind and she recited it to herself now as she lay in bed in the dark train compartment:

"He who is strong above all else
He who is blessed above all else
He who is great above all else
May He bless the bridegroom and the bride."

Then they had each sipped wine from the same goblet since in Jewish tradition as Sarah's father had told them, "there is no joy without wine." Then the father's voice had risen in the achingly sweet Hebrew chanting which in English meant:

"Blessed art Thou, O Lord our God, King of the Universe, who makest Thy people Israel holy through Thy commandments and hast commanded us concerning marriages that are forbidden and those that are permitted when carried out under the canopy and with the sacred wedding ceremonies.

"Blessed art Thou, O Lord our God, King of the Universe, who makest Thy people Israel holy through this rite of the canopy and the sacred bond of marriage."

Sarah had hoped that her marriage was truly to be permitted by God. She remembered how Farrel had placed a plain gold band on her right index finger and with her father's coaching had said to her those most binding words: "Behold thou art consecrated unto me with this ring according to the law of Moses and Israel."

The final act, Farrel smashing the wine goblet under his heel, signified that as smashing a glass is an irrevocable act, so too is marriage which should last forever and ever. Then the parents and the two close friends who'd been invited to act as witnesses

21

shouted, *"Mazel tov!"* Everyone kissed and hugged and Sarah smiled and smiled and smiled. It made Sarah smile again now to remember.

The Christian ceremony that followed shortly thereafter was also impressive, of course, as was the elaborate reception during which Sarah felt sure she must have danced with every boy and man in Richmond, but it was the simple home ceremony which made Sarah feel truly married. She wondered how Farrel would compare the two experiences. Perhaps someday she'd feel comfortable enough with him to ask, she thought, as she drifted off to sleep.

Farrel, just across the narrow compartment a few feet away from Sarah, had also found his thoughts circling around the events that had occurred near to their marriage, but it wasn't the marriage itself upon which his mind focused. Rather, he felt himself drawn back to the terrible scene he'd had with his mother when he'd told her he was about to marry a Jewish girl, a pharmacist's daughter. Farrel's father, who would have been his ally he felt sure, had died when Farrel was fifteen. It wasn't that he'd died prematurely—he was seventy-three years old at the time—it was just that the elder Hurstwoods had had Farrel so late in their lives. He was their only child.

Farrel's mother, Phoebe Walmsley Hurstwood, was thirty years younger than her husband. Always a reserved woman, she had turned into an icicle of a woman after her husband's death. She had taken over her husband's wine-importing business and ran it with a hard hand and hard heart. She based every decision on profitability.

When Farrel, after college graduation, had chosen to become one of Edison's *Wunderkinds* and then, more recently, to start his own business, his mother had taken it as a personal rejection. If he didn't want to be a part of the family business concern, she reasoned, very well, but in that case she felt no obligation to supply him with funds. Money equaled love in her mind. If he wouldn't give the one—love—on her terms, then she wouldn't give the other—money—on his. He'd had to seek all his financing independently.

That had been all right with him, but as to this marriage issue, that was an entirely different matter! He could not accept that his mother seemed to view it, too, in terms of profitability. She expressed her horror at his plan in no uncertain terms.

"She's a nobody, Farrel. A pharmacist's daughter. Really! It will destroy your chances of success, this alliance. She has no social connections whatsoever and no breeding. A Jewess on top of everything else. Do you want to kill me, is that it? Why don't you just plunge a knife into my heart? It would be kinder."

"Stop, Mother," Farrel said. "It is my choice." He told himself to stay calm.

"No, I cannot give my permission. I absolutely forbid it!" Her eyes flared, challenging him.

He'd paced the length of the room as she had spoken, back and forth like a leopard in a cage.

"That's my final word," she repeated, "I forbid it!"

23

He told himself not to say words that he might regret later. He told himself to stop and think. He told himself . . . Then he'd exploded and nothing that he told himself made any difference.

"Don't you dare talk to me that way, Mother. Not ever again. I am a man, not a child, and I am not to be told what I may or may not do. Not to be forbidden!"

"Farrel," his mother broke in, using a tone that stopped him. They stood facing each other like fencers in the en garde position. "Please leave this house at once." .

A growl filled his throat. "I shall have a wedding invitation sent to you, madam, in case you should change your mind. I am having a house built for us in Richmond, Virginia where we shall make our home." He turned on his heel then marched toward the door, but before he reached it, his mother's voice filled the air.

"Richmond," she cackled. "Richmond, Virginia! I mean it's *nowhere,* you fool."

After that, he'd slammed the door and heard no more. Those were the last words his mother had spoken to him. They had remained indelibly clear in his mind during the months since then. She hadn't come to the wedding. She hadn't even sent a message. Neither a message, nor a present. He supposed that he was essentially an orphan now having neither father nor mother. Strange that it should cause him so much pain when he'd never felt really close to either parent. But to be alone like a bird with no nest . . . His thoughts began to spin in the slow and lazy circles that indicated he

was moving toward sleep. His mother's words . . .
the streetcar accident . . . you fool, she'd said . . .
two critically injured . . . asleep. Sleep.

"Richmond, Virginia," the conductor called as
he swayed down the aisle past their car door.
"Richmond next. Half-hour stop."

Two

It was midday and Sarah had had her things gathered together for more than an hour, but still she felt a rush of nervousness at the conductor's call.

"Hurry, Mr. Hurstwood," she urged. "We're here."

She picked up her bag of handwork—she had been working a motto to frame over their back-parlor mantel—her small copper-beaded purse, and the copy of Mrs. Browning's love sonnets which her mother had given her for the honeymoon journey, only to discover that she had forgotten to put on her hat and gloves. Sarah dropped everything back down onto the seat and hurriedly adjusted her little blond straw bonnet aslant on her forehead. She had to crane her neck to see herself in the round gilt-edged mirror that hung on the compartment door. She smiled at the whimsical touch of the blackbird with his out-spread wings perched on the narrow brim. The new hat was a purchase she'd made in New Orleans during their honeymoon tour. She noticed how pale she looked, but hesitated to pinch her cheeks rosy with her husband watching. She hated for him to learn of her subterfuge. Instead, she lowered the black net veil over her face. Then she picked up her fawn kidskin gloves and eased them onto her hands finger by finger. By this time the train had steamed into the station and come to a complete stop. Passengers and townsfolk milled about on the station platform searching each other out.

"My God, Sarah," Farrel fretted, tapping his foot, "I thought you were ready long ago. Weren't you the one who was rushing me awhile back?"

"I'm so sorry," Sarah said contritely. "I'm afraid I'm just not used to travel. You know that this is the first real trip I've taken since my parents brought me to Richmond as a little child."

"You're right, my dear. I should be more patient, and I will try to become so. Only for now do please try to hurry."

Farrel slid open the heavy door and held it for her. Sarah's long, full beige linen skirt brushed against his legs as she passed by. He caught a whiff of her perfume, a rich oriental blend that he found out of keeping with her youthfulness. She'd never worn it before. She must have purchased it in New Orleans especially to impress him, he figured, but he made a mental note to tell her it just wouldn't do.

Sarah climbed down the steep metal stairs to the stepstool, then onto the cobblestone platform

27

aided by the conductor who supported her gloved hand. Farrel, close behind, signaled to one of the colored boys lounging against the pillars and arranged for him to pick up the luggage in their compartment. Sarah stood to the side watching Farrel hand over some coins and felt the thrill of knowing she was rich. Farrel said not, but she knew they really were. Or very well off, at any rate, and would be really rich soon.

The train, as though relaxing after a hard struggle, gave a great hiss, and bursts of steam poured from its underbelly and chimney. Sarah jumped, dropped her book, which she immediately bent to retrieve, and glanced around to see who'd noticed. Ashamed of looking the fool, she glared at the huge black monstrosity whose windows were almost completely covered over by the grime of the road. Steam began to fill up the space under the station's corrugated metal canopy. Sarah regarded the whole ugly, dirty, noisy scene and wondered how Farrel could love it.

Farrel came over to her. "The boy will bring our baggage along," he said. "Let's go get a buggy."

With Farrel's arm to lean on, Sarah climbed the long flight of stairs to the waiting room. She looked around her trying to take in every detail. She felt thrilled to be here, a returning traveler. Even the unfortunate accident which was calling them back couldn't dim her delight. Before her marriage, she had only seen the railroad station from the outside. Now she noticed the polished marble floor, the solid wooden benches where people sat waiting for their trains to be announced, the mahogany counters behind which stood the men who bore the glamorous title of railroad agent. It was a striking contrast to the world of the tracks and the trains just below.

She stared up at the domed ceiling far above her head. The plaster ornamentation with its elaborate curlicues seemed particularly beautiful. Tall windows more than a story above the main floor let in stripes of daylight. Gaslights on the columns around the room added their flickering light. The entire scene seemed sheer magic to Sarah.

Farrel, on the other hand, was oblivious to the station which he'd passed through many times before. He tried to speed Sarah along to the street. "Sarah," he hissed, "please hurry! I must get over to the office and find out what's going on."

Sarah increased her pace a little, but she continued to cast her glances about this way and that so as not to miss anything. Outside, the air, though bright and sunny, had the feel of autumn. She welcomed its tang after the summer which had been tiresomely hot. She stood in the shade of the portico wishing she'd brought along her parasol, while Farrel went to organize the placing of their luggage in the carriage for their trip home. She had to admit that it did not make her unhappy to be back in her familiar Richmond. At least, here at home she knew what was expected of her. This honeymoon business, she decided, was a great strain.

As she waited, she thought back to the first time she'd ever spoken to Mr. Farrel Hurstwood. It was in her father's apothecary shop where she worked after school. She felt privileged to be allowed to continue her schooling even though she was already sixteen, so she didn't object in the least to helping out with the family business. That day, though, she'd arrived late, having stopped to see the progress the men were making laying the tracks for the new streetcars. She'd hurried in and begun to wash the glasses and plates for the afternoon crowd. When she looked up, there were two men waiting for her service and one of them was Farrel. He'd been pointed out to her before at the work site as "the brains from up north."

Her father rushed over from his place behind the high pharmacist's counter to greet the important out-of-towner.

"Mr. Hurstwood," he boomed, "welcome to Seewald's Apothecary Shop. This is my daughter, Sarah. She'll get you whatever you want."

Farrel shook hands with her father and indicated the man next to him. "Mr. Pat Rankin, my number-one worker and the best foreman a man ever had." Then Sarah's father was called away by a customer wanting medication.

"May I serve you, gentlemen?" Sarah asked nervously.

"I'd dearly love a beer," said Rankin, "but since my boss here chose this soda shop instead of a saloon, I'll just have a piece of that cake and a cup of coffee."

"And you, sir?" Sarah asked, raising her eyes to Mr. Hurstwood's face for the first time.

"I know exactly what I want," he answered with

a wink that made Sarah blush. "A chocolate egg cream. That's what I haven't tasted during the entire time I've been working in Virginia!"

Sarah looked at him blankly. The frown she used to practice in front of the mirror to look grown up came to her face unrehearsed. It had its planned effect—Farrel Hurstwood realized that this lovely child he'd seen often at the construction site was actually a beautiful young woman. A flower bud that had just begun to unfold its tightly curled petals.

"I'm terribly sorry, but I don't know what that is," she said. "Perhaps if you could tell me how . . . creamed eggs, you say?"

"No. No!" Farrel threw back his head and laughed. "Oh, my. It doesn't matter, Sarah," he hurried to add, afraid he'd hurt her feelings. "Why don't you get Mr. Rankin's order and then get back to me?"

Sarah removed the glass-dome lid that protected the cake. She sliced a large wedge and placed it on a dessert plate. The cake was her mother's butter cake with the burned sugar praline icing drizzled across the top. Sarah replaced the cover noticing her hands with their too-long and too-square fingers as she did so. She felt suddenly self-conscious of her school outfit with its navy-blue skirt and white shirtwaist and the matching blue bow in her hair. She pursed her lips thinking of how she must look to Farrel Hurstwood of New York City.

Sarah served the cake and poured out a cup of

coffee. Then she turned back to Mr. Hurstwood who smiled his beautiful smile at her. She stuck her hands in her apron, glad for a place to hide them.

"How would you like a cooking lesson?" Farrel asked.

"I don't know. . . . What do you mean?"

"I'll show you how to make an egg cream! Goodness knows I've watched them made enough times." He jumped up, setting the stool spinning. "Here, Rankin, I'll leave you in charge of my coat." He stripped off his coat energetically and rolled up his cuffs. Then he marched around the gray marble counter and up to Sarah who felt slightly alarmed at his approach.

"We start with a soda glass." Their hands touched as they both reached for the glass. Sarah pulled back as though burned.

"I'm sorry," she mumbled.

He had to laugh again. "You're lovely, Miss Sarah Seewald," he said. Then he grasped her hand and put the glass firmly into it. "There."

His skin felt warm—warm and soft. Sarah dreamed of that touch over and over again in the days to come.

"Drip some chocolate syrup along the side and into a puddle along the bottom. Where's your cream? Next comes cream."

Sarah brought the pitcher from the ice box and Farrel guided her hands in measuring out the right amount. She was painfully aware of her father glancing over at her from where he was helping customers with medications.

"Good! Almost done," Hurstwood announced.

Her heart fell. She didn't want the moment ever to end.

"Last of all, you add seltzer and stir as you're adding it. That's it. That's a chocolate egg cream!"

She turned to place the drink in front of his stool and bumped squarely into him. Only his quick leap and her tight hold on the glass saved Mr. Farrel Hurstwood from wearing a chocolate egg cream across the front of his starched shirt.

"I understand, Sarah. You want me to go sit down," Farrel responded with humor, "but couldn't you just say so?" He went back to the stool, much to Sarah's chagrin at losing their closeness.

"I'm so sorry for my clumsiness, sir," she said as she put the egg cream down safely in front of him.

"You have no clumsiness to apologize for," he answered.

"Good lord," Rankin interrupted, "is that the everlasting egg cream you're always talking about? A bit of a letdown, I'd say."

"Only because you haven't tasted it, Rankin, I assure you."

"Well," Rankin added, his tone showing some doubt, "I'm about done with my refreshment, Mr. Hurstwood. I think I'll leave you to yours. You have a bit of a sweet tooth, I think." He looked pointedly at Sarah and winked. "I'll get back to the men. No time to let up now, eh?"

"You're right, you're right. I'll be along shortly."

"Very good," Rankin said. He rose, clapped Hurstwood on the back, and walked out of the shop.

"Sarah," her father had called then.

"Yes, Father," she replied, half-turning.

"Sarah," she heard the soft whisper of her name from Hurstwood at the same moment. "Can I see you later?" he urged. "Could we go for a walk?"

"Oh," Sarah gasped. She wanted so much to say yes, but knew she mustn't.

"Sarah," came her father's call again.

"I'm coming," she answered her father.

"No, Mr. Hurstwood, I'm afraid not," she said softly. "I wouldn't be allowed." She looked him full in the face for a moment, hoping her look conveyed her feelings. Then she went to see what her father wanted.

By the time she had returned from running her father's errand, Sarah found an empty counter stool. More than enough silver coins, gleaming and beautiful, lay on the countertop. She picked them up one at a time enjoying the cool hard feel of them. Then she tried to sense the special magic they held from Farrel's touch. She fondled them, letting them slide from one hand to the other, as though they were bits of candy. She recalled the sweet feel of Farrel Hurstwood standing next to her. She knew she had to see him again.

"Sarah. Sarah Hurstwood!"

Farrel's call, with that strange name that had

become her name now, penetrated her reverie. She saw her new husband signal frantically from within a carriage that stood at the curb. Its pair of large white horses pawed the ground and snorted. Hurstwood jumped from the carriage as Sarah walked down the few broad stairs. He held the door open, waving at her to hurry. Sarah felt miffed that he hadn't come up to fetch her. Northern gentlemen certainly had an indifferent sense of courtesy! None of her Virginia beaus would have dared holler to her. Why he might as well have whistled, for heaven's sake!

She stepped up into the buggy, settling back onto the somewhat worn red velour seat. As soon as Farrel pulled the door to behind him, the coachman flicked his whip and the horses started up with a jolt. Sarah's head banged against the hard wooden back of the seat. She straightened up quickly, feeling for her hat to make sure it was in place.

"My goodness, Mr. Hurstwood, did you set the fiends of hell on his tail?"

"Yes, I guess I did. I told him to push those horses and there'd be extra money in it for him."

Within minutes the carriage pulled up before an all-too-familiar gray stone house on Cary Street.

"Why are we stopping here?" Sarah asked. "At my parents' home?"

"Sarah, I really must get down to my office. I thought you would be better off with your parents than in a strange new place alone. Come along now!"

His peremptory tone allowed her no room for argument. He hurried her along into her parents' house where he deposited cartons, trunks, and his new wife. Although it was past time for the midday meal, Farrel rejected offers of food and stormed off to the offices of the Richmond Electric Street Railway Company.

Three

Sarah, left standing among the assorted pieces of luggage, tried to smile at her mother. She vowed to herself that she wouldn't cry even though she felt stranded in this familiar, yet uncomfortable, territory—neither her mother's child nor the mistress of her own province.

"Come, dear," her mother suggested, "take off your hat and gloves. We'll share a bite of food. I'm sure you're tired and starved after your long trip. Why don't you just go and have a wash."

Like a little child, Sarah followed her mother's directions. As she poured the pitcher of water into the wash basin, she felt like a child again. Here she was back home doing the things she'd always done. She held the wet cloth to the back of her neck and closed her eyes letting the coolness refresh her. Inside her head she could live again the exciting days of a year ago, her last year in high school, when it seemed that the laying of the streetcar tracks was the only thing she could think about. She could almost hear the sound of the school bell at which the children, like a flock of starlings startled into flight, flew out of the schoolhouse door.

The youngest students, of course, went in a direct line through the schoolyard, past the fence, and off toward their homes. But after them came the slower almost amoebalike spread of the upper grades. Once out of the schoolyard itself, they broke into clusters and moved at different speeds in different directions.

"Sarah," a boy said. She'd looked at him over her stack of textbooks and notebooks. "Do you really study all that much or do you just carry those books to get sympathy?"

"Al, are you going to start up again?" Sarah's best friend, Maxine, asked. "If you want books so badly, why don't you carry ours? Here." She pushed her books at him. "You can have mine *and* Sarah's!"

Al backed away. He raised one hand in mock horror. "No, thank you, Maxine. This hand has not been sullied by either hard labor or book-carrying. I don't want to ruin my reputation now when we're less than six months from graduation."

"I'll carry your books," a shorter, rounder boy offered, "if you'll come watch us play football."

"You have made a deal, Sam," Maxine said. She handed over her small pile of books at once. "Come on, Sarah," she urged, "that'll be fun. Besides, you'll get your books carried."

Sarah hesitated.

"C'mon," Maxine urged. "Anyway boys are stronger and so they *should* carry our books."

"I'm strong enough to carry my own books, thank you," Sarah answered. "Also, I thought we agreed that you'd go with me today to see how far they've gotten on the tracks."

"Not again with your tracks," Al howled. "Aren't you bored with them yet?"

"No, I'm not. I find the street railway construction utterly fascinating," Sarah said haughtily. "Well, Maxine?"

"It *is* a little boring, Sarah," Maxine answered sheepishly. "Would you mind awfully much if I didn't go with you?"

Sarah frowned at Maxine.

"I'll come with you, if you really want me to," Maxine hastened to add.

"No," Sarah laughed, "it's all right. You go on with the boys. It doesn't matter. Maybe we can get together after supper."

"What about that problem Mr. Muggins put on the board?" Sam interrupted. "Does anyone have a clue as to how to answer it?"

"It's not as hard as it looks," Sarah said. "It's really just a variation on that proof we had yesterday."

"Hey, come on," Al called. The others were cutting through a field to get to their makeshift playing ground.

"I know the one you mean," Sam said. "I'll look it up in my notes." He hurried to catch up with the others.

"'Bye, Sarah," Maxine shouted.

"Good-bye, good-bye, good-bye," Sarah answered. Then her friends moved out of sight and she sped up her pace. She hurried along the dusty street toward the construction site. Throughout the fall, workers had been laying track for something her father called an electric tram. He had told her it was a special kind of one-car train that would carry people back and forth along the streets of Richmond. It would do away with the horse-drawn streetcars. Sarah found the idea of an electric train so exciting she could hardly concentrate during the day at school. And after school she spent every moment she could watching the crew of men at work.

As she rounded the corner, the sight of a larger-than-usual crowd surprised her. She edged into the group. The mayor was here today, she noticed, and four or five other dressed-up men. She'd seen one of them here before and knew he was the man responsible for bringing this excitement to her town. Mrs. Cleary, a neighbor who also spent her spare time watching the tracks' progress, caught Sarah's eye and signaled her. She was standing close to the cluster of important men.

"Sarah, look," she called, "they're almost finished." Then she lowered her voice as close to a whisper as she could and still have any hope of being heard. "That fellow there's that New Yorker, Mr. Hurstwood, you know."

She'd already met him at the soda fountain, but she kept her peace. Nonetheless, her excitement glowed from her large gray eyes, but Mrs. Cleary didn't notice.

"I heard him say," she continued, "that they'd finish before dawn if it took keeping a road crew hard at work all night."

"Today?" Sarah broke in. "They'll finish today? Are you sure you heard right?"

"Oh, yes." Mrs. Cleary nodded firmly, her lips tightening. She was not used to being doubted. She paused, to show she was peeved. She untied and retied her apron before continuing with her biggest news.

Mrs. Cleary leaned her head close to Sarah again. Their heads were almost on the same level, she noticed; the Seewald girl was just about full grown. "I heard Mr. Hurstwood make plans for a trial run at dawn tomorrow!"

Sarah shifted her books around in her arms in an effort to ease the pain in her shoulders. She couldn't think of any worthy answer to the amazing statement Mrs. Cleary had made. Sarah shook her head slowly back and forth so that her curls trembled. Her eyes traced a line between the shining rails and the lanky man named Hurstwood.

Sarah had never seen anyone quite so handsome. He was old, of course, maybe even thirty, but she so admired his elegant mustache and his hollow cheeks. How she wished she'd been able to go for a walk with him.

Once when he scanned the crowd, he caught her watching him and nodded. He even smiled. A smile that looked like the silver lining in a cloud. Her breath caught in her throat. She couldn't tear her glance away from his steel-blue eyes.

41

' "Sarah." She vaguely heard someone call her name. "Sarah!" The call was more insistent this time and Mr. Hurstwood winked as she reluctantly turned back toward Mrs. Cleary.

"Yes, Mrs. Cleary," she answered dreamily.

"Sarah, your father's calling you from up the hill."

"Oh, no! I forgot," Sarah wailed. "I'm supposed to work at the fountain today. He will tear me limb from limb." Sarah found it easy to be melodramatic at any time and even more so this afternoon with the tension of Mr. Hurstwood's presence and the promise of the streetcar's completion. "I've got to run. 'Bye now." Sarah hurried up the steep hill toward her father's Main Street shop.

Mr. Seewald, the town's only pharmacist, was a man respected for his integrity and his calmness during emergencies. But now, as he watched Sarah struggle up the hill toward him, he felt anger boil up in him like steam in a teakettle.

He tapped his foot and rested his hands on his hips as his wife came up behind him.

"David," she called softly. "Don't upset yourself so. What does it matter if I stay a few minutes extra? My wages you don't have to worry about," she teased. Her voice still held the slight Russian accent that so often made him homesick for his native land.

"I know, Rachel, I know," he began in an angry tone, "but she should learn! You have a job to do, you do it!"

"Darling, you're right. I know you're right. But she's a good girl. You know that I'm right, too."

Sarah overheard the argument as she rushed up to them full of apologies. Fortunately for her, due to her mother's ministrations, her father limited his scolding to a few brief sentences.

"Sarah Leah Seewald." She stopped in her tracks. His use of her full name told her how serious he thought it was. "When you make a promise, it is your seal. You must act as you have said you would."

"Papa, I'm sorry. I forgot. I forgot for a few minutes only."

Mr. Seewald turned away. With his back to her he muttered, "That's no excuse. There's no excuse for breaking your word."

Then he walked slowly back into the shop. Rachel and Sarah followed. Sarah felt confused and desperately unhappy, but she fought off the tears that threatened to appear. This was no time to cry. I'm in charge of the fountain, she told herself. Her father appeared from the back room, his starched stand-up collar poking out above his white lab coat. He busied himself with orders that had been piling up all afternoon.

"I'll just put my books away and slip on my apron, Father. I won't be a moment."

He nodded, but refused to speak. She knew he wouldn't. Even after he forgave, he didn't readily forget.

The next morning, Sarah had awakened to a drizzling rain which dripped steadily down her windows. She sat up and stared at it in distress. It was a bad omen. She knew she had to hurry so as not to miss the start of the trial run. She wondered if they'd cancel it due to the weather. She moved silently so as not to awaken her father who would surely order her straight back to bed.

Sarah wriggled her flannel nightgown up over her head and shivered as the cold air bit at her skin. She hurried to replace her night clothes with underclothes. Then she layered petticoats over them. She picked up the dress she'd decided on the night before: a beige sailor waist with a full skirt. She tied a black silk scarf under the collar. Sarah buttoned up her best shoes. Her last step was to brush and brush her hair until it gleamed with auburn lights; then she wound it into a coil and pinned it up with golden butterfly clips.

She eased her bedroom door open and slipped into the hall, but she couldn't resist stopping a moment to inspect herself in the round gilt-edged mirror that hung there. She couldn't get a full-length view, but what she could see looked grown-up and ladylike. Sarah folded her cape over her arm as she tiptoed toward the door. At the heavy front door, she paused to take a deep breath. Then, saying a small prayer that it wouldn't squeak, she pulled it open. A blast of cold wet air stung her face. She rushed out pulling the door tightly closed behind her.

Despite the darkness, she didn't dare slow her pace. It might already be too late. But when she neared the bottom of the hill she saw by the hubbub that she had arrived in time. Specially constructed lights hung from temporary poles. They cast light down on the cluster of workers and the huddled group of watchers. For yes, despite the attempt at secrecy, there were more than a dozen people gathered on the sidelines. They simply looked on in silence as workmen rushed around oiling gears and polishing fittings. From where Sarah stood, she spotted Mrs. Cleary in the very center of the crowd and moved toward her. As she did so, she caught sight of Mr. Hurstwood up on the platform of the test car with his hand on the throttle.

"Sarah, Sarah," Mrs. Cleary greeted her. "I hoped you'd make it. You've been my most faithful companion on this electric-street-railway watch. I didn't want us to miss seeing this event together."

"Oh, I know," Sarah answered. "I could hardly get to sleep last night, and then when I did I was afraid I wouldn't be able to wake up early enough."

"They'd better hurry up. I have to get home to my babies in a little while—and to make Charlie his breakfast. They almost started, oh, maybe ten minutes ago, but that wagon just bucked once, gave a cough, and died. Don't you hate this weather?"

Sarah pulled her cape tighter around her and nodded, but she never took her eyes off Mr. Hurstwood as he gave orders, made adjustments, leaped up to the car and back down again, and moved among his men with authority and graceful ease.

At last he gave a sign. Mr. Rankin climbed up to the platform next to him followed by a nervous portly fellow in a black suit and bowler hat. The three men shook hands. Hurstwood took his position at the front and Rankin at the back. The round fellow clung to a shiny white pole just behind Hurstwood. Hurstwood pulled on a chain and a whistle shrieked through the air. The small crowd laughed and cheered. Hurstwood turned a lever. The machine shook. It began to move. As it rattled away, the crowd rushed after it. By the end of the block the streetcar had picked up speed. The demonstration seemed to be a success. Excitement surged through the spectators when suddenly there was a bright yellow flash followed by a muffled explosion. To Sarah, in the crowd, it looked like a little sunrise. The car stopped dead in its tracks. The black-suited man bolted from the car, his bowler hat flying off behind him into the gutter.

"Wait, Mr. Marden," Mr. Hurstwood yelled. "It was nothing. Only a fuse."

But the round man rushed into the crowd, pushed his way through it, and disappeared in the dark street. Mr. Hurstwood, watching, knew he had seen the last of Mr. Marden forever. And the last of his hope for Marden's New York money as backing.

"Christ, Pat," he said to Rankin, "how will we get this street-railway project rolling now? Damned bad luck. There goes the last bit of money we needed. Damn!"

"Well, I'd say our first worry," Rankin answered, "is how to get this one car rolling back to the barn for repairs."

By this time people had begun meandering over

to where the single car stood stuck on its tracks. Farrel knew they could hear him so he tried to put a brave face on it.

"Mr. Rankin," he called loudly—too loudly if his goal were only to reach Pat, who stood a mere yard away—"I'm afraid you'd best go get the special equipment necessary to make these minor repairs."

Without a murmur of dissent, Pat nodded and started off to the car barn almost a mile away. Farrel sat down on the hard wooden bench of the trolley car. He calmly lit a long skinny cigar. A tight smile played across his lips. The watchers began to move off, their excitement for the day apparently at an end. When most of them were gone, Farrel slunk down onto the seat virtually out of sight. To a townsperson on his way to work, the car would look empty.

"What a disappointment," Mrs. Cleary said. She and Sarah, not having followed the car's progress down the street, stood in their original places.

"Yes," Sarah agreed.

"In her heart, she felt Farrel's shame keenly. She saw him slide down out of sight and felt she understood.

"I can't wait around anymore, Sarah. Are you going to come along with me?"

"No, Mrs. Cleary. I'll wait here just a bit longer."

"Don't forget school, child. First things first."

"Yes, ma'am," Sarah said. She smiled. Mrs. Cleary patted her on the shoulder, then turned and began to trek back up the hill.

Sarah moved into a doorway so she wouldn't be noticed. A trio of men stood a little way off gossiping. Across the street a man and a woman Sarah didn't recognize watched in silence. Except for that, the street was empty now as dawn's pink fingers smoothed the night out of the sky. For a while nothing changed except the gradual shift of the light. But then, just as Sarah was about to move out of her hiding place and make her way home, she saw Mr. Rankin returning along the tracks. She expected to see a tool kit in his hands or some piece of machinery being lugged along the tracks. Instead, she watched him lead four big mules toward the stationary car. The trio of men noticed, too. They burst into rude laughter with one of them calling out, "By golly, here comes the 'special equipment'!"

"It's special all right," returned a second; "it's got four legs!" Then they laughed again and the couple across the road joined in and even Sarah giggled for a minute until she caught herself and thought, in horror, of Mr. Hurstwood's humiliation.

Without waiting another second, not even long enough to see the mules harnessed up to the car, Sarah dashed from her hiding place and raced for home.

"Poor Mr. Hurstwood," she thought as she ran, "poor, poor Mr. Hurstwood." The cruel sound of laughter echoed in her ears. She reached home breathless and without an idea of what she should say to excuse her absence. But luck was with her. She eased into the house unnoticed and could

48

pretend she was just coming from her bedroom for breakfast. Her mother stood at the stove stirring a steaming kettle of rolled oats.

"Hurry, Sarah, hurry," she said as soon as she spied her. "I thought you'd never get in here. One more minute and I was coming after you. Get a bowl and sit down. Hurry or you'll be late for school."

Sarah wondered as she rushed about the kitchen setting the table whether her mother knew she'd been out. In any case, she asked no questions and Sarah was grateful for that.

Sarah ate quickly, then went to get her books, and left for school calling, "'Bye, Ma."

The rain had stopped, and the air smelled fresh as hay. The bell was just beginning to chime as she walked along the hill's crest to School Lane.

During the day, she'd tried hard to concentrate on schoolwork, but at recess she grabbed Maxine and dragged her off into a corner of the schoolyard.

"Maxine, I've just got to talk to you or I'll die."

"Sarah, what in the world is the matter? You look flushed. In fact, you look crazy! Are you sick?" Then when they were out of hearing of their classmates she added in a whisper, "It better be important, too. Did you see that cute Johnny Bollier? He was talking to me for the first time. He's so shy it will take him another two weeks to build up his nerve again!"

"Oh, it is, Max. It's the most important thing that's ever happened to me in my whole life and I need your advice."

49

The two girls found an empty bench and sat down close together with their heads almost touching. From a distance they could have been taken for playmates gossiping. Or, with a different angle of vision, politicians deciding on a campaign plan. Instead, Sarah was busy with her explanation of her almost-imaginary romance. Just as recess ended, she got to the part about the invitation.

"Shall I agree to meet him, Maxine, do you think?" she asked as they walked back toward the school building. Maxine remained silent for a half-dozen steps. She slipped her hand into Sarah's arm. Then she answered.

"Yes, Sarah. Risk it!"

"But what if he doesn't ask again?"

Sarah, suddenly activated by her friend's answer, panicked at the thought. They were almost at their seats. Miss Stanley was ready at the chalkboard. "Tell me," Sarah urged.

"Write a note," Maxine answered. "When you see him again, slip it into his hand."

"Oh, Maxine, you certainly have a lot of nerve!" Sarah gave a little hoot of laughter which she stifled as heads turned in their direction. They both took their seats. The afternoon's lessons began. But, a little later, when Sarah had finished a problem the others were still at work on, she tore a piece of paper from her tablet, and began a note in her careful schoolgirl script:

> *Dear Mr. Hurstwood:*
> *Forgive my rudeness yesterday to a request for*

an interview. In fact, I regret my negative words. If you would care to walk tonight, I should be pleased to accompany you. Is seven o'clock at the foot of Main Street acceptable?

> *Most sincerely yours,*
> *Sarah Seewald*

"Hsst." Sarah tried to get Maxine's attention. She passed the note folded into a little square across to Maxine who read it on the sly. A few minutes later her note and another made their way back to her. When she got another break from Miss Stanley's attention she held it down on her lap and unfolded it. Maxine's note said:

Dear S,
  You certainly beat around the bush. I'd have said, "H, honey, how 'bout a stroll in the moonlight tonight?" But I'm sure yours will do the job. Good luck!

> *M*

Sarah smiled, but then Miss Stanley called on her for her recitation. She put the notes and further thoughts of Mr. Hurstwood away for the rest of the afternoon.

When the schoolbell rang releasing the classes for the day, Sarah walked outside with Maxine. For once, she had no books in her arms. She gave Maxine a hug and a kiss before she rushed off to her duties at the fountain. After yesterday afternoon's scene she didn't want to anger her father. During the course of the day, the rain had been

51

replaced by a sun which was bright enough to fool her about the cold. But after a few blocks Sarah wished she had remembered her gloves this morning.

She pulled open the door and hurried inside setting the little bells over the door into a crazy jangle.

"Papa," she called breathlessly as she rushed across the floor to where he stood at the back counter, "see how I hurried here straight from school?"

Sarah threw her arms around her father's neck and kissed him on one cheek and then the other. Despite himself, he chuckled.

"Enough, enough already. You're freezing, *bubbele.* Go warm yourself a little before you get ready. Mama has some cocoa made." Then he reached over to pat Sarah's hand gently. That gesture of affection made Sarah so happy she skipped into the back room and felt warmed even before the cocoa made a hot streak straight down into her stomach.

Sarah washed out her cup. Then she reached for her special apron. At the first touch of its silkiness, an image of the note to Mr. Hurstwood folded in her cape pocket flashed through Sarah's mind. She fastened her apron, then transferred the note into its pocket. Just in case, she told herself.

The afternoon fountain trade kept Sarah rushing about. Some of her schoolmates dropped in, demanding service right away, overflowing the fountain stools, and throwing jokes and riddles at

Sarah. When her father had first opened the pharmacy, Sarah had been only eleven, but she'd been expected to help. She could hardly stand the shame then of having her friends order her around. She'd finally overcome her false pride. Her friends were still her friends. Their jokes reminded her of that. She laughed and teased back as she filled their orders.

Other townspeople came in as well, of course. In fact, Sarah began to wonder if everyone in Richmond had decided to gather at the fountain today. It was almost closing time before she realized sadly that the one person who had not shown up, who was conspicuous by his absence, was the one person she secretly waited for—Mr. Farrel Hurstwood. Perhaps, she thought, he's given up on Richmond after the morning's debacle. Maybe he's left for someplace else. Her heart fell. I'll die, she thought. She turned away from the door. No point in staring at it. She began to wash up the last of the glasses and dishes so the fountain would be set up for tomorrow. She heard the bell's tinkle announcing a last customer, but she could hardly bear to turn around for fear it wasn't the man she awaited. She knew, though, that she must. She shut off the water and turned. Farrel Hurstwood sat astride a stool, alone, not five feet from where she stood.

"Mr. Hurstwood," she exclaimed. "Can I get you a chocolate egg cream, sir? I remember how to make them."

"Well, I knew you would be an apt pupil, Sarah," he answered softly. "Yes, I'd love one. I'm sorely in need of comfort this afternoon."

Sarah could see a deep pain behind his dark eyes. She bent her head to her task, biting her lip. She followed exactly the steps he'd taught her yesterday. When she placed the glass in front of him, she said, "I had a good teacher, is all." Then she reached into her pocket, drew out the note and placed it next to his hand.

"This is for you, too," she said, her voice just a shade above a whisper. Her hands trembled. She felt heat rise up to her face. Farrel raised his eyes to hers, full of questions. Sarah bit her lip again, a trait she thought she had outgrown years ago. Neither of them moved. Then slowly, Farrel looked down at the note. His egg cream sat neglected. He looked back up at Sarah who remained rooted where she had been. "Yes," he said and nodded, "yes." Sarah's heart pounded and pounded in her chest. He put the note in his jacket pocket. Then he began to sip his drink, all the while watching Sarah as she completed her dish-washing chores.

As the meeting hour neared, Sarah approached her mother where she sat knitting in the parlor next to the fireplace.

"Mother, I've done my work," she began. "May I go out for a while?"

"But Sarah it's so dark already. Why do you want to go out?"

Sarah froze, her mind a total blank.

"I suppose it's Maxine," her mother half-asked, but then hurried on. "You may go, only don't stay out too long, because it's cold and also you know how I worry about you, my precious."

"Yes, Mamma. Thank you."

"Father is in his study. Don't bother him."

Sarah wondered how much her mother knew or suspected. She gathered up her cape, wound her scarf around her neck, and remembered to bring her gloves. She hadn't exactly lied, she comforted herself. She hadn't said she was going to see Maxine. Still, she felt guilty as she closed the door behind her on her way to meet Farrel Hurstwood. It was the first date she'd ever had and it was the biggest deception of her life.

There he was, waiting. She could see his lean shape when she was still a square away. She waved.

"Hello," he called back. He moved toward her so that they met at midpoint. Impulsively, he put his hands on her shoulders. "Miss Hurstwood, thank you for meeting me. It's been a day when I needed something good to happen."

"Yes, I know," Sarah answered boldly, freed from the constraints of the fountain with her father always watching and where her surroundings reminded her of her childhood self. She went on, "But temporary troubles should cause only temporary sorrow."

It sounded so much like a school maxim, Farrel laughed out loud. Then, he hurried to say, "Thank you. You are both wonderful and kind." He didn't want to offend this doelike creature, nor did he want to scare her off. "Which direction shall we walk in?" He made his arm into a loop and, quite naturally, Sarah slipped her hand through it while she answered his question.

"Let's head over past the school." She pointed with her free hand. "There's a lovely park there with grand old trees."

Farrel smiled at Sarah's way of expressing herself. "Fine," he said. Then, as they began to walk, he added, "Tell me a little about yourself. You have quite the advantage of me, you know. I know nothing about you except for the fact that you are the pharmacist's daughter. I think you know more than that about me."

"I know you're from New York City. Were you born there?"

"Why yes. My family is one that would be referred to as 'old money,' I'm afraid. But that's all the more reason why this streetcar project is so important to me. I want to succeed on my own. Not because of my parents' money or my family name." He fell silent and they walked on with heads bent against the wind.

"Oh, look," Sarah cried, glancing up. A soft snow had just begun. It snowed so seldom in Richmond that when it did the snow felt more magical than in northern cities. The white blaze of dots haloed the lights and softened the look of everything. Farrel, too, felt lightened by the snowfall. He was able to turn his thoughts away from streetcars and back to Sarah.

"You still haven't told me," he said, "about yourself. Were you born here in Richmond?"

"Oh, dear, no. Can't you hear my accent?" Farrel shook his head no. "Well, I'm glad of that," she went on. "I was born in Russia. Odessa. My parents and my parents' parents were Russian. I, too, was a Russian for the first ten years of my life. Then bad things happened there and we moved to America."

"How did you manage to land in Richmond?"

"We lived first a year in Boston where I went to school and we learned English. Then, six years ago, my father accepted the position here as pharmacist. So now I am an American. Forever. An American from Richmond, Virginia!"

Sarah felt lucky to be an adopted American. She treasured the country in a way she thought most native-born Americans didn't. Farrel realized as he heard the pride in her voice, that he'd never really given much thought to what being an American meant to him. It was just what he was.

"Now it's your turn again, Mr. Hurstwood." Sarah looked up at him. Farrel felt a tug of protectiveness toward this innocent girl.

"First of all, I insist on being called Farrel!"

Sarah smiled and said, "I'll try."

"I'm afraid," he went on, "you'll grow bored of my favorite topic of conversation. To me, right now, there's nothing more exciting than streetcars, streetcars, streetcars. They fill my mind all day and they fill my dreams at night."

"I can understand that," Sarah said. "I watch fascinated as the tracks inch their way across the town. I even sneaked out of the house this morning before school in order to see the first run." Suddenly Sarah remembered that he would probably rather not be reminded of the morning's misadventure. "I mean—" She began again, but could think of no way to continue her thought. The silence between them lengthened, interrupted only by the staccato rhythm of their footsteps. Suddenly Farrel Hurstwood threw back his head and laughed.

"Oh, God," he said between hoots, "I must have looked the perfect fool!"

"No. Oh, no," Sarah said. She placed her hand on his arm. "I felt so sorry for you I could hardly stand it. But, tell me, did you get it fixed?"

Farrel closed his large hand over hers. "Yes, at once. As soon as we got it back to the car barn. That's not the worst part about the morning's disaster."

"Disaster?" Sarah asked alarmed.

"Well, that might be putting it too strongly. But it certainly feels like a disaster."

"What do you mean?"

There was a brief silence, as they turned a corner and started up the hill. Then Farrel began to talk in a tight, low voice.

"I'm short of the final funds. Today's test was going to impress the banker I imported from New York, so much that he'd give me the money I need. Well, you saw how impressed he was!"

Sarah stopped walking; she faced Farrel. "I'm so sorry," she said simply. Farrel gazed into her eyes. They stood near one of the infrequent streetlights so he saw the somber set of her full lips, the slight frown between her brows.

"Sarah," he began, placing his hands on her shoulders. Then he shook his head once or twice.

"I guess we should head toward home. Your parents will begin to worry about you."

Sarah's heart pounded. She'd hoped he'd lean over and kiss her. How many times had she dreamed of a real kiss! Her lips tingled in anticipation. Instead, he turned away. They again took up their deliberate pace; only this time they turned at the next corner to head in the direction of the Seewald home. They fell silent. As they neared the house, a figure loomed out of the shadows of the porch. Sarah gasped and took a step backward.

"Sarah!" Her father's voice followed her. "Come here at once!"

Four

"Sarah!" There was a loud knock at the door. "Sarah, are you all right?" It was her mother's concerned voice. Sarah had no idea how long she'd been sitting there with the cloth on her neck, daydreaming.

"Yes, Mamma. I'm coming just now."

Rather numbly, she found herself seated beside her mother at the familiar dining-room table.

Aunt Jane, the Seewalds' only servant, the fierce Negress who had but to shake her head so that her large gold ear hoops trembled to terrify Sarah throughout her childhood, said, "Welcome back, Miz Sarah." Her white teeth flashed out in a bright brief smile as she served the two women bowls of chicken and dumplings.

"Thanks, Aunt Jane," Sarah replied, thinking to herself, You can't give me orders anymore; reminding herself: I don't have to be afraid.

"So tell me," her mother urged, "how was New Orleans? You know, I've never been there so you have to tell me everything."

"Hot mostly. Hot and humid and with streets so narrow, yet full of people, that I felt terrified I'd get crushed—or murdered. You know, there are a lot of murders down there near the harbor. Oh, wait. I brought something for you."

Sarah ran back to the foyer where she searched out a foot-long wooden box inlaid with mother-of-pearl which she presented to her mother with a kiss.

Rachel delighted in the beautiful workmanship of the box. Then she opened it and stroked the plush red velvet lining. Inside, Sarah, aware of her mother's fondness for sweets, had packed divinity fudge squares and big round praline wafers.

"You darling." Rachel smiled at her only child. "On your honeymoon yet you still had time to think of your mother. Thank you. But now come sit and eat before it gets too cold. Then you'll tell me more about your trip."

Sarah hardly tasted the food before her. Sitting here with her mother in her old place at the table, she almost felt as though her marriage had been part of the old fantasies and had no reality at all. Maybe she'd only dreamed it. How often she had dreamed of it during those days and weeks after that first walk with Farrel. She hadn't seen him for a long time after that. Finally, he'd written her explaining that he'd had to return to New York to find additional financing. He'd also confessed how attracted to her he was! She'd read that letter over so many times that she soon knew it by heart and could still remember every word.

"My dearest Sarah," he'd begun, and at those first words her heart had started to flutter with the speed of a hummingbird's wings. "I have endeavored to follow your father's request and refrain from seeing you, but I find it impossible to do, since every time I close my eyes or pause in my day's activities I see your face before me. You've quite bewitched me with your innocent charm; I've never known anyone like you before."

She'd known, of course, about her father's advice to Mr. Hurstwood on that night of their first walk. After he'd talked with Farrel, her father had come in and explained about how the differences between them were too great for anything serious to take place. That had been the first of the innumerable talks she'd had with each of her parents about "differences" and love. She'd cried herself to sleep so often she expected her pillow finally to dissolve from her tears. Then the letter had arrived. She carried it with her still in her little purse. Later, when she took a rest she could reread it, but for now she must pay attention to what her mother was saying. Her darling mother who had eventually convinced her father to allow the wedding to take place.

"Always," her mother said now as though it were the climax to a story. Sarah had to admit she hadn't been listening. She didn't know what story her mother had been telling her.

"What, Mamma?" she asked. "I'm sorry, but my mind drifted out the window into the meadow beyond!" It was an old family saying, and she knew it would bring a smile to her mother's face.

"Oh, you know me and my old stories. I was thinking back to when you were a little girl in Russia. How even then you were sweet and considerate. And smart, too. When we came first to Boston here in America you were put into the baby class. So insulted you were! Your little body shook with anger when you told me about it."

Sarah had heard the story a thousand times. At least a thousand times. But she never tired of hearing it. The old stories of her life in Russia and then in America when they first settled here were what fairy tales and good-night stories were to other children. This time, though, she was aware of her mother's accent. Her mother had never lost that strong Russian-Jewish accent. Sarah wondered why she was suddenly disturbed by that. Ever since her engagement she'd felt ashamed of her parents at moments. And ashamed at feeling ashamed. Am I already becoming a snob? she asked herself. Too good for my own mother? God forbid! The Yiddish words to protect her from such unbearable thoughts sprang to her mind.

"Go on, Mamma," she urged. "Tell me again."

"You were so little. Just a little peanut of a girl. Yet you spoke Russian and Yiddish and poppa had already taught you to read in Hebrew as well. But now suddenly we were in America and you didn't speak any English at all. None of us did. Still, it offended you to be put into the baby class when you were already so grown-up. I told you to be a little patient, that you'd soon enough learn this new language and then you'd be with your own age group. But you know, Sarah, patience has

63

never been your outstanding virtue!"

Sarah laughed at that and leaned over to give her mother a hug.

"By the end of the year," her mother went on with the story that they both knew so well, "when we were making plans to come to Richmond, you had already made up all the grades you'd missed. You came to Richmond and went into the fifth grade just as if you'd lived here all your life. What a *schön kindele,* a marvelous child. I bless you every morning in my prayers, Sarah. May God only be good to you forever and ever, my precious daughter."

That moment, as they sat together holding hands, eased away all of Sarah's confusion and pain. The stories, yes, the stories, she told herself, they connect the days of our lives together into one beautiful whole. Into a work of art, she hoped. She would try to put her life together that way. The way her parents had, or at least so it seemed to her during this perfect moment.

When Aunt Jane came in to clear the dishes, the day returned to normal.

"I know you must be tired. How about a nap, Sarah?"

"Yes, I'd love that, but I have to make plans for tonight. I have to check over the house and make sure everything is in order. The moving was to be done while we were gone, you know. There's so much I should do." She wondered if her mother could sense the terror she was feeling at suddenly being the lady of the house—the mistress of a huge house she'd never fully explored. The builder had only finished it while they were gone. She was the mistress of a household of seven servants. No, it was more than she could manage. Why had she ever considered it?

Now she realized that she hadn't really ever considered it. She'd simply loved Farrel Hurstwood and wanted to be his wife. Everything else had seemed unimportant at the time. Now, though, the details of life seemed to be taking on a whole new importance.

"Oh, Mamma," she gasped, "I'll never be able to do it!"

Her mother understood, of course, what Sarah was feeling. She'd already thought through some small things she could do to make this transition a little easier for her only living child.

"Take your rest, darling. Then we'll go over together and supervise everything. The meal is already ordered. I made plans as soon as I learned that you would be coming back. Daddy and I are going to be with you this evening. That will be a glorious treat for us, to welcome in the Sabbath 'like a bride' as they say—with our daughter who *is* a bride. Now go and rest awhile. One step at a time is the only way to walk any road!"

As Sarah lay back on the smooth sheets of her childhood bed, she breathed a sigh that indicated the nostalgia she already felt for the easy days of her childhood. Nostalgia, she thought; well that is certainly a new sensation for me. Nostalgia at seventeen! Am I then already growing old? A married lady, she thought. Yes, growing up must mean growing old too. She remembered the times she had flung herself into this same hard-mattressed bed and prayed to be more grown-up. Then she thought again of Farrel's letter. The only letter he had as yet written to her. It was a sort of tangible evidence of the reality of their marriage which had otherwise a sort of murky unreality today.

She climbed back out of bed and rummaged in her purse for the envelope. Then, back in bed, she smoothed out the tissue-thin pages and began to read. At the part about her father asking Farrel to stop seeing her she paused. She remembered vividly how angry her father had been that night. He'd stood on the porch and ordered her to her room. Then he'd talked awhile privately with Mr. Hurstwood. Only then had he come to her room to talk to her.

"It will not do," he'd thundered. "You will cause yourself grief, grief, and more grief." She shuddered now as she thought back to those words. God, Papa, I hope you're wrong. She felt less certain now than she had then. Then she'd simply insisted that nothing else mattered except for true feelings between people.

"You're a Jewess, Sarah, and though you and I might like to think it doesn't matter, it does. For a while when we first came to America we tried to hide our Jewishness, but that was wrong. It is not something to be hidden. We haven't gone to *shul* here, haven't joined a synagogue, or sent you to classes, and that was probably wrong too. But there are so few Jews. We didn't want you to feel so different. Now this whole Reform Movement that's starting to take over! It's like we wish we were Christians. There's talk of Sunday services instead of our own Saturday Sabbath, and organ music instead of a cantor, of becoming goyish, in short."

He'd gone on and on. It seemed that the situation with Farrel Hurstwood had caused Sarah's parents to rethink their lives in America. They'd decided they'd made mistakes, and they wanted to correct them. A reaction to the Reform Movement was just starting to take place. It would mark a position midway between the Orthodox and the Reform movements and the Seewalds were going to become part of it. The Conservative Movement, he told Sarah, was a way for American Jews to leave behind the parts of their European heritage which no longer seemed appropriate, but to hold on to the precious parts of their Judaism. After all, he reminded her, they were the chosen people.

She'd never before given much thought to being Jewish. Only that she didn't go to church and couldn't have a Christmas tree like the other kids. Her mother said prayers on Friday nights and her father in the mornings, but these rituals had become as automatic as brushing her teeth. She never really saw them anymore or thought about them. Suddenly her father was telling her that being Jewish changed everything. But how could that be when for all of the years of her life it had changed nothing. She knew that her parents were saddened that she had married a Christian, but she felt it was too late for her suddenly to become Jewish. She turned her attention back to the old letter she was rereading.

"*I must tell you that part of what differentiates you from the other women I have known is your eager mind and especially the interest you have in every detail of my streetcar operation.*

"*Richmond, Virginia will soon be my city as well as yours as I have decided to move my company headquarters there permanently. I write you this from New York, the city which has been my home for more years than any other, the city which provided my mother and father, God rest his soul, the only home they ever knew. I am making final arrangements to leave here and will soon be back in Richmond. When I return, I intend to call on your father. Surely he will not refuse me when I request his permission to court you, but I write you this first because I must be sure I have your permission.*

"*I also cannot resist the chance to boast a little. New York, too, needs a streetcar system, and they are considering my plans for an elevated line, but they have not been as forward-looking as Richmond. However, I had a glorious victory just yesterday. As part of a demonstration meant to impress the money people and the city politicos as well, I linked up sixteen cars on one small piece of experimental track and started up and ran all sixteen units simultaneously. I know it could not have failed to impress everyone present, because it has never before been attempted. What a vain and boastful man I am to write you this; but I hope, nonetheless, that it has impressed you, also.*"

Sarah closed her eyes after she read the last line.

Almost at once, she was asleep. When she awoke, it was with the comfortable awareness of being home. She saw that the sky at her window held the look of afternoon as it dipped toward the deeper purples of evening, and she went at once to seek out her mother. Together, then, they traveled the distance that was so short in terms of number of streets and so far in terms of significance between Sarah's childhood home and the new home which was to be her married home.

At Sarah's urging, they hardly paused to take in the impressive look of the house from the outside. Sarah found it overwhelming, in fact. Inside, where she could consider one room at a time, she reasoned, she would be much more comfortable. Once inside the door, they stopped in the foyer. There was no need to comment on the beauty; they both felt it. The parquet wood floors, inlaid in an intricate pattern of small wooden chips, shone with the rich warmth only beautiful wood possesses. The elaborate crystal chandelier held flickering gaslights that sent off brilliant bits of light which sparkled and danced across the walls. The stairwell and a hall to the side of it divided the space just ahead of them. The formal sitting room was on their left and Sarah just glanced in at it a moment to admire the rose damask love seat, the soft fall of light through the Monticello window, and the carvings in the pink marble of the fireplace. Then she led her mother into the dining room with its huge wood table and chairs so elaborately carved in patterns of grapes and vine leaves. A matching sideboard topped by a huge beveled mirror covered one entire wall. Another huge mirror filled the space above the dining-room fireplace. The mirrored walls multiplied the large room's sense of space. Sarah saw an endless tunnel of room after room reflected in their surfaces. Again the chandelier added its magical effect. In addition to the gaslighting in this room, though, were the elaborate candelabra on the table and the sideboard.

"Oh, how grand!" Rachel sighed. "Here my little girl becomes a queen!"

"Mamma." Sarah's hands had flown to her mouth when she'd first entered the room. Now she smiled at her mother through her fingers. "Look at the walls. My husband told me they're real silk. He had an artist paint the willow pattern on them by hand."

The mother and daughter stood still, smiling and shaking their heads. "Let's go on," the mother said then. Sarah led the way once more into the back section of the house, the servants' working section. First, the butler's pantry; then, the regular pantry; finally, the kitchens. Servants were already busily at work on dinner preparations. Sarah had met them before but only once, and she felt shy about meeting them again without the protective guidance of her husband. Instead, she nodded briefly, and retreated back out the door.

"So?" her mother asked. "Who is this shy and retiring violet? This can't be my Sarah who would risk anything at the first hint of a dare."

"I'm sorry, Mamma. I haven't figured out how to act around the servants now that I'm not a child in the household but the actual mistress."

"Well, I'm sure it won't take you long to feel more comfortable. After all, the main thing to remember is that human beings are human beings. With Clara, of course, you'll have no problems, since you grew up as playmates together in our house."

"I don't know; that may make it all the worse. Now I have to be able to give her orders."

"Never mind all that now," her mother suggested. "Let's take a quick look at the second floor."

As they walked together up the steep stairway, Sarah wondered what Farrel had been doing this afternoon. Soon, surely, he would return home and then she would truly begin her life as Mrs. Farrel Hurstwood presiding over her first dinner in her new home.

At about the time Sarah and her mother sat down to their midday meal, Farrel burst through the doors of 810 Main Street with such energy that papers fluttered from desks and heads were raised from their work in both of the outer rooms.

"Mr. Hurstwood! Good day to you," the surprised receptionist managed, unconsciously touching the roll of hair at the nape of her neck to check for stray hairs out of place.

"Yes," Farrel nodded curtly. "Where's Mr. Rankin?"

"He's in your office, sir. But there's a gentleman with him. A magistrate." She bobbed her head nervously.

Farrel nodded again, then marched toward the closed door of his office struggling for control. The muffled sound of voices came to him through the door. He knocked once sharply. Then again.

"I asked not to be disturbed!" Rankin's hearty bass voice rumbled out like a thunderclap.

Farrel swung open the door, his face clouded with anger. "What's this! A week away and a man can't enter his own office?"

"Farrel!" Rankin rose and made his way around the oak desk that dominated the room. "For Christ's sake, I didn't mean you, man. I hadn't any idea when you'd make it back. Come meet Inspector Pressman. Inspector, Farrel Hurstwood."

They shook hands, took their seats, and Farrel said, "Tell me. Everything." He leaned back in his leather chair. For the first time since he had received news of the disaster, he felt at ease. He was back where he belonged and he would take charge. Whoever was at the root of this trouble would pay. He'd make sure of that.

By the time the inspector left a half-hour later, Farrel knew that sabotage had caused the accident, just as he'd suspected. Two out-of-towners had dynamited the tracks. They'd been caught and were in jail now whimpering about how the streetcars meant doom—loss of jobs, worship of the machine, ungodliness, et cetera. Farrel was familiar with the argument. Specious reasoning, he told himself, but typical. A frightened reaction to anything new: destroy it!

Rankin came back from showing the magistrate

out. "Well, boyo. That was some scrape we was almost in. Let me tell you, it scared the bejeesus out of me that we'd be ruined. Until they found those damned crooks." He ran out of steam then and collapsed into a chair across from Farrel, who had been staring at him steadily throughout his speech.

"Pat! Cut the baloney." Farrel leaned toward Rankin. "With the number of sticks they used? If those tracks were right, Pat, it wouldn't have done enough damage to harm the rail, let alone derail the car. Now I want to know the story from you. The *whole* story."

Farrel made a bridge of his fingers. His face was stern. Pat shifted uneasily in his chair.

"Boss," he began in a booming voice.

"The *truth,* Pat. I'll check it out; you know that. And I'll *know.*"

The room was growing dark, but Farrel made no move to light the lamp. Pat stood up. He turned his back to Hurstwood seated behind the desk. He seemed to almost fold in on himself as Hurstwood watched.

"You're right. I am to blame. The rails aren't up to specs." When he spoke these words, Pat's voice sounded like sandpaper scraped against metal.

"Why, goddamnit?" Hurstwood shouted and plunged toward Rankin. "How could you let that happen, Pat? You're my number-one man. You never came to me with problems on rail construction. God knows we had problems enough without that."

"Problems enough," Rankin echoed, then his

voice broke.

When Hurstwood heard sobs shake Rankin, he relented. After a moment, he put his arm around Pat's shoulders. The two men stood that way awhile in the gloomy half-light. It was to be their last close moment.

"Tell me about it, Pat," Farrel said finally, and so Pat began to explain the bad decisions he'd made that had led to the streetcar disaster.

The sky was a dark lavender streaked with deep purple before Farrel opened the ornamental wrought-iron gate to enter the Seewalds' front yard. In his distracted state he strode straight past the huge oleander still in bloom which would normally have received at least an appreciative glance.

Farrel pounded on the door with the brass knocker. The gray stone house seemed unnaturally dark for this time of day, but he assumed they must have drawn the heavy draperies against the night.

"Farrel, welcome back!" Mr. Seewald himself opened the door. "Come in, come in."

They stood in the entrance foyer. Farrel noticed the floor cover of rust-and-white diamond-patterned linoleum pieced together to fit exactly between the black enamel baseboards. It looked gaudy to him, and he was secretly glad he'd taken his architect's advice and installed parquet flooring. He enjoyed the idea of being a bit avant-garde. The single gaslight above their heads was not really to his liking either. Privately, Farrel looked down on the Seewalds as provincial—salt of the earth, he would have said of them aloud. But he thought of himself as superior. He looked into the future and saw himself becoming richer and richer. He hoped Sarah would be able to grow into the role that would be demanded of her: the wife of an important man.

"Rachel and I are so sorry about your troubles," David Seewald said.

"Thank you, I appreciate your sympathy. But where is Sarah?" Farrel asked, looking around uncomfortably, eager to be on his way.

"Why, she's at your home—your new house, Farrel, waiting for you. Mamma's with her and I am to go along with you. I'm afraid we've invited ourselves to join you for your first dinner home."

"That's just fine, Mr. Seewald." Farrel strained to say the appropriate thing. All he could think about was Rankin and the streetcar wreck.

"Please call me David. I've asked you before."

"David, yes. I'm sure we'll both be glad for the company. In my present mood I'd be no fit companion for Sarah, I'm afraid."

They walked together out the door. David pulled it closed tight behind them.

"The women went over in the buggy, so I suppose we'll have to walk. You don't mind, do you?"

"Not at all, Mr. Seewald—Dave—the air might help clear my head."

"Dave, yes, that's good. I'm not a very formal person. But as to the air helping your head. Feh! It's enough to bring tears to your eyes. Literally.

Who could imagine horses do so much pissing? And the droppings! That's even worse."

Farrel laughed in spite of himself. What a comical father-in-law he had acquired. They walked along Cary Street with its beautiful inlaid brick sidewalk in an elaborate crisscross pattern. The thoroughfare between the sidewalks, though, was still just packed dirt that turned to swampy mud after a rain. Judging by its present condition, Farrel assumed that it must have rained this morning before their train got in.

"Just you wait awhile. When people fully accept my electric street railway, we'll get most of the horses off the streets!"

"The horses that draw the old streetcars, sure. Those, of course."

"Those will be a good place to start. Did you know that each horse produces twenty to thirty pounds of manure every single day?" As Farrel walked along, he held his white linen handkerchief up to his nose to filter out some of the smell. "Getting rid of the horse-drawn cars will help some with this stench. Get rid of some of these damned flies, too," he said as he swatted one that had been buzzing around his neck. "But we'll get rid of a lot more horses from the street than that. People will start to use the streetcars instead of their buggies, because it will be cheaper and easier for them. As for the town as a whole, well, as you say, we'll be doing it a tremendous favor. Not just the aesthetics of the thing either. Runaways kill people. More than you could believe. I was astounded myself."

Mr. Seewald trotted along beside him, taking two or three steps to each of Farrel's long strides. He shook his head at his son-in-law's grandiose ideas. Richmond, Virginia without horses . . . why it was inconceivable. But let Farrel dream on. Dreams were the province of the young anyway.

The sky was darkening, almost indigo. Across the street, moving slowly toward them, Dave saw Otto Schmitt, the lamplighter. Behind him, down the length of the street, lights had sprung up along the edge of the sidewalk. He paused almost directly across from them raising his pole to set the flame to the lamp.

"Good evening, Otto," Mr. Seewald called. "I think we'll cross over and take advantage of your lights."

"Who's that?" Otto called back startled by the presence of people, so intent was he on his job. "Why, Mr. Seewald, sir, good day to ya. Or good night, I should say. I'm a little late tonight." Otto lowered his pole, checking to be sure the light held. He raised his shabby top hat in their direction. His clothes had certainly seen better days, but were once the makings of a fine dress outfit right down to the white gloves through which the ends of his fingers now poked. He replaced his hat, picked up his lantern, his pot, and his pole and shuffled on toward the next street lamp.

As the two men began to pick their way across the mucky street, the older man lost his footing and slipped. Farrel with one quick motion grabbed his arm and held him steady saving him from a nasty fall.

"Thank you, son," Dave Seewald said when he had caught his breath. It scared him how hard his heart beat over any little thing lately, but he hadn't mentioned it to anyone. "That's another thing you can add to your list of pluses for getting rid of the horses. Not so many people would get hurt in falls. Why, Doc Lathrop—you know Sam, don't you? No? Well, I'll have to introduce you—he told me about a case he treated just last week. Fell over on Main where the cobbles are always slick from horse stuff. Cracked his head open and died two days later. And that kind of thing's not unusual either."

But Dave Seewald could see he'd lost his son-in-law's attention. Farrel seemed deep in thought about something else. The men walked on for a few blocks each closed into his own private world. They turned off Cary Street and headed toward Monroe Park. Mr. Seewald wondered why Farrel had chosen to build a house way over here. He knew that some property agents around town touted this new section as the coming "in" place. They called it the Fan district because of the odd way the streets branched out from the park. He had to admit there was enough empty land to allow for extra yard space and Richmond did appear to be growing in this direction. But it still seemed to be taking a big risk. If the town went in another direction, or if it stopped growing altogether . . . well, Dave didn't like to think of the loss Farrel would take. He knew his son-in-law had spent a small fortune on the house. They were on West Franklin now and approaching the house before David broke the silence.

"Farrel, are you still worrying about your streetcar accident?"

Farrel shook his head abruptly as though to call himself back to the present.

"No, strangely enough I was on another topic altogether. I admit the accident's been about the only thing I've been able to think about since I heard. Some part of my brain keeps nagging at it like a dog with a bone. But watching the lamplighter just now turned my thoughts another way. I was thinking about lights. The streetlights. They should all be electric and get turned on at one time from some central location. I was trying to figure out how I could somehow link it up with the electrification of my trolley lines as I extend them."

"Wait a minute, boy, wait a minute. You're about to pass by your own house."

"Oh, so I am."

Dave laughed and Farrel laughed with him. They stopped and looked admiringly at the broad brick-and-brownstone house. It had a stylishly asymmetric front with a round turret cresting the third floor to the right and a square structure extending top to bottom on the left. From where they stood they could count five chimneys, and there were another two around back. The large window of the front parlor was a beautiful work of beveled and leaded glass which found its counterpart in the two panes that bordered the solid oak front door.

An intricate scrolled metalwork railing edged

both the four steps leading up to the porch and the porch itself. It was locally done work that was gaining a national reputation. In fact, it was becoming a Richmond trademark. The wrought iron was a product of the Richmond Foundry, a manufacturing concern that managed to survive not only the war but also the fires and other horrors of the postwar period. Now the foundry, the burgeoning tobacco industry, and Farrel's company formed a hub of industry that couldn't help but draw continuing development to Richmond. Farrel felt sure that the old capital of the Confederacy would rise again as the capital of the new South.

"The Hurstwood mansion," Farrel said as he gazed up at his three-story twenty-two-room house.

That was just what it looked like, David thought, although he knew Farrel must be joking. A mansion. Maybe he was only half-joking at that. All his ideas were pretty extravagant. I wonder, David Seewald said to himself, what my little Sarah is going to make of her marriage to this man. I just wonder. . . .

Farrel opened the ornamental wrought-iron gate and led the way through the yard, up the stairs, and onto the front porch. He grasped the wooden handle to the side of the door, pulling it out and then plunging it back to set off a jangle of bell chimes within the house.

"That's pretty." His father-in-law laughed.

"It should really be electrified, of course. The whole house should. But I guess the time's not quite right yet. Things always move too damned slowly, don't they?"

The door opened before Sarah's father could answer that he thought they often moved too fast.

A beige-colored girl who couldn't have been much more than thirteen stood smiling in the doorway. She nervously smoothed the crisp white apron over her long green plaid dress. Her head, wrapped up in a matching plaid turban, bobbed as a signal for them to enter. A broad smile never left her face.

"Why, Clara, don't you look fine? You know," David Seewald continued as they followed Clara into the front parlor where their wives waited, "she was a tiny girl when we first settled in Richmond and her mamma, our Aunt Jane, has been our mainstay all these years. I'm glad she's come to be of service to you now that she's grown."

"My dear," Farrel said as he bent over his wife's raised hand. "Forgive our tardiness." He smiled at his mother-in-law who sat close beside Sarah on the small rose settee. "It was my fault. This accident is bad news in every way. Even to spoiling our first dinner in our new home."

"Oh, but it isn't spoiled." Sarah smiled. "It's waiting for you. You and Daddy might like to go ahead and wash up a bit and then you can join us in the dining room."

Farrel nodded and walked toward the stairs. David, before following him, went over to his wife and rested his cheek against hers. Rachel smiled up at him and patted his hand. "It's quite a moment, isn't it, David? Being here with the children. Our Sarah, a married lady in such a fine home."

David shook his head, saying nothing, then followed Farrel. When both men were out of sight, Sarah jumped up and pulled on her mother's arm just as she'd done when she was a child impatient for a treat.

"Oh, hurry, Mamma," she begged. "Let's check everything over once more. It's just got to be perfect."

Rachel pushed herself to her feet. Sarah, seeing that she'd gotten her mother moving, rushed ahead to tell Bessie, the cook, that it was almost time. Then she checked her appearance in the long mirror above the sideboard and glanced over the dining-room table for the hundredth time. The hand-embroidered linen cloth covered the shining wood with ample folds draped over the sides. The china and crystal glittered. Sarah couldn't remember ever having seen so many beautiful treasures as she now owned. Farrel had outfitted the entire household from New York City's finest stores. Sarah almost felt her hope-chest items were too homespun by comparison. Yet she couldn't help but admire the band of wheat stalks and flowers that edged the tablecloth. She thought back to the many evening hours she and her mother had spent on that project. Well, it had been worth it; she could see that now. Her mother was rearranging the candles, placing the two heavy brass candlesticks near Sarah's place.

The men joined them then and they all took their seats, Farrel at the head, Sarah at the foot, and her parents at either side.

"It's Friday night, the start of the Jewish Sabbath, Farrel," Rachel spoke out as soon as they were settled. "Although we don't go to *shul,* we do say the prayer and light the *lichten.* You don't mind?"

Farrel shook his head no, offering a strained smile, but he looked uncomfortable as he did so. He had mostly ignored the fact that Sarah wasn't Christian; after all he wasn't really much of one himself. It was true they'd had a little ceremony before the wedding, but they had been really married in church. So, paying it no mind was easy to do up until now. Except for his mother's attitude, of course. He knew so little about the Hebrews, he suddenly realized. It was quite an awkward situation for him.

"Go ahead, Sarah," her father urged, taking his *yarmulke* from his pocket and putting it on the back of his head. Sarah sensed her husband's discomfort and tried desperately to think of a way out of this predicament.

"Mother," she said, "my husband and I haven't discussed this yet. We may have other customs. . . . I mean," she stammered, "won't you light the candles tonight?"

"Of course." Rachel, taking her cue from Sarah, moved the two special brass candlesticks with their graceful white tapers to the sideboard. Then Rachel lit them. Three times her hands circled around and over the flames as though to bring their light into her heart. She covered her eyes with her long fingers before beginning the ages-old prayer: *"Boruch Atah Adonoi. . . ."*

Her voice came through clear and shining as the candle flames themselves filled the room. Sarah was moved as she always was by the exotic Hebrew sounds, by the meaning of the simple prayer of her people: "Blessed art Thou, O Lord our God, King of the Universe, who hast sanctified us by Thy commandments, and hast commanded us to kindle the Sabbath lights." After the blessing, Rachel remained a moment with her eyes covered saying a prayer for each person in the room and for all people. When she finished, she said "Amen" aloud and then Sarah and her father shouted "Good *Shabbas,"* happy holiday.

As Rachel sat back down, she said to Sarah, "You'll have to instruct the servants not to put out the Sabbath lights."

"Why is that?" Farrel asked.

"It's God's light," Rachel answered without embarrassment. "We welcome it for as long as it lasts; then we carry it with us in our hearts."

Farrel, to his surprise, found the ceremony quite beautiful. It echoed through his mind in the same way as the Jewish wedding ritual. These home ceremonies, he decided, had a special charm. Perhaps the Jews had stayed closer to their sense of being a tribe blessed individually and especially by Yahweh, their own particular God. He knew they still called themselves the Children of Moses. The tallow candles flickered, making shadow patterns on the hand-painted wallpaper and endless circles of light in the huge mirrors.

"Mr. Hurstwood," Sarah said, formally, enjoying her role as lady of the house, "shall I have Samson light the tapers before I ring for the first course?"

"I'll light, if you'll ring," he offered, smiling across the length of the table at his beautiful young wife.

Sarah lifted the little brass bell shaped like Queen Elizabeth in a wide-skirted gown. She shook it back and forth and a lovely, delicate sound filled the room. Farrel made his way around the table, setting the half-dozen tall graceful tapers in each of the two candelabra alight. By the time he sat back down Clara and Samson were already coming through the door. Samson, Farrel's old manservant, carried a silver tray with a huge soup tureen on it which had been Mrs. Seewald's. The tureen was one of the few things Rachel had managed to carry with her out of Russia when they'd fled. The tray also held four intricately decorated hand-painted soup bowls that had been a wedding present. Clara unloaded the tray onto the sideboard, taking care not to knock over the Sabbath candles. Samson made a second trip to the kitchen and returned with a basket piled high with corn muffins. He moved silently around the table placing hot muffins and a miniature crock of whipped butter on each bread plate. Clara began to ladle out the thick yellow country chicken soup when Sarah rose unexpectedly and reached for the ladle.

"I'll serve, Clara," she said forcefully.

"Thass all right, Miz Sarah. Ah'll do it," the girl answered, refusing to relinquish her hold. For a moment the two struggled for possession of the ladle the way children might fight over who would lick the batter bowl. Then Sarah, remembering that they were no longer children together in the Seewald household, but mistress and servant in the Hurstwood household, her own household, raised herself to her full five feet two inches and said in a newly firm voice, "Clara, that's enough! Go help Aunt Bessie prepare the next course for serving."

Clara, chastened, dropped the ladle at once. She glared at Sarah, then turned and fled back to the kitchen.

Sarah felt the bittersweet joy of victory. She hoped her husband noticed how prettily her round arms shone as she ladled the soup into the bowls. The candles, shining off the silver and the crystal, filled the room with soft yellow light. My new life, Sarah thought happily, this is really the start of it.

She carried a bowl of soup over to Farrel, moving slowly so as not to spill a drop.

"Serve your parents first," he whispered.

Was he criticizing her, she wondered, as she served first her parents, then Farrel, and last of all herself. When they were all eating, Sarah thought back over her behavior to Clara with less satisfaction than she had felt at first. She had been wrong, she decided. Servants can't be expected to understand. As a result, she decided, she had probably looked rude and childish. Oh dear, she added, delighting in a crumbly mouthful of buttery muffin, I have so much to learn.

"Sarah, dear," her mother said softly, "perhaps

you should ring now; I think everyone is ready."

Sarah washed down the last bite of muffin with a hasty swallow from her goblet. It was bitter and made her wince. Farrel believed in good wines with dinner, but Sarah was unused to drinking anything but the sweet kosher wines her parents had on Friday nights. Still, she recognized that the deep maroon wine was considerably more beautiful than the "James River straight" which was what Richmonders called their drinking water which came from the muddy James River and never lost its dull yellow color or earthy taste.

Rachel caught Sarah's eye and nodded. Sarah rang for the next course. She appreciated her mother's coaching. She was more ready than ever before to acknowledge that she was going to need help in her new life.

One servant cleared the bowls while another brought out the main dishes: shrimp and Smithfield ham over dirty rice, a side dish of hot spicy applesauce, and another of summer-squash casserole. Sarah noticed that Clara did not reappear. The Hurstwoods and the Seewalds busied themselves with eating. Their conversation consisted of idle comments about the food, or the new house itself.

Finally, when the meal was completed and they were awaiting dessert, Sarah could stand it no longer and broached the subject of the streetcar accident.

"Tell us what you learned today, Mr. Hurstwood, won't you? You haven't said a word about it."

Farrel held up a cautioning finger. Samson was scraping the last few crumbs from the cloth with a special crumb blade. When the door to the kitchen swung shut behind him, Farrel spoke.

"It was sabotage, just as I suspected."

"But who? Why?" David Seewald was stunned. He couldn't conceive of such a thing happening in Richmond. An accident, yes, that could always happen. But this! "Hoodlums," he said, "hoodlums. I knew we should be doing something about those hobos that are always around, always passing through town. I read in the newspaper just the other day how there's an army of hobos drifting across America causing trouble whenever they can."

"No, Dave," Farrel said, stopping the enraged outburst from his father-in-law. "This was the work of outsiders. They came here just for this purpose. Not organized even. Just ignorant men trying to stop progress single-handedly."

"Anarchists, you mean, like those Chicago mobsters?"

"Yes, that's certainly possible." Farrel knew Dave was referring to the bloody Haymarket riot of a couple of years ago. Since then the word "anarchist" had become one of the worst insults one could hurl at an enemy.

"What happened in Chicago?" Sarah asked. She didn't read newspapers, having until recently confined her reading to schoolbooks. Now she began to see that she was going to have to become up-to-date unless she wanted her husband to consider her pretty but dumb, and she knew he had always liked the fact that she was so smart. She'd begin tomorrow, she told herself.

"It took place a couple of years ago. When you were still in the cradle," Farrel teased. "A labor group went out on strike against a factory in Chicago. Some anarchists organized a street demonstration to protest the way the police were treating the workers out on strike. Somebody threw a bomb and that started a riot. By the time the smoke cleared, there were a dozen dead bodies—eight of them were policemen's bodies, I think."

"God forbid," Rachel whispered. "Such talk on the Sabbath."

"It's life, Rachel," her husband said. "Life and death. So what did President Cleveland do, that do-nothing fellow?"

"You know that's not fair. Even if you don't like the man, you have to admit he's done plenty."

"Said 'no,' that's what he's done over and over."

"You're right, Dave, but that's plenty. Saying 'no' or saying 'yes' is doing something—if you can make it stick. Mind you, I don't think he's the businessman's friend—too much sympathy for the little guy—but I have to admire his guts. He's tough."

"Enough. Enough," Sarah broke in. She felt more and more ignorant as they went on talking. "Let's get back to the streetcar business. How do you know it was anarchists?"

"Yes. Do you know who did it?" Rachel asked.

"They're already in jail, but—" Farrel paused as he saw Samson enter the room with the large silver

89

coffee urn. He didn't believe in discussing personal issues before the servants.

Sarah, picking up the direction of his thoughts, said, "Here's coffee. Let's not spoil dessert with any more talk of this horrible accident. Look, Mr. Hurstwood, it's pineapple snow, one of your favorites. And Jumbals, such delicious cookies they melt in your mouth."

"I'm sorry, Sarah, I haven't much of an appetite left," Farrel replied unable to raise himself from the torpor that the memory of Rankin's words had once again sunk him into.

"Oh, do have some," Sarah coaxed. "I had the cook bake the Jumbals specially for you from Mamma's recipe."

"Sarah," her mother interposed to relieve the tension, "that peach silk really did make up into a fine gown. You look quite the lady with that small waist and fancy bustle." She beamed at her daughter.

"Thank you, Mother."

"It's true," her father agreed, "but we have our new son-in-law to thank for Sarah's happy eyes."

Farrel tried to smile at his new family, but his face felt so tight he thought it would crack apart. He didn't mean to spoil this dinner, but he knew that was exactly what he was doing. If only he could put the business of the derailment out of his head . . . But he couldn't.

Five

Later, after the Seewalds left, Sarah had Clara help her prepare for bed. Clara undid the dress and the corset stays, then put the numerous layers of clothing away as Sarah tossed them to her.

"I'm sorry 'bout before," Sarah said, laughing. "Clara, I really am, y'know?"

"'Tain't nothin' no way," Clara answered, nonetheless appeased by Sarah's words.

Sarah slipped into a silk night dress that fastened, empire style, under her full firm breasts. She took the clips out of her hair letting it flow over her shoulders.

"Brush me out, Clara," she pouted.

Clara picked up the brush and brushed and brushed and brushed until her arms were sore. Sarah's blondish hair shone silkily in the candle's soft light.

"It's mighty purty," Clara said, "and now I thinks I'll go to bed, too."

"Is it nice, Clara? Are your quarters nice? I

haven't seen them yet."

"Oh, yes'm. Bessie and me have rooms up over the kitchen. I could've stayed on with my mammy if I wanted, but I figgered as how if you wuz on yer own it wuz time fer me to be on my own too." At that she sniffed and stuck her nose in the air.

"What about the others?" Sarah asked, smiling.

"Most of 'em stay in town. They can ride Mr. Farrel's cars back and forth. Mr. Samson stays near to Mr. Farrel, of course. And Bertie, he stays nearby them horses of his in a room above the carriage house."

"I'm glad you're here with me in my new house, Clara, truly I am. Now before you go to bed will you stop and ask Mr. Hurstwood to come see me in my rooms?"

Sarah waited anxiously for Farrel's appearance, imagining the pleasure of their first night in their new home. But when Farrel knocked it was only to tell her how tired he was and to give her a perfunctory kiss, before retiring to his own suite of rooms.

Sarah, although distressed by this latest rejection, surprised herself by falling asleep quickly and easily. But then, just as suddenly, sometime in the middle of the night, she awoke. It took her a moment to realize where she was. For all of her seventeen years she had slept in a narrow bed in a room down the hall from her mother and father. Two weeks ago all of that had changed. Was it the strangeness of her new house that had awakened her? No, she was sure it was something else.

She quickly slipped into a peignoir and, barefooted, felt her way to her door and down the hall to the faint flickering light that came from a room in Farrel's suite. She knocked and entered. There, in the small room between his bedroom and bath she found Farrel staring into the glow of a small fire. Sarah didn't speak. There was no sense in asking him what was wrong. She already knew that. She bent to put another piece of wood in the fireplace and Farrel stirred as though he'd just become aware of her presence.

"Sarah," he said, "I didn't mean to disturb you. I couldn't sleep and I was cold. I thought I'd make a fire."

She pulled a chair close to his and sat down beside him. Without answering, she reached across to pat his hands. It already seemed a hundred years since that February day when they rode the streetcar together at the grand opening, since he asked her to marry him in the triumph of that moment. Yet it was only a little more than half a year. They were different people now, different from those two confident souls. She'd come to feel that in a dismal way during the long, painful return trip, and this strange, strained first day back.

"Sarah, I have a serious problem to resolve." Farrel's voice broke, as he spoke these words aloud. "I've been sitting here spinning it over and over. I'm beginning to feel like a wheel on a track. I'd like to tell you about it, if you're not too tired to listen."

"I'll be glad to listen, darling," she answered,

93

"but I don't know if I can be of any help." Sarah felt her youth and inexperience as an inadequacy tonight in a way she never had before. What could she possibly say that would be of any help in the real world of affairs . . . in the world of men. Then she shook that dismal thought out of her head. She was very smart, she reminded herself; everyone said so, even Farrel. Being young was no sin. Maybe she could be of help to her husband.

"I explained at dinner about the saboteurs. Damned fools!"

"Yes, yes, I know. They'll be held for trial, you said. Is that the problem, the dreadful anarchists? Have they somehow seriously hurt your streetcar line?"

"No, no. The streetcar repairs are almost complete already. Tomorrow we'll be back on schedule. No, it's a more complex issue involving my foreman, Pat Rankin."

"Mr. Rankin? I don't understand, I'm afraid. Was he involved in some way with the criminals who set the dynamite?"

"No, no. Nothing like that. But the tracks weren't right. You understand? If they had been constructed the way I ordered them, the accident would never have happened."

"But the dynamite . . ."

"It would have done no real damage, I tell you."

"And Mr. Rankin is somehow responsible for the bad tracks?"

"Yes. He's to blame. He shorted the supplies. Got lower quality rails. Weaker rails." Farrel's words trailed off into silence.

"Are you sure, Farrel? Did you ask him?"

"Of course I did," Farrel burst out. He went over to the fire and poked at it causing a cascade of sizzling sparks. "He confessed to everything."

"But why?" Sarah asked, appalled.

"That's exactly what I asked him. He had my trust, my confidence . . . my friendship. Not to mention a good salary." Farrel was pacing from one end of the little room to the other as he spoke.

"Well, what did he answer?" Sarah gripped the arms of her chair.

Farrel turned and stared at her. Then he came back to where she was sitting and sank down heavily into the empty chair beside her.

"He said he needed extra money. A *lot* of extra money. His baby son needed an operation. Why didn't he come to me? I'd have given him the money. Instead, he sold me out. Christ, I'd have trusted Pat with anything! But I was wrong. So wrong." There was silence, then he asked, "Now what do I do? That's the problem I face."

"Darling, what *is* there to do?"

For a few moments, the husband and wife sat on, sharing the dark night and the heat from the fire. They could almost feel comfort just out of their reach.

"I suppose I have two choices. I could expose him publicly. He'd go to jail. Or I could simply fire him. No one else would ever know. My sense of justice, our friendship, and my outrage at having been betrayed are all at war within me. I can't decide which course to follow. It's clear he must be punished one way or the other. I could never trust him again."

"Surely if he did it because of his baby's medical expenses, you can't send him to jail. Isn't firing him punishment enough?"

Silence again. Then, softly, Farrel said, "Perhaps it is punishment enough. With no letter of reference from me, he'll have a hard time finding work on any kind of rails anywhere in the country. But no doubt he'll find somebody who doesn't care about references to hire him. Damn it. I ought to expose him publicly!" The war within Farrel obviousy still raged, Sarah thought.

"It would be a scandal," she said. "You know how the papers love a scandal. There seems to be a new one every day: politicians who buy their elections, merchants who pay off the police to cover their dishonest practices. Your enemies would love to see the streetcars involved in scandal, wouldn't they? And you know how people are. They don't read enough to learn the facts, but simply take the headlines and imagine the rest. I wonder if it would do Mr. Rankin nearly as much harm as it would do you. Imagine! A streetcar scandal!"

Sarah knew her words were a kind of torture to Farrel, but she felt she had to speak strongly in order to penetrate the gloom he'd sunk into. She seemed to have succeeded because he stared at her speechlessly.

"You're absolutely right," he managed at last. "I'm lucky this didn't come out in some other way. The anarchists will take the full blame and my streetcars will quickly return to public confidence.

My God, and here I am ready to bring it all down like Samson with his pillars. And, like him, to die in the rubble! Thank you, Sarah. You've certainly helped. Of course, I'll have to find a good replacement for Pat. Maybe, though, I'll start to look for a partner instead. It would help the cash position and guarantee that the person would have the streetcars' best interests at heart."

He leaned toward Sarah and kissed the curl at her ear.

"I think I can sleep now," he said. "I'll walk you to your room."

He led her back to her bedroom where she paused at the door awaiting his kiss. She lifted her face toward him. He bent toward her, but instead of kissing her soft lips he kissed her closed eyes, one after the other. A soft "oh," escaped from Sarah's parted lips. Farrel slid his arm around her waist pulling her to him. The kiss he gave her then, left no doubt of his interest. His free hand caressed her full breast as he whispered, "Shall I join you in your bed for a while?" To which she answered, "Oh, yes, my dear. My bed and I have been waiting on your pleasure. Let's hurry," she added, opening the door and drawing him in with her.

After the shared misery of the last few days when it had been more a burden than a pleasure to be together, this night provided the healing magic of closeness. Farrel had never desired Sarah more ardently. Sarah had never so fully given herself to Farrel. It was nearly dawn before he left her to return to his own bed. Then Sarah fell into a deep sleep, one blessedly free of dreams. Their hours together had been dream enough.

The next day and the many days that followed seemed to strain Sarah's adaptability to the limit. She had to learn new ways to deal with servants, she had to learn how to manage a huge household—she who had never managed any household at all—she had to find ways to spend her time during the hours and hours and hours while Farrel was at work. Then there were the many times when Farrel was out of town when those hours stretched not only from sunup to sundown, but also from sundown to sunup.

Samson, who had been Farrel's manservant before the marriage, now took over the major function as household administrator. He took his orders directly from Mr. or Mrs. Hurstwood and the other servants took their orders from him. Under his control were Bessie, the main cook; Clara, the girl from the Seewald household; Flossie, the laundress; Beulah, the upstairs maid; Hector, the man who did general repairs and heavy work; and Bertie, the young groom. Samson had enjoyed the closeness of his earlier relationship with Mr. Hurstwood when it had been just the two of them moving about together from place to place. He knew how to serve without obtruding, and he believed that Mr. Hurstwood appreciated the care he took. Women had always seemed to him frivolous creatures, who deserved no significant place in a man's life. Now all that had changed. He knew he could handle his increased responsibilities, but he felt there had been more loss than gain in the change. This young mistress would need his most sensitive guidance, because she must be led while not feeling herself insulted. Well, he hadn't lived these almost fifty years without learning how to deal with folks. All kinds of folks, but especially the ones he liked least: white folks and womenfolk.

Each morning he would meet with Mrs. Hurstwood and they would plan the household's needs for that day. Together they planned the meals, the shopping needs to supply those meals, the cleaning chores so that the entire house seemed always at the peak of polished perfection. Then he would consult with her during the day only if she called him to her, which she seldom did.

By noon, then, Sarah found herself breakfasted, dressed, and freed of her day's major chore. What was she to do next? She spent some time with her mother but felt reluctant to express her dissatisfaction, her feeling that somehow marriage had cheated her out of romance. She took it upon herself to visit with the families of the two people injured in the streetcar wreck, and she hoped Farrel would find that a help in relieving his feelings of guilt over the whole incident.

One of the injured was a young boy, Tyler Moss, no more than eleven years old, whose legs had been crushed. At first the doctors had feared that they would have to amputate his legs, but fortunately the rapid healing powers of youth had served him well. He simply had to maintain patience while the bones healed. Sarah visited him at least once a week, because so much of the time he was left alone. Tyler's father worked in construction when there was anything being built. He'd even worked for a while on the streetcar tracks. Tyler's mother worked in the tobacco factory where Tyler had worked with her before he got hurt. Now he explained to Sarah how the family could hardly get by with him stuck at home. His dad was out of work just now and his mother only earned a dollar and twenty-five cents a week—not enough for the three of them. Sarah, horrified at his words, always managed to bring a huge basket of food with her and stuck several dollars at the bottom of it. She didn't want their gratitude; she just wanted their continued survival. What a hard life some people had, she thought, and felt guilty that she spent so much of her easy life feeling sorry for herself.

"Tyler," she said on what would probably be her last visit as he was now able to move about some and had told her he would be back at work in a few days, "shall I read you a story?"

"Yes, miz, how 'bout the one with the lion and the thorny paw." His eyes were bright coals in his grayish skin. He had that look about him that bad eating and too little laughter bring to young faces making them old before they're even grown up.

"Androcles it is. Why is he your favorite? You like him better than any of the others, I know."

She settled herself in the wicker chair whose cushion, though it had stuffing poking out in a half-dozen places, still protected her clothes from being torn by the broken pieces of stick. Tyler sat on the unmade bed. She had tried to lure him onto her lap, but he knew he wasn't supposed to get too close to rich folks and always said no. What if his mum or dad had come in and seen 'at, why he'd get a lickin' sure. Now he tried to think of an answer to the lady's question, but he'd never given it much thought.

"I just do, I guess. I guess maybe there ain't no reason. Does you have reasons for liking stories?" he asked, really curious now about this business of liking things.

Sarah laughed. "I guess I do. Or I try to think about it. Maybe sometimes I just make up a reason. Anyway, it doesn't matter at all. I'm just glad you like it. I could leave the book here with you so that you could have it even when I'm not here."

"But, miz, I cain't read the words. I never been to no schools, y'know."

Sarah's heart felt like a sky heavy with rain. Never been to school and never would be. What's worse, she realized, his life was representative of so many many others. Children who were quickly turned into workers. Workers instead of citizens. Well, she shook off her gloom; smarter people were going to have to figure out that problem.

"The book has lots of pictures and you can look at them," she told the little boy now, "and remember the story so you can tell it to yourself."

"Good!" he cried; then a shy look she'd seen whenever she'd left him the basket of food came over his face as he remembered his manners. "Thank you, miz." She'd rather he hadn't thanked her. It seemed to stretch the distance between them

101

into miles instead of mere feet. But there was nothing she could do, she told herself, and so she began the story he wanted to hear.

The other injured person presented her with fewer complex feelings. He was an old man with an injury to his back. He had nothing to do but wait for death before the accident, he told her bluntly, and he could wait just as well sitting upright in his chair at home as anywhere else, so nothing had changed. His life had been good enough as those things go, but not anything worth clinging to. Sarah could hardly believe that anyone felt that way. At seventeen, life seemed to her like the tight bud of the magnolia blossom which held within it the possibility of nothing but more and more beauty. Beauty upon beauty. She was eager for her share of it and thought that she could never get enough.

Only one problem marred her sense of a near-perfect life. Well, it was true she experienced a certain restlessness because of the huge amounts of time she felt she really ought to find useful ways to fill, but that was hardly a problem. No, there was really only one problem that she could think of, one problem that she thought of over and over: that she wasn't yet expecting a child. At first, on her honeymoon, Sarah felt almost terrified of the prospect of being with child. She assumed, never having been told otherwise, that once a woman lay with a man she bore him a child as a result. But then a month passed and she learned that she was not about to bear Farrel a child. She had to tell him, in fact, that she could not entertain him in her bed because . . . that was an embarrassment for her. Then a second month passed and yet another and then she began to worry that perhaps she was unable to have children. It was a worry she shared with no one—not her husband, not her mother. She simply waited, finally believing that if only she would become pregnant then her life would solve itself.

Six

During these fall months when Sarah had been trying to find a pattern to fit her new life, the two men who had dynamited the streetcar remained locked away in jail awaiting a place on the court docket.

Farrel had fired Rankin the very next day after returning from New Orleans, the next day after he had learned of Rankin's betrayal of his trust, the day after Sarah had pointed out how important it was to minimize any scandal even remotely connected to the streetcars. Farrel continued, though, to spot Rankin on occasion lounging around town, although his home was in New York City. It worried Farrel that Pat might be planning some sort of courtroom shenanigans.

As the trial date approached, Farrel became increasingly miserable and anxious. Instead of the accident fading from his mind with time, it seemed clearer than ever. The week preceding the trial, nightmares plagued his sleep. Over and over he watched helplessly as streetcars careened around too-sharp curves or collided head-on into each other. Other, more bizarre images he could only half-remember: the overhead wires ripped loose and crackling with electricity while a baby crawled along the muddy tracks toward them, reaching out its hand; or huge and hideous spiderlike creatures tentacling their way across the top of a streetcar in search of a way in to the unheeding passengers, reaching the rear platform, at the open door, beginning to advance as the first passengers see them and scream. Farrel's own voice woke him as he called out in warning.

The day of the trial finally arrived. Richmond turned out in full force. The courtroom filled rapidly, and groups of people unable to gain seats lingered in the hall outside. Suddenly a hum of noise like bees around a hive filled the air, as the whispered news that the injured old man had died hummed through the courthouse. Almost at the same time, the court's officer called out the traditional "Oyez, oyez, all rise," and the judge took his place behind the high desk. The prisoners, looking like rabbits just let out of a cage and uncertain where to run, stood up to hear the charges against them read out.

The initial charges, which were serious enough, included criminal conspiracy, malicious mischief, and destruction of private property. But, due to the old man's death, murder now led the list. At that dreadful word "murder" a hubbub arose among the spectators drowning out the remaining charges. One of the prisoners sagged against his comrade who struggled to hold him up. The sounds of amazed voices in the packed room were like the rumble of a gathering storm. One woman's voice penetrated through it shrieking, "Malcolm, Malcolm." The small foreign-looking prisoner whose name she called gazed wildly about seeking the source of the sound, seeking his wife in the mass of faces before him. Farrel sat frozen during this drama. He gripped Sarah's gloved hand so tightly she thought she must call out herself from pain. The judge pounded his gavel and gave his warning about clearing the courtroom if there was another outcry.

The trial itself was brief. There was no real defense as the two men had readily admitted their guilt, almost proudly, the day the police arrested them. Farrel had trouble listening to even the brief testimony, though. He heard each of the prisoners present his story in a broken English which was probably going to weigh more heavily than any evidence as proof of guilt. He noticed that their clothing was of an odd unfashionable cut and emphasized the fact that they were outsiders. Of such irrelevancies, Farrel thought, is justice composed. Previously, he had felt that one should take charge of the events in his life, but in the courtroom today he began to suspect that events could take the control out of one's hands. That, in fact, the sense of control over one's life might be a fragile construction.

The judge pronounced the two men guilty as charged. They would be sentenced in a week's time.

As the prisoners were led off to their cells, the spectators milled about; Farrel remained motionless beside a concerned Sarah. He never before had felt such a keen sense of pity. Guilty of murder, the judge said, when all they had really been guilty of—those foreigners—was mischief. How we have erred and strayed like lost sheep. . . . He remembered that from Sunday-school classes. His mind slipped back to his childhood Sundays when he had heard the minister talk about life and sin. He might have been poor. . . . Might have been an immigrant himself except for good fortune. It was certainly neither to his credit nor due to his ability that such was not the case. "The race is not always to the swift," he remembered reading from the Bible, "nor the battle to the strong; but time and chance happeneth to them all."

The following week Farrel tried to concentrate solely on the job of keeping his streetcars running on schedule and sending out feelers to neighboring communities to see about forming an even vaster streetcar network. Thoughts about the two men locked away in jail intruded at intervals. When his receptionist came in with the name of a woman who wanted to see him, a Mrs. Malcolm Persniak, Farrel breathed a sigh of relief almost as though he had been waiting for her visit.

He knew at once it was the prisoner's wife. He straightened his jacket, preparing himself for a furious assault, but then a woman who looked more like a servant than a goddess of wrath came through his door.

"Good afternoon. Have a seat," Farrel offered.

"I would just as soon stand, sur," she answered, twisting her handkerchief nervously around her raw-looking hands. "I come to ask. You got to hulp them men."

"What in the world do you mean?" Farrel asked, immediately on the defensive. "I have nothing to do with their situation. Nothing at all. Surely you'd be better off talking with the lawyers."

"The charge is murder, sur, murder! The man what died wur jist old is all. You kin talk to the judge 'bout dropping the murder charge. Put the charges back the way they wuz."

"No. I couldn't do that. It's none of my affair." Farrel began his habitual pacing, but then he turned his back on the woman and stared out the window.

"You're a powerful man, sur. And they wuz your streetcars hurt. The men sez they're guilty, sur, but not murder!"

Farrel blanched. He turned back to the woman and saw the frayed sleeves on her coat; he noticed the flowered babushka, that funny scarf poor women wrapped around their heads and tied in knots beneath their chins. He felt as though his conscience had taken shape before him.

"Yes," he mumbled, as though to himself. Then, louder, he repeated, "Yes. I will go and talk with the judge. I'll see what I can do."

The woman made the sign of the cross and uttered a blessing in what Farrel thought was Polish. "Thank you," she said; then she turned and left.

Farrel left the office shortly after. He hurried along the street as though somehow his speed could compensate now for actions he hadn't taken previously.

Judge Weston greeted Farrel warmly. He clapped him on the back as he welcomed him into his private chambers. While they talked, the two men swirled rich amber brandy around in expensive snifters. They sipped on the fiery drink during the pauses between their words. Fifteen minutes later, as Farrel was leaving, the judge rested his arm on Farrel's back in a fatherly gesture. Farrel's smile would have looked to anyone watching like the smile of a good friend saying good-bye.

From the outside, no one would have known that Farrel felt as burdened as though he were a barge loaded down with tons of steel rails. He turned back toward his office because he couldn't bear to face Sarah until he had thought through his conversation with the judge. The office had closed down for the day, but he let himself in, glad of the dark rooms and the silence. As he turned to lock the door behind him, though, Pat Rankin came up to the doorway.

"I'd like to talk with you," he said. He had his hands stuffed in his pockets, and his jacket collar raised against the chill wind. Farrel signaled him in and locked the door behind him. They stood in the gloom of the half-light from the street; Farrel made no move to light the lamp.

"Go ahead," he said tersely, when the silence seemed to stretch uncomfortably between them.

Pat shrugged his jacket collar down, took his hands from his pockets, blew on them, and gazed at Farrel trying to work up the courage to begin the speech he'd planned. "I'd like to come back. We worked together good enough, don't you think? This was a bad thing I did, and I'm damned sorry! But there's no real harm done. Streetcars are more important to Richmond every day. The company's still in fine shape." Having run out of words, he stopped.

"No harm." Farrel repeated the phrase. His eyes had a fierce glow as they picked up just a glint of light from the street. Rankin backed up a step.

"What's the matter, man?"

"Those two men are going to hang! Two poor bastards too dumb to get out of town before they got caught. I'm not excusing their actions, but I still lay their lives at your feet."

"What are you talking about? Hang? They'll spend a couple years in jail. Probably teach 'em a trade. I'm talking about us working together. To hell with those guys."

"Get out, Pat! Get out of here and get out of town. You will never work for me again. Nor for any man who does business with me. Talk about learning a new trade—well, I think that's a mighty fine idea for you. Just don't let me see you again or I might just change my mind about bringing you up on criminal charges."

"Christ, Farrel, you've gone off your rails," Pat spoke as he backed toward the door. He'd never seen his boss this way. He knew that if it came to a fight he could clobber this fine and dandy Mr.

Farrel Hurstwood, but with the bad times he was in already that would probably be the worst thing he could possibly do. "Well, that's it then," he said at the door. "You won't see me again." He fumbled with the door, trying to get it unlocked. Farrel came up and pushed him out of the way, unlocked the door, and held it wide for him to leave. After Pat walked out, Farrel locked the door once again before he slumped into the receptionist's chair. He let his head sink onto his arms on top of the desk as he thought about the judge.

The judge wouldn't change a thing. The public wanted the foreigners punished, he had said, and besides he had plans for himself. He intended to run for Congress. This trial, with a public execution at its conclusion, would get him a lot of attention. Everyone would know his name. That's what mattered in an election. "You understand," he'd said to Farrel, "that that's the way these things work. After all, those men are no good anyway. It will be no loss to the world to get rid of them, and it will be a hell of an effective lesson to others to stay out of Virginia if they want to make trouble!"

On January 15, 1889, one month short of a year after the Richmond Electric Street Railway Company had begun operation and almost halfway through the Hurstwoods' first year of marriage, the two men were sentenced to be hanged by the neck until dead. In summation, Judge Weston made a speech that he hoped would be quoted by the newspapers:

"Progress is necessary and inevitable. It is the triumph of the American spirit. Although some commercial problems such as temporary unemployment may result from new inventions and innovations, it is imperative that no barrier be allowed. You two scoundrels in your attack on progress have spit on the American flag. We are empowered to pass sentence upon you and will do so to the fullest extent of the law. Let others heed this warning: we won't tolerate anarchists! America is the land of progress: God bless it!

Farrel never told Sarah about his discussion with the judge. When she tried to raise the subject of the sentence's harshness, he avoided the topic completely. When the day of the public execution came, he stayed at home, and Sarah made no comment. Neither of them had the heart to attend such a piteous event in any case.

To Judge Weston's amazement, the aspect of the trial which elicited the greatest commentary was the public nature of the execution. The newspapers focused their attention on the fact that surely as America approached the start of the twentieth century it was time to abandon the cruel and barbarous custom of public executions. In general, the readers agreed. People associated the judge's name with this issue so strongly that when election time came he decided it would be unwise to run. Perhaps by the next election, he thought, people will have forgotten.

Seven

It was almost spring of 1890 before Farrel Hurstwood finally found a replacement, and more, for Pat Rankin. By that time and after lengthy deliberation he had decided that he should seek additional fiscal security for his company, which meant, in short, that he would take a partner. After a period of searching and feeling out, he'd found the right person; at last they were in the midst of final negotiations.

At a soft knock, the two men looked up. They had their heads bent over a table littered with papers, charts, maps, and official-looking documents.

"Come in," Farrel called.

Lizbette Willis, the receptionist who had been with the Richmond Electric Street Railway Company since Farrel had opened the office, stood in the doorway.

"I'll be leaving soon, sir," she said. "Is there anything more you need before I go?"

"Yes, Mrs. Willis," Farrel answered, "as a matter of fact there is. If you would bring in the original city council ordinances, that should do it." She nodded and left.

"Mr. Spencer," Farrel said, addressing his companion, "I had no idea I'd kept you working at these papers all afternoon. Perhaps we should call it a day."

"No, no," George Spencer responded emphatically. "If you're an angler, Mr. Hurstwood, I have no doubt you're a good one. You've hooked me solidly with the bait of your streetcar, I confess. Let's go on a little longer. After I look over that first route plan in the city council records, let's explore the expansion you have in mind."

Mrs. Willis returned and handed Farrel a file. He nodded and she left closing the door behind her.

"Oh, and as to our partnership," Spencer continued, "your terms are perfectly acceptable to me. Tell your attorney to draw up the papers and I'll have my banker send over a draft."

"Splendid!" Farrel exclaimed. "This deserves a drink. Will you toast our new affiliation with a brandy? I have some Courvoisier that should be worthy of the occasion."

"Of course," George agreed. He sensed that he and Farrel shared the good breeding developed in the sons of sons of main-line Americans.

"You know," Farrel went on as he arranged two snifters and poured the amber liquid two fingers deep in them, "as soon as I heard that speech of yours on the need for electrification to increase

Richmond's power base, well, I knew we had to get together!" He passed one of the glasses to George and raised his own in a salute. "Here's to us," he said.

"Yes, to us and to streetcars, bless 'em." George inhaled the brandy's bouquet. Then he took a deep swallow and placed the half-emptied glass back on the table, saying, "Now let's see that ordinance for the original routing."

Farrel, still warming his glass in his hands, smiled and pointed to the file. This new partner was certainly eager, he thought.

"I'm the fourth generation of Spencers to have lived in Richmond, y'know. I don't say it to brag. Only that it may help us get permission for certain passageways. Access to information and such, too."

"Really!" Farrel pretended surprise. "I never thought of that."

George looked up from the file to regard his partner in a new light. Yes, he told himself, of course Hurstwood had already discovered and evaluated that bit of information. Probably long before contacting him. He shook his head. Then, smiling, went back to examining the ordinance again.

"First, a double track on Laurel Street," he read, "from Broad Street to Main Street. Second, an additional or second track from Main Street down Rocketts Street to Denny Street; then with a single track along Denny Street to Williamsburg Avenue, along said avenue to Louisiana Street, along said Louisiana Street to the point on

Seventh Street where its present right of route terminates." There was more, of course, much more.

While George Spencer read the rest of the document, Farrel Hurstwood imagined a stairway with collapsible risers carried on a mechanical moving belt. The motor needed to drive such a contraption wouldn't have to be too powerful. He changed the angle of ascent in his drawing and wrote out a new formula to describe the resulting situation. Even as a schoolboy, Farrel had kept a pencil and paper stuck away in his pocket for the random moments when nothing special was going on when he could imagine spectacular inventions. Mechanical devices yielded their secrets to him, and he could move easily from what already was to what might possibly be.

"Done," George announced at last. "I think I see where we travel now and where we need to extend the lines. What's next?"

"Nothing more for today, partner. Tomorrow morning will be time enough." Farrel piled his projected streetcar route maps on the side of the desk. He placed his stairway plans in a special folder of future possibilities which had a place right at the front of his desk drawer. Then he stood up, stretching his back a bit. "What do you say we retire to my house for dinner. My wife would enjoy meeting you, I'm sure. It would cheer her a bit too, I think. A childhood friend of hers is in some sort of trouble and my wife is in quite a funk about it. I don't know the details, but I'm sure a festive evening would be just the thing to bring her around."

"I have no dinner plans; I'd enjoy meeting my new partner's wife!"

"Shall we ride the streetcar?" An impish smile crossed Farrel's face, making him look younger than his thirty-two years. "That way we can take today's thoughts and transfer them deep into our bones."

"I suppose," George answered as he slipped into his jacket, "that's the Hurstwood way of saying that a trolley-car ride relaxes you, eh?"

"Guilty. I admit it. This streetcar business drives me to despair, but I love the wonderful rattle-buggies nonetheless."

The unhappiness Farrel mentioned had come about in Sarah due to a visit with Maxine less than a week earlier. Sarah had been sitting in the back parlor playing at embroidering a sampler for her parents when she heard a tap, light but persistent, at the side-porch door. She wondered who would avoid the front door and come here. A hobo begging scraps of food or a job would go around back to the kitchen. Sarah considered calling out to Samson for help.

An article in the *Dispatch* last week had put a scare into her. It told of a gang of young hoodlums called the Red Devils. They were only one of many gangs people had grown used to seeing around the city. The gangs mostly drank and yelled insults at the folks who walked by, but last week they had robbed and beaten up an out-of-towner. Then they had left him lying in his own blood in front of the elegant new Jefferson Hotel. The *Dispatch* demanded that the police get the gangs off the streets. "If they have nowhere else to go," the editorial stated, "let's put them in prison. That will teach them about work. The chain gangs are a hard school but an effective one."

The knock came again. Sarah stood, uncertain what to do. Now the tapping was on glass and Sarah saw a child's dirty face smile at her through the window. Ashamed of having let her mind run away with her, she hurried to the door.

"Maxine ast me tuh bring yuh dis," said the little boy. Sarah recognized him now as Maxine's youngest brother, Roy. He handed over a pale yellow envelope sealed with wax to ensure privacy.

"Thank you, Roy. I hardly recognized you, you've grown so. But why aren't you in school in the midde of the afternoon?"

"Ah, I played the hook. Said I had a stomach ache to Ma." He grinned, waved his cap at her, and ran off down the path alongside the house to the street.

Sarah pulled the door shut against the raw March wind that swept into the room and over the small fire in the grate. Blue-and-orange tongues licked at the air in response.

"Samson," Sarah called, "Clara." She wanted someone to come and add a log to the fire. The combination of the sharp air and the unexpected letter had quite chilled her. Since her marriage, Sarah had mostly lost touch with Maxine. She sensed that this message meant trouble. Maxine had never sent her a letter before.

Samson came in and she asked him to fix the fire. When he'd gone out again, she curled into the bentwood rocker that was the most comfortable chair in the room. She flapped the envelope against her open palm, reluctant to open it. Pandora's box, she thought; lift the lid and out fly troubles.

Then she tore a strip off along the side of the envelope, her special way of opening letters. It let her leave the seals intact. She saved the envelopes because of the seals which she admired for their beauty and individuality. She had quite a collection of them. Sarah unfolded the letter trying to keep her hands from shaking. She smoothed it so that she could make out the spidery writing that covered the tissue-thin paper.

"Sarah," Maxine wrote, "I must see you. You were always a sensible person and a good friend, and I have need of both at this particular moment. My subject is of a sensitive nature and I must see you alone.

"Would it be possible for you to meet me during my supper break at three outside the tobacco factory where I now work? We wouldn't have much time, but even a few minutes would allow me to outline my situation to you and hear your response.

"The bell rings promptly at three. I'll wait by the door closest to the river. If you can't make it, you can't, but I pray that you can and will. For old friendship's sake!" She'd signed it Jug, the nickname from their childhood.

The letter's tone scared Sarah. What, she wondered, could be the trouble? She could hardly picture Maxine at work in a factory. She knew the Cooper family had more children than money, but she had always imagined a finer destiny for Maxine than this. Of course, when they were schoolgirls they'd only shared schoolgirl dreams. They would run off together and become actresses, that was their favorite fantasy. If it hadn't been for her marriage, she realized, she would still be at work in her father's pharmacy.

It was already past two o'clock. She must hurry or she'd miss Maxine. Sarah rose at once and went in search of Bertie. She'd arrange for the closed carriage which would allow them the privacy Maxine wanted. By a quarter to three, Sarah sat in her fashionable black brougham in front of the factory anxiously watching the huge metal doors. Precisely at three the factory bell sounded, the doors swung open, and workers flooded into the courtyard. They were mostly women and children, these workers, many of them black people, with only a sprinkling of white men who were, no doubt, the bosses. It shocked Sarah to see the number of children, the youth of the children. How had she managed to remain unaware of these troops of children during the years when she and her comrades spent their carefree days in school? Before she could give further thought to this subject, the carriage door opened and a dark wraith slipped in beside her.

It was Maxine, Sarah realized, this ghost who

leaned over and planted a cold kiss on her cheek, but a Maxine she could hardly recognize. A Maxine, in fact, whom she hadn't recognized as she'd approached. Sarah had stared out at the throng of humanity in search of her laughing school friend but didn't spot her. Now she scanned the troubled face of the woman beside her trying to find traces of the Maxine she knew.

This woman, thin as a skeleton, looked old enough to be Sarah's mother. Her eyes were dark marbles sunk within dark rings. They dominated the small face and burned with a terrible intensity. Maxine's dark hair, once a mass of curls, frizzed around her head now like a worn-out scrub brush with splayed-out bristles. Sarah feared for a moment that her friend would spring upon her in a murderous rage, so mad did she appear. Instead, the face crumpled before Sarah's eyes, becoming a contorted mask. Convulsive sobs shook Maxine's body.

"Oh, Sarah, my life . . . my life is in ruins."

Sarah could not conceive of any forces that could have wrought these changes in her friend. Less than a year ago they had sat together busily planning their graduation party.

"Tell me, Maxine. I can help. Whatever it is you need, I can help." So she spoke in the overconfidence of youth, certain that nothing could be beyond repair.

"It's too late! There's no help to be had, I'm afraid. I've shamed myself, and I've shamed my family as well. In a matter of months—" Here she stopped, unable to go on. She dabbed at the tears which dripped down her cheeks as though they flooded from some inexhaustible underground spring. "In a matter of months I'll give birth to a bastard!"

The words and the manner, both, shocked Sarah, as did the fact, the reality, behind the words.

"But how?" She stumbled over the questions she wanted to ask. "Who? Maybe you're mistaken. I certainly can't tell by looking at you."

"I've eaten nothing. Practically nothing. I thought if I kept losing weight it wouldn't show as soon. Or maybe it would die! But no. I'm more likely to die than it. It's the life force itself. Determined to be born. Isn't that what the fancy philosophers say?"

"Don't talk that way," Sarah pleaded, unable to bear the bitter tirade that poured from Maxine's lips. "It can't be as desperate as you think. Do you love the father? Could you marry him?"

Maxine threw back her head, but the sound that burst from her throat bore no resemblance to laughter. It was the braying of a mule as it falls from a cliff wall. It was the squeal of a rabbit clamped in a hound's teeth.

"It's my foreman at the plant. He offered to take me home one day and he forced me." She burst into fresh sobs as she remembered her innocence. She'd felt flattered that he wanted to be alone with her. Often as he walked past her during work hours, he'd stop and make some friendly comment, sometimes even pretending to point to something so that he could brush his arm against

122

her in an almost accidental way. She'd felt sure he liked her, but she'd been wrong, her interpretations completely mistaken.

He'd driven the carriage out to the edge of town. Her heart pounded in anticipation of the romance that was about to begin for her. She'd looked down at her lap demurely and then back up at him. What she saw then made her heart pound even more furiously.

His eyes gleamed like an animal's. His hands fumbled with his pants. He lunged toward her. There was no room to move, no time to escape. In one swift move he was on top of her; his thick body pinned her down as he tore at her skirts, forced her legs apart. The moment which she had envisioned as holding a tender kiss turned instead into searing pain as he thrust his way into her body. Her only further memory was of the agony in both her mind and her body.

That was dreadful enough, of course, but it was not all. No, not by any means, because when a week had passed and then another, she'd learned the meaning of despair. There was no need to go to a doctor for confirmation. She knew with a certainty that dulled her senses: she was carrying his child.

As Maxine finished her story, she thrust her head back, with eyes closed and jaw clenched. Her bony fingers formed fists. She began rhythmically to pound on her stomach as powerfully as she could.

"Stop, oh, stop," Sarah begged. Horrified, she grasped Maxine's hands. Sarah could feel the round swell of Maxine's belly which her full black dress had hidden. She dressed as though she were in mourning.

"Oh, my poor Jug. Have you talked to him?"

"I did, even though I could hardly bear to look at him. He laughed in my face and threatened to fire me if I ever said another word about him."

"You have to tell your folks then."

"Oh, God," Maxine gasped. "No! I want it to die." Her voice sounded like the olden-day prophets to Sarah's ears. It called upon God to bear witness.

"Don't say that, you'll mark the baby. It's a sin to say such things." Sarah babbled on hardly knowing what she said, unable to think of what she could say to ease her friend's pain. Even through her confusion, though, the irony of Jug with child against her will when she yearned to conceive struck her. God's will be done, that was the hard part to accept, she thought, as she held Maxine in her arms.

The factory whistle split the air with its short blast. Maxine straightened.

"Thanks for coming, Sarah. I had to tell someone. I wake in the mornings and it's still night inside me. I move through the days like a sleepwalker."

"Don't give up. Maybe I can come up with an idea."

"It doesn't really matter. He called me a slut and he's right. He made me into a slut."

She pushed open the carriage door and stepped out onto the cobblestone street.

"It's not true. You're good and pure just as you've always been."

Maxine almost smiled at that—Sarah couldn't tell if it was a smile or a grimace of pain—then she was gone. She hurried across the yard to where the factory's gaping mouth swallowed her.

Sarah stared after her. Their meeting had had an eerie effect on her. She felt as though sad and pitiful events were flooding across the world. Any moment of happiness was a chunk of rock you had to use to build a dike to hold back the raging sea of misery. Or else it would drown you. She felt herself being pulled under. She was in deep water, felt helpless to fight against the pull.

"Drive home," she called up to Bertie who dozed on his seat. He clucked to the horses and the carriage began to roll across the stones. The sound, once so cheerful to Sarah, now seemed like a drum roll. The long, slow drum roll before an execution.

When Sarah arrived home, she went directly to bed saying she didn't feel well. The next morning she didn't get up. Clara brought her breakfast on a tray. But when she returned awhile later, she saw the food still uneaten.

The next morning Sarah stayed in bed also, but when she tried to do the same thing for the third morning in a row Farrel came to her room.

"If you are feeling so poorly," he said, "I'll bring the doctor around." His look had just the tinge of the look her father sometimes wore when he felt she was bluffing about something.

"I'm not sick, I'm just sad." She meant to sound

like a tragic heroine, but her voice sounded merely petulant, she decided. "Maxine's in bad trouble."

Farrel remained standing at the foot of the bed. He took his watch from his pocket and checked the time. Sarah knew he must be restless to be off to the office.

"What kind of trouble?"

"Nothing. Never mind. I know you're late. I'll get up today. I'm just being self-indulgent, I guess." She hoped he would urge her to tell him the details, decide it was more important to be with her than to rush off to work. But instead he looked relieved to be able to leave.

"Good," he said, as he planted a brisk kiss on the top of her head. "I'll be home late tonight, but you'll be fine, I'm sure."

He strode from the door, glad, she was sure, to be headed toward the real world, the world of streetcars. Damn them! Sarah realized she was beginning to sound like a jealous wife. Jealous of her husband's work!

She called for Clara and forced herself to begin a normal day. She had to think of something to do for Maxine, but she just couldn't. That day passed and the next one began. Farrel had said this would be the day he hoped to establish his new partnership. Well, Sarah figured, that would probably mean another late night at the office.

By midafternoon, she retired to her suite of rooms for a rest. Unable to breathe in her tight stays, she called for Clara to help her undress, to unbutton the thirty-two satin-covered buttons that ran down her bodice to below her waist, to lift

126

the heavy russet taffeta gown up over her head, and finally to loosen the strings on her corset. At last, freed from confinement, Sarah lounged across the fainting couch, dismissing Clara with a wave of her hand.

The couch was the newest addition to the house. Sarah had pointed it out to Farrel in a shop window the month before, admiring the aqua velvet upholstery and the gilt scrollwork across the high headrest. He'd had it delivered the next day as a surprise. Sarah lazed back against it, determined to begin *Madame Bovary,* a novel which had quite a scandalous reputation and which Sarah had gone to some pains to obtain from the Rosemary Library, but which she hadn't opened yet.

Eight

When Farrel and George left the office, the sky had just begun to turn rusty. Days were getting longer as spring approached. Crowds of people restless for home filled the sidewalks. Women and children who had just gotten off from the factories mingled with townsmen closing up their shops for the day. Horses hitched to carriages pawed the ground awaiting the flick of reins. Hurstwood and Spencer stood anonymously in the cluster of people at the trolley stop. It wasn't long before they saw the car rocking along toward them with its yellow headlamp casting a light onto the tracks in front of it.

When the streetcar screeched to a stop, people surged forward to get on. As Farrel climbed the two iron steps, he thought, "This is mine. I made this." He breathed in the familiar smell of the heated grease. He and George let the others rush ahead of them for the two-person seats on the right or for a place along the wooden bench that ran the length of the left side. He read again the sign prominently displayed over the front of the car: "Colored patrons will please fill the seats from the rear. White patrons will please fill the seats from the front. Thank you. Richmond Electric Street Railway Company." Looking about him, he saw that the folks obeyed the rules. No trouble there, he thought.

As the streetcar lurched into motion, the standers reached for the leather straps which hung down from the long brass overhead bar that ran the length of the streetcar body. Although the car was eighteen feet long, it seated only twenty people. Farrel thought, I'll have to talk to George about increasing the capacity. A small coal stove on the rear vestibuled platform kept the air comfortably warm, but street dust swirled in through the open sides. I'll have to think of a remedy for that, Hurstwood told himself, coughing.

"Fares, please. Have your money ready."

Farrel stayed George's hand and pulled two nickels from his own pocket. He knew he could easily arrange for a pass on the cars, but he preferred to be treated like any other passenger.

He paid for both of them now, saying, "How's it going, Mike?" The uniformed man tipped his cap and smiled in greeting, "Mr. Hurstwood, sir, an honor," and moved on to collect other fares.

The motorman, who pulled a heavy curtain across his back as he started the car, was invisible between stops. There was a romance already developing around his role, Farrel thought. The car slid smoothly along the rails between stops. The noise from the motor, though, made it hard to talk.

"There's a flexible suspension system below the car springs," Farrel shouted to George, "which minimizes shock and jar and prevents the possibility of stripping the gears."

George nodded and smiled. He was thinking about ways to lower the noise level. Also, the lights in the car were too dim, George thought, and dimmed still further when they crawled up a hill or approached a turn.

At a particularly sharp turn, the motorman called out to the rear man, "Broom, Sol," as he came to a full stop. Metal scrapings, accumulated over the last several runs, blocked the tracks. Sol jumped down, swept the tracks ahead of the car, then leaped back on board. As the trolley started up again, Farrel asked, "What do vou think, George?"

"I think we should put a streetcar line in every city in America!"

Sarah had read her novel up to the point where the young Emma Bovary had begun to doubt that she had ever really loved the man she had recently married. When Emma yearned to know the meanings of the words that she had found so beautiful in books, "bliss," "passion," "ecstasy," Sarah felt such terrible pain she had to put the book down. Tears blurred the room around her. She wasn't sure whether her sorrow was for Emma Bovary, for Maxine, or for someone else. Better not to think about it, she decided, as she let herself drift into a drowsy state which was neither sleeping nor waking.

Sometime later, the slam of the downstairs door startled her. She heard voices. She thought she heard Farrel and another man. Feeling vaguely alarmed—was she supposed to have prepared for company?—she jumped up and rang for the maid. Without help, there was no way she could fasten her stays. Where was that girl? Sarah fumed. But then just as she started to ring a second time, there came the familiar knock.

"Come in, Clara. Don't you know I can't fix myself up by myself? Isn't that Mr. Hurstwood's voice I hear? Is there someone with him?"

Sarah fired this volley of questions without a pause. Meanwhile, Clara shut the door and moved behind Sarah in order to tighten her corset.

"It's him all right and asking where you is too. With a big man along."

"What did you tell him? Did you say I was reading?"

"Reading," Clara snorted, giving a final fierce tug to the laces. "Dreaming, I'd say. And when's you gonna teach me reading like you promised?" Clara held the gown up for Sarah.

"No, not that same one, Clara. Fetch me the teal blue with the little lace collar and the bustle. I like the look of those gray velvet ribbons down the skirt." She struggled into the gown smoothing it over her crinoline petticoats. "I'll teach you to read, Clara, really."

"Thass what you allus says."

131

"I will, I tell you. Oh, wait! I just had a marvelous idea. I have a friend who needs work. Maybe I could get her to come here and teach you how to read. But do me up now and no more sass. I have to hurry and get downstairs."

Sarah felt a visible change in the room as though the light had just brightened turning the marigolds in the vase beside her bed from bronze to a golden orange. Could unhappiness actually dim vision, she wondered for a fleeting moment. But then Sarah turned her thoughts away from her unhappiness which was only a faint echo of Maxine's original cry of despair. Maxine could move into the house until the baby came, and she could feel useful by teaching Clara to read. Then later, maybe she could get a real job teaching. Maybe Farrel could help with that. Oh, she could hardly wait to tell Maxine. First thing in the morning, she promised herself, she'd go to Maxine. Tomorrow was Sunday. Maxine would be at home. Yes, that's what she would do.

By now, Clara had Sarah's dress fastened and her curls carefully arranged. Sarah hurried down the stairs to her waiting husband.

"There you are at last, my dear," Farrel said as she appeared at the door of the front parlor. She could tell by his voice that he was peeved with her and she felt her heart tighten. Why was it that he always made her feel as if she'd done something wrong, failed him in some way? He guided her over to the mantel where an unknown man stood smiling at her.

He was shorter than Farrel and rounder, not

much taller than Sarah's five feet two inches, it seemed. Actually he was more than five seven, quite a startling difference from Farrel's six feet. "I'd like to introduce you to my new partner, Mr. George Spencer. George, my wife Sarah."

George took her extended hand, bent over it, and kissed the soft white skin. Sarah felt the slight scratch of his beard and shivered unaccountably. She could feel the moist print of his lips long after he'd risen, after they'd murmured their hellos, after they'd taken seats and were drinking their sherry.

She thought it amazing that this stranger, surely fifteen years her senior, and not at all handsome, certainly much less handsome than Farrel, should have set her imagination spinning with just a polite kiss on the hand.

"You're lost in thought, Mrs. Hurstwood," he said. Farrel had excused himself to wash up for dinner so they were alone for the moment. Sarah blushed.

"I'm sorry," she stuttered. "I'm being rude. I should be congratulating you and my husband both."

"I understand you were reading when we arrived. Do you mind my asking what? I'm quite a reader myself."

He sat back placing one shiny black-booted foot onto his other knee. Part of his appeal, Sarah decided, was that he seemed to be so comfortable with himself. She envied his composure. She herself felt as tense and awkward as she had on the day she had made that chocolate egg cream for

Farrel, the day they had first met. As tense as a wave about to crash onto the rocks, she thought, as awkward as a falling star. She surprised herself with these odd and poetic thoughts. She wondered where they came from.

"The book you were reading?" George Spencer asked again as she continued to look at him with an alarmed and blank look. He was afraid she might faint.

"*Madame Bovary,*" she managed. "Do you know the scandalous book?"

"Yes, as a matter of fact I do. I try to keep up with books. That one is by a French writer with an amazingly clear eye for reality, I'd say. Not pretty, though. It's strong stuff. Have you gotten very far into it?"

"Well, that's a funny thing." Sarah lost her self-consciousness as she began to talk about the book. "I got to where she had married. I don't think he's the right man for her, do you? Then when she felt unhappy, even though I thought it was inevitable given their respective natures, I felt so unhappy myself that I had to stop reading. Isn't that odd?"

"You seem to have quite a grasp of what the author is trying to say. As to your reaction, no, it doesn't seem too strange to me." What he meant was that this young, young, young woman before him probably shared with Emma Bovary an intensely poetic and romantic appreciation of life. If she read it one way, the book could serve as a warning to her to guard herself from extravagant reactions, but on the other hand, it might simply encourage her natural inclinations. God forbid, it might encourage the same self-deception that led to Madame Bovary's suicide. "If the book troubles you too much," he said, "you might want to give it up. There are so many others. Equally wonderful. Many by women, many by Richmonders, for that matter."

"What's that?" Farrel asked, reentering the room.

"*Madame Bovary,* a novel, is the subject," George answered. "Have you heard anything about it? It caused quite a scandal in France. Even some sort of court trial, I believe."

"No," Farrel said definitely, as he threw himself down into an overstuffed gray armchair across the room from George and Sarah. He lit up a cigar, holding one out to George, who refused it. "I have no time for novels. The reading I do is practical. Reality is my only world. One world at a time, I say. And this one is plenty. No need for foolish make-believe to add to our troubles, eh?"

Sarah and George exchanged a special glance that spoke of the values they shared and which left Sarah flushed and excited. George noticed the color rise in her cheeks and felt a dangerous attraction to this woman he'd just met. He mustn't let himself feel such things nor think such things; no, he must not even imagine the things he found himself already beginning to imagine. This was his partner's wife, George warned himself, but even as he warned himself he realized that his reaction to those words was a happy awareness that he would see her again—many times.

"George Spencer is a native Richmonder,"

Farrel said. "I bring you this tidbit because I know how women concern themselves with the personal rather than the professional. But as to any other gossip, my dear, you shall have to find out for yourself."

"Why, Mr. Hurstwood," Sarah began half-angrily, "Mr. Spencer will tell us what he wishes us to know. There's no need to pry." Why was Farrel behaving in this way, so crudely? Sarah asked herself. He seemed offensive tonight, a bit vulgar in comparison to Mr. Spencer.

"My friends, I'd be happy to answer any questions at all that you might have, although my life has been so relatively bland there may not be much to interest you. I believe I'm a little older than you, Farrel, but I've conquered no city the way you've conquered Richmond."

"Too modest, too modest," Farrel broke in.

"Are you married, Mr. Spencer?" Sarah could have bitten her tongue the moment she uttered the words. Of all the questions to ask, she scolded herself.

"No. To my sorrow, I never have married. Perhaps the right woman was not where I was. Perhaps she will be someday."

"So, then, do you live nearby us? Perhaps with your parents?" Sarah couldn't stop herself from asking personal questions. She was intensely curious about this new partner of Farrel's. If he was a native Richmonder why hadn't she met him before? she wondered. He had a fascinating way about him.

"That's a bunch of questions in one. Or at least it

seems to need a group of answers."

"Whoa," Farrel broke in, when he saw Samson at the door, "it's time to eat. You can deliver your answers over dinner."

While they began their soup course, George filled in some of the details of his life. He lived, he told them, on Church Hill, an older part of Richmond, in a house he had inherited which was far too large for him. He described the Ionic pillars around its square granite porch. "Your basic Greek-revival style," he'd said. His parents, who enjoyed the leisure of a moneyed life, had raised him to be a "gentleman of leisure." They'd sent him to England for his college; he had attended Cambridge University. Then, in the manner of a gentleman-to-be, he had gone on the grand tour, visiting the important cities of Europe. He'd had his turn at the cultural salons in Paris and Berlin, for example. "My elders hoped culture was like the dust on train-compartment window ledges that would brush off on me wherever I came in contact with it," George said, with more than a trace of self-mockery.

Because he didn't think death was an appropriate topic for the dinner table, he didn't explain that he had come back to Richmond two years ago for his parents' funeral, didn't bring up their terrible deaths in a hotel fire while they were on a trip to Chicago. It was then, though, that George, suddenly orphaned at thirty, had begun to question his useless, refined life.

He had discovered that he was ready, even eager, to abandon his dilettante ways. He had a

137

good mind, he had been well-educated, and he had seen plenty of how the world worked. He thought he could be an asset in a business. As Farrel's partner, he intended to prove it.

In order to turn the conversation away from himself, George returned to the earlier topic of books.

"It lingers on my mind as an amazement, Mrs. Hurstwood," he said, "that a charming young woman such as yourself should have chosen such serious reading matter as Flaubert."

"Oh, Sarah's got a sharp mind," Farrel bragged. "Even my dull one spotted that as soon as I met her."

"Stop, stop. I'm unworthy of this praise. I have a confession to make! I really went to the library to choose some perfectly ridiculous book. You know the kind I mean—a popular romance or some such. Maybe Bertha M. Clay's latest. But as I stood at the counter, I heard the librarians arguing about a book that lay on the counter before them. They questioned the wisdom of allowing such a shocking book to sit on the shelf where just anyone might come across it. It was, of course, *Madame Bovary*. They decided to lock it in the drawer. They would only bring it out if someone asked for it specifically. Well, of course, I had to ask for it! So there you are—the whole sordid story."

Sarah looked ashamed, but George found the story another of her charming ways. Farrel thought the whole thing amusing.

"What a clever way to get you interested in good

138

literature!" George said. "Now, of course, you must read it in order to be able to make an intelligent comment when you return it." They all laughed at George's notion.

"It's like that marvelously comical scene in Mark Twain's Tom Sawyer book," he went on, "where the boy gets someone else to whitewash the fence for him by pretending it's a great privilege."

"Mark Twain, do you read him?" Sarah asked. "I heard he was a bit on the vulgar side."

"Not at all. Not at all. An American genius as I'm sure time will prove. We're the ones who are a bit vulgar—the American people! He just holds the mirror up to us so we can see ourselves. Maybe we don't all like what we see."

"Anyway," said Farrel, "in my mind, Sarah doesn't have to read that French book at all. She can just return it and make some neutral comment about how it had good description, or something."

"A politician amongst us," George cried out. "But no, that politically wise approach would be intellectually foolish. It's a book worth reading."

"Enough about books," Farrel insisted. "You two have ganged up on me. I forbid any more book talk for tonight. Agreed?"

Sarah ducked her head in agreement, but also to hide her smile. To see Farrel Hurstwood, always the man in charge, feeling left out delighted her. A smile just crept across her face. She couldn't stop it. Since they were just about done with their meal anyway, Farrel suggested a brandy and a cigar to George.

"Very well," said George, "but only if we discuss your proposed new streetcar routes at the same time."

"Oh, Lord," Sarah sighed. "That's my signal to leave. I'll return to *Madame Bovary*. Ooops, I promised to say no more about books. Congratulations to you both on your new partnership. Good-bye, Mr. Spencer. I trust I shall have the pleasure soon again."

George and Farrel stood when Sarah did.

"Until our next chance to talk books without your husband's interference, my dear Mrs. Hurstwood, I bid you adieu. Please don't allow that French lady's romantic notions to give you bad dreams."

"Yes," Sarah said; then, "I mean no." She flushed and curtsied, a habit she'd abandoned when she married and became a grown-up lady. This George Spencer, she thought, makes me feel like an awkward girl again. Yet she felt light-hearted as she hurried up the stairs to her rooms. The world did contain more than sorrow and bad people after all.

The next morning Sarah awoke to a belief in sunlight behind the heavy satin drapes which covered her two windows. She bounded from bed and hurried to the window. She was right. The sky held the azure clarity typical of certain spring days that speaks directly to the unbroken heart, speaks of new love and new life.

On the branches of the dogwood tree, Sarah counted seventeen redbirds. Soon tight buds would burst into leaf. The air, now full of sounds, would fill with color. The air, she thought as she swung open the casement to breathe it deeply in, the air is full of hope.

Clara came in to awaken Sarah and couldn't believe it when she saw Sarah's shadowed form against the bright sky. "Up early?" she asked unbelievingly. Sarah spun around.

"Yes. When will the bells begin? The Sunday bells."

"In a little bit. For nine o'clock services, I reckon."

"I want to be dressed and gone by then."

With Clara's help, she just managed to make her planned departure time.

She pulled the front door closed as the first burst of bells split the air with their silver sounds. Sarah decided to walk to Maxine's house which was near where her own parents lived.

Sunday brunch with her folks, yes. They had always had that as a special time to lounge and eat goodies while the Christian world scurried about to church. The thought of church made Sarah wince. She had left Farrel a note saying she would not be going to church with him. It explained her idea about Maxine—she had not been able to talk with him the night before because he and George Spencer had talked streetcar talk until late. He didn't know about Maxine's condition, of course, and she wasn't sure that he would approve of her idea if he did know. She remembered the despair in Jug's coal eyes, though, and knew she had to risk his disapproval.

141

He would not like her not being by his side at church either. She walked faster as she remembered the several arguments they had already had on that subject. He didn't seem to care about church as a way to get closer to God; he never urged her to convert. It was instead a social necessity to Farrel to attend church. And he wanted to have his wife beside him. Well, after today she would accompany him without comment no matter how uncomfortable the sight of the poor tortured body of Jesus made her feel. She would just concentrate on what her mother had taught her as a child about Jesus Christ: he was a wonderful teacher, he was a good Jew who tried to make his people into better Jews, he was one of the chosen people—but he was not God, not the long-awaited Messiah.

She had reached Maxine's street. Down the block of row houses, in front of Maxine's door, Sarah saw Doctor Sam's buggy. Fear set her feet into motion, and she began to run. Her cumbersome petticoats and heavy skirt thwarted her. She felt as though she were struggling to climb up a hill of sand.

Then the pain across her chest began. The tight corsets required to form the perfect small waist didn't allow much breathing space. Sarah felt sure that was the reason women were always fainting when men didn't seem to have that problem. Why couldn't life be simpler? she asked herself as she rushed toward Maxine's. She wasn't sure whether her question had to do with the fashion of the day or the overall sense of life getting so scary now that she'd grown up.

"Maxine," she called out when she finally made it to the door. She began to pound on it, certain that the doctor was there for Maxine, that something was terribly wrong, that her friend needed her. To her utter amazement her own father opened the door, and for a moment, in her confusion, she imagined that she'd gone to her own house by mistake. But the gray color of her father's face, his shocked look as he said, "Sarah, how did you know?" convinced her she was at Maxine's after all.

"Father, what is it?"

"She's dead. Your friend is dead." He lowered his voice as he spoke. He reached over and took hold of Sarah's arm to support her in case she needed it.

"No! Not dead!" Her voice sent birds back into their winter hideouts, denied the fact of this morning's sunlight. She heard footsteps approach, and she wanted to run, to fly. She couldn't bear to face Maxine's parents. Then she saw it was the doctor she'd known all her life. Thank God, Sarah thought, not Jug's parents.

"Thank you for coming as soon as I called, Dave," he began, then called out, "Sarah," as he recognized the young woman beside Dave See-wald. "What are you doing here? Are you all right? Would some smelling salts help?"

Sarah shook her head no, too miserable to speak.

"Take her home with you," the doctor suggested. "There's nothing else to do here. I'll stay

143

"with the Coopers until the undertaker comes."

"How?" Sarah asked in a pale voice.

"Your father will tell you everything. Take her home to Mamma and a cup of good strong coffee. Go on." Doctor Sam pushed at his friend's arm as he spoke. He wanted to get Sarah away from the gloom of this doomed house. Not good for young people to be near death, he thought. Especially this kind of death, self-chosen, self-inflicted, unnatural.

Sarah turned a blind face toward her father. She felt the world becoming less solid and struggled to stay in contact with it through him. He'd protect her. Her daddy would protect her.

His arm around her back, his hand around her upper arm, made a band of warmth that kept the world real. She could see the room's wallpaper again. She'd go with her father. To her mother. She'd be at home. It would be all right. So went the thoughts that accompanied her slow footsteps away from Maxine's door.

Some minutes later, minutes that disappeared from Sarah's memory even as she passed through them, she sat morosely at the table between her silent parents. She clutched her cup of coffee in order to feel its heat in her hands, took swallows of it to feel its heat in her throat. I'm alive and Maxine's dead. I'm alive. Maxine's dead. Dead.

"How did it happen, Papa? When?"

"They're not sure what or when. Either at work or soon after she came home from work she took some sort of poison. She said she didn't feel well and was going to go straight to bed; told her

144

mother not to bother the doctor, that she'd be better by morning."

"Oh, God, poor Jug." Sarah could hardly stand to hear the story, yet she felt a terrible need to know. "Then what?" she asked.

"Just about daybreak her parents awakened to her screams. They rushed to her room and found her already in convulsions. Of course they sent for the doctor. He sent for me hoping that I could guess at the poison or run tests. Suggest an antidote. There wasn't time. It was too late."

"No," Sarah almost shouted. She stood up so abruptly that she knocked over her chair. "I could have saved her. It's my fault." Then her sobs choked off her words. She leaned against the table, her head hung down, her chin pressed against her chest.

Her mother and father exchanged pained looks.

"Come, *bubbele,* lie down awhile," her mother said. She gathered Sarah to her bosom and began to lead her out.

"She left a note that mentioned you, Sarah."

At these words the women froze where they were.

"It said she couldn't bear to bring shame on the family. From what you say, you know more about that than we do, I suppose."

"Not now, Daddy," Sarah said. She shook her head as though to toss curls out of her eyes—or tears.

"The note ended, 'Tell Sarah I love her.'"

"No more! I can't . . ." Sarah wrapped her arms around her mother's neck as she'd done when she

145

was a little girl. She hid her head in the soft curve.

"Later, David dear, later." Rachel helped her daughter, whose knees seemed about to buckle under her, toward her old bedroom. Then she covered her and left.

When Sarah finally stopped crying and came to herself enough to realize where she was, she thought: this is the place I always come back to. This is my heart's home. She remembered the part of her marriage ceremony that spoke of forsaking all others, but she couldn't believe that really meant to forsake your parents. Anyway, she wouldn't. She needed them. They understood her in a way Farrel never would. Or anybody else either, probably.

The funeral, a few days later, was a small private affair. The family tried to hide both Maxine's pregnancy and her suicide. A sudden sickness, the paper called it:

> *Maxine Cooper, in her twentieth year, has left her earthly family to join God's heavenly family. Taken suddenly ill one evening, she did not survive to see the day break. Instead, her soul flew away from this troubled earth to that eternal happier place above.*

The minister, too, talked in these lofty terms. Sarah, leaning on Farrel's arm, bit her handkerchief. Why don't they tell of her mischief and her fun? she wondered angrily. Why don't they tell how she could throw a ball as far as any boy? They always speak such meaningless drivel, she reminded herself in an effort to stay calm. He didn't ever really know Maxine, not really. If the minister had been the person he should have been, Maxine could have gone to him for help. She knew she was being unfair. She just felt mad at everything and everybody.

Unfair. Maxine shouldn't be dead. Unfair. The word kept running through Sarah's mind. Unfair. Maxine and the baby she would have had were both dead. It was all so unfair. At night, when she tried to fall asleep, other words haunted her. Mainly the tragic hopeless words: if only. If only I'd sent a message . . . If only I'd thought of the idea sooner . . . If only I'd said the right thing when I saw her . . . if only . . . if only . . . Those words marked Sarah's first great regret.

Nine

Sarah moved through the spring as though she were a tired swimmer struggling to stay afloat. She read *Madame Bovary* and frequently dampened her pillow with tears over the sadness of life in general and the plight of women in particular. Maxine's death, which felt like an abscess that would not heal, and Farrel's increasing neglect of her in favor of work, compounded Sarah's pain. She returned the novel as soon as she finished it, glad to get it out of the house. But its presence haunted her. Women's lives seemed too sad, too empty.

Until her marriage, Sarah divided the hours of her busy day between schoolwork and work at her father's pharmacy. Now, alone too much with nothing to do, she began strangely to feel the need of more and more sleep. The more empty her days were, the more exhausted she felt. She could hardly manage to get up in the mornings and she went to sleep at an earlier and earlier hour in the evenings.

If only she had a child, she dreamed, her life would have a purpose, a purpose that could match Farrel's sense of purpose in his career. Her days would be full of important activities. She knew it would solve everything, having a baby. But month after month she continued to make the unhappy discovery that she was not yet with child. Her misery grew. Though she felt an ever greater need of something or someone in her life, Farrel was more and more unavailable to her.

During the hot and sultry days of that summer of 1890, during the brief, crisp fall that released the city from the hold of the heat, during the biting, miserable winter that lived on in people's minds as the "Winter of '91"—one of Richmond's worst—Farrel Hurstwood and George Spencer spent endless hours in one or another of their adjoining offices. They refined their present operations and made elaborate plans for expansion. They had already doubled the number of miles of track and tripled the number of cars on the lines.

In the evenings, Farrel parted reluctantly from George outside of 810 Main Street. When he started for home, more often than not, he carried a thick briefcase of unfinished work along with him. After the evening meal, frequently eaten alone because Sarah had given up waiting for his later and later arrival, he would sequester himself in the largest room of his suite, which he had set up as an at-home office. He emerged for a nightcap only when he could hardly keep his eyes open. Sarah had, by that time, already retired for the night.

One Friday in June, Sarah appeared in Farrel's office at noon to request his presence at an early supper. She had thought through this plan and hoped that her sudden appearance would charm him. Charm him enough, she hoped, so that he would agree to dine with her. Perhaps it would make the beginning of a new and better phase of their marriage. So she hoped anyway.

Although he seemed distracted, not quite the charmed reaction Sarah had wanted, nonetheless he did agree that he would take special pains to be home for the meal.

"I plan a meal of your favorites," Sarah promised, "if I can still remember what they are," she added before she could stop herself. Lately she had begun to feel so bitter toward Farrel, toward the loss of her youth—the theft of her youth by Farrel really—that bitterness had become the mark of her words and her thoughts. She had meant not to let this show, however, during this conversation and the evening that was to follow.

At her words, Farrel's lips tightened into a narrow band. "I am busy now, Sarah," he said. "I'll see you at home later. I'll try to be there by five." He had turned away and she had crept out of the office. Nothing I do works out right, she sighed as she made her way back home.

That evening Sarah awaited Farrel in a special gown she'd just had made for her. It was similar in style to the gowns Farrel had so liked when he had first courted her. What she failed to realize was that eyes change in what they see or care about, even though what they look upon remains unchanged. Farrel, in fact, tired and still annoyed by her afternoon's comment, failed to notice her new outfit.

"I'm here, Sarah," he said gruffly. "I'll wash up and be down in a minute."

Sarah's smile of greeting slid off her face. He was here under protest, she thought. He refuses to be charmed. She walked slowly to the dining room to check on its readiness. The heavy white linen cloth emphasized the length of the huge table. She began to doubt that she could reach Farrel across its length. Nonsense, she told herself. You're giving up the battle before it's even been fought. She shuddered at her unconscious use of war imagery.

"Shall we sit?" Farrel asked. She hadn't heard him come in.

"You sit, my dear," she said. "It's Friday evening, just about sundown, which marks the start of the Jewish Sabbath. Remember the first night back from our honeymoon? Our first night in this house. My mother lit the candles to welcome in the Sabbath. I thought it would be a nice custom for us to start. No one else need ever know." She'd been thinking of this idea for a long time. Longing for some of the comfortable old ways of her childhood.

"Is this going to be the prelude to another discussion about whether or not you wish to attend church with me?" Farrel's voice was edgy. He held himself stiffly, looking almost like a cat who senses danger—arched back, raised fur, a hiss of warning that says beware.

"No indeed. Nothing of the sort. The two issues have absolutely nothing to do with one another." Sarah's response was as quick as the way a flame catches up dried twigs.

"What has happened to your logic, Sarah? To your good mind? The subject of a Jewish custom of worship and going to church with me are unrelated, is that what you are trying to tell me?"

"Please let us try not to be angry with each other. I just thought it would be nice to develop a custom together that would be special. I want tonight to be special. We have been apart so much." Sarah came over to Farrel's chair and laid her arm on his shoulder. The gesture quite melted him.

"I'm sorry. You're right. These years of my life are all business. Perhaps I shouldn't have married at all. Perhaps George has the right idea."

Sarah sighed. These were hardly the words she had hoped to hear. He was sorry, but not for their drifting apart. No, sorry he'd ever married her at all. She walked woodenly to the candles, which she had set up on the sideboard the same way her mother had done that night almost two years ago.

She said the prayers, made the gestures, sat down at the table, all as though some other person were acting for her. Sometimes she felt as though she were simply the observer of her life. She wondered who, then, could be living it.

"Shall we eat?" she asked.

Farrel had watched her movements and was reminded of the light way she used to move. This didn't seem to be the same person just a short time later. He felt guilt. Guilt that made him want to run away. Guilt that made him want to deny the evidence of his eyes. It couldn't be his fault. Although he was a busy man, his success was important to her future, too. Guilt, instead of leading him back to her, only drove him further away.

She must be sick with something, he reasoned as he ate silently. Perhaps a trip would help. A trip Sarah could take alone—or perhaps with her mother. Yes, that would make more sense. He began to feel better even as Sarah, aware that she could not make Farrel love her, began to feel worse.

"You seem to have spring fever," he said. Sarah didn't respond. "Perhaps a trip to Boston with your mother might cheer you."

"Can you so ill abide being with me that you must banish me?" She spoke without plan. Anger spoke for her, in fact, anger and hurt. Like a child, she just wanted to hurt back.

"Boston, after all, is where you first lived when you came to this country. You lived there for a year. I just thought you'd like to retrace that year. Along with your mother it might be quite a sentimental journey." Now, having been so badly misjudged by his wife, Farrel felt a flow of self-righteous indignation. It was a welcome replacement for his guilt.

"I lived in Boston when I was ten years old. Do you really think I remember much about it—or care?" She felt so bitter against him that she couldn't stop herself, although she knew she

153

should. Knew that she was probably saying words that she would later, in the calm quiet of the empty house, regret. She even dimly recognized that once a word is spoken one can never wholly call it back. "No, I don't need a trip, sir. What I need is a husband. Do you know where I could hire one?" She stood and fled the room although her meal was only half-finished.

When Samson came in to clear the plates, he found the room empty. The front door slammed as Farrel left the house to go who knows where? Sarah in her room overhead sobbed herself to sleep still wearing the new gown with which she had planned to charm her husband. Samson shook his head over the troubles of these married folks. Onto his list of things he'd never understand, things he didn't care much for, he added marriage.

The next day over morning coffee they both made ineffectual attempts at apology without having to utter the words. It helped, but it didn't heal. They parted for the day with a light kiss which spoke of pattern more than feeling.

Sarah decided to visit her old school and play with the little children there. That would cheer her up.

Farrel decided that he must talk to George about coming over more often. A buffer, that's what they needed. Especially since he would have to do a great deal of traveling over the summer to set up systems in three other cities. George could fill in for him around here, he reasoned. George always found a way to make Sarah smile. He himself no longer knew how, he admitted. But the thought left him as he began to plan the system for Chicago. That would be real excitement!

At Farrel's insistence, George began to spend more time with the Hurstwoods at their home. His feelings for Sarah, which he struggled to keep in check, were like a willful horse constantly working to get the bit between its teeth and take charge.

Especially did George find it a problem when Farrel was away on trips. But, on the other hand, he yearned to see Sarah and hated the idea of her being alone in that big house. In August of 1891, therefore, when Farrel was off in Germany where so much important electrical work was being done, George decided to accept Sarah's standing invitation to dinner.

In the afternoon, he used the new telephone system which Farrel had insisted they install to call her up.

"Hello," he shouted into the mouthpiece. He held the ear cone tightly against his head, afraid he would not be able to hear her answer. He had not really made his peace yet with this gadget.

"George?" Sarah too still felt it was impossible that someone miles away should be able to speak words into her ear.

"I need a good meal! Do you hear me? I'd like to come to dinner sometime during this week that Farrel still remains away. We shouldn't let him have all the fun."

"Wonderful. Come tonight. I can't wait!"

When they'd both hung up, George sat on reliving the excitement in Sarah's voice. Surely it was just that when you're lonely you want some company. But he didn't believe it. He believed that Sarah cared—more than she would even admit. Just as he would never admit his feelings either. He wanted to be fair to Farrel, but the man refused to give the proper amount of attention to his wife. If she were a motor, he thought, ah, that would be different. He'd never met anyone quite so addicted to work, to success, and to the infernal contrivances of electrical motors, damn them!

As George stood in the parlor awaiting Sarah's arrival that night, he recited some Greek verse to himself. He'd almost forgotten the ancient languages now that he'd given up the role of nonworking gentleman. But it still pleased him to remember the verses he had committed to memory so long ago. This one, part of the chorus in a tragedy, spoke of man's inability to avoid his destiny however much he might try. Odd that it should come to his mind. Perhaps not so odd after all, he acknowledged as he realized his impatience to see Sarah again.

When she entered the room, though, he was shocked. Her face was paler than he had ever seen it. She seemed drawn and tired. Her hair no longer curled in ringlets across her head. Rather, she had pulled it tightly back into a bun fastened at the nape of her neck.

The dress she wore was simple—a gray shirtwaist tucked into a deeper gray skirt. It would have been beautiful if the woman inside it hadn't looked also somehow gray. She belied the season.

156

Outside was the radiance of the August summer, but Sarah presented a picture of winter's bleakest day.

"Sarah—" He stopped himself on the verge of asking what was wrong. Perhaps she would tell him unasked. Surely if he asked directly, she would have to deny that anything at all was wrong. "I have wanted us to get together more often during Farrel's long journey. But I didn't wish to infringe upon your time. Here we are at last though." He stretched out his arms toward her.

"Mr. Spencer you are most welcome." Her voice almost contained a sob. She moved toward him and they shared a brief embrace as two distant relatives might. "Let us sit awhile and talk before we eat, shall we?"

"Yes, yes, I would like that better than food."

Sarah led the way out to the little side garden which she had planted in herbs and spices. It had been her main project during the early summer months and she was quite proud of it. A small table and two chairs, all of white wrought iron, sat in the shade of the crape myrtle tree. From there they could see the careful color arrangements of her plantings. The spices filled the air with the exotic fragrances of foreign lands. Rue, she'd planted, and thyme, basil, and oregano; mint, of course, for what would a southern garden be without its mint? She pointed out each plant to George and described how she had sketched the colors in on her pad to be sure that the final effect would be pleasing. Yes, she admitted, it is quite as delightful as I had hoped.

As she spoke, George could see the spark of the old Sarah reignite. Her cheeks began to turn pink, her eyes to sparkle.

"Now, I suppose, you just sit about here and admire your handiwork."

"No. The work itself was the best part. Since it is done I seldom think about it. I'm glad you are here to see it because it allows me to feel pleasure in it again. In fact, this project has helped me to understand my husband a bit better—the absorption in work. Yes, it is a drug. One could become addicted, I can see that."

"And he has." George had said it to test her reaction. He'd meant it to come out as a question. Unfortunately, it stood as a fact uniting them on one side of some question or other and leaving Farrel over on the other side.

Sarah stared at George a moment before answering. "Yes, he has." She crumpled a basil leaf in her hand and passed her hand under George's nose. "Smell this. Isn't it lovely?"

He sniffed so deeply that he almost choked, and they both laughed. "It *is* lovely," he said, "but you are lovelier by far." When he saw the happy smile she tried to hide beneath a frown at his fowardness, he felt no remorse. She needed a few compliments in her life.

"How do you manage to be a good worker without being a madman?" She knew as soon as she had spoken that she had gone too far. To call her own husband a madman. "I did not mean that the way it sounded, sir," she tried to amend it.

"No need to apologize for the truth, my dear

Sarah. Your husband is a special kind of person. I don't pretend to admire his ways at all times. Particularly not on the personal level. But his genius in terms of electrical power forces me to make allowances."

"I don't think I understand what you are trying to tell me."

"Perhaps we should just drop the subject. It's really not my place to be talking to you about your husband anyway."

"No, no, no," Sarah insisted. "I need someone to talk to me about him. And you are the only logical one. The only one who knows him well. The only one who knows both of us, I should say, know us both well."

"What I was trying to say—" George paused. He looked off into the back yard where the graceful trees drooped toward the lawn. How could he explain this to a young woman who really didn't care much about progress, who probably yearned for laughter and romance, and who would probably find neither. Not with the man she'd married. He had his own special destiny. "Exceptions must be made to normal rules when we discover people with greater than normal ability. Such a person is Farrel Hurstwood. I don't use the word 'genius' lightly, but I believe that he is a genius. His mind is always active in new directions. He lives in the future on a plane of existence that is different from the reality of the streets of Richmond where you and I walk."

"You mean I can't expect the same things I might have from a more common man—conversation, evenings together, a day that includes little remembrances of each other?"

How deeply disappointed she sounded, George thought. As well she should be, he supposed. "That's right, Sarah. I don't think you can ever count on those commonplace pleasures in your life with your husband. Perhaps, though, we could find a way for him to share more of his insights with you."

"No. That's just more unreality. I have no special knowledge such as I would need. Nor, I must admit, have I much special interest. I'll have to make my peace with the situation in some other way."

It felt comforting to sit together this way sharing a common problem. George, before he let thought stop him, reached over and took hold of Sarah's hand. Although two spots of color appeared in her cheeks, showing the struggle she was going through, Sarah did not move her hand away. In fact, she seemed to respond to his hand's pressure with her own. The moment had a perfection of its own. They didn't speak. There was no need to try to capture it in words. At one point a flock of small birds, perhaps fifteen or so, clustered in the sky over the back yard, then settled into the various trees. Their spread wings folded in on themselves. This enfolding movement symbolized something to George and Sarah that made them smile.

Farrel returned from his trip, and the pattern of their days reestablished itself much to Sarah's dismay. The fall came and winter would soon be here. She felt that if she didn't do something to get her husband's attention, she must die.

Finally, one bleak November night Sarah could stand it no more. At the close of a strained supper, she interrupted her husband as he started to excuse himself from the table in his usual manner. She had planned for this moment all afternoon, but still her voice shook as she said, "Mr. Hurstwood, I assume you plan to disappear into your mysterious office?" She paused for his reply, but when he simply stared at her, she forced herself to go on. "I must insist," she said boldly, "that you spend this evening with me."

There was a short silence during which Farrel stroked his mustache into the droopy shape he was cultivating. "I'd love to, Sarah," he said finally in a steely voice, "but it's absolutely impossible. There's a report on Peterboro's street usage that was just completed and I have to get to it immediately."

Without a second look at her, Farrel tossed his crumpled napkin onto the table and stood.

"You spend more time with Mr. Spencer than you do with me," Sarah flung at him. Her voice trembled dangerously. Farrel ignored the comment and left the room. Impetuously, Sarah rushed after him. She caught up with him at the foot of the stairs. Grasping his arm, she shrieked, "Maybe you should have married him instead! At least you should never have married me, when you're already married to that damned company of yours." Here her voice broke. She began to weep and wring her hands.

Farrel stared at her as though she were a madwoman. He knew females had their special moods, but he never imagined he'd encounter anything like this. Enraged by this breach in good manners, Farrel took his wife by the shoulders and shook her.

"Take hold of yourself right now, Sarah. Right now," he roared, shaking her still harder until she thought he was going to kill her. Terror silenced her cries. Then he pushed her from him. She stumbled back slamming her head against the wall.

"Disgraceful behavior," he mumbled, and wasn't sure himself whether he meant hers or his, or perhaps both. Not to mention the horror of their raised voices within the hearing of the servants who might have their ears pressed to the butler's pantry door at this very moment.

Farrel straightened his jacket and smoothed back both sides of his hair from its center part.

"We'll discuss this later," he said in as close to a normal tone as he could manage, "but for now, madam, you will excuse me while I go to do my required work."

Without a backward glance, Farrel stolidly climbed the carpeted stairs. Sarah, seeing him turn his back so easily on her distress and shame, felt her heart sink. Avoiding her image in the huge mirror that hung across from her, she lowered herself down onto the hard horsehair settee that stood against the foyer wall. Her tears blurred the gaslight chandelier into a constellation of twinkling stars. Oh God, she sighed, what misery this life is. Can this be what my life is to be like forever? She remembered George's words last summer about how Farrel was an extraordinary person and could not be like other people. Yes, she thought, a sob escaping from her, this misery was what her life was to be. Uncaring if the servants heard her or not, she leaned her head back against the wall and succumbed to the sorrow inside her.

Ten

The timing of Sarah's increased demands upon Farrel couldn't have been worse. He was involved in a critical legal battle over extending the territory of the streetcar line. The first painful scene between Farrel and Sarah became a pattern for others. At one point Farrel, stopped from leaving the house one morning by a wild-eyed Sarah in an unfastened housecoat, pushed her from him and then in a move that left them both horrified slapped her across the face as hard as he could. That was the nadir of their fights. From that moment on they began to avoid each other. Farrel spent little time at home, in part because of the legal struggle, but to an even greater extent because he could not bear any more confrontations. He had struck a woman. He must now somehow include that fact in his self-evaluations. As he could not resolve his feelings regarding his behavior, he simply put it out of his mind and went on with his work.

Farrel was positive that the wave of the future was the interurban—a streetcar line that would travel between one city and another on a regular schedule. He had spoken so convincingly of this to George that even George had come to share his vision.

In a routine move, the Richmond Electric Street Railway Company had applied for the permits necessary to begin work laying track between Richmond's city limits and the nearby town of Peterboro. Farrel expected immediate approval and was confused, then annoyed, and finally outraged when obstacle after obstacle had to be surmounted. It was six months after the initial application and still the permits seemed no closer to being granted.

During a mid-April afternoon a puzzled Farrel stood looking out the window at the flowering dogwood trees and the disturbingly cheerful azure sky. He snapped the Venetian blinds shut closing out the bright spring day. Everything was going wrong: his marriage, his work. Especially and specifically this interurban deal.

There was a rapid series of knocks on the door and George rushed in thrusting a sheet of paper at him.

"I've found the trouble, man! God, why is it so damned dark in here?" George jerked on the rope to reopen the blinds, flooding the room with daylight. They both blinked like moles emerging from underground.

"Read this, Farrel, read it!"

It was a letter of some sort, Farrel saw as he took

the paper over to his desk. He sat down heavily in his chair with a grave sense of foreboding and began to read. George lit the wick in the desk lamp to give him more light and couldn't help but admire once again as he did so the spider pattern in the Tiffany glass. Farrel certainly had flair, George thought. Then he turned his attention back to Farrel whose face reddened as he finished reading the letter.

"Where in hell did you get this?" he demanded looking up at last, his quiet voice ominous.

"I've been hearing rumors at the club. I tracked down the source and bought enough drinks so that a noisy fellow talked even more than usual. Then I promised to provide money if he'd provide proof—put the authentic material into my hands. Today he gave me the original of that. I copied it out so he could return it before it was missed."

As George spoke, Farrel began to pace back and forth between the window and the desk, a habit he hadn't been able to abandon although George always urged him to sit back down.

"A competitor, yes, that I've been expecting. But this sneakiness and downright dishonesty—"

"Sit down, Farrel, for the love of God. You're making me dizzy."

"And who is it?" Farrel went on as he sat down behind the desk. "Who's paying this Monsieur Zorbini to present the arguments against our requests? The whole damned thing is so anonymous!"

"Yes. Like a Chinese box, eh? You open one and find another. One defecting board member. That's all it took. I found him and he gave me the next name, Zorbini. How to go beyond that, though, I don't know. There's the clear implication that whoever it is, isn't beyond spreading around money to the board members for their votes. Farrel," George paused, aware of the naïveté, the refined sensibilities of his partner, "perhaps we should try that ourselves. Fight fire with fire, they say."

"I know who it must be, you know," Farrel went on, ignoring for the moment his partner's words, "the goddamned railroads, that's who. But how to prove it?"

"The railroads?"

"Yes, indeed. Whose toes would an interurban step on? Even though the trains don't handle that local service adequately now and have no plans to. I don't know." Farrel thrust his hands into his hair, weaving his fingers through the thickness at both sides of his temple. He jumped up from his chair, perched momentarily against the edge of the desk, then began to pace again. George rolled his eyes to the ceiling, but refrained from further comment.

"So that explains it, anyway," Farrel muttered. "One problem after another."

"Well," George concluded, as he stood up, "we have to make some hard decisions fast, that's sure. How about a brandy at Sloane's to smooth the ruffled feathers and then we'll get down to it."

Farrel nodded, tugging absent-mindedly at his mustache. "I'll send word to Sarah not to wait on me for supper. In fact," he added, realizing that he

167

must get a grip on himself and that George was right, there was work to be done—fast, "I'll tell her not to wait up at all."

That night they mapped out a strategy that moved them squarely into the main action of the war. Even as an old man, Farrel would trace back a deep strain of sadness, an initial loss of innocence, to that night's decisions.

It turned out that the machinations were on behalf of an underground system that was being promoted despite the obvious disadvantages, particularly its higher cost. Because of this, the sponsors felt it necessary to discredit the streetcar lines in order to strengthen their own position. It wasn't the railroads at all, Farrel realized. Zorbini, the underground's man, was even responsible for the establishment of a special commission on electrolysis to explore and then advertise the danger of damage to underground water pipes from the ground return of the streetcars' electric current. The Benchley Corporation, the group behind it all, the group paying Zorbini to appear disinterested while promoting their cause, hoped that by attacking streetcars on many fronts at once they would weaken the company's ability to fight back. Their reasoning, had Hurstwood and Spencer decided on "fair play" instead of "all's fair" as their motto, would have provided the underground system with the inevitable ultimate victory they anticipated. Once the streetcar people began employing equally underhanded techniques and since they had the advantage of playing on the home court—the Benchley group was in England —the odds rapidly shifted in their favor.

Zorbini and Hurstwood were never to meet head-on, but they fought each other fiercely nonetheless. They each spent a great deal of money and they each made carefully prepared speeches in numerous public arenas. Few people ever realized how little the board's decision had to do with the words spoken before it. The money spoke louder than all the words.

Zorbini, the spokesman for Benchley's system, declaimed before the board: "The primary cost of the overhead system is a great deal cheaper; but we claim that in ten years or more the underground system will be cheaper, because of the economical operation in the first place, and the doing away with all the wear and tear as we have it now in the overhead system, the rottening of the poles and the dropping of trolley wires, and numerous other troubles they encounter in the overhead system when sleet comes, and when heavy wind storms come; and these things will be done away with in this case, because it will be underground."

He stood no more than five feet tall, but every inch was superbly prepared to give the impression of a man one could never call in question. He wore a worsted suit carefully tailored to emphasize his slim waist. His black shoes gleamed with a polish that was so severe you could see your face in them. His small mustache was clipped close to his lips and, except for it, he was clean-shaven. His foreign accent added just the proper note of intrigue without scaring anybody.

Wherever he appeared, women went out of their way to be introduced to him, and yet he never acted personally interested in them, so that their menfolk were not threatened. In truth, the sturdy young man who traveled with Zorbini under the guise of being his valet was his only love. They had been faithfully and deeply in love for half a dozen years. So, with his personal life so happily resolved, Zorbini found it easy to play to whatever his audience's interests were. He was, he himself acknowledged, a superb actor and cared not a whit which side won as long as he earned every penny possible along the way. Not quite a scoundrel, perhaps, but available for hire to scoundrels—or to whoever paid the highest price.

Meanwhile, at a public celebration, Farrel Hurstwood spoke out for the streetcars with the elegance and terse wit for which he was becoming known: "Every man knows that clean, quick, and uninterrupted streetcar service is nowadays one of the common necessities of city life. Every community needs it. Every wise community demands it."

When the final vote was taken both parties' words had less to do with it than whose vote was in whose pocket and how much the winning number of votes cost. The vote of six to four went in favor of granting the Richmond company the privilege of an interurban line and, additionally, the service within the town of Peterboro itself. Farrel, ecstatic over the results, dragged George home with him to share a celebration supper.

*   *   *

"George Spencer, it's been too long," Sarah said, holding out her arms to George in greeting.

George took her hands in his, smiling appreciatively at her slim figure in its soft gray shirtwaist with mutton-leg sleeves tucked demurely into a black silk skirt.

"Kind of you to say so, my dear, when I virtually haunt your doorstep, not to mention your groaning board."

"Nonsense," she giggled, slipping her hand through the crook he made of his arm. "I haven't had a good chat with you in weeks. Let's sit in the window seat. We can talk about our reading again, if you like. My husband will see to the sherries, I'm sure."

She wondered to herself why it was so easy to be teasing and friendly with this almost-stranger when it was practically impossible to utter a single friendly word to Farrel, her husband and the man she should be closest to in the whole world.

"My pleasure," George replied as he playfully squeezed her arm to his chest. He'd come to feel comfortable enough with Mrs. Hurstwood to risk these familiarities. The fact that each contact made his heart pound was something he tried to hide not only from her, but also from himself.

When she looked at him now with widening eyes, he was afraid she'd noticed, but then she said, "Oh, Mr. Spencer, I just remembered I have something special to show you in the carriage house. Come along," she urged, tugging at his hand.

"More important than reading?" he teased,

following after her as she rushed him through the rooms, out onto the side porch, down the steps, through the little herb garden and to the carriage-house door.

"Voilà!" she cried, as she flung open one of the doors. There inside the dark recesses of the huge bare room stood a magnificent vehicle. "A lady's basket phaeton," Sarah exclaimed, "for me. A gift from my husband. He had it sent around while you two were at your infernal work. Isn't it gorgeous?"

George circled the carriage admiring its shape and sparkle. The bright yellow wicker body sat atop high wheels with a softly cushioned seat for the lady of the house and a firm tiger's seat behind where the groom could sit and control the reins when the lady tired.

"Quite splendid," George admitted. "Have you taken a turn in it yet?"

"Right away. But only a short way. I only got it last week, and the weather's been so bad. Maybe tomorrow I'll be able to take a real trip, out into the country. Now that your work on the Peterboro project is finished perhaps I can talk Mr. Hurstwood into joining me."

George felt a sense of alarm, knowing how far from finished the Peterboro work really was. This was just the beginning. And he sensed the young woman's need to believe that now her time with her husband would increase dramatically.

"Yes," he agreed, "an outing would be fun. Sometime I'd be honored to join you in one of your outings. I'd provide the picnic lunch in exchange for a ride in your buggy." He paused,

172

realizing that this time he really had gone too far. She gazed up at him, her lips trembling. Her gray eyes were wide and tender as a fawn's, George thought, wishing he could unsay his bold and thoughtless words.

"Perhaps the three of us," he amended. "The three musketeers, eh?"

"Yes, yes," Sarah said quickly. She lowered her eyes to the tips of her pointy patent shoes which stuck out from under the gathers of her skirt. "I think we ought to return to the house now, don't you?"

When Sarah raised her moist eyes to his, George saw two red circles high on her cheeks. Could it be, he wondered, that she returned his feelings? Or was it just that he had embarrassed her? Probably the latter, he decided, as he followed her shame-facedly back to the main house. Imagine, he reprimanded himself, flirting with your partner's wife. Why, it could only lead to trouble.

"Well, well," Farrel greeted them upon their return to the front parlor, "was Sarah showing off her new toy?"

"And quite a toy it is," George answered, accepting a sherry in a beautifully cut Waterford crystal glass from Farrel. "When did you have time to pick it out, old man?"

Sarah excused herself to check on the dinner arrangements, leaving the men alone to their sherry and cigars, a luxury they wouldn't otherwise have indulged in.

"I didn't, actually. Just phoned up and ordered the damned thing to placate the missus for my frequent absences. The only time it cost me was a call. Now money, though, that's another issue!"

"You'd better watch out," George warned, "or your little bird could fly away during all these days when you desert the nest."

Farrel threw back his head and guffawed.

"George, you old sentimentalist, what do you know about the subject of keeping wives happy, eh? I ask you that."

"Perhaps not much," George nodded amiably, with a tight smile on his face, "I admit." But enough, he added to himself, to know you're not keeping yours happy; that's for sure.

"I hope you never marry and find out how different the reality is from one's dreams," Farrel said with a bitterness to his voice that surprised both men. "Let's drink to that, eh?"

Over dinner, Farrel brought up an issue he'd been avoiding mentioning to Sarah. He hoped George's presence would soften her reaction.

"Once we get the Peterboro project laid out, I think I'd better do some of the traveling I've been putting off."

"Yes, I suppose so," George answered, suspecting Farrel's motives in raising this topic just now. He dusted the crumbs out of his beard. "Where would you go first?"

"Chicago, I think. Those Chicago dealers have been wanting to discuss my plans for an elevator motor for some time now. Can you hold the fort, George? And you, Sarah, can you make do without me around for a few weeks?"

Sarah stared at her wineglass. The sight of the clear amber liquid gave her a way to calm herself. She'd imagined that with this bad Peterboro problem out of the way, Farrel would make time for her. Now she realized that wasn't to be.

"Sarah," Farrel repeated, "did you hear me?"

"Yes, Mr. Hurstwood. You're going to Chicago. When do you plan to leave?"

"Oh, not until next month, my dear. We still have so much work to do setting up the interurban."

"Fine. I'll begin tomorrow to get your travel needs organized, if you like."

"No need, no need. Samson can handle all that easily."

Sarah bent over her plate. So she was to be robbed of even this small sense of being of use, she thought. She found herself cutting chunks of meat off the Cornish ham in front of her, pushing the wild rice stuffing around on her plate, but eating nothing. She lifted a forkful of rice and meat to her mouth and began chewing mechanically. As though from a great distance or over the telephone wires, she heard Farrel ask George to keep an eye on her while he was out of town.

"The Hurstwood house is my home away from home," George answered. "If Sarah can bear me being around—"

Sarah was still chewing on the same mouthful of food, a mouthful that had become so rubbery that she could neither swallow it nor spit it out. Now, though, with an answer demanded of her, she forced herself to swallow, coughed once, and struggled for composure.

"Are you looking for compliments, Mr. Spencer?" Sarah responded at last. Then, realizing her answer was too sharp, she amended it. "Surely you know you're always welcome in this household. Mr. Hurstwood has told you that many times, I know, and I add my voice to his."

"Thank you, Sarah," George answered simply, feeling for her pain.

"Sarah," Farrel broke in, "ring for coffee, won't you? Then George and I must get back to work. Too bad you don't have a wife, George, so that Sarah would have some company, eh?"

Farrel chuckled at his little joke, raised his glass in a salute, and downed it. Sarah met George's eyes and felt a thrill that gave her goose bumps up and down her arms. What special meaning did that look have? she asked herself. It was a mixture of many things. An awareness on Sarah's part that George had no special woman in his life . . . no one else, that is, she told herself; on George's part a recognition that the one woman he longed for was another man's wife. Before the moment's tension could touch Farrel, the servants were busily clearing the table and preparing for the final course.

Eleven

The next day Sarah told Bertie, the young groom, to ready her phaeton. She planned to visit her mother and intended to complain ferociously about Farrel's neglect. She'd suffered silently as long as she intended to. Sarah had previously associated the concept of rancor with the notion of a villain. Now, though, she had to reshape her notion to accommodate the feeling building within her toward her husband. Rancor was, it seemed, the only appropriate word.

She dressed with special care for fear that her mother would otherwise fault her for not doing her part of the marriage contract. Though where Sarah had acquired the notion that looking smart was her function, she couldn't for the life of her say. Nonetheless, she knew she was right, that it was terribly important.

"Bertie, Bertie," Sarah called impatiently as she descended the stairs, lightly trailing her hand along the walnut bannister.

"He's already out front, Miz Sarah," Clara answered from the parlor where she was polishing the metal drawer pulls and bric-a-brac. "I saw him through the window dressed up like a fool and marching up and down in front of the house like he was Mr. Farrel hisself."

"Maybe you'd finish your work faster, Miss Busybody, if you didn't look out the window and flirt so much!"

"Hoo," Clara laughed, enjoying the exchange of teasing words that reminded her of their old days of friendship. "Say hello to my mammy, if you say hello to yours," she called after Sarah, suspecting her destination. Sarah slammed the front door, in place of an answer. Outside, she took a deep breath hoping for freshness and flowers, but instead found the sweet smell of wisteria overpowered by street stench, like a foul slop pail that needed emptying but instead had been doused with perfume. She choked and coughed, reaching into her little crocheted string bag for a hankie.

"Oh, Bertie," she called rushing down the brick walk to where the sturdy young man held the gate for her. "Please won't you drive us? I'm sure you'll be faster and less sparing with the whip. My eyes are stinging so, I can hardly see. I swear this air isn't fit to breathe."

"Yes'm, yes'm," he agreed, rushing ahead of her to give her a hand up into the high carriage, gleaming brighter than the day it arrived from his constant loving attention. "After a minute you'll be used to it, missy. It don't bother me none. But I'd be mighty pleased to drive, ma'am. I surely do love to drive. We'll be at your mamma's before you know it."

Sarah found herself smiling at his mannerisms. Farrel told her she was too lax with the servants, but she enjoyed their sassiness and vitality. Secretly, Sarah wished she could share in their energy, be part of their lives. Sometimes she'd hear a group of voices singing of an evening out behind the carriage house and she'd hum along from her rocking chair inside the house. Often they sang spirituals. "Rocked in the Cradle of the Deep" was a favorite. Sometimes just for fun, songs like "Jim Crack Corn."

She watched Bertie unwrap the reins from the hitching post. She saw him slip a piece of carrot to the restless bay before sprinting to his place behind her. His white-gloved hands seemed to be a thousand places at once as he set the phaeton in motion.

She was a cautious and somewhat timid driver herself, but she loved the terrifying thrill of being recklessly flung through the Richmond streets at breakneck speed. If we overturn and I die, she thought in a burst of melodrama, I won't care at all. Not at all. The excitement would make it perfectly well worth it. She turned her head to look back at Bertie whose pink tongue was clamped between his teeth in concentration and who rolled his eyes at her until they seemed all whites. Just then they careened around a corner tipping precariously onto two wheels, then bounced back onto four wheels with a painful jolt. Sarah laughed out loud.

Bertie, though, was scared by his own abandon. If Mr. Hurstwood heard, it would mean his job for sure. "Whoa," he called, pulling on the reins until he'd slowed the galloping horse down to a gentle trot, a more seemly pace. Flecks of foam spun out into the air from Graylady's mouth, after her exertion.

Another square and Bertie pulled the carriage over to the curb in front of the Seewald house. He jumped down to tie up the buggy and offer his arm to the lady of the house. "I'm sorry, missuz," he muttered.

"Don't be a fool, silly boy," Sarah answered, "I loved it. Only," she hesitated a moment, "let's not mention it to anyone. Especially not to Mr. Hurstwood."

Bertie grinned at her, relieved by this declaration of silence.

Sarah paused just inside the gate and gazed at the garden of her childhood, her mother's garden. The crape myrtle glistened and a rainbow of azaleas bloomed everywhere. Despite the popularity of formal gardens, Rachel Seewald continued to believe that more was better. The yard reflected her countless hours kneeling in the rich Virginia earth shaded only by her linen sunbonnet, happily oblivious to the city noises around her. She often told Sarah how the hours in the garden took her back to her own childhood in Russia and the little garden that her dear mother, may her soul rest in peace, had urged from the reluctant soil.

Sarah, as she meandered along the brick path through the yard, admired the wildly beautiful space her mother had created. The garden, the walk, the porch railing with its ornamental wrought-iron scrollwork, brought back the feelings of her early childhood; all were as familiar to her as life itself. Each scent, each sight cast its magic so that she arrived at the front door cloaked in nostalgia. Sarah tentatively turned the large brass knob wondering if her mother still left the door unlocked, a habit that Sarah had carried into her own household until her husband's repeated ragings about the risk of theft had forced her to abandon it.

The door opened at her touch and swung in on an empty hallway. Suddenly, Sarah had a terrible feeling of urgency. What, she thought wildly, if her mother were dead? What if she'd waited too long? Now, when she needed her mother so badly, she first realized the possibility of her loss.

"Mamma," Sarah called out in a timid child's voice. "Mamma?"

The sound hung heavily in the air a moment like the heavy swag of a dark thunderhead just before a storm, then a clatter of noise broke out upstairs almost like the expected thunderclap. A door opened and slammed somewhere, there was the sound of footsteps, a rustle of skirts.

"Sarah!" her mother called down to her from the top of the stairs. "Sarah, I can't believe it's you. Actually coming for a visit without my urging. My goodness!"

Hearing these words, Sarah realized how much she had closed her mother out during these first years of her marriage. She hadn't meant to.

Instead she'd kept hoping that she'd never have to stand here like a beggar telling her pathetic little domestic tale, hoping never to have to admit what a mess she'd made out of her young life.

Her mother reached the bottom stair and clasped Sarah to her, only then noticing how her daughter's large eyes brimmed with tears.

"Sarah, my dear, what is it?"

The sympathy and concern in her mother's voice broke through Sarah's last bit of reserve and she burst into sobs.

"Mamma," she finally managed to gasp when she caught her breath, "I'm so very unhappy. Oh, why did I ever marry?"

"Sh, sh," her mother comforted her, patting her shoulder and gently leading her into the back parlor where they could be comfortable and where, with both doors firmly closed, they might speak in privacy.

"Tell me," she said quietly when at last they'd settled themselves on the sofa.

Sarah struggled for control. Then seeing the pity in her mother's face, she burst out, "I hate him!"

Rachel was shocked by her daughter's fury, but when Sarah threw herself across her lap sobbing, her mother's heart melted.

"There, there," she crooned, stroking Sarah's head. This was no time for lectures on propriety and restraint. Let her cry it out and then I'll learn what this is all about, she thought. "There, there," she whispered again, "there, there."

Finally, Sarah's shoulders stopped their heaving. The sobs subsided. Sarah straightened.

"He never talks to me," she said, beginning her recitation of the list of grievances she'd held in for such a long time. "He's always at work, Mother, always. Even when he's at home. He prefers time with his partner to time with me." Her voice cracked. Sarah cried again, muffling the noise with her handkerchief. "I'm so unhappy," she concluded, burying her head in her mother's neck as she'd done when she was a child.

Rachel remembered the early years of her own marriage too well not to sympathize—the surprising loneliness, the hurtful, angry words, the tears. But part of her worried that Sarah's problem might be more than just the normal adjustments. After all, she'd married a non-Jew and who knew what disasters that might produce? A non-Jew, poor Sarah raised as a non-Jew herself for the most part. And after that decision to hide their Jewishness in this new country, what else could they realistically have expected but that Sarah would marry a gentile? Realistically, yes, but in the private place of the heart she had hoped otherwise. Sarah's marriage to Mr. Farrel Hurstwood had hurt, Rachel couldn't deny. Now she saw how it was hurting Sarah, too. She couldn't separate out her mixture of responses. So, for a while, they sat in silence together, the mother and the daughter.

"Sarah, now to be fair you must tell the other side. He buys you everything you want, doesn't he? Look at your fine gown, your house—the showplace of Richmond with the latest of everything."

"Yes, but why?" Sarah broke in. "I always loved our hall with its brown-and-white linoleum. The way it smelled of lemon polish. Why must we have parquet floors, the hard wood, sticky with wax and the smell of wax always in the air? Just because it's the newest thing! It's not for *me*, Mamma. It's for his blessed image. And as for buying me things—"

"Enough, Sarah," Rachel said sharply, but Sarah, now that she had finally brought herself to speak at all, would not be stopped.

"He buys me things, that's true, and I can predict each gift's arrival. When he's been out of town, of course, or about to announce yet another trip, or when he's stayed at work through the dinner hour for an entire week. They're not gifts at all, you see, Mother, they're bribes. He buys my silence. So I won't complain. Silence."

And, as though called back to her duty by the very word silence, Sarah fell suddenly silent. A soft slow blush made its way up from the firm flesh revealed by her low-cut bodice to her slender neck and from there fanned across her previously pale cheeks.

The awkward silence extended for only seconds, but seconds that seemed to both mother and daughter like eternities.

"Tochter," Rachel began at last using the Yiddish term with which she herself had been raised, *"Ich hob* herring and sour cream. Could you eat a little something?"

Sarah burst into laughter. "I am starved!"

Sarah jumped up dragging her mother to her

184

feet at the same time.

"Oh, Mamma," she cried, "it's so good to be home. I love you, Mamma."

Rachel hugged Sarah to her, murmuring, "My darling, my darling." But despite their affectionate closeness, Rachel couldn't avoid a shudder of apprehension that after almost four years of marriage her daughter should still feel that this was her home.

Although her problems with Farrel were not actually resolved by her talk with her mother and their day together, nonetheless Sarah returned home feeling more light-hearted than she had in many, many months. She'd found that her mother could also be her real friend, a recognition that perhaps more than any other marks the end of childhood. Sarah had already discovered the virtues and delights of another friend, so that after dinner, when Farrel retired to his home office to continue his day's work, she hurried to her own suite. There she rummaged through one of her drawers where under her dainty camisoles she had secretly hidden her little treasure, her leather-bound diary. Yes, it was her diary in which she recorded each day's events and more importantly her feelings about those events that she had come to regard as a true friend—until today, the only friend she had confided in about the personal aspects of her marriage.

She settled herself on the soft chaise and stroked its velvet surface distractedly. Biting at her underlip in concentration Sarah opened the diary to a new page, her place marked by her pen. As soon as they were marketed commercially, Farrel insisted upon fountain pens for his home and office and by now Sarah had grown used to them and enjoyed the smooth flow of the ink across the page.

"July 15, 1892," she dated the top of the sheet with a flourish. "Today at last I spoke with Mother. I poured out my self-pitying feelings, indulging myself completely. Strangely and wonderfully, it sounded not as horrible as I'd imagined. I felt myself to be less than the nasty and ungrateful wife. Even Farrel became simply an extremely ambitious man and not the unfeeling monster I have been making him into in my mind.

"On the first of September we will celebrate our fourth anniversary. Mother suggested that we plan a party. She thought perhaps in this way I might be able to establish a shared project. The plans themselves would require us to spend a good amount of time together. Time spent in ways other than arguing, I'm sure she meant. It's really an exciting idea. Perhaps I'll approach Farrel at dinner tomorrow and see what he thinks. Oh, please let him approve."

As she wrote the last word, there came a knock at her door. Sarah jumped, guiltily slamming her diary closed.

"Yes?" she called in a nervous voice.

"Sarah, may I come in and talk with you for a moment?"

It was Farrel. He rarely chose to seek her out

after dinner. She flung the diary back into the drawer and shoved it closed. Ignoring her pounding heart, Sarah rushed to the door and opened it.

"Mr. Hurstwood," she said, her voice revealing her surprise, "are you done with your work so soon?"

"Done?" he echoed, as he strode past her into the room. "No, I'm not done. It's never done, really. There's always more."

She stood frozen with her hand still on the doorknob, alarmed by Farrel's agitated manner. He paced back and forth between the window and the bed as he spoke, his words coming out in a gush.

"I've been unfair to you, Sarah. Beastly really." He chewed at the end of his mustache. "The company has been growing bigger and bigger, the issues ever more complex. There just hasn't been time for anything else." Suddenly he paused. "I do love you, Sarah, and I just realized how long it's been since I said it."

He strode back to the door and pushed it closed.

"Mr. Hurstwood," she whispered, as his arms slid around her back. Then he was kissing her. She clutched him to her. He nibbled at her neck.

"Sarah," Farrel said, his voice hoarse with urgency, "give yourself to me."

He led her to the quilt-covered bed where he pulled her down on top of him. His hand caressed her satin bodice, exciting her by the repeated pressure and the unusualness of the entire scene. He lowered his head, nuzzling the beautiful flesh exposed at the top of her bodice.

"Farrel," she whispered.

Their passion increased with each touch, each kiss, until, pushing aside layer after layer of her skirts, he thrust his way into her and, with a great tortured groan, found the ecstasy of release. They had never before shared such an impetuous moment. The disarray of their clothes and the stain on the bedcover bore evidence against them. But surely, Sarah mused, lying languidly beside Farrel, married people need not be so mindful of indiscretion. Sarah laughed aloud with happiness.

"Vixen," Farrel teased, struggling to open his eyes and glare at her.

"Oh, husband," she said, throwing her arms around his neck, "I do love you so very much."

Within minutes their passion had mounted again to the point where the sound of galloping horses seemed to resound in their ears, the pounding of hoofs to reverberate within their bodies.

Farrel didn't leave his wife's chambers that night. The morning light filtering through the loose-woven curtains awoke the Hurstwoods who lay still entwined in each other's arms.

Over their morning biscuits and coffee, Sarah, her bright eyes sending out secret messages, broached the subject of their upcoming anniversary and its celebration.

"A party! What a perfectly splendid idea," Farrel agreed. "We can repay some social debts at the same time. Some important business contacts from out of town as well. Yes, we'll do it."

Sarah's delight was slightly dimmed by the way

in which the party seemed already to be slipping out of her control, but it had been her mother's idea that it be a shared project after all, she reminded herself. Business was Farrel's world and it must necessarily impinge on her space. If only she had a child, she knew she would not be so restless and so jealous of Farrel's work. However, she continued to discover to her regret that she was not yet with child. But last night, so wild and passionate, surely last night, she silently prayed, would lead to the pregnancy she so long had yearned for.

Long after Farrel had kissed her forehead and left for the office, she sat on over her coffee dreaming of how much it would mean to her to have a baby of her very own. How much happier she would be, she mused, how very much happier. Finally, she forced her thoughts away from that topic which so often hounded her, and back to the party. She must start making lists at once. What fun it was going to be.

With all the planning and the work, Sarah's days seemed at last no more than twenty-four hours long. She made an extensive list of names. Anyone who was anyone in Richmond found a place on Sarah's list. Farrel added his names to hers—the business people, the out-of-town money. The numbers mounted. She made out menus and then tore them up and made new ones. She consulted with Farrel on the plans for alcoholic and nonalcoholic beverages. She oversaw the servants' preparations around the house.

Each of the twenty rooms, after all, had exquisite, carved, wooden wainscoting that went halfway up the walls and which must be polished back to its original lustrous beauty. Sarah wanted the parquet floors completely refinished, the carpets cleaned. The list of requirements went on and on.

During this busy time of Sarah's, Farrel was making final preparations for the opening of the Peterboro-Richmond interurban. He reviewed the cars with George. The wheels were larger than the regular streetcar wheels, as were the motors—they generated more than fifty horsepower as against twenty-five horsepower—so the interurbans could run at forty or more miles per hour. The cars were heavier, so the ride would be smoother and quieter. Passengers had choices, too, as to their seating arrangements. There was a main section and a smoker. A sliding door divided the two compartments. The seats in the main section were plush and allowed for a relaxed ride—time to read the daily paper perhaps. In the smoker, where men could sit and smoke and not annoy the ladies, the seats were rattan. Both sections had beautiful polished hardwood wainscoting. The fittings—doorknobs, window latches—were solid brass. All in all the two partners felt pleased that they were providing a luxurious way to travel.

Sarah, involved with her own project, found life remarkably pleasant. She even forgot about counting the days to check on whether or not she might possibly be pregnant, a task that had turned from a silly habit into an obsession. Then one day toward the end of July, with the party only a little more than a month away, Sarah awoke with stomach pains which became severe enough by midmorning to force her back to bed. They didn't feel like normal cramps to her and, when she checked her calendar, she discovered they were more than two weeks late to be her ordinary problem. She rang for Clara and asked her to call Mr. Hurstwood at work.

"Tell him I'm ill," Sarah said. "Ask him to call the doctor."

To Sarah, who had led an unusually healthy life avoiding the influenzas that swept through the town on occasion, it was a new and frightening experience to be in so much pain that she felt the need of a doctor. In fact, Dr. Sam hadn't seen her professionally since she had the chicken pox at eleven. The fear was worse than the pain. She felt a thrill of fear that made every breath seem like a jagged lightning strike. And each breath went from her throat into her lungs and then, with a barbed red pain, into her abdomen. My God, what is happening to me? she cried to herself. This couldn't be what it felt like to be pregnant. Surely it could not.

"Clara," she called again, "ask my mamma to come here too, please."

Yes, she decided, she really needed her mother more even than the doctor. Her mother she could question. She would be too shy with the doctor. It had never entered her mind before, but now she wondered how women managed to overcome their natural shyness with men in order to have babies with male doctors. She thought the older system with women as midwives was better. If she was pregnant, that was what she would do—find a midwife.

By the time the doctor arrived, Sarah had grown feverish and was groaning in pain. He took off his jacket, rolled up his sleeves, and called for a basin to wash his hands in. Then he asked to be left alone with his patient.

"Oh, Farrel," Sarah's mother said in alarm, "she looks so little in that big bed. So little and so alone."

"Come now, Rachel, we'll have a cup of something hot downstairs while we wait. The doctor's here now and it will be all right." He put his arm around his mother-in-law and led her downstairs, although he, too, felt concern, and his words had something of the whistle-in-a-cemetery-to-seem-unafraid quality to them. Nonetheless, they served to assuage Rachel's fears for the moment. If Sarah had been sick more often, they wouldn't have felt this amount of worry. But for Sarah to ask for a doctor—it seemed impossible. They had a cup of tea, refusing any food to go along with it, and waited.

Sam Lathrop's footsteps lumbered down the stairs, and they exchanged tense glances.

"Back here, Doctor," Farrel called.

Farrel stood up as the doctor appeared in the doorway. Rachel remained seated, her hands two knotted fists in front of her.

"Is she all right?" Farrel asked. "What's wrong?"

"Calm yourself. Sit, sit." The doctor sat down heavily across from them. "Rachel, I could use a

192

cup of tea," he said as he noticed their cups and the earthenware teapot. A third cup stood empty. Rachel filled it with the hot amber liquid and passed it over to her old friend.

"Thank you, dear. Hot tea makes even bad news a bit easier to bear. There must be an old Russian proverb that goes like that, don't you think?"

"Tell us," Farrel insisted. These people with their old-country ways would test the patience of a saint, he thought. Why didn't the man get on with it, for heaven's sake?

"She'll be all right with a little rest," Sam said. He blew on his tea and then slurped at it. "It's better if you make noise when you drink," he said and winked at Rachel.

"So what does she need rest for?" Sarah's mother asked.

"She was going to have a baby. Just a little bit pregnant. That's what she needs rest for."

"*Was* going to have?" Farrel repeated. "Is she going to have a baby or not?" He only felt comfortable when he was dealing with facts. Now he demanded them.

"No. She lost the baby. She's a strong young woman, though. She'll have another with no problem, I'm sure."

"How can you be sure? We've waited all this time for one. Now this." Farrel was angry. This old man was probably a charlatan. He'd have to get Sarah a real doctor, a New York doctor.

"How is Sarah?" Rachel asked. "Can I go up to her?"

"I gave her something to make her sleep.

Laudanum. It won't hurt her. It was so early that the body will recover almost immediately. It's the broken heart that will be her problem. It'll be up to you, young man, to convince her that it doesn't matter. That you love her and just want her to get well. Understand?"

Farrel nodded. "Was it a boy?" he asked.

"Too early to tell. Probably it's a blessing in disguise. Mother Nature correcting a mistake. That's what these early abortions usually mean."

"Poor Sarah," said her mother. "Shall I stay with her until she awakens?" she asked her son-in-law.

"I'd appreciate your staying with her," he answered. "I must get back to work. Some final negotiations are in a crucial stage or everything will fall apart. If I knew you were here, I could feel at ease. Sarah probably needs you more than she needs me just now."

"She'll sleep until evening at least," the doctor said, "maybe until morning. Then when she awakens, she can do as much as she feels up to."

"I'll go up to her room. Sit by her side."

"Good. Doctor, can I give you a ride any-where?" Farrel asked out of politeness. Actually he was eager to get away from the house and the whole tense situation as fast as possible. He couldn't work things out in his mind until he had a private time to mull them over.

"No, son, go on ahead. I have my buggy here. I'll just walk Rachel upstairs and check on Sarah once more before I leave."

With a sense of relief, Farrel kissed his mother-in-law on the forehead, shook hands with the doctor, mumbled his thanks, and headed for the door. Once outside he took a deep breath, but found the hot muggy air no refreshment.

When Sarah awoke, she saw her mother's kind face beside her bed, looking at her with loving concern.

"Mamma," she said in surprise; then she remembered. "The baby!"

"No, Sarah, don't even speak of it so. There was no baby. Soon, I feel confident, you will have a baby, but this was just a time of being sick. No need to mourn for something that never really existed. Too many real things to mourn for in our lifetime."

"But I didn't even know! I didn't even get to enjoy those few days when I could have looked forward to having a baby."

"That's a blessing. Think how much greater the sorrow would be now, if you'd had those high expectations. No, darling. Let it go. Pretend that you just had a bad sickness, like the time you had the chicken pox and croup at the same time. Let your mind help your body to heal and to forget."

Sarah could sense that her mother's words were wise. She was right that it would be better to just go on from here. But Sarah wasn't at all sure that she could do that. She'd try, though, she decided.

When Farrel came home he approached her warily, afraid that she would be in an emotional state that he couldn't deal with. But, thanks to

Rachel's advice, he found Sarah pleasant and calm.

"I'm so sorry," he said, pressing his lips to her pale cheek.

"Oh, my dear, I'm the one who is sorry for you. Well, no, I guess that's not right either. It's a loss to us both." She tried to smile so he would know that the tears that trickled from her eyes, along her cheeks, were a reflection of a sorrow she knew that they both shared.

By the next morning, Sarah was able to sit up in bed and continue her directing of the party from there. When Farrel suggested they cancel the party, she insisted that they do no such thing. The busy work of the arrangements was just what she needed now to keep her mind off herself. Within the week she was up and about and actively involved in the party plans.

Rachel thanked God that she had been able to find the right words for her daughter. She knew how easily Sarah could have used this incident to slip into a deep, distant, depressed state. Sarah, with her flair for melodrama. But instead she'd behaved in a mature way. Thank God, she sighed again.

Twelve

By the night of the party, Sarah and Farrel and all seven of the household's servants had reached such a high pitch of nervous excitement that each had on one or more occasions privately wished the party idea had never come into being.

The table linen had been blued and sun-bleached and starched and ironed—each napkin, each doily, each cloth. The silver had been polished, polished, polished until the reflected light bounced back from its surfaces. Even the elaborately wrought handles and borders on the large platters shone wonderfully. Everything and everybody was in readiness.

Awaiting the first guests, Farrel stood dressed most handsomely in a black worsted suit. A rustling sound caught his attention and he turned to see Sarah descend the stairs. There are special moments when some perfect sight transforms itself into an analogous image of beauty. Farrel stared at his wife and suddenly saw the first snow he could ever remember as it fell past the flickering gaslights onto the silent night streets. Sarah smiled at her husband's appreciative gaze. She moved across the foyer to take his arm. Her dress had been handmade by Aunt Jane, the Seewalds' fierce black seamstress. Sarah's mother had overseen the process, of course, every step of the way. The result was exquisite. The gown had a tightly fitted pale apricot satin bodice, the neckline edged in seed pearls. The full striped skirt was a deeper shade of the same color and shimmered whenever Sarah moved.

Farrel leaned close and softly kissed the upswept curls at the top of his wife's head.

"You look delicious," he whispered.

Sarah thrilled to his words, to the beauty of her dazzling home at its party best, to the thought that with this party she would take her rightful place as one of the leading young matrons of Richmond. She smiled up at Farrel and was about to speak when a flurry at the window caught her eye. Carriages were arriving. Involuntarily, she clutched Farrel's arm. "They're here," she breathed. "Oh, my God!"

Farrel led her toward the door to greet their first guests. "Happy anniversary, Mrs. Hurstwood," he said.

The house rapidly filled with sounds and movement, the smell of food, the gay colors of society ladies vying with one another to be the brightest, boldest beauty at this first gala party of the fall season.

*   *   *

Shortly before midnight, Sarah found herself standing alone in front of the punch bowl and smiling at her own image in the mirror across from her. George Spencer, who had been waiting to have a moment alone with his radiant hostess, moved to her side.

"Mrs. Hurstwood," he addressed her. She raised her head and their eyes met in the mirror. In the instant it took her to swivel around and face her husband's partner, Sarah thought, What a handsome couple we make. The thought, appearing out of nowhere, embarrassed her.

"George Spencer," she beamed, "I cannot believe how much of the evening has passed without our spending a moment of it together." She wrapped her arm inside of his and looked directly into his eyes as she added, "There are many eligible girls who would like to know you better, you know." The question in her voice hung in the air like an early-morning mist.

Now George felt embarrassed. "Sarah," he stumbled, "Sarah . . . my time with you . . . and Farrel, of course, is enough . . . companionship enough." He stared blankly ahead. Sarah knew she had blundered, had somehow hurt her friend. She tried awkwardly to make amends.

"Would you like some punch, Mr. Spencer? Come, the party is slowing toward its inevitable farewells. No one will mind if we steal a few moments from the general company. Let us retire to the back parlor."

The pressure of her arm against his urged him to move. In truth, some time alone with her was what he'd most wanted. He patted her hand which rested so delicately along the sleeve of his dark suit.

"Yes, I've been wanting to talk with you. This will give us a chance."

They each took a new cup of punch as much for something to hold as for something to drink. They made their way into the back parlor. Only a single pair of tapers burned and the silence as Sarah closed the door behind them, combined with the dim flickering light, gave the room the feel of a chapel—a mysterious, almost holy, place.

"How I wish everyone were gone," Sarah sighed petulantly. "I would unbutton my shoes and loosen my waist cinch and collapse in comfort."

George laughed. "I suspect you've loved every minute of it though. To a recluse such as myself, throwing a party on this grand scale would have resulted in a solid case of nervous exhaustion."

"Yes, I have loved it," she admitted. "It has been something to do with my time. Too much time, that's my problem. I shouldn't say that," she quickly amended. "It must be the reckless mood of the evening combined with your kindness."

"You've said nothing wrong. I know, don't you think I know how the idle hours while Farrel and I work and work must fret you?"

Sarah avoided meeting his eyes.

"And please, Sarah, won't you try to call me George? It's quite a common practice really in much of Europe, but because we're a younger culture we seem determined to maintain these boring, formal, out-of-date customs."

"What a tirade!" Sarah responded, a smile playing on her lips.

"I'm sorry."

"No, you are right. But only when we're alone, only between us . . . George. Oh, George, it does feel wonderful. Like when we were children. But quick, tell me, how can I make better use of my time?"

George, hearing her call him by his first name and clearly aware of the warmth of her response to him, could hardly talk for a moment. His heart pounded in his ears. What he really wanted to do was grab her in his arms and kiss her eyes, her lips, her neck. Oh God, he thought, help me not to ruin everything. He closed his eyes.

"George," Sarah said, alarmed.

His eyes sprang open. "It's nothing," he assured her. "Just the party mood and the lateness of the hour. What I wanted to talk to you about was the work I have been hearing about that some women up north are doing. Making people realize that children should not work in factories. We have children in the factories here in Richmond, Virginia. Little seven- and eight-year-olds working twelve hours a day or more. Maybe half the children of ten are at work for wages, not in school the way we were at their ages."

Sarah's pulse raced. She couldn't get her breath. "You mean *I* should try to change that? Go out in the streets carrying signs? I have seen photos in the gazettes. Maybe get arrested? Good Lord, you are asking too much of me. Too much. I'm not—" Here her voice failed her. Words refused to come.

She rose from the sofa and began to walk agitatedly back and forth in front of George.

"Wait, now wait," he urged. "That's not the only possibility. It's just that I know how much you love children, is all. Please, Sarah." He stood and took her by the arms in order to stop her. "Sarah." He shook her gently. It quieted her. She looked deeply into his eyes and saw there what his words had never said and what she had never before allowed herself to acknowledge. He loved her.

"George," she whispered, not struggling to escape.

He knew they were on the brink. On the brink of, if not disaster, then at least a terrible indiscretion. I must not, he warned himself.

"Sarah, sit back down."

They moved apart.

"Why do you even bother with my trivial 'lady's' problem?" Sarah asked in a tight voice.

"Oh, I don't know," George teased. "I just use your problems to ignore my own, I guess." They smiled at each other. "Anyway, you do like children, don't you? That's the key. So start there. What could you do that would put you in touch with them?"

Sarah frowned. "You are serious, aren't you?" she asked.

George nodded, then waited while Sarah thought.

"I suppose I could go over to Mrs. Madley's school and see if they need help in the baby class," Sarah amazed herself by saying.

"Good, Sarah. Let's drink to that."

As they raised their glasses, Farrel flung open the door.

"There you are," he called. "Hurry, Sarah. Our guests want to say good-bye to you."

She glanced at George apologetically.

"I'm coming," she said. "George," she whispered, leaning toward him, "stay a few minutes more. Have a last drink with us after everyone else leaves." Then she hurried toward Farrel's outstretched hand and the waiting guests.

It had been quite an evening, Sarah mused later as she sat before her mirror brushing and brushing her almost copper hair. Farrel had already retired. It was well past midnight. Yet she felt no inclination to sleep just yet. She had so much to think about—her anniversary, the four years of her marriage, this new idea of how she might be useful to society, being with the little children. Oh, why hadn't she thought of it sooner! And, finally, nagging at the very edge of her consciousness, stood the message she had read in George Spencer's eyes.

It took time before Sarah could put her plan into effect. She made each move tentatively and without comment to her husband. She knew he would probably disapprove, but she pretended to herself that he would not. So time passed. Finally though, she could no longer put off their confrontation. It was already December of 1892. The children's new school term would be beginning.

"Mr. H," she began in her boldest tone, "I have

203

been talking with Mrs. Madley at my old school. . . ."

"That's nice, dear," Farrel interrupted, rising from the table, "but I really have to run now. You can tell me all about it later." He dusted a kiss on the curls atop Sarah's astonished head. It had taken her days of planning before she could make herself approach the topic of her going to work. At last, though, with a pounding heart she'd begun, only to have her attempt foiled by Farrel's infernal drive to be working every moment that he was awake. Sarah's heart sank, but only momentarily. The sound of the front door slamming shut as Farrel made his whirlwind escape fortified her in her determination to carry out her plan with or without his permission. She saw Mrs. Madley again that very afternoon and confirmed her intention to help the teacher in the baby class three mornings a week beginning when classes resumed in the middle of the month.

When Farrel finally got around to listening to Sarah, what had been merely a scheme had become a *fait accompli*. Perhaps it was this fact more than the idea itself that caused Farrel to rage.

"Work!" he bellowed. He stood towering above her, threateningly. "A wife of mine? Never. What would people think, for God's sake, if they saw Mrs. Farrel Hurstwood going out to work?"

"They would think it was nice that rich people could also be kind. After all, I would be helping at a school. It is quite a proper and ladylike profession."

"Profession! Now we are talking about a

profession for you! I tell you, I will not tolerate this."

"Besides, who cares what people think? You never paid much attention to that when you were starting out. Only now that you are so successful, now you suddenly care about appearance, propriety. The name for that—the correct name—my dear husband, is hypocrisy!"

She had never been so bold, but she felt a sense of desperation. She would fight Farrel on this; she must win. If not, the dark days of winter, of boredom, of despair, would begin again, and that was something she could not tolerate. For him, she thought, it is only a matter of peacock pride, whereas for me, it is my very existence.

"Do not ever again speak to me in such a manner, I warn you." Farrel pounded his fist on the table in front of her. The silverware jumped and so did Sarah. This terror of being hit, beaten, killed—how often must men use it as a means to control their women? Brute force. Our fear. I must withstand it, she told herself. Unless he hurls me into unconsciousness, I must withstand.

"I will accept no money. I already explained that to the schoolmistress."

Farrel struggled with himself. He would not strike her. A gentleman does not, and he would not. His hands formed fists at his sides.

"Why has this suddenly become an issue?" he asked.

"It is not sudden. Not really. I have too much time and too little to do. I need something more to do with my time," she answered back though tears blurred her eyes.

"This house provides work enough, I am quite sure," he sneered.

"Important work, I mean," she insisted, holding her ground. "I'll be helping with the littlest children, the baby class. I always loved the babies. I even helped teach them when I was in school myself."

"Then have one of your own, damn it! That would keep you busy enough."

"You know I want that more than anything," Sarah answered, tears finally mastering her self-possession. "God, how cruel you are!"

Farrel stomped out of the room without another word. In his mind, the issue had been resolved and there was nothing more to say. Sarah, however, left behind sobbing, was far from broken. Her husband's harsh words had hurt her feelings, but not her inner resolve to do something valuable in the world. The words that George had spoken to her at the party were seeds on fallow soil.

Two weeks from today, she promised herself, I'll report to the head teacher.

Farrel circled the desk in his office that morning like a hurricane's winds. Then, as with a hurricane, the excessive fury passed; as with a hurricane, a stillness deeper than any church silence took its place.

He stared out the window, but saw nothing. He stroked the drape pull, but felt nothing. Divorce, a word he had heard more and more often of late, but which he had never let himself think about in connection with himself, now tolled in his ears until it was the only thing he could hear. If the marriage was a mistake, then he ought to end it. He was, however, a man who did not admit mistakes readily. He was particularly reluctant to do so in this case. Not reluctant out of love, he had to admit—not at this point—but reluctant out of a sense of dignity. He did not wish to appear the fool in the community. Divorce, moreover, although it was becoming less uncommon these days, was still a bit scandalous. Also . . . he frowned . . . there was his mother. That was the thorn which pricked his skin. To allow her the victory. To show her that she was right in the first place. Because, indeed, he reasoned, that is exactly what a divorce would do. No words would be necessary. The action would state it more clearly than words ever could.

No, for the moment at least, he would not contemplate so drastic an action as divorce. Perhaps, though, he ought to have a drink at the club this afternoon. He could easily seek out his attorney there. The topic of divorce seemed on everyone's lips these days, so it would be easy enough to ask questions without arousing suspicion. That was what he would do.

With that settled, he could return to the work he was doing on a motorized belt to increase production speed at the tobacco factory. No one had asked him to design it, but he knew the Begglers would be glad of the help. Besides, he couldn't stop the ideas from entering his head, and once they were there he had to develop the plans for making them a reality. That was just how he was built.

Dear Diary,

Happy New Year! Farrel drank too much last night, I fear. He still sleeps on as I sit with my breakfast tray already finished. Nonetheless, I am not annoyed, since it gives me a chance to bring you up to date, my dear diary. I see I have been naughty and neglectful and not written here since back in September. On my fourth anniversary. Although I don't know what I accomplish, the time rushes by full of busy things and so I neglect you. In a short time, I will begin to help at the school working with the littlest children. Such darlings. It seems impossible that year after year I still have no children of my own. The one moment of hope ended all too soon. I begin to think that perhaps I never shall have. Oh, I must leave off this topic of children or I shall cry and I have shed too many tears already.

So. As to Farrel, his streetcars are a glorious success. Some people call them trolleys because of the little trolley wheels on top that roll along the electric line. I think that's a cute name. The electric motor in all its variations is Farrel's life. Work takes up his time, his mind, and his heart. Nothing changes there except, I must admit, my growing resentment. Which is unfair, I know. After all, Farrel told me from the first that streetcars were his life. I chose to share that life. But I still resent his total absorption.

I remember our first meeting so clearly. Can it really be five years since then? Since that day when a long lanky stranger walked through the door of Papa's pharmacy. I must admit he is as beautiful to me now as he was then with his dark deep-set eyes and hollow cheeks. His beard is

208

*new, but it only adds to the elegance I saw in him
at first glance. He leaned on the counter and
smiled at me as my father introduced us. That
wonderful smile. Although I didn't let on, I already knew who he was because I spent every
spare moment after school watching the construction of the tracks. He impressed me right
away because he seemed so powerful and so sure
of himself. Different from the Richmond folks. I
asked around and learned he was the streetcar
mastermind from New York City, and that impressed me even more.*

*Ah, my schoolgirl dreams after that! He would
fall in love with me and take me away to someplace romantic. Then, unbelievably, it happened—at least the falling-in-love part. As to
the someplace romantic—well, here I am still in
Richmond, Virginia, probably forever. It seems
Farrel was looking for what he calls a "base of
operations" away from New York. He says Richmond is perfect. Ironic, is it not?*

The crisp, blue mid-January morning that was
to be her first day at work, Sarah greeted with a
mixture of excitement and fear. Imagine, she told
herself, her first day helping at the school. Sarah
had been lying awake hours waiting for it to be late
enough to get up. She had chosen, rejected, and
reselected her outfit for this first day a dozen times
over the past weeks. Finally she decided on a navy-
blue wool dress over which she would wear a
simple white organdy apron to protect herself
from the chalk and paint and crayons and who
knows what other messy things.

Not another word on the subject of her working
had been spoken in the household. Indeed, few

words of any kind had been spoken between Mr. and Mrs. Farrel Hurstwood since their last fierce and angry ones.

Sarah hurried now, hoping she could leave before Farrel, but even as she stood sipping and blowing at her hot coffee, she heard him descend the stairs.

"What's this?" he asked, surprised by Sarah standing beside the table fully dressed and obviously getting ready to leave. A dark cloud gathered in his face.

Sarah's trembling hands threatened to spill the coffee. She placed her cup back in its saucer on the table with as much composure as possible.

"This is the day I begin at the school." She held her head tensely, determined not to shrink before him.

His face flamed. He tightened his lips, but said nothing. They stood frozen. Farrel asked in cold tones, "Are you taking your phaeton or do you want me to drop you off?"

"Thank you just the same, but I shall walk."

He nodded abruptly. He walked to the kitchen door to order his breakfast. Sarah's heart turned into stone. The morning's thrill drained from her. She held herself firmly as she said, "Good-bye for now, Mr. Hurstwood."

When Farrel didn't answer, refused in fact even to turn toward her, she left. Despite her tension and misery, she felt a little tingle of delight to be the one leaving. The breeze that caught her as she pulled the front door shut seemed to welcome her into the world. A smile burst over her face, and she hurried on eagerly.

By week's end, Sarah felt happier than she had at any time since the exciting period of her courtship. Her schedule varied little from day to day, but each day felt full. Sarah knew again the joy of being wanted, the thrill of being needed. She arrived at the school early enough to sit with the head teacher over a cup of tea and plan out the day. Sarah's first assignment was to help the children practice their letters. It made her smile to see their baby faces frown in concentration as they struggled to form an A or a B on their slates. One tiny girl pressed so hard on the chalk that it crumbled in her hand, and she looked up with fear in her eyes at Sarah who simply hugged her and got her a new piece. Another day a boy no bigger than a mite put his curly head down on his desk and sobbed because he could not form his Q's properly. As Sarah comforted him, she thought how easily the heart breaks. Later on, when she saw him at play outside, seemingly forgetful of the morning's tragedy, she realized it can break over and over, the heart, but also it can heal itself again and again.

When the children had their quiet time, heads resting on their desks, Sarah would read them stories. Sometimes she would close her book and tell them a story, instead, of when she was little. They seemed to like that better, so she began to try to recall her babyhood adventures in Russia. She told them about the Cossacks with their shiny boots. How they would ride through the village

211

looking beautiful and cruel. She told of how she hid behind the water barrels because she thought they would steal her away if they saw her.

Sarah described the glitter of the soldiers' spurs as they urged their horses into a gallop, the sleek sweat of the horses' flanks. As she spoke, she had flashes of other memories, too scary to tell to the children. She didn't tell them about the time a poor Jew returning home from *shul* was struck to the ground and killed by a Cossack for no reason. She didn't tell them how the Cossacks had murdered her sister, her only sister.

When her group of youngest children left at midday, Sarah began to visit her mother's house to learn new stories. They had never before talked about the old days together. Rachel had locked those memories away in pain and sorrow. As she reopened the gates now, she found that for every scene that brought tears there was some other time some other place that gave her joy.

She shared these memories with Sarah who, after all, was a woman herself now. Rachel told Sarah about the influenza epidemic when they refused to give Jews any medicine. Told her that, as a result, many of the village's Jews died. That was, in fact, the way Rachel's own mother, Sarah's grandmother, had died.

Rachel described the way her mother used to sing and clap her hands to make music for the children to dance to. She told how her mother loved to watch plants spring from the earth, how she talked to her fruit bushes.

"She would tell them, 'You better give me plenty

212

grapes, you hear me? I have wine to make!' The bushes would give a *bissele* shake, the leaves would rustle. They understood. By morning, there would be more ripe grapes!"

"Oh, Mamma, you are telling me fairy tales." Sarah laughed.

"Of course. Of course I am. You want I should give you stories for your school babies. What should be better than fairy tales, I ask you? But anyway, I believe them. When my mother talked to her plants, they listened. You tell the children that for me."

And Sarah did. She would go into the classroom each day and tell the children the latest story that her mother had told her. She described these days in her diary as "all chalk dust and stories." On one page, otherwise empty, Sarah wrote the two words, "SUDDENLY HAPPY!"

Sarah found that she and Rose, the head teacher, were becoming friends. Since Maxine's death, Sarah had really had no women friends. She had avoided her old schoolmates because she could hardly bear the memories they brought back to her of their old days together, days full of adventures with Jug. With Rose, though, the talk was of shared days, shared problems, shared plans. Their talk lived in the present or in the future, not in the past. This fact allowed Sarah to relax into the friendship.

Thirteen

After a month, with Farrel still ignoring her outside activities, but with a semblance of peace reestablished between them, Sarah felt absolutely certain that she had made a lifesaving decision. Thanks in large part, she admitted to herself, to George Spencer's conversation at her anniversary party. She wanted to see him, to tell him, to thank him. But of late, George had not been visiting as often as he used to. The days went by and the weeks, and as winter's crust melted from the earth uncovering spring, she decided she was going to see George.

So it was that on the first day of April of 1893, while Farrel was visiting Peterboro for the day, Sarah Hurstwood appeared in the office of the Richmond Electric Street Railway and asked to see her husband's partner. It was a school holiday so her time was free.

"Sarah Hurstwood," George explained as soon as he caught sight of her, "what a treat to see you!

Come into my office, won't you?"

She took his proffered arm and let him lead her away from the curious eyes of the half-dozen or so office workers that comprised the staff.

When they were alone, George whispered, "You look divine!" She laughed in delight.

"Mr. Spencer," she began.

He interrupted. "George, remember?"

"George," she began again, shyly. "Do *you* remember the day I first showed you my little carriage?"

George nodded, surprised at having her here, warm and lively beside him.

"On that day you suggested a picnic and I, like a ninny, failed to insist you make good on your word. I hope you have no plans for lunch today because my carriage is outside packed full with an enormous hamper of goodies. What do you say, George, are you ready for a spring picnic?"

George saw a different Sarah before him. She held herself in a regal way, as though newly conscious of her body. Her eyes shone. It was a Sarah who had just come into sharper focus. George had recently taken up photography as a hobby and now saw the world in a new pictorial sense. He had bought one of the new Kodak cameras, won over by the advertisements that claimed: "You just press the button, and we do the rest."

"I must take your photograph. How wonderful you look," he repeated. "Has something happened?"

"Come with me and I promise to tell you all

about it."

"I wouldn't miss that opportunity, believe me. If I bring my Detective Camera along—did you know that's what they are called? Did you know that I had become a photographer?—perhaps I might get a likeness of you." He rolled down his sleeves, fastening them with gold cuff links retrieved from his vest pocket. He struggled into his jacket, stuck his bowler hat on his head, grabbed his Kodak, and said, "I am ready. I am yours. Shall we go?"

Sarah had stood by beaming during this rapid transformation. Now she nodded and followed George as he led the way to her waiting carriage.

"I brought no driver," she whispered, "but we can manage alone, can we not?"

A sense of danger flashed through George as he set the pony to galloping, and his mind outraced the rattling wheels. This behavior was so unlike Sarah. He felt that she was basically a free spirit, but she had so long controlled that part of herself he could hardly believe her actions today. Could she possibly be offering herself to him? No, he must control his fantasies, he reminded himself.

"George, George dear."

He heard her call him as though waking from a deep sleep.

"Oh, I am sorry, Sarah. What did you say?"

"I asked where you were leading us at this breakneck pace. Who are we running away from?"

He reined the horse in. He had not realized how far they had come.

"Anywhere along the river here would be fine, I

guess. I was so lost in thought we might have ended up in Canada, had you not spoken."

They climbed down into the scratchy dead winter grass. Spring had not fully burst upon the scene. Sarah spread out a large red-plaid blanket; she circled and swooped at its corners until it lay, a smooth soft surface, before them. George hoisted the basket down.

He led the horse over to a clump of trees and tied him loosely. Sarah had already begun to spread the food, but George called her and she stopped, rose, and went to him.

"Leave the food for now. Let us walk a bit, beside the water. I must hear what you have come to say."

They strolled to the riverside path. Sarah breathed in the smell of water, of sunlight. Everything smelled green as though it were the first day of the earth. She began to tell George about her days in the classroom, about the love the children gave her, the sweet way they hugged her neck. He asked about Farrel's response and she told him that, too. She described how she had stood up against him, even revealing their current coolness. Finally, having run out of words, it seemed, she stopped. She laid her hand on George's arm.

Despite her words, tears filled her eyes. George reached over and wiped a single tear off her lashes. They stood awhile so. He brushed another tear from her cheek. A smile trembled on her lips. Their eyes met and held. He felt as though she could see into his soul. With slow deliberateness he put his hand on the back of her neck. Sarah shivered, but did not pull away. As though drawn by a force he could not resist, he leaned forward and just barely touched her lips with his, so tentative a touch it could hardly be called a kiss. Yet he had frightened her. He could feel her pull back from the pressure of her head on his hand.

"No," she hissed. "We must not."

But it was too late. Having come so far, at last, he would not retreat.

"Hush," he whispered. He gathered her into his arms and kissed her again. George allowed himself to feel the soft fullness of her lips, the press of her bosom against his chest. How long he had waited. After a shocked moment, Sarah responded. She passionately returned his kiss. Their kisses felt like spring. Their kisses felt like the first rush of warmth into the chilled roots of plants. When at last they pulled apart, there were no words. George kept his arm around Sarah's waist as they strolled back toward their picnic lunch.

To Sarah's surprise, their friendship, though now so much more intense than ever before, still felt comfortable and easy. They allowed themselves tender kisses. They laughed and talked as they enjoyed the food Sarah had brought—ham baked in a flaky biscuit crust, crab-meat salad with peas and scallions, a bottle of glorious French champagne. Then George insisted on taking photographs.

"Sit, sit," he commanded, as she started to stand for an appropriate pose. "I want to capture you sprawled amid the debris of delight. No more

218

propriety, please. Allow yourself a little self-indulgence. If the resultant picture is too shocking, we will hide it from Farrel!"

As Sarah heard these words, she sensed they were moving into new areas of complicity, George and she. She had not, she realized, mentioned the picnic idea to her husband and had given no thought to telling him about it. She dismissed the idea now. It felt delightful to bask in George's admiration. She smiled and smiled as he took photographs.

"Now," he said at last when he had satisfied himself with picture-taking and sat again beside her, "now this perfect moment will remain forever. It will be a part of history."

Sarah took his hand and said, "Even without a photograph I could never forget. It is already part of our history."

He raised her hand to his lips and kissed each fingertip. Later, on the way back into town, Sarah asked, "Am I wicked?"

"No, Sarah," George answered. "With all the hatred that exists in the world, how can any little bit of love be evil? If there is one thing I am sure of, it is that you are absolutely good."

Sarah's work at the school had added a new complexity to her relations with Farrel, who continued his course of silent disapproval. The intensification of her friendship with George, though unknown to Farrel, added yet another barrier for Sarah to overcome in her effort to respond to Farrel as his dutiful wife. But as the months had passed, so had the extremity of the strain between them. During the Easter holiday, in fact, when there were no classes, Farrel arranged not to travel, and the Hurstwoods managed to heal their wounds well enough so that only a narrow area of scar tissue marked the rift. Sarah's friendship with Rose grew stronger and stronger. It was of a different order from anything Sarah had ever experienced. Rose Endicott was an independent woman with unusual ideas. She was unmarried and spoke of marriage as a second but more subtle form of slavery, a condition where one class of people completely controls another. It surprised Sarah that when Rose came to dinner Farrel took an instant dislike to her. He called her mannish and rude, but Sarah found her worldly-wise and provocative.

"Her ideas are different," she explained to George. "But that's what I like about her. She reads constantly and forces me to consider issues in a larger context than just their effect on Richmond, Virginia. I have to defend opinions I have that I just absorbed and never really decided upon. The way you force me to think about things," she said and nudged George who smiled, happy as always to be near his beloved Sarah. "Only she concentrates more on the political side of things. I believe she is a bit of a radical—wants women to get the vote; insists that the government is full of corruption and is basically bought out by businessmen."

"Is she a Populist, then?"

"I don't really know what that means."

"Oh, the Populists are folks who like neither the Democrats nor the Republicans. Folks who think government would do better in the hands of the poor and the uneducated." George, being one of the businessmen the Populists were attacking, felt little sympathy for their position.

"Oh, then that is surely not what Rose is. She is the most intellectual woman I ever met. You would surely like her. Shall I arrange a meeting between you two?"

That—the meeting between George and Rose—was the real issue Sarah had been leading up to in their entire conversation.

"Perhaps at another time," George answered. "There is already a woman in my life at this particular moment." He grinned at Sarah who caught her lip between her teeth and blushed. "Anyway, enough about your new friend. I brought a copy of a journal with some portrait reproductions. Look at these." He flipped through the pages until he came to the photographs. "See how she gets close in. Just the head, that is the only thing which concerns her. Yet look how much personality one can see."

"She? Is the photographer a woman?"

"Yes indeed. Unfortunately she is no longer alive. Julia Margaret Cameron, her name is. Look at this photograph of Alfred, Lord Tennyson, the famous poet."

"Remarkable. Truly. But a woman photographer?"

"Yes. Yes. Why not? What would your friend, Rose, say to your skepticism? It is light enough to

221

carry, the camera. Also it is simple to operate. Talent, that is the required quality and I believe that men and women both have that."

"I know," Sarah laughed. "You just press the button." She had heard George quote the advertisement a million times it seemed to her.

"Would you like a camera, Sarah?"

"No, dear. Between my work in the school and at home, and my visits with you, with Mamma, and with Rose, my days are at last too full to take on a new activity. You be the photographer! Besides, soon it will be time to tend to the herb garden again."

Fourteen

Warm days had arrived of a sudden in Richmond. Sarah began to spend many afternoons out of doors. At times she played at gardening, the heavy work of which she left for the servants. At other times she simply sat or wrote in her diary. Sarah continued to confide in her diary about everything, in George about everything but the true depth of her feelings for him, and in her mother about everything but George.

April 25, 1893

Dear Diary,
  Spring, glorious spring! I feel like a schoolgirl again with my moods changing as fast as the clouds scoot across the sun on a windy day. The whole household is affected. We are all in a turmoil, except for Bessie the cook (bless her) who keeps her equanimity. She laughs at us, jollies us out of our sour faces, and bakes us strudel for dessert. Who, dear diary, could stay unhappy when strudel steams its apple-cinnamon-

buttery smell under your nose? Certainly not I. I eat every fattening crumb, then complain to Bessie, a mountainous woman, who laughs at my worrying. Farrel teases me by saying my plumpness is as delicious as the strudel. So I go on eating everything even though my clothes do seem to be getting tighter.

May 13, 1893

Dear Diary,

Haven't I been getting better, dear diary? That was one of my New Year's resolutions: to write in my diary regularly. No more six-month gaps.

Another resolution was to stop brooding over the fact that I have no children of my own. That resolution I have been less successful in maintaining. Too often I still lie awake at night unable to sleep. Too often I burst into tears at the school when one of the tots says "I love you" or hugs my neck. Too often when Farrel comes to me in the night I feel myself grow tense and resentful.

But that is all over now because—dear diary, I have been saving the best news for last—today Dr. Lathrop told me definitely that I am going to have a baby! Toward the end of the year, he said. I haven't even told Farrel yet so you are the first to know. If I could, I would wait until next month and tell him on my twenty-second birthday. But that would be too cruel and anyway I could never manage that much restraint. So I shall tell him tonight at dinner. I must say goodbye for now so I can run down and coax Bessie into making an extra special meal. Then I shall dress myself in the plum taffeta which is Farrel's favorite gown. But however shall I find the right words to say what I have yearned to say for so long?

The study is too hot tonight, Farrel thought.

Although it is only May, I feel as though I cannot breathe. I am sure Sarah is asleep by now. Thank goodness, because I need this time alone to take account of my feelings. A baby, she tells me. At last, a baby. That seems a clear and simple statement. Why, then, I wonder, did I have such an extraordinary response—wanting to run, feeling trapped. My face felt as flaming as the candles and my collar suddenly grew so tight it choked me.

It seems I am at last to become a father. Do you hear that, Dad, wherever you are, in heaven or hell? Do you hear that, you old S.O.B.? Now I get a chance to mess things up the way you did working so hard you died too young—leaving behind a son who needed you and a wife who grew old and bitter without you.

Christ, where is my handkerchief! My nose is runny. It can't be tears. Not tears now when I have never shed a one for you since the day you died. Oh, poor you, Father! Poor me.

Well, a new baby is a new chance. My chance. I wonder if I can do any better. Mother always used to say I am you all over again, an exact duplicate. I hope not.

Sarah will be a good mother, I am sure of that. Just to watch her play with the baby class at school would prove that. And thank God she shall have her chance. Still, she seems not much more than a baby herself.

I remember my impressions of her when we first met. What a lovely child, I thought. It was afternoon and she still had on her school clothes under her apron. Her little breasts barely puffed out the ruffles. Her eyes sparkled with mischief. She seemed to know how charming she looked. I wanted to grab her there and then and take her. There amid the pastries and whipped cream— just one more delicious dessert.

225

*But her innocence. Ah, her innocence was very
real. I learned that soon enough. Then after our
wedding—well, I discovered that her first provocative glance was real, too. Sarah, my dear, you
can be a passionate tigress when you are aroused!
What a strange blend of many different qualities,
this wife of mine. Almost five years we've been
married. Unbelievable. This must be how life
slips away from us. One day we have lived it all
out and we look back and sigh that we cannot believe it.*

*It will be dawn soon. I had better get myself off
to bed. I wonder if Sarah would mind being disturbed from her sleep. Surely pregnant women
are still allowed to play games under the
blankets.*

Since the school year had only a month left
before the summer holidays, Sarah decided to
continue on there as a helper until then. Although
Farrel made a feeble attempt to convince her that a
lady in her condition should remain at home, he
realized that in a matter of weeks she would leave
her job forever. He had won.

Sarah's last day felt scratchy in her throat. Next
year there would be a new baby class and she
would not be there to tell them stories. She
reminded herself that in a short time she would
have a baby of her own. That was what she had
waited for all during these years. She swallowed
hard, and then she kissed everybody good-bye. As
she walked home, arms full of flowers from the
mothers, she felt a special strength in having
chosen to work despite Farrel's resistance. She

could do that; she would always have that knowledge within her. After all, she had won.

During the long days of summer, Sarah lounged about enjoying the changes in the season and the changes in herself. Her mother came by often to make sure that Sarah was eating enough, resting enough, happy enough. She warned Sarah not to raise her arms above her head for fear that the cord—some mysterious entity Sarah could not really imagine—would strangle the baby. She warned Sarah not to carry anything heavy for fear she would rupture the casing—another mysterious entity—and deliver the baby too soon. It seemed to Sarah that her body was suddenly full of unknown parts and full of dangers.

Rachel warned Sarah not to think angry thoughts nor to look at anything violent (not even the killing of the chickens by the servants) for fear it would somehow mark the baby. Sarah was suspicious of all this advice, viewing it as old-fashioned and probably based more on superstition than science. Nonetheless she tried to bear with her mother in good spirit, recognizing mother's love from which the warnings sprang.

She began to notice that her mother was showing signs of her age, and noticing that made Sarah kinder and more patient too. Her mother's hair had turned almost completely gray over the years since Sarah had married and left home. The soft skin under her chin sagged now which made Sarah feel tender and frightened at the same time. The laugh lines around Rachel's eyes and mouth had turned into definite wrinkles. It made Sarah sad to see these changes. Still she felt relieved when the weather grew so hot that Rachel stayed at home and would not venture out. Her extreme attentiveness had become a strain.

On the other hand, Rose's visits were a refreshment. They were rare since Rose used her summer holidays for adventures. She went by steamer down the Mississippi River; she learned how to bicycle and bicycled around the growing city of St. Louis; she even hinted at romances in the picture post cards she sent back to Sarah. She was really the "new woman" that all the magazines were talking about, Sarah thought. When she did visit, she came with breezy advice: "For heaven's sake, stop wearing corsets and let your insides have some room." "Come on along for a good walk. The exercise will strengthen your body for the time ahead." Sarah followed these prescriptions gladly. Then the fall came and Rose went back to work and the visits became even rarer.

Also by the fall, the novelty of the pregnancy had worn off. As cold weather closed Sarah in, she began to feel like a prisoner despite her spacious house. The song about the bird in the gilded cage frequently floated through her mind. She had never been a patient person and her new condition had done nothing to increase that quality. Farrel, when he came home at night, often found her in tears. Damn it, he cursed, totally confused by the seeming illogic of a woman crying over what she had so long wanted. Damn it, what more does she want from me?

228

Dear Diary,

Well, here I am still heavily encumbered by the grotesque shape my body has assumed, the traitor! Christmas came and went and still no child. Obviously even if I am impatient the little one within me is enormously patient. It is only here that I dare admit that I sometimes ask myself why I ever wanted to have a baby at all. I know that is an unnatural thought for a mother-to-be to have. How I envy Rose her freedom!

That winter of Sarah's pregnancy was a bitterly cold one. Temperatures plunged below zero nightly. The first week in January, 1894 set a record with the coldest weather in Richmond's history. The wind howled up and down the hills making the days seem forbidding and the nights ominous. The stars were such tiny glints of icy light up in the sky that they seemed to have lost interest not only in Richmond, but in all of humanity.

It was in that frozen January that Sarah lumbered around the house awaiting the birth of her first child. It was already a week into the new year, she thought, and Dr. Lathrop had said the baby would be here for Christmas! She grudgingly admitted that he always reminded her that babies did not run on streetcar schedules and that the little darling would be here whenever he or she was ready to arrive. Dr. Lathrop was more than attentive, pounding on the door every few days to check on the daughter of his old friend, Dave Seewald, the pharmacist.

"Clara," Sarah shouted down the stairwell, "please get the door and if it is Dr. Lathrop show him up."

Clara took a moment to check her cap in the foyer mirror before she opened the door.

Dr. Lathrop stood huddled against the door. He held his hat on with one gloved hand and clutched his coat lapels together with the other.

"Good afternoon, Clara," he greeted the maid as he hurried past her into the house.

Clara leaned against the door to get it locked. The wind whistled as it pushed back at her.

"Lordy, sir," Clara exclaimed, "this is the devil's own winter. I hope it don't mark the baby-to-come with evil ways. Let me take your coat. Miss Sarah's upstairs. She knew it was you at the door. She's waiting."

"Clara, don't let her hear any of this devil talk, you hear me? That's just foolishness." He started toward the stairs.

Clara asked, "You want me to lead you up?"

"No," Sam Lathrop answered, "I know the way well enough after all these months."

He climbed the thickly carpeted stairs easily despite his sixty years. "Halloo," he called, pausing a moment at the top. How many more babies would he be able to bring into this world? he wondered. The thought caused him no particular pain. Since his wife, Hannah, had died two years back, Sam had been ready for his own death whenever it was ready for him. That's what he always told his old friends at the barber shop, but they'd say "No, Sam," and "Don't talk like that,

Sam." Why not face it? he wondered. Death was just the other side of being born. And he had dealt with that all his adult life.

"Come in, Doctor," Sarah called from her room at the end of the hall.

He entered the room to see his patient seated prettily on the bed's edge. A face like an angel, he thought. He almost could have fooled himself into believing he was seeing his Hannah many years ago. Sarah wore a yellow wool robe belted together above her bulging belly.

"Any news, young lady? This baby should be just about ready to make an appearance."

"I am not sure, Doctor, but I think something has started." Her voice was edged with excitement.

"Well, well? So tell me."

"Oh, I cannot."

"What do you mean by that?"

"It's too embarrassing."

"Nonsense!" Sam Lathrop exploded. "To your doctor you can tell everything. In fact, you must."

There were a few seconds of silence. Then Sarah began to speak, twisting the belt of her robe in her fingers.

"When I woke this morning. Well, there was a stain on my nightgown."

"What kind of stain? Describe it."

Another strained silence followed, as Sarah reminded herself that she was an adult and must act like an adult. Nonetheless, she flushed as she spoke.

"It was a glob of mucus. Rust colored. You taught me that was one of the ways it could begin."

The doctor nodded. "Let's check," he said. He sat near Sarah on the bed and placed his hand under her robe. He pressed on her globe of a belly, now here now there, while Sarah wondered and hoped that this would be the time.

"Anything else?" he asked.

"I felt some cramps. A strong one or two just in the last hour." Her voice betrayed her excitement. "Could it be?" she asked.

"Yes, yes. It seems to be starting," he agreed. "Have you gotten a room ready to use for the birth, as I directed?"

"Clara prepared it just the way you asked."

"Good. I'll be back later tonight to check on you or if you need me sooner, send Clara for me."

"But what should I do in the meantime? What should I do now?" Sarah's voice rose in panic.

Doctor Lathrop patted her on the shoulder. "Easy now, Sarah. For as long as you are comfortable, you can do anything you want. Read a book. Walk around the house or take a nap. No baths, though. Oh, and tell Bessie just light foods. It looks like your baby wanted to wait for the new year to get himself born."

"When will it be, Doctor?"

"No one can answer that exactly, Sarah. Sometime soon, though. Tonight or tomorrow. Tomorrow night at the very latest. Just relax, it won't be too long. You have waited all these months. Now it is just a matter of hours!"

"Yes. I will try to relax," Sarah answered nervously, sounding to herself like an obedient child.

After the doctor left, Sarah sat on in the bedroom. How, she asked herself, could she be feeling so much like a scared little girl when she was about to have a baby of her own? Having a baby must surely be the most grown-up thing a woman could do. Even more so than gaining the title of Mrs. Farrel Hurstwood.

Where was Farrel now? she wondered. He could calm her, if anyone could. He could sit and just talk to her and she would know everything was going to be all right. But he was probably at his office. Even now, with his first child almost two weeks overdue.

She pushed herself up from the bed clumsily. She must not get angry, she reminded herself. She should concentrate on the baby-to-come—her baby and Farrel's. Sarah moved toward the head of the stairs. She would go down and ask Bessie for a light supper. Suddenly, a powerful spasm caught her in its grip. She staggered and clutched at the newel post leaning her weight against it for support.

At that very moment, before Sarah could catch her breath, the downstairs door burst open and a bareheaded Farrel rushed into the house.

"Sarah," he called. "Sarah."

"What is it, sir?" Clara asked, appearing at the dining-room door. "Is there something wrong that you in that much of a panic?"

"No, no, Clara. Just tell me where Mrs. Hurstwood is, please."

"Up in the bedroom, sir, I believe. Least she was when Doc came by a few minutes ago."

Farrel handed Clara his coat, then took the stairs two at a time. As he rounded the curve at the landing and bolted the last few steps, he almost collided with Sarah who still clung doggedly to the ornately carved wooden post at the top of the stairway.

"Sarah!"

"Farrel!"

Her relief matched his surprise. He removed her hands from their stranglehold on the post.

"Are you in pain?" She shook her head no and he led her back toward their room. His protective arm supported her as they walked.

"It has started, Farrel," Sarah exclaimed as they sat together on the pair of matching chairs in the window nook. "I'm going to have the next baby born in the whole world! I'm the most pregnant woman in the world!" She was ecstatic. Her flushed cheeks and the damp curls across her forehead made Farrel think of a Rubens sketch he had seen of a young girl. He laughed at the image and at her exaggerated statements seeing them for what they were—pride.

"I know, sweetheart. Sam Lathrop stopped at the office to tell me. I rushed home to be with you. Are you sure you are not in any pain . . . ?"

A great groan interrupted his words. Sarah squeezed his hand until he thought she would break the fingers right off. Uncertain what he should do, Farrel sat and did nothing. In less than a minute, Sarah sagged against him.

"I am so scared, Farrel. What will it be like? What is to come?" Sarah's voice broke and tears glistened on her lashes.

"Honey, do not cry. Soon we shall have our little baby. It won't be long, darling, and it will be all over. And we will have our baby at last. Remember that."

"You are right. I will just keep my thoughts firmly on that. Our baby." Sarah smiled at her husband. "Thank you for coming right home, dear. In the middle of your workday, too!" Farrel easily recognized her teasing mood and knew the pain must have passed and with it the fear.

"Why don't you lie down, Sarah?" he suggested. "I can have Bessie bring you some tea and toast, if you like."

"Yes, I think I would feel better lying down, but perhaps you should help me get to the birth room first."

"Why I suppose so. I'd forgotten all about it."

Sarah leaned heavily on Farrel as they made their way back down the hall to the small room at the other end. There Farrel settled his wife into the narrow bed with its crisp white sheets. The room had a stripped-down look and a vaguely antiseptic smell that made Farrel uncomfortable. He would not admit that it scared him, though, or it would alarm Sarah. Instead, he excused himself saying he would be back with a cup of tea in a few minutes. When the door closed behind him, Farrel breathed a sigh of relief, then headed down the stairs.

Left alone, without the need to hold herself under control for Farrel's sake, Sarah breathed a sigh of relief, too. There are some situations where no matter how much love is shared, sharing a room pushes intimacy beyond its natural limit.

The tea turned into cinnamon toast and cocoa under Bessie's hand. Farrel kept Sarah company as she enjoyed every bit, then she asked him if he would mind lighting the lamp as it seemed already to be growing dark.

"I think I will try to nap awhile," she added. "Then I will be rested for the hard work later on. You don't have to stay by me, Farrel. I understand."

"Nonsense, Sarah," Farrel said with a heartiness he only feigned. "I shall sit right here next to you and read while you take your rest."

Awhile later Sarah began to toss and turn in her sleep. She groaned. Then she grew calm again. Farrel put down his paper and gazed at her. He told his heart to stop pounding. It would probably be hours and hours yet. No need to fetch Dr. Lathrop around just now, he told himself. Still, he knew he would feel more comfortable if the doctor were near at hand.

Farrel had just about convinced himself to send the girl off for Sam Lathrop when Sarah sat bolt upright and screamed. Sweat popped out above her lip and across her forehead.

"Farrel," she shouted frantically. As she woke more fully her eyes focused on her husband seated nearby. "Farrel, it hurts so much. I never had such a bad stomach ache in all my life."

In no space of time, he was on his knees beside her bed.

"Oh, Sarah, poor darling," he murmured.

"What can I do to help? Try to relax, Sarah, I remember the doctor said how important that was. I'll send Clara for the doctor. He will hurry right here, Sarah, dear." Farrel kept repeating reassurances even after Sarah nodded and eased herself back down onto the pillow. "Don't worry, Sarah," he went on. "Everything's going to be just fine. Don't you worry about a single thing."

Sarah opened her eyes. "Farrel," she said, stopping the flow of his words. "Dear, go get the doctor!"

The baby, a large healthy boy, was born just before dawn. Farrel had to be awakened to hear the news. He had dozed off downstairs before the fire. He rubbed his eyes, then smiled up at the doctor and offered him a drink.

"Brandy or Scotch?" Farrel asked.

Bessie's voice boomed out from the kitchen. "Now never you mind, Mr. Farrel. Hot toddies been ready this past hour waitin' on the good news. I'll bring 'em right out."

Fifteen

One week later, the Hurstwoods took their son to Sarah's parents' home where he was ritually circumcised according to the age-old patterns of the Jewish people. The Seewalds had, after losing their daughter to the Christian world—that is how they thought about it sometimes—returned to the practice of their religion. Their decision was made in part because of the activity of the Reform movement people. They seemed more like Christians than Jews, for heaven's sake. They had given up the Saturday Sabbath with the excuse that when in Rome you should do as the Romans do. That seemed to mean that in America you pretended to be a Christian and you tried to make as much money as possible so you kept your stores open on Saturday to that end. The Reform temple even exchanged the traditional cantor and his beautiful chants for organ music like the Christian churches. Rachel and David began to view their actions in hiding their religion as parallel to these other actions of other Jews. Suddenly they saw clearly that, if followed to their logical conclusions, these actions would mean the essential end of the Jewish people. No, they decided, they must take a stand—for themselves, for their heritage, for Sarah, as late as it now seemed in that regard. So they joined the newly formed Judah Israel Synagogue. As Conservative Jews, they could keep the best of the old, reflected in the Orthodox tradition, and incorporate changes that reflected a new time, such as allowing men and women to worship together. They were happy, too, to be able to celebrate now with their new friends the welcoming of their first grandchild—a boy—into the tribe.

Although it was a party, it had almost the feel of an underground meeting with only the select few there who, like the Seewalds, had followed an arduous route away from their religion and then back to it by means of the new Conservative movement.

Wine was on every table, in every glass. The kosher sacramental wine with its sweet heavy taste that always reminded Jews of their childhood and their first Sabbath celebrations. Farrel, on the other hand, raised on French wines, trained to know grape types and to recognize vintage years from a single taste of the wine the grapes produced, could hardly imagine people drinking this strange sticky stuff—though he noticed that everyone else drank it with pleasure. To his surprise, they even gave the baby wine. David dipped the corner of a napkin into his wine, shaped it into a nipple, and stuck it in the baby's mouth for him to suck on.

The wine was to keep the baby from crying during the minor surgery. The anesthetic quality of the alcoholic beverage and the comfort of sucking had their desired effect, to Farrel's amazement. He held his tiny son in his arms averting his eyes from the silver shine of the straight razorlike blade. Then it was over. Farrel was in reality more upset than the baby who gave only one little jump and then lay still again in his father's arms. Farrel felt a sudden surge of love for this frail creature who depended so completely upon him.

He was somewhat ill-at-ease among so many people of the Jewish persuasion. It had surprised him that Sarah had planned on this ceremony. She seemed never to question the fact that they would, of course, have the baby circumcised. Well, as long as there would be a christening, he decided, this rather primitive bit of hocus-pocus surely would do no harm.

The Hurstwoods waited until the baby was a month old before they had the christening. After their long wait for a child, Farrel thought that a public ceremony and an elaborate party to celebrate the event would be in order. Despite warnings from her overly concerned mother that she should still be in bed, Sarah dressed in her finest gown on which certain seams had been let out so it would fit. The minister poured water three times on the baby, saying "Lawrence

240

Seewald Hurstwood, I baptize thee in the name of the Father, and of the Son, and of the Holy Ghost." They had chosen the name, Lawrence, in honor of Farrel's father. Baby Lawrence screamed lustily, despite being the center of attention, as he was transferred from hand to hand in the crowd of well-wishers. He calmed down when Sarah carried him out of the noisy parlor and into the quiet of the nursery. As she nursed him, he fell asleep against her breast and she gave silent thanks for this miraculous gift in her life. He wore the white lace and beribboned dress and bonnet that had been Farrel's christening outfit. Now that he was asleep, he looked like a little angel in it.

The special guest at the party was Farrel's mother, Phoebe, who had come down from New York City for the event. After a personal invitation from Farrel, she had agreed to come. It was her first such visit. She had arrived the day before and was staying with the Hurstwoods.

She definitely stood out from the other guests, Sarah thought. Partly because of the striking contrast presented by her exquisite emerald-green brocade gown and her heavy black hair swept up on top of her head, and partly because of her erect, almost rigid, posture. Sarah watched her as she stood beside the mantel. Farrel got his good looks from her, no doubt about that. Sarah noticed her signal to Farrel. She saw him put down his glass and make his way to his mother's side. Then he escorted her to the room he used as his home office. Sarah puzzled about it for a moment, then let it slip from her as she turned back toward her guests. How gay the house looked with so many smiling people dressed in their party clothes in it. She had grown to love this house over the past years. It was truly home to her now, she thought. She saw her mother bend over the buffet table to move the platters of food around. Even with Clara, Bessie, Jane, and the other servants to do the work, Rachel could never resist making changes and suggestions; helping whenever possible.

"Just taste this chopped liver," she said now to Carolyn Smythe, the banker's wife.

"Mamma," Sarah interrupted, "it is pâté, not chopped liver." At the same time, she slipped her arm around her mother's waist. They smiled at each other and anyone watching would know how much affection there was between the mother and daughter.

"See how much alike you two look," Carolyn Smythe remarked. "Like sisters!"

Sarah and her mother both sought their image in the elaborate gilt-framed mirror over the mantel. Sarah saw two smiling women dressed in silk gowns; one gold, one blue. She immediately spotted the thickness around her waist where she carried the extra weight left over from Lawrence's birth. She thought her mother looked splendid, though, younger than her almost fifty years. But she could see that just now, tired from the baby and puffy from the pregnancy, she herself looked older than her twenty-two years. As she stared into the mirror, Sarah thought about the closed door to her husband's office and wondered again what was going on behind it. She could never forget that her mother-in-law had been so extremely displeased by Farrel's marriage that she had refused to attend the wedding. Sarah hoped that whatever was going on would not be something that would leave Farrel upset as he had been then.

If she could have seen through the door to Farrel's office, she would have been relieved to see Farrel and his mother in an embrace that appeared no less fond than the one she shared with her mother.

"Now, Farrel," his mother was saying, "enough idle chatting, eh? I want to discuss something important with you." She moved a few steps away and seated herself in the damask overstuffed armchair. "Come, dear," she said, signaling the matching chair nearby. Farrel joined her.

"Our falling out over your marriage was a regrettable incident which is fortunately long in the past. It is time to forget it completely. I hope you agree."

"Nothing would please me more, Mother, than to have our angry words of that day forgotten. Erased, in fact." He wondered why he always became so formal when he talked with his mother.

"At that time," his mother continued, "it was a great shock to me that you were planning to marry a Jewess. I foolishly said that I would disown you. Those words have echoed in my ears. At last I have met your wife who seems to be a lovely girl. More important, you have a child, so the matter is settled."

"You can surely see by today's christening that

Sarah does not acclaim her religious heritage." He didn't mention the earlier *briss* or the Seewalds' new ties to the emerging Conservative movement in the area.

"You can see that your fears were needless," he said, instead, although he never had understood what her fears were. She wasn't much of a Christian herself, after all.

"That is neither here nor there," she answered him. "This issue is closed and we need never mention it again, if you will allow that to be the case."

Farrel bit his lip. Just remembering that time, the anger rose in him again. But nothing would be gained by going back over it. His marriage was a good one, and neither it nor Sarah really needed defending.

"You are one hundred percent correct," he said, nodding. His mother held out her hand and they shook hands on it as though closing a business deal. Well, he thought, that makes sense since my mother is the best businessman I've ever known. "Past is past," he added. "Today we share a special moment. My first child, your first grandchild. Let us reunite on that." He began to stand, holding out his hand to help his mother up.

"Wait," she ordered. Farrel sat back down. "I brought a gift for you that I would like to give you now."

"You mean a gift for the baby?"

"No. A special gift for you. On the occasion of your child's birth."

She reached into her purse, then handed him a

check. Farrel accepted it from her, taking in the amount at a glance. He raised his eyebrows.

"Mother!" He whistled. "That's much more than generous."

She raised her hand, halting his speech. "It's your due. No need to wait till I'm dead for you to be able to enjoy it. Or if you need it for your little business, just go ahead and use it."

His gratitude was tempered by an awareness of how much more that money would have meant at his wedding when his streetcar company was more of a novelty to the people of Richmond than a means of transportation. Now the money was merely icing on the cake. But, he realized, it was also as close to an apology as his mother would probably ever come. She was a proud woman. And he knew he had inherited his own stiff neck from her.

"Thank you, Mother."

"Shall we rejoin the party?" she asked. "I want another look at my beautiful grandson!"

February 18, 1894

Dear Diary,
The party for Lawrence's christening was wonderfully splendid, if I do say so myself. The townspeople seem to accept Farrel fully even if he is an outsider. Everyone came. And they happily ate their way through table after table of Bessie's and Mamma's food, I noticed.

Farrel's reconciliation with his mother seemed to please him, though he really would not tell me much about it. His mother had absolutely refused to attend our wedding so I knew I was the cause of their falling out. Although I asked him repeatedly, Farrel would never tell me why. Was I too young, or too poor, or too small-town? Perhaps all three, I imagine. But I suspect that the major reason was that Farrel made the mistake of telling her I was a Jewess!

It's strange to think about my being a Jew. In my life, the fact has had more of a negative reality than any power over me. When I was a baby and a small child in Odessa, before we escaped from Russia, my parents raised me as a Jew, of course. Then it was something to be proud of, a special blessing from God. We are the chosen people. Then came the Odessa pogrom. How often has Papa described the vicious raids, the beatings, the murders? Throughout my childhood that bloody outrage has formed my vision of how cruelly people mistreat Jews. It was then, after that terrible time, that we came to America and Papa decided if simply being a Jew could lead to so much abuse, then we would never admit to being Jews again. So I'm a Jew and I'm not a Jew!

But, of course, I told Farrel after he proposed marriage to me. He didn't seem to care at all; he said he didn't care about labels anyway. He only cared about what I was inside, and he already loved me for that. Bless his heart.

But he must have assumed his mother shared his values and I think she had an entirely different point of view. Perhaps Lawrence's birth has changed all that, thank God. I find the emphasis on differences among us so foolish. Especially when we all believe in God. One God of love!

At times it troubles my mind to think that the baby has been welcomed into the Jewish faith and also made a Christian. What a strange burden I have placed on those tiny shoulders. In Jewish belief he is a Jew if he has a Jewish mother. So that is what I believe. The fact that

246

some water fell upon his brow does nothing to change that! When he is grown, he can choose what he wishes to believe. Meanwhile, as with everything else in my life, he is neither fish nor fowl. May God—anybody's God—protect him. I waited so long for this child, I only hope and pray that he will have a very special life.

Days blew by with the speed of wintry winds. Suddenly baby Lawrence was almost two months old and Dr. Lathrop approved a daily outing.

"Brisk air is good for you," he assured a worried Sarah, "and the baby will have apple cheeks. Also, he'll sleep better at night."

"Farrel," Sarah said, passing the word on, that evening, "tomorrow Lawrence and I are going out for a constitutional!"

"Isn't it too soon, Sarah!" Farrel asked, looking up from the journal called *The Electric Age* which had engrossed him since he came home from work. "It's still so cold out."

"Not another word," Sarah insisted, although secretly she agreed with Farrel and thought perhaps Dr. Lathrop was making a mistake. "The outing is on doctor's orders."

Farrel reached out his hand and took Sarah's. He pulled her down beside him.

"Well," he said, "in that case, that is great news then! I have a surprise I have been waiting to show you when you could get outside for a bit. How about planning a noon outing? I'll come by and pick the two of you up." Farrel slipped his arm around his wife's shoulders. He gently massaged her arm letting his hand slip down every now and again to brush against her breast. It had been a long time since they had been together, he thought.

"How myterious you are being," Sarah said, smiling up at him and licking her lips. His touch was affecting her and she could feel her heart begin its old slow and heavy thump. The doctor had also told her that it was time to resume marital relations, but she hadn't known quite how to mention this to Farrel. Maybe he realized it without her having to speak the words. She leaned toward him and nuzzled his neck. Her breasts, still full from nursing, pressed against Farrel's chest. The contact excited her, and she hoped it was giving Farrel ideas too. In fact, Farrel had had ideas all along, as Sarah would discover later that night in the welcome darkness of their bedroom.

When Farrel came to his wife's room that night, he found an aroused Sarah awaiting him. Her beige silk nightgown fell gracefully off of one shoulder revealing her soft bare flesh. When he wrapped his arms around her, he could feel her breasts flatten against his chest. He moved his body slowly back and forth as the excitement in the pit of his stomach tightened like the coiling of a spring. As for Sarah, the touch of Farrel's body against hers sent electric signals coursing through her. Her nipples flamed. She reached up to stroke the back of Farrel's neck where the hair curled against his soft skin. It was a favorite love spot. It reminded her that Farrel was human, vulnerable— not the hard money-making machine he often seemed to her.

Farrel's hand moved down Sarah's back to the base of her spine. To the place where the round bulge of her buttock began. He cupped her buttock in his hand and pressed her against him. They stood so, groin to groin, for only a moment before Farrel swept Sarah up in his arms and carried her to the bed. There he laid her down, slid her gown out of his way, and quickly found a way into her. He could hardly hold back his response due to the long period of required abstinence. Farrel thrust straight and true to Sarah's center. She gasped at his weight upon her, his power in her. He pounded into her, then quickly reached the peak of his pleasure, rolled off her and was almost instantly asleep. Sarah, though happy to offer her husband the gift of herself, was left feeling aroused and somehow restless. She lay long awake unable to slip into the release of sleep.

At noon the next day, Sarah heard a strange horn bleat outside the house. She plucked the curtain aside to see what it was. She was awaiting Farrel. A strange contraption sat parked before the house. Sarah had seen sketches of similar machines in Farrel's magazines. Horseless carriages, she'd heard them called, but knew Farrel preferred the term "automobile." Now one sat before her house. And Farrel was inside it waving and smiling at her where she stood half-hidden, peeking out the window.

"Clara. Clara!" Sarah called. She wrapped her cloak around her, buttoning it from neck to waist and letting it flow freely below that. Clara appeared with the bundled-up baby cuddled inside a fleecy bunting.

"Here's the boy, ma'am," Clara said.

Sarah finished stretching her kidskin gloves the length of each finger before taking the baby in her arms. While this wrapping was taking place, Farrel dismounted from his vehicle and bounded into the house with the energetic movements more typical of their courtship days than their married rhythms.

"Hello, sweetheart," he called. "Here's my little ily. Did you see the surprise, Sarah? Did you? my present to us—to our little family!" His nusiasm also reminded Sarah of her first vision of him when he was racing around town trying to get his fledgling streetcar company going. She loved it then and found it touching now.

"Oh, Farrel, yes," she exclaimed. "Is it really ours? More important, is it safe?" Sarah couldn't help giggling at the horrified look on Farrel's face.

"Safe!" he cried out. "Of course it's safe. Would I take you in anything unsafe? Would I risk that? Of course not. It's as safe as my streetcars! Has the same power source: electricity. Come now. I'll take you and the baby for a ride around town and show you."

Farrel guided Sarah, who clutched the baby to her, down the steps to the street, avoiding the few remaining icy patches and mounds of dirty snow. There they stopped before the two-seated carriage to admire it. The gleaming body was an almost iridescent black with gold trim.

"Look, Sarah," Farrel said excitedly, "isn't it beautiful the way the fenders flare out over the high tires?"

Sarah gazed at the machine skeptically. The wheels were certainly high, she had to agree, but they seemed too high in proportion to the rest of the automobile. She kept her doubts to herself, though, not wanting to ruin Farrel's pleasure.

"There are even lights on it for night driving!" Farrel exclaimed, pointing. "Get in, get in. I'll take you for a turn around town."

Farrel helped Sarah climb up into the passenger's seat. She squeezed his hand. His excitement was contagious. Sarah settled her skirts and her cloak around her legs. The baby in her arms never stirred. There was a canopy overhead, but except for that the car was open, leaving the passengers exposed to the wind and weather. Farrel went around to the other side and climbed into the driver's seat. He started the car. Sarah couldn't help being impressed as he easily maneuvered it into the street. They moved along smoothly.

"My, isn't it quiet!" Sarah remarked, trying to please Farrel. It *was* a thrill.

"Not very fast though. We could probably make just as good time running alongside it," Farrel answered. "I'll have to tear down the motor in the shop to see if I can adapt it for faster speeds."

"Yes," Sarah smiled, "a new toy for your workshop."

"Now, Sarah," Farrel began, but was interrupted by Sarah's excited questions.

"What shall we call it, Farrel? Has it a name?"

Then before he could answer, she added in a whisper that reminded him of the schoolgirl he'd met so long ago, "Will you teach me how to work it? We're the first ones in Richmond to have one, aren't we? Oh, this *is* exciting." Sarah waved at a cluster of gawking townspeople as she motored by them.

"You'll love the name of this electric automobile, Sarah. The name itself was almost reason enough for me to buy it."

"Well, tell me," she urged.

"It's an Electrobat!" Farrel laughed.

Sarah joined in. "Electrobat," she echoed. "That's a wonderful name. Knowing you, by the time you finish tinkering, it will go like a bat, too. A bat out of you-know-where." For a few moments they rode on in silence. "But, Farrel," Sarah continued then, her voice edged with fear, "what if they become popular? They will, won't they? How will that affect your streetcar?" Sarah dreaded the possibility of a loss of position, she admitted to herself ruefully. She knew she should be more noble and wished she were. But she remembered only too clearly how poor her parents were when they'd first brought her over from Russia with them. Even though she had been only seven or eight, she retained vivid images of skimpy meals stretched out by cabbage soup, of carefully patched clothes. Now that she had become a mother she more than ever wanted to put those memories out of her mind and out of her life.

"No, Sarah, no," Farrel reassured her. "This motoring machine will never be very important to the American economy. It couldn't possibly replace my streetcars. After all, it's expensive—not many people could afford it—and it's inefficient. No, there's nothing to fear from the automobile!" Again a brief silence fell. Sarah smiled down at the still-sleeping baby in her arms. All would be well, she promised him silently; Farrel would take care of them.

"What's more," Farrel went on as though there had been no pause, "it's not only the first one in Richmond, there are only a handful in the entire country. It's 1894, after all, and I thought we might as well get a jump on the new century!"

Farrel glanced over at his wife with a mischievous look. She smiled back at him. They continued motoring happily up and down the Richmond streets enjoying the comfortable sense of being young, rich, and full of new ideas.

Sixteen

Despite riches and servants, Sarah found the care of the baby exhausting. She seemed to make a continual round of cleaning Lawrence, comforting Lawrence, nursing Lawrence, rocking Lawrence, until she wondered how, if this were the way of things, people continued to have babies at all. Each morning she would promise herself anew to work out a better schedule that would allow her some time for herself—time to visit neglected friends or time to read or simply time to take a needed nap. She found herself often edgy and depressed, unaware of what might be going on in the world outside her own home. Occasionally she and Farrel would recapture their bold and gallant mood of that first motorcar ride. But more often some seemingly innocuous remark of Farrel's would send Sarah rushing to her room in a flood of tears.

Farrel's moods these days were equally unreliable. The idea of having a son pleased him more than the reality of this noisy creature who disrupted the pattern of life and seemed to be the constant focus of Sarah's attention. The thought that his son had already replaced him in his wife's affection left him rigid and unfeeling. He urged Sarah to let the servants care for the child, urged her to leave him in the nursery, but she insisted on intruding him unnecessarily into their lives. Underlying Farrel's displeasure at the domestic distress was his concern over the lagging recovery from the bad economic times just behind them—what was being called the Panic of '93.

More than seven hundred banks had closed their doors for good and, although he and George had diversified their holdings enough to have lost little money directly, Farrel found the still-surviving banks unwilling to invest the moneys they held. For many it meant the loss of their homes, their jobs. For Farrel and George it meant only that they would have to delve into their own capital. Nonetheless it was a damned nuisance!

Farrel, always alive with new speculative schemes, dared anyone to say him nay. When the bankers, despite his power, did turn Farrel's loan requests down, he went home in a black rage. Gradually, though, the recovery did take hold and Farrel could once again put full energy into expansion and diversification.

For a while things went along smoothly. Eighteen ninety-four turned into eighteen ninety-five. Lawrence became recognizable as a member of the human species—someone who would someday be a boy and then a man. Sarah was pregnant again and, though both she and Farrel were taken by surprise at the realization, they were happy enough at the prospect of being parents of another child. Both Farrel and Sarah regretted not having had siblings to play with in their own lives, and they were glad that Lawrence would not be an only child. They had planned on waiting a bit longer, but they accepted the reality of what was to be.

Then new tensions arose. George was becoming almost fanatical, or so Farrel thought, about the new conservation movement. He insisted that they develop parks at each end of their trolley lines— parks where people could walk and enjoy a bit of nature; parks where the woodlands of the area would be guaranteed preservation. Also, he began to travel. He went out to see what he called the "glorious West." He went north to explore the Canadian borderlands. He seemed always to be on one trip or another. The worst part of this, to Farrel's way of thinking, was that when George was gone, Farrel had to remain in town to take care of business. Never before had there been any need for him to curtail his travel, and he felt caged, which was an entirely new and entirely unpleasant sensation to him.

Upon George's return from an important trip to Washington, D.C., as an official representative of the American Association for the Advancement of Science, he was fairly bursting with news that demanded a sympathetic audience. He already knew that Farrel would have no interest in hearing any more on the subject of conservation. Farrel's view was that the land was there to be used. Misused and abused would be more to the point, George thought. So they avoided most discussions of the subject.

Sarah, though, would be the perfect person to talk to, George reasoned. He knew that in part he was simply seeking an excuse to see her again. It seemed so long now between their times together and ever since the picnic she had held herself in greater reserve from him. He knew she was again expecting a child. She was so far along, in fact, that she had confined herself to her house and gardens. She must be desperate for company, George decided, reaching for the telephone.

It was a brisk day although the calendar announced that spring had arrived. Sarah waited for George to arrive with an eagerness that she told herself was due to the loneliness of her life just now. She checked her looks in the mirror. If one looked only at the face, she thought, there is a certain rosy charm. But as to the form, alas, that was probably gone forever. Sarah could hardly bear to contemplate her roundness. She felt certain that the waistline would never be eighteen inches again. Not even with the help of corsets! Just then the doorbell chimed. Farrel had electrified the system so that the chimes sounded throughout the first floor.

"Never mind, Clara," Sarah called out. "I am right here." She hurried down the hall and opened the door herself.

George, unprepared to see Sarah at the door, held out his arms spontaneously. Without a thought, without taking time to consider, Sarah moved into his embrace. Immediately, she felt self-conscious of her bulky shape. George had a quite different response. The warmth of Sarah in his arms made him acutely aware of how lonely his life had been without her. God, he thought, can I go on this way? They moved apart and smiled at each other.

"I could hardly wait until you got here," Sarah admitted. "How long has it been since our last visit?"

"Only one answer to that: too long. Always too long."

George followed Sarah into the back parlor where a friendly fire sparkled and sputtered.

"Ah, just the thing to take the chill off the air."

"Yes, a fire is a lovely comfort," Sarah agreed.

"But my dear," George teased, "I didn't mean the fire at all. I meant seeing you!"

"Shame on you."

They both smiled again. It seemed that the smiles would never leave their faces. They both enjoyed luxuriating in the comfort of being together. George saw the special radiance that lit Sarah when she was with child. Sarah reluctantly recognized that George touched her in a way no one else did. He made her heart soft and fluttery. If only life could be other than it is, she sighed.

"I understand you are busy exploring this great country of ours. Is that because you want to see the wild lands before they disappear as my husband indicates to me?"

"Not quite. You see, I would like to make sure

that the wild lands, as he calls them, will never disappear entirely from our land. I came to see you to tell you about my latest exploits in that regard, in fact." He edged up closer to her as he spoke. His enthusiasm made his face look shining to Sarah who nodded at him encouraging him to go on. "I have just spoken with President Cleveland. He spoke as all politicians do, so that one never really knows on which side his vote shall be cast. But I know it is an important issue. I feel that. The woods, the streams, the mountains—I tell you this country can match anything Europe has to offer!"

"Surely there is enough land that is undeveloped that no harm can ever really come to it. Why do you feel so much concern?"

"Now it seems so. Plenty of land. Plenty of air. The land of plenty. But greed, my dear, human greed, that is what we must take into account. If that land can be turned into a profit then the land will go. The water, the air, the animals, and birds—all will fall before the desire to make an extra dollar. I see it already in the history of the railroads. If Farrel has his way we will follow in their tracks, no pun intended."

"It is hard to take the issue seriously, my dear. With the cities filling up and more and more land being left bare of people."

"True. True. People are moving into the cities in ever-increasing numbers. All the more reason for us to save the wilderness so that we have a place to turn to for refreshment."

Sarah could hardly understand the cause of George Spencer's passion, but passion it was, she could see. And she knew better than to question it or doubt its validity. Instead, she skirted the issue and asked about the group to which he belonged.

"My group is one of many. There are a number of groups forming over these issues. The Audubon Society is another. The Boone and Crockett Club. The idea is right, I just know it."

"What of the idea that involves the streetcars, parks I think my husband said . . . ?"

"Yes, yes. We can build up the areas at the ends of the lines so that people will ride the trolleys on the weekend and holiday times just to get out to a place to picnic." He stopped short at the mention of picnics. It almost took his breath away how clearly he remembered the feel of Sarah's lips on his. He looked over at Sarah who was looking down at her hands. Her face looked flushed and he felt sure she was sharing the same memory with him.

"Yes, a place to go for a nice walk under trees and so forth." Sarah sighed. "I like that idea. Especially for the poor factory children who hardly have time to notice that there are trees and beautiful things that grow under the heavens."

"Good. Maybe between the two of us we can prevail upon Farrel. I think my best approach is actually to point out that we will increase our market by being able to lure people onto the cars on their days off from work. You know, your husband is what they call nowadays a pragmatist. Always with an eye to the practical advantages."

"Yes." Sarah frowned. "I know."

*　　*　　*

For whatever reason, Farrel did agree to George's suggestions regarding the development of the parks. He put George in charge of the work, of course, which meant that George had to stay close to the office. That set Farrel free to wander.

His own view of the biggest concern to the nation was that America should stop being impressed by Europe. He saw America as the next great power and believed that, by God, Americans had better start taking their role seriously.

When Sarah gave birth to her second child, a daughter they named Jessica Lynn Hurstwood, Farrel was out of the country involved in some big money deal in Switzerland. It was June 11, 1896. Once more Sarah found herself overwhelmed with the responsibilities of a new baby. With two babies really, for Lawrence was not even two and a half yet.

"Two babies," she told her mother during a teatime visit during which the baby cried to be nursed and Lawrence whined for attention, "is eight times the work of one. I do not know which mathematical formula measures such things, but I am quite sure I am right."

As the summer heat took over the town's energy and the babies took over Sarah's, the absence of Farrel and George—both of whom seemed constantly occupied with more important things—went almost unnoticed. When Sarah managed to have a few moments alone, she was happy just to spend the time writing in her diary which continued to be her major confidante.

*   *   *

In the fall of the year, Rose came to say good-bye. She had gotten a job as a fledgling reporter on the staff of the New York *World*.

"The world is full of excitement, Sarah, and I just have to get in on it. Teaching children is a valuable thing, but I want more. Do you know what I mean?" She bounced Lawrence on her knee as she spoke. He giggled and his little legs kicked furiously at the air.

"Oh, I do know, but whatever shall I do without you? You're my only real contact to the outside world, you know."

"Every article I get printed I'll post to you the day it hits the streets." She put Lawrence down on the ground. They sat in the back garden. She leaned over and kissed Sarah's cheek. "I wish you were coming with me," she said.

"Oh, I must confess that I am bitterly envious. Does that make me a monster, Rose? Here I have everything that I ever wanted: a husband, children of my own, a lovely house and life. Then why am I so dissatisfied?"

"My answer to that would not be welcome to your ears, I'm afraid. I believe, you see, that women should never marry. Men only use us for their pleasure. They never consider us their equals in mind or body. If it were the way I would like it, you could come with me to the big city. You'd bring the babies along and we'd find a way to raise them. We would both work and be comrades. Oh, that would be the life!"

"Please say no more." Sarah had paled. Rose looked at her anxiously.

"What is it, Sarah? Have I displeased you?"

"What you speak of is impossible, of course."

"Doesn't it excite you just a little, though, the prospect?"

"Excite me? Yes, of course. It makes me wild with excitement. But it can never be and we must not speak any further about it."

"Very well then. I must leave soon. It won't be good-bye, though, Sarah, because I intend to keep in touch with you. And you must promise me faithfully that every time I write, you will answer. Agreed?"

Sarah and Rose were standing now. The baby, Jessica, was asleep in Sarah's arms and Lawrence played with the leaves that fell in the grass.

"I promise," Sarah said solemnly. "But you know, Rose, I always meant to have you meet my husband's partner. I believe that you two could have been great friends."

"Perhaps when I return on a visit," Rose suggested lightly. She had little interest now in meeting anyone else from Richmond. In fact, she could hardly wait to be on her way. New York City, she thought; at last a city big enough for my ideas. The two friends kissed, and then Rose left. Sarah remained behind wondering what her life might have been like had she not chosen to marry, wondering why she had never seriously made the effort to bring her two dearest friends together . . . Well, she thought she probably knew the reason she had never introduced Rose and George. Jealousy. Afraid she might lose them both. She was not proud of that, but it was the truth.

'She called to Clara to come and help her with the children. Then she hurried to her room. She desperately wanted to have some time alone. Not time to think, she realized, but time to not think. Vaguely, she remembered the story of Madame Bovary and her unhappiness with life. She would put that out of her mind as well, she told herself.

It seemed to Sarah that when she closed her eyes that afternoon she let herself disappear into a dream of days. She awoke and slept and woke again, but she never really left her dream world. From what felt like a great distance, she sensed her life passing her by. She cared for the children in a mechanical way. She felt vaguely distressed that she was not a more natural mother, a more natural woman.

For a while no one seemed to notice her absence from the scene. Baby Jessica continued to grow more and more sturdy throughout her first year. Jessica and Lawrence were specially attuned to each other, and developed a private language of their own. Their nursery play became a second dream world in the Hurstwood household.

The larger world, too, seemed to have moved into some other reality. It was 1897 and the bloody mess in Cuba was arousing American sympathy. Why would the Spaniards not allow Cuba its freedom? people asked. It stirred feelings in the population that were a bizarre mix of concern for a people who were perhaps like the early American settlers in wanting their independence, and of jealousy of a people who were taking over other countries when the Americans were not, but should be. No matter whether one decided on the concern side or the greed side, the vote seemed to be for America to get in on the action. The newspapers screamed for intervention.. Farrel, caught up in the mania, backed up that message one hundred percent.

At last, Rachel noticed her daughter's increasing withdrawal from life. She spoke to Dr. Sam about it, and he stopped in on Sarah as though for a friendly look at the children. When he returned to Rachel's house that afternoon, he looked somber.

"So, *nu?*" she asked. "Am I right that she is sick? Something has to be wrong; this I know. She just does nothing. She seems to be fading away into God-knows-where."

"You were right to call on me. She is not really herself, I can see. How, I wonder, has Farrel missed it?"

"Husbands and wives are not always the ones who see each other most clearly, Sam. You know that. Sarah has her problems there. But tell me what's wrong."

"Don't allow yourself to get unduly alarmed. We'll allow nothing to harm our little Sarah, eh? But this condition she presents . . . it is an odd one. A problem of the mind, I think. The journals call something like it, neurasthenia. But a name for it is not a cure for it."

"So what is?"

"There seems to be little in the way of cure, to tell you the truth. To me it seems that time itself is the main cure. Love, of course, is always a magic medicine of its own. But you hint at trouble with Farrel."

"Not such serious trouble as to cause this."

"Trouble is trouble. The babies need her care. That will probably bring her back. But I think maybe you should start dropping in on her in the afternoons and see if you can get her interested in anything. Does she do handiwork of any sort?"

"Not really. What she always most loved to do was read!"

"Good enough. Find a special book. Take it to her. Maybe even read to her for a while each day."

"But what book, Sam? What do I know from books? It took me years in this country before I could even read the paper."

"Something neutral. Nothing morbid, of course. Try to make her laugh. Let me think."

They sat together in the twilight. Rachel got up heavily and moved about preparing them tea.

"I know," Sam said, as she set the cup down before him. "It's supposed to be a children's book, so you can pretend you are bringing it for them and that is why you are reading it also. Called the *Prince and the Pauper*. Makes fun of the British. By that Twain fellow."

"Perfect!"

"I think so myself."

They both breathed easier as they drank their tea. Surely this idea from these two concerned conspirators would save the day. Save Sarah from sinking forever into a darkness where no light could reach her. Humor. A book. Some love from

Mamma. These would be the cures. Yes, it would work. It had to work.

Rachel put the plan into effect the next day, and persevered day after day. She did not allow herself to get discouraged, and slowly Sarah did begin to respond. The afternoon they finished the book and Sarah asked, "Well, Mamma, what shall we read next?" Rachel knew they had been successful. She could safely leave her daughter again to the business of her life: her husband, her children, her household. Sarah was back among the living!

By the time Sarah opened her eyes to the world around her, it had become a world she could hardly recognize. Newspapers were being hawked from every corner and the headlines always screamed about the Spanish-Cuban situation. Then, unbelievably, the morning papers of February 16, 1898 told of the American battleship *Maine* blowing up in Havana harbor where it had been sitting on a friendly visit. Hundreds of Americans died.

Hysteria swept the country. "Remember the *Maine*" became the slogan on everyone's lips. Farrel offered his services to President McKinley. Sarah felt scared by all of this, but clung to her domestic routines to keep her safe. Would Farrel really go to war? Where was Rose now . . . Was she perhaps a reporter in Cuba? That would be just like her. Foolhardy and daring. She was Sarah's ideal of the woman hero. Please God, she prayed, keep those I love safe. She loathed the concept of war and had trouble thinking of what some people called justified wars. Killing could surely not be right. Even hunters upset Sarah. How much more so, then, the hunters of people!

Farrel Hurstwood gained an appointment in the government to help with the problems of the communications systems that would be a necessary part of the military effort if war became a reality. In a way, Sarah was just as glad that he was gone for a while. Then the war news seemed more easily buffered. But even she could not avoid the news that America had declared war! It was April of 1898. She began to have nightmares that she would not live to see the new century born. War. Blood on the American doorstep, the papers said.

She shared her fears with George when they were together. He, too, felt that war was antilife and that rather than see America moving into other people's lands and taking over, he would like to see America saving what it already had. But once all that had been said, their basic agreement in attitude realized, Sarah and George went on to other topics. Despite war and Farrel's involvement in it, life seemed mostly composed of food for the table.

"Is it always so?" Sarah asked. "First feed the belly and then worry about others?"

"Oh, Sarah," George laughed. "You are always so hard on yourself. You are the least self-centered person I know. But, yes, I do believe that is the human way of things. First feed the belly . . ."

They were drinking sherry and waiting for dinner to be announced. Farrel remained in

Washington, D.C., so he was safe, but at a distance.

"Perhaps," Sarah went on, "I am simply jealous of the people who do the acting when I sit at home and do so little. That could be it, of course. Maybe I would yearn for a war if I could be the one to strap on a gun and go be a hero."

"You have some imagination. I think you ought to become a writer! That way you could be everything! There are some darned fine lady writers around, too."

"Well, George, you're the first person I've told, but I am a writer."

George looked at her amazed. His mouth fell open. Then she laughed, and he knew it was only one of her teases. He waited for her to explain.

"I keep a diary. I write in it quite regularly, as a matter of fact." She smiled coyly at him wondering if he guessed how often his name appeared in her diary.

"Am I someday to be allowed to read this special volume?"

"Oh, no!" Sarah had to laugh at her own horror at his suggestion. My God, if he read what she had written there! All the bad things about Farrel and all the good things about himself. No, she must not show the diary to either of those two men. "Maybe someday I will leave it to my children."

"Do you ever mention me?" His voice was so soft that at first Sarah was uncertain whether he had spoken.

"More often than I should have, I am sure," she

269

answered. She reached over and stroked his full cheek. The touch said even more than her words. He clasped her hand to his mouth and kissed it fervently. She closed her eyes and gave herself to the sensual feel of his lips on her skin. Reluctantly, she pulled her hand away. "The dinner must be ready. I had cook make your favorites. She is becoming quite good at them with all this practice!" They both laughed, changing their mood into a lighter one.

"Will the children be joining us?"

"Oh no. They eat in the nursery. You know we have Sassafras now to care for them. She can read and write and can teach them their beginning lessons. Also," they moved as they spoke into the dining room, "she is helping Clara to read and write. I promised her that when I first married. She probably gave up hope by now."

"Good for you. Reading is such a joy that it is hard to think of anyone not being able to share in that." George slid his arm around her waist as he helped her to her seat. Just that least touch set him aflame for more. Would there ever be more for him? he wondered. Surely someday there must be. They must have their time, he felt. He believed that with all his heart.

Four months after war's declaration, the peace agreement went into effect. The sudden victory left the country flushed and ready for more. Farrel came home full of excitement. Plans for expansion into other countries that would soon be part of the American family, he said.

Then it was New Year's Day, 1899. Only one more year and there would be a new century—the twentieth century. Communities all across the nation made preparations for the following year. Along with the sense of America as the greatest nation on earth went the feelings of a new world ahead in terms of dates. A new century!

Farrel became the vigorous leader of various organizations. He seemed always to be involved with one thing or another. In the end, he managed to tie everything together with his blessed streetcar lines, though. They were millionaires now, he assured Sarah. She found it hard to realize that being so rich should make so little difference in one's happiness. Surely being poor would not have made her life better. Oh no, she did not for a moment imagine that. She had the latest fashions. She had servants to do whatever work she chose not to do. She had any number of acquaintances who called upon her for various charity functions. Oh, and the parties! Why she and Farrel were out dancing every weekend that he was in Richmond. It was a grand life, she had to admit that. A grand, miserable life.

But Farrel would have recognized none of her melancholy description. To his eyes everything was going just as he had planned it—or even better! Oh, it was a grand life all right. Good now and going to be even better. He had never felt so full of passion. He worked hard during the day and into the evening, and when he was at home, he took Sarah with a fierceness that he had seldom felt since their early days together. Now he seemed to want a woman constantly. And he found that his wealth was a powerful aphrodisiac among the ladies. Wherever he traveled there was a fair and friendly lass ready to spend time and money with him. Ready to show him a good time in exchange for the good time he would buy for her.

Occasionally, when Farrel was returning to Richmond after one of his trips where he had dallied, he felt a twinge of guilt. But, after all, that was the nature of men, he told himself. A drink, a cigar, and a woman. That was the perfect recipe for a good evening. Followed by a good night, of course.

He had put a streetcar system in just about every city in America and linked most of them to an interurban route, as well. With some of his money, in fact, he had bought into the railroads so that the transportation in America was his lifeblood.

He had begun to drink heavily. He noticed that when he woke in the mornings he could sometimes not remember what he had done the night before. But he was sure that nobody else noticed. It was just to help him relax. A hard-working man needed to relax.

Sarah had noticed, of course. She saw the amount he drank when he was at home. She saw the way he sometimes lurched against the door when he came to her room in the night. She saw, and she became afraid.

The one time that she had tried to have a serious talk with him about his drinking he had roared at her that by Jesus he would do any damned thing he felt like doing. It was his house, he told her, and his money, and she was his wife. He had slapped her then so hard that the side of her face had swollen and she had had to hide away in her room for days. Now she no longer mentioned his drinking directly although she could seldom resist a snide comment which he either ignored or responded to with a sneer.

Then, to her distress, she found herself pregnant again. The baby would be born in the first quarter of the first year of the new century. A new life. The baby of a drunk, she told herself mournfully. But she submitted to Farrel when he pounded on her door although she began to think that her body had forgotten how to respond. It took an act of will simply not to pull away from Farrel; her instinctive response would have been to shrink from his touch. But she knew better than to do that.

At one point, in despair, she wrote of men who took women whether they wanted to be taken or not. She wrote of this to her friend, Rose, who continued to stay in touch. The answer she got was so full of sorrow and venom, so painful to read, that she knew she must never speak of these things again. Rose just hated men, Sarah told herself. And I, she pondered, perhaps I just hate Farrel. God help me!

Seventeen

Dear Diary,

Today we celebrate the birth of a new century and life seems cluttered as it usually does around the time of a birth. All is chaotic and moving too fast. It was not too very long ago when I wrote repeatedly in these pages about my fear of remaining childless. Here I sit today with a son and daughter already and a new baby due before spring. Mind you, I am not complaining. At least I hope not. The children do often bring me joy with their baby play and silly prattle.

Then what is it that has me in this dissatisfied state? you may well ask. In part, I believe, it may just be the result of being so big and awkward again and often feeling too tired to play with the babies or to properly care for them. We have Sassafras, Bessie's oldest daughter, to be a mammy, but though she is kind to the children and teaches them, she does not do enough to encourage the growth of their little minds. Of course, that is really what I should be doing. And I do, too, when I am not too cranky or tired.

Still, the major source of my dissatisfaction, I

am sad to admit, is quite other. It is the same as always. It is Farrel, Farrel, Farrel. More specifically, Farrel's drinking and Farrel's absence. His occupational involvement increases yearly and seems to require greater and greater periods of travel. Even when he is in town, he is not here for me. I mean, he is at his office for long hours and then he spends more hours in his club or in his study at home. When we are together and he is sober, he is reading one of his damned journals.

The one time when he is with me, in a sense, is in the middle of the night. Then he comes to me and takes me the way one beast must mate with another. There is nothing in the act that resembles lovemaking. Oh, no. It feels more like making hate. Perhaps he does not even know that I am the woman beneath him! I often wonder, of late, whether he has other women. I feel sure that he must. But what is worse is that I cannot even feel jealous. I am sure he has no real lover. He surely cannot really love anyone. Not the way he is now. His work is the only thing he may still love—his work and his money.

Do I sound as though I complain all the time? Well, I do. But not aloud. No, I have grown too afraid of Farrel for that. I complain most often right here in these pages. What a poor little rich girl I have become!

On Valentine's Day, Sarah gave birth to a second baby boy. They had decided in advance that if it should be a boy they would name him Franklin Goodrich Hurstwood. Franklin came into this world with an ease for which Sarah was grateful. My little heart baby, she called him.

The routine of baby and child care felt more easy in general to Sarah this time and the spring brought with it sweet gifts of new life, new possibilities. Even Farrel seemed to relax a bit and become more bearable when he was at home. To a great extent, Sarah realized, she had come to accept—no, to welcome really—his trips away from the home. The little family unit moved more smoothly through their circle of days without his burly presence. She felt almost like one of the babies. All nursery playmates, that was how she thought of herself and the children during this time.

Farrel seldom wrote personal letters, but that summer he discovered that it was Sarah's birthday and he was many miles away in the great metropolis of Chicago, so he sat down to send her a greeting. He would bring a present home later.

June 30, 1900

Dear Sarah,

Chicago is a glittering city at night. A far cry from even our wonderful Richmond! It is hard to tell the sky from the streets, what with all the lights. I am sure you would love it and love, too, the fashionably dressed people who parade the streets.

If you were here with me, we would see the sights. But alone it is too much effort, so when I finish my day's work I return to my hotel where I eat my dinner and retire to my room. I am sincerely sorry we are apart, especially as it is your birthday! But things will calm down and then I will make it up to you, I promise.

The people I am meeting with here are talking about the possibility of using my elevator motor in buildings even taller than the ones they have

*already built. Taller than any now in America.
"Skyscrapers," they said they will call them. Isn't
that a marvelous name? It is poetry really. Poetry
for the twentieth century.*

*My darling Sarah, at home with our three
babies, can you share this excitement with me?
Send Jessica and Lawrence their papa's love.
Franklin, I am sure is too young to care. He is
happy enough just so long as Mamma and meals
are nearby.*

*I have asked George Spencer to look in on you
now and again. I am sure as my associate he will
not mind that little chore which, since he is so
fond of you, will be a pleasure for him. I know
you are far from alone with your parents mere
blocks away, but I thought he might provide you
with some fresh conversation.*

> *As ever, your loving husband,*
> *Farrel*

As Farrel put the pen down, the gloom of sitting
alone in even a splendidly appointed hotel room
affected him. He had been trying to avoid spending too much time in the saloons, but tonight he
wanted some gay company. He slipped back into
his jacket, refastened his starched collar, and
arranged his silk tie; then he left the room carrying
with him the letter to Sarah which he would put
into the care of the front desk.

Within minutes of this scene of departure,
Farrel found himself being comforted by the warm
thrill of Scotch whiskey in his throat and his
innards. The lady who sat at the end of the
gleaming bar was obviously for hire. Why else
would a woman be in a bar? But her teeth flashed
in a welcoming smile when she caught his eye, and

Farrel felt the desire for a companion. For the evening, he told himself. Just a friendly ear to talk into, a woman's scent nearby—no more than that. He signaled the bartender, and told him to offer the lady a drink on his account.

Soon they were at a dark table in the corner drinking together. She was a regular fellow, Farrel thought. Able to match him whiskey for whiskey. No "lady's drinks" for her.

"My name's Estelle," she told him leaning forward so he could hardly avoid noticing the cleavage revealed by her tight black satin bodice. "What's yours?"

"Call me Larry," he said, using his oldest son's name. No need, he figured, to tell her who he really was. He had no undue trust in the lower classes, of which Estelle was obviously a member. He would be glad to pay for her company, but he would try to protect himself from having to pay for any blackmail attempts.

By the time the saloon was ready to close, any virtuous thoughts Farrel had had about spending the night alone had disappeared. Sarah and his three children had vanished from his thoughts, too, and been replaced by a flaming desire to do more than brush his fingers against this woman's breasts. He wanted to bury his head between their fullness. He wanted to learn whatever tricks she had to teach.

It took no urging to convince her to join him for a nightcap in his room. But the minute they closed the door behind them all thoughts of another drink had left Farrel's mind completely. That had never really been in either of their minds anyway. Estelle felt herself clutched to this man's chest with a fierceness that disturbed her. After all, a poor working girl had so little protection. She always heard about vicious beatings and even murders that the police did nothing about. The police were on the take, of course. She paid them her share. But they would certainly be for sale to the highest buyer. This Larry fellow, or whatever his name really was, sure had a lot more money than she did.

"Easy, easy," she murmured when she could work her lips free of his. "You're too strong for me. I can hardly breathe."

"Come here," he said, dragging her along toward the bedroom. "I want you, lady."

She dressed in the fewest clothes she could arrange to look desirable and respectable enough to get into the saloons. So it was an easy matter for her to undress in a hurry. Farrel watched her as she did so. The rustle of her gown as it slid to the floor aroused him wildly. Yes, he thought, this will be a long night and worth every penny it will cost.

She came to him and began tugging at his clothes.

"Hurry now, lover, don't you see that I'm ready for you?" She urged him on hoping that she could get him going and be on her way again. But if he wanted her to stay the night that would be all right. Of course, he would have to pay extra, but she could see that there was no problem here with money. His clothes told her that. So did the suite of rooms he occupied.

He struggled to undress in a hurry, but the

amount of Scotch he had drunk slowed him down. Finally though, he stood over her where she lay legs askew on the bed. Strange, he thought in some dim way, but I hardly care about going through with this. Nonetheless he closed off that part of his thinking and stretched beside her. Soon her hands had reawakened his waning interest. He pulled her on top of him and made her do the work. After all, he thought, I'm paying for the service. She was good at her job, too, and he quickly spent himself. Too quickly, he thought. His mind still yearned for more.

"Estelle," he began, as she began to move away from him toward her clothes. "Come here. I want something else before you go. I'll pay for it."

She moved closer and he grabbed hold of her arm so strongly that the marks from his fingers would leave a bruise by morning. With his other hand he began to push her head down along his body. Down to his stomach. Down still further. Her mouth found its goal.

"Yes," he urged. "Yes. Do that. Then you can go."

She began to lick his body. Kissing and sucking on him until she could feel him grow in her mouth. Then she tried to pull away, thinking that he would want to mount her. But he would not release the pressure on her arm, on her head.

"More," he demanded.

Damn, she thought, but went on with her work. Soon she could feel him strain up toward her and knew he was getting close. Then he began to groan and buck, and he spurted his juices into her mouth. He flung his arms free of their hold on her. She pulled back from him and spat out what she could into the sheet beside her head. The rest she swallowed with a shudder at its bitterness. When she moved up to lie down beside him, she saw that he was already deeply asleep or unconscious. As quietly as possible, she dressed. Then she searched his pants pockets for money. There was more than she had hoped to find, and she took it all. I hope it was worth it, buddy, she thought, as she stuffed the bills into her black beaded bag and stole from the room.

Eighteen

A few days later, on the same day that Sarah received the letter from Farrel, George Spencer arrived at her door.

"Miz Hurstwood, it's Mr. Spencer at the door asking if you be free." Clara paused at the door.

Sarah looked up from her play with the babies. "Oh," she said, only half-surprised. "Do send him in. He can help me read these rascals their bedtime story."

While Clara went to convey the message, Sarah straightened her gown and tossed her head so the curls would rearrange themselves loosely. At a noise from the doorway she turned and glanced up into the smiling face of her husband's partner.

"George, how nice," she said. He took her hands in his, squeezing them gently.

He nodded toward the three tots giggling together on the rug.

"I've interrupted bedtime, I'm afraid," he said.

"Not really," Sarah assured him. "They're in

their nighties already. I was just about to read them a story. You can help."

"Good. It is such a steamy night and I thought you might spare me some company. As to the story idea, I can be a terrific wolf, if you want to play Little Red Riding Hood. After they are in bed, perhaps we can have a chat. Unless you are too busy," George added, sensing some nervousness in Sarah. She is so beautiful, he thought, more beautiful even than she was before the babies. There's a new ripeness to her.

"No, of course not," Sarah said. "I'm not too busy. I'm hardly busy at all with Farrel out of town again. But you know he is out of town, of course; that is why you are here. On Farrel's orders," she said with a note of bitterness in her voice.

"Hardly," George laughed sincerely, then stopped himself as he realized the pain Sarah was feeling. "Sarah," he went on, "these times we have had together with your husband on his many trips around the country have become the most important part of my life. I do not want to speak too boldly, but I cannot allow you to think that I came here out of duty to your husband. Oh, no, hardly that!"

Sarah gazed solemnly into his eyes. She saw there the direct look of an honest man and a true friend. Tears came unbidden to her eyes and she leaned her head against George's chest a moment.

"There, there, my dear," he murmured as he wrapped his arms around her. For the first time in years he felt the warm pressure of her body against his again. He stroked her head enjoying the silky softness of her tresses.

"Sarah," he whispered, "put the babies to bed so we can be alone for a bit. Perhaps they could miss their story this one night, eh?"

Sarah straightened, dabbing at the remnants of her tears with the cuff of her sleeve.

"Yes," she said. "I'll be back in just a few minutes. Please help yourself to the brandy on the sideboard while I am gone." Then, turning to the children who had been so busy arranging and destroying their doll babies that they had hardly noticed their mother's distraction, she said, "Come now, my angels, let us find Sassafras. It is past your bedtime." She lifted Franklin out of his little rocking cradle and took Jessica by the hand. Lawrence, already six years old, trailed behind, unwilling to be linked with "the babies."

George watched them leave and, as so often before, felt the bitterest envy of Farrel Hurstwood. He has it all, he thought, swirling the brandy into burnished circles, but I don't think he knows what he has. Otherwise why would he be gone so much? He could send me on some of the trips. Or just not be so enamored of the promotion of his engines. Never satisfied, but always thinking of new applications. Well, he's a genius, there's no doubt about that. But not with men and women; oh, no, a genius with machines. Always urging me to spend as much time as possible with Sarah to keep her from feeling blue. He'll get no better than he deserves, I'll warrant.

He closed his eyes and imagined a time alone with Sarah. The sense of her made magic pictures

284

in his mind. An occasional shadow seemed to ripple across the images bringing the thought of Farrel—his partner, his friend, Sarah's husband—to his mind. Then dreams took over again.

"George," Sarah spoke his name softly as she laid her hand on his shoulder. He remained a moment unmoving, seated in the wingback chair before the fire, enjoying the intimacy of the experience. Then he turned and raised his glass toward her.

"Sarah, may I get you a brandy or perhaps a blackberry liqueur?"

"No," she answered, "I'm perfectly comfortable, thanks. Just being here with you."

"Well, at least come sit with me. This chair's large enough for the two of us." George took hold of Sarah's hand and guided her around the chair and onto the cushioned space beside him. Both of their hearts were pounding as they felt again the forbidden contact of their bodies.

"Sarah, dear," George began, but Sarah put her finger against his lips. He cupped her hand in his and kissed each finger. Sarah knew she should protest, but the magic of the moment carried her along unresisting. She leaned her head back against the chair with her eyes closed. Almost soft as a breath, Sarah felt the press of George's lips. For a time, she yielded wholeheartedly, then she pulled away horrified at herself. Not that she hadn't dreamed the scene a hundred times over since their picnic kisses years ago, but she was a married lady, she reminded herself. She was a mother of three children!

"George, I think you had better leave." Sarah struggled to rise. George offered his hand to help, but she refused it. He stood, too, beside her.

"Forgive me, Sarah," he said stiffly.

"There is nothing to forgive, George," she answered slowly. "It is my own behavior I question. My feelings are so terribly confused right now. I really need some time alone—time to think things through."

"Of course," George agreed at once, "but it is not thinking that is at issue, you know. It is more a matter of the heart than the mind."

Sarah cupped her forehead in her hand in a gesture of such anguish that George at once relented and tried to think of the fastest means by which he could make his departure.

"I'm sorry to have overstepped my limits as a guest in your home," he offered. He walked quickly toward the hall that led to the front door. Then, as though helpless against the force of his feelings, he stopped midway and turned back once more. "Sarah," he said, a question hanging in his voice, "you must know how I feel about you. I won't say any more for now."

Then he was gone. Sarah sat back down, staring blankly ahead. Stop it, she lectured herself; there is neither reason nor sense for tears at this point. She brushed angrily at her cheeks with the back of her hand, but new tears mysteriously appeared.

"Whatever has happened to us, Farrel?" Sarah silently questioned the air around her. Sitting now in this richly appointed room, she pictured the dreamy schoolgirl she had been more than twelve years before when she had first met the dashing Farrel Hurstwood.

Farrel had always been so beautiful, to her, that she could never get enough of looking at him. Not like George, poor homely fellow. When Farrel had introduced her to George shortly after taking him on as a partner she remembered thinking he looked a bit like a walrus—sad eyes that drooped to parallel his mustaches, both face and body a little puffy as though stuffed with marshmallows. It was wondrous, she thought now, how dear that silly face had grown over the years and especially during these months when Farrel was always gone and George had spent so much of his time looking after her and the family.

If she had known so many years ago what she knew now, she wondered what choice she would have made between the two men in her life.

December 10, 1900

Dear Diary,
There is not much in my life that is new or worth writing about, I am afraid. Farrel, however, is having ever greater success. This very day Farrel is in Paris being decorated as an Innovator in the Physical Sciences, or some such title, by L'Académie. I am proud of him, of course, but not as proud as a wife should be when she has such a successful and important husband. I still resent his overinvolvement in work. More to the point, I resent being such an unimportant part of his life. So you can see that things go on substantially as they were. Farrel hopes to return in time for us to celebrate the holidays as a family. Dare I plan on it?

Farrel is so busy elsewhere, so involved with what he calls "diversification plans," I sometimes wonder how our little Richmond streetcars keep running at all. They probably would grind to a stop, of course, and the company would fail as so many others have over the past decade, if it were not for a certain Mr. George Spencer. Choosing him for a partner was probably Farrel's wisest move; certainly his most practical one, in a business sense. He stays in Richmond, while Farrel moves about. It is George who takes care of the shop, as my father would say.

It is also George who spends a great portion of his time as the man in this family. Good, old, reliable, dear George. Mother spoke to me yesterday suggesting ever so subtly that people might get the wrong idea about his attentiveness. She has been very forbearing not to have spoken sooner. I am sure Daddy has been after her for a long time to do so. I reassured her that George's attentions were a result of Farrel's wishes in the matter.

Dear diary, I was telling the truth as far as I went, you know. But, oh, there is so much more I could have said. It is only here, though, that I can tell the whole truth. Mother and I have the deepest affection for each other. We have been close ever since she protected this curly head from Father's rigid rules and anger. But of the behavior between men and women we have seldom been able to speak.

She senses my continuing unhappiness and loneliness, I am sure, but neither of us approaches that painful topic. Instead, we talk of goings on around town and of the babies. We talk of the family pharmacy, too. It still has its faithful following despite the modern competitors. Daddy refuses to consider retirement, of course, so Mamma is kept busy doing the baking

*and helping out. At least he has taken a school-
boy on to work at the fountain after school and
weekends. I suppose in a way he has hired someone to replace me. Those are the topics Mamma
and I stick to when we talk.*

*The main topic I avoided bringing up yester-
day was George's idea that we take a little day
trip. Yes, just the two of us. A drive into the
country to pick out a Christmas tree and a stop
along the way for a meal. Oh, I know I should say
no, but I just cannot resist any longer. So when
he stops by this afternoon to check on us, I am
going to tell him yes. And tomorrow I will leave
Sassafras in charge and run away—just for a
little while—with George.*

The snow swirled around them as they drove the
Electrobat toward the mountains.

"Are you too cold, dear?" George asked,
glancing over at the huddled shape beside him.

"Oh, I am absolutely fine," Sarah beamed, her
eyes twinkling at him from under her fur hat. "My
chills are due more to excitement than to the
weather, you can be sure. Did you plan this sudden
storm, George?" she teased. "No sooner do we
escape the boundaries of Richmond than we
become enveloped in a wonderland."

"You have caught me! I confess," George
answered, picking up her playful mood, but not
taking his eyes from the road on which he was
navigating. "Weather control was my first course
in magic school. How do you like my work?"

"I love it!"

The shiny black motorcar, already half-covered
with snow, scuttled along the road like a field

mouse scurrying for cover. The road wound through the countryside which was mostly deserted, but which was dotted occasionally by a farm with its outbuildings. Cows stood by the side of the road balefully gazing out at the world from under the snow blankets which made them barely visible. As Sarah and George drove on, the storm grew worse and worse. Abruptly, the car skidded, almost landing in the ditch. George struggled for control. Then they were all right again and the tension eased.

"Is it too dangerous to go on?" Sarah asked suddenly alarmed.

"It is pretty slick," George answered, "but just stopping by the roadside doesn't seem too smart an idea. There's an inn I know of that we should come to in only a few more minutes. Let us keep going until we get to it. Then we will stop and consider the situation."

Sarah nodded. In the silence that accompanied their slow progress she thought, Even if we crashed it would have been worth it—worth the excitement, the adventure, the feeling of being carefree for a short while. Then, staring ahead, through the milky snow, she thought she saw a flickering light in the distance.

"George," she said, pointing.

"Yes," he answered. "That's it!"

Shortly, George steered the car into the inn's front yard. It was with some relief that he helped Sarah down. They picked their way across the snowy yard to the front door. Once inside, they stamped their feet clear of the snow, then unbundled themselves. George looked at Sarah with her cheeks flushed from the cold and was struck again by her handsomeness. She smiled at him as he took her arm and led her into the dining room.

"After that scare, I should have lost my appetite, but instead I am absolutely starved," Sarah whispered, squeezing his arm. "Don't you think I am perverse?"

"About you, Sarah, nothing is perverse. Everything is perfectly natural."

"Welcome," their host greeted them, ushering them into the inn's cozy dining salon. "How brave to have ventured out on this snowy day. Will it be just the two of you for lunch then?"

"Yes," George agreed, "and the table closest to that lovely fire, if you don't mind."

When they were seated, had placed their orders, and were sipping their sherry, they smiled at each other, extraordinarily pleased with themselves.

"I feel like a kid playing hooky," George said.

"Me, too. Thanks to you, George. You provided the idea, the opportunity, the setting." Embarrassed, she fell silent.

The food was smoothly served so that Sarah and George were hardly aware of the waiter's presence. They were the only diners today so the room took on the essence of a private mansion. They toasted the occasion in shimmering glasses of Pinot-Chardonnay. The reflected flames cast dancing circles of light across the ceiling. Sarah saw them, lifted another bite of Norfolk crab to her lips, and felt that her problems were floating upward, too, like those circles. George shared her delight and knew that just then he was the luckiest man in the world.

When they finished eating, George checked on the weather conditions. By this time, instead of dissipating as he had expected, the storm had grown angry, adding a howling wind to its dense snow. The snow had already obscured the road and was well on its way to burying the Electrobat.

"Sarah," George said, returning to the table where she was waiting. "I am afraid we had best plan on staying here overnight. It looks too dangerous to attempt going either forward or back. I am so sorry, but I seem to have unintentionally placed you in a difficult position. If you agree, I will go arrange for rooms for us."

"Please do not fret one moment about it," Sarah reassured him. "I will not allow anything to spoil this perfect afternoon."

They fell silent then, gazing into each other's eyes, both aware of the change taking place in their attitudes toward the holiday outing. Sarah felt reckless and free. She could have blamed it on the wine, but knew it was more than that.

"Perhaps you ought to see about getting us rooms," Sarah said. Her heartbeat deafened her.

In a matter of minutes, George was settling Sarah in her room.

"I will be just across the hall," he told her. "Would you like me to go now so you can have a little rest? Would you like some time alone?" He paused. Sarah continued to stare at him, smiling slightly.

"George," she said, "I don't want to be alone."

"Sarah," he whispered, his voice hoarse.

She walked to the quilt-covered fourposter and sank onto it. "Come here, George," she said softly. She smoothed the space beside her. George moved toward her as though in a magic dream. He sat next to her, hardly daring to hope, hardly daring to breathe.

"George," she said again. "Let us spend the afternoon here. Together."

He clasped her to him then, stopping any further words she might have spoken with fervent kisses.

"Sarah, darling," he whispered again, sliding his hand up along her satin bodice until it cupped her breast.

"Oh, that feels good, George," she sighed, stretching out languorously.

How bold I am, Sarah thought. How bold, and eager, and yearning. Will there be remorse later? she wondered. Will there be a terrible price to pay? And, if so, will I be strong enough to pay it?

George, too, wondered at Sarah's boldness. I know she is all purity, he told himself, and I know she does not really love me, so what is the explanation? It must be her loneliness, he decided. Farrel's devotion to work leaves her virtually abandoned. Perhaps, he thought, just perhaps she could come to love me.

As he leaned above her, his hands reaching for her breasts, he put thought aside in favor of feeling. Sarah yearned up toward him, also abandoning herself to the moment. George's hands moved in rhythmic circles around Sarah's breasts while his own chest pulsed with the passion he felt. Sarah closed her eyes.

"Shall I close the drapes?" he asked.

"It doesn't matter," she answered leading him down until he lay beside her. "The blizzard itself provides us with a beautiful white drape. Whirling and alive . . ." She stroked George's cheeks as she spoke, traced the shape of his lips with her softly trembling fingers. "Spinning wildly," she added, "just like my feelings."

George began to undo the row of tiny buttons that ran the length of Sarah's salmon-colored gown. "Sarah, my dear Sarah," he spoke softly as he worked, "you look very beautiful in that lovely outfit, but"—at this point he eased Sarah's shoulders and arms out of the sleeves—"you will be ever so much more beautiful without it." With Sarah's assistance, George succeeded in removing her heavy gown. Now he gazed at her as though at a vision, seeing her creamy skin against the dazzling whiteness of her starched camisole. Sarah smiled at him only a little shyly.

"George," she said, calling him out of his dazed condition, "you are still fully dressed. Would you not be more comfortable if you shed some of those binding clothes?"

He laughed then and became himself. "Yes, yes," he muttered, "but first just one more kiss, I beg of you." He leaned over and they shared a soft kiss. His tongue gently probed her lips until he reached her teeth which parted allowing him entry to her mouth, her tongue. When at last they moved apart and he began removing his jacket, his tie, his shirt, she said, "You need not *beg* for a kiss, George. I offer you my kisses wholeheartedly." At her words, he sat down by her again.

"Sarah, my love," he whispered, taking her hands.

"Wholeheartedly, George," she repeated, "and with gratitude." A tear traced a crooked path down her cheek, trembled on her chin a moment, then dropped onto George's hand. He could not think what to do or say, so he returned to the task of undressing. He removed his shoes, his trousers, his socks. All that remained on was his union suit. Sarah, meanwhile, had crept between the sheets to remove her underthings. Now she lay completely naked, but hidden from George's sight by the quilt.

As George climbed out of his all-in-one, Sarah noted the differences between his body and Farrel's, the only male body she had ever seen. George's was thicker and had dark coarse hair curled across his chest and belly. Every part of his body was thicker than Farrel's. His belly, she saw, was too full and shook as he moved toward her. I don't care, she told herself. The surface is nothing, the person within is all. I yearn to be close, she thought, to become part of him and have him become part of me.

George got into bed beside her. Sarah felt the shock and thrill of his warm flesh against hers.

"Sarah," he asked, "may I take down your hair?"

She smiled and nodded, sitting up on her

elbows. As he slowly removed pin after pin, her ringlets fell into long slow curls along her shoulders. He shook his head.

"I don't know how to say what I want to say," he began. "For so long I have forbidden myself even to think, let alone utter, the words. I suppose the oldest phrase of all is still the truest and will have to do. Sarah, I love you."

Sarah stopped smiling and lay back down on the pillow. "I know that, George," she said. "That is why I feel safe wtih you, why I trust you. I hope you know how much I care for you, too."

She knew he wanted to hear those same words, but she could not bring herself to say them. She had only ever said them to Farrel. Even now, she thought, in bed with another man, to utter them would seem the final betrayal.

"George, I want to hold you," she said instead. "Please come to me and hold me."

With a groan, he moved above her and lowered himself over her.

"Sarah," he called out as he entered the dark wetness of her body. "Sarah," he called again pumping, pumping, pumping into her, against her, toward her until with a final cry he arched away from her and his powerful hands lifted her up, too. For a few endless moments they remained poised half-sitting. Then, at last, the tension changed into that special heavy relaxation only accessible after fulfillment. Within a few minutes, Sarah could feel George's breathing become a sleeper's breath.

She loved the feel of his head cradled on her

breast and his arm across her hip. The differences between George and Farrel along with the forbidden nature of the act made this love-making spectacular. Adultress, she called herself, but the word seemed to have no connection with her life or with this particular afternoon. She eased her hand down to where she could touch George's liquids leaking out of her body. Her finger pressed on that special button she had discovered and she jumped slightly. George shook himself awake.

"Oh, my God, Sarah. Thank you."

She kissed his ear, then blew in it, making him smile. He could see she felt playful and, happy that she was not suffering feelings of remorse, he gladly joined in. They began to tickle each other until they were both giggling.

"Are you getting hungry again?" George asked. Sarah frowned, uncertain whether he meant food or love. While she paused, he reached between her legs and began stroking her body.

"Oh, George, yes, yes, yes," she sighed leaning back against the piled pillows.

Within a short time, he too had found that special place and moved his fingers on it, adjusting his pace to her responses. As he began to move faster, she raised his free hand to her mouth. First, she kissed it and then, at the fastest peak, she bit the fleshy part at the base of the thumb.

She could hardly believe the feelings that coursed through her. Nothing had ever felt like this before. Suddenly, though, along with the release of tension came shyness.

"George," she whispered. "What happened to

me? I have never felt that way."

So then George knew. "Nothing, darling," he answered, "but love. Love is supposed to feel that way."

"Oh, George," she cried out. "Oh, George." Then continued in a whisper, "I must be completely shameless, but I want you again."

At that, George laughed out loud. "You are, darling," he said, "you are. You are perfectly *wonderfully* shameless. Now come here, hussy, and get up on top of me. You want more, and more you shall get. I shall give you a ride you can never forget. And just maybe," he added, "by morning we will both have had enough."

Sarah laughed, too, then pulled his ears and climbed astride his sturdy body. She wanted to try it. She wanted to try everything. She saw now that George was a far more experienced lover than she had ever imagined.

"Teach me, George, my dearest darling," she said to him then. "I want to learn. I want to learn everything."

George thought that his heart must burst with joy. Over the course of the afternoon and evening and night, he discovered what an apt pupil Sarah could be. It was a space of time that neither of them would ever forget.

Nineteen

When Sarah and George returned the next day to Richmond with the most beautiful huge tree that ever graced the Hurstwood house, only they knew how changed they were from the two people who had left for that tree. Sarah amazed both George and herself by retaining the best of spirits and feeling no obvious remorse or guilt. The sadness that tinged their parting was the realization that the delights of the night could not go on. Sarah had made it quite plain over their breakfast that she would not ever repeat this journey. Oh, no, she insisted, that would strain her ability as an actress. No, this one time would be their only time. George accepted her verdict though it rang like a death knell on his ears. But deep within him he resisted her words. There must be other times, he told himself. There just must be.

Sarah and George shared that Christmas season just like a happily married couple with George sitting at the head of the table over the elaborate turkey dinner. Farrel could not return in time to celebrate with his family, it turned out. For once George blessed the slowness of boats, the thoughtlessness of his partner in making plans. Although he and Sarah avoided any touches, they shared looks and words and, he was sure, memories. For that brief shining season George could pretend that this was his wife and his family. He felt completely happy and had no trouble finding a prayer of thanksgiving when the family gathered for their holiday dinner.

Of course, Farrel did eventually return and George went back to his lonely life. The winter dragged by. Gradually January's short days turned into February's long nights. Farrel blew in and out between trips, like a cold wind whistling in the chimney. George continued his visits, but the memory of their December tryst often blazed up making their times together uncomfortable. By March, everyone's tempers were strained.

Sarah knew she was with child again, but she made every effort to conceal the signs. She told no one. Until, that is, the mid-March afternoon when because she felt vaguely unsettled she decided to take her needlework and spend the afternoon at the Rosemary Library. Yes, she told herself, gathering her threads and putting them along with her needles and hoop into her crewel bag, a restful afternoon with the ladies will be a good change.

She took the trolley, paying her nickel fare like everyone else. She could have walked really. She remembered Rose's advice and often took long walks. But she felt a bit self-indulgent today. She was in a strange, restless mood altogether. The trolley stopped at Fourth and Franklin almost at the library's door.

Once inside, she hung up her cloak and made her way to the fireplace which held a Latrobe stove. A coal fire burned behind its isinglass doors. It was wonderfully cozy and she sat enjoying the fire without busying herself about her handiwork, but she soon became aware of someone standing behind her. She turned her head and discovered George Spencer, derby hat in hand, no more than a few feet away.

"Why, George, what on earth are you doing here?"

"I'm a member, too, Sarah. I come here every few days to get a new book to read. You ladies do not have a total monopoly on that habit yet!"

"Oh, I am sorry. You know I meant no rudeness. It is simply that I have never seen a man here in the library." She paused a moment, looking around to make sure no one was within hearing before adding, "Nor anyone doing very much book reading either! And I am as guilty as the next one. Why, I can hardly remember the last book I read. But tell me, what book have you got there? You always inspire me to begin again."

George sat down in the chair next to hers. He leaned forward, excitedly pointing to the books clutched in his hand.

"I am about to read a history. Well, really more of a philosophy. You mustn't tell your husband," he remarked as an aside, "because he thinks philosophy is nonsense."

"Yes," she added, smiling at his pleasure, "he thinks anything that has no electrical application is a bit of nonsense, I am afraid."

"This book I just borrowed is *The Destiny of Man*. But you know that I also read other things— novels, even poetry."

"Well, suggest something for me." She found his excitement contagious.

"The book I just returned! Then when you finish it we can have a good talk about it, eh? It's a historical romance. About colonial Virginia, so it is a subject dear to both our hearts. The name— Oh, damn, I just finished it; how can I have forgotten already? Oh, I remember. *Prisoners of Hope*. By a woman, too. I can just go up to the desk and sign it out for you. Shall I?"

"Yes, George, do! I am as excited about this new project as you are."

As he wrote out the card to have the book charged out, George thought of the exchange he had just had with Sarah. It was the most comfortable that they had been with each other since their night together almost three months earlier. Maybe just getting away from the "Hurst-wood Mansion," as he'd come to think of her house, made the difference. He walked back to where she waited. Her smile lit his world like the sun breaking through clouds.

"Here you are." He handed her the book, then held her hand a moment. She looked up with questions in her eyes. "Sarah," he said in a low tone so that only she could hear him, "I need to be alone with you."

"But, George," she said, tugging slightly against his hold, "we are alone."

His face remained somber. "No, Sarah. I mean really alone. I need you. Please, Sarah, do not tell me no and send me away. I have never before asked this of you, have I? But I'm begging you now."

Her already pale face became a shade whiter. "Oh God, George!" She thought for a moment. It had been so long since that glorious night when they were together. Yes, she admitted, she wanted to be with him, too. Longed for him to hold her. "But, George," she went on, "where would we go even if I said yes?"

"To my home. I have thought of it a million times, but never dared to broach the subject with you for fear you would banish me forever from your life. I could never stand that, Sarah."

"Neither could I," she admitted, "but what of our ever-watchful Richmond neighbors?"

"It will be all right. Trust me, Sarah. I would never place you in danger. You know that, don't you?"

She nodded. George offered her his hand and together they walked out of the library into the glory of the almost-spring day.

Their time together in George's rooms was more gentle than their first time together, but it was equally sweet. Sarah felt happy just to lie beside George and kiss his cheeks, his eyelids, his brow. George felt contented just being in a private place with his Sarah. At last he could take kisses at his leisure, look his fill on Sarah's lovely face, stroke her body. Time for comfort and time for passion. A lifetime in one afternoon, that was how he viewed it. His feeling for this woman gave him pain, joy, excitement, despair—in short, everything one could ever imagine receiving from life. During this unmeasured time with her, George did not even question whether they would ever be together this way again. The moment held its own fulfillment.

The moment did end, of course, and they prepared reluctantly to return to their normal roles. By the time George's carriage drew up before Sarah's house, bringing her back home, the day had the feel of late afternoon—time slowed to a honey drip. They both felt an equal reluctance to slip on their other faces. They both shared the desire to keep a bit of the moment they had just had for a while longer.

Even after the carriage stopped, neither of its passengers made any attempt to step from it. They smiled into each other's eyes. Finally, George stepped down and held his arm up to Sarah. She sighed as she took his hand to alight from the protection of the carriage.

"Do you have time for a brief cup of tea?" she asked him. "I hate to see today's chance meeting draw to a close!"

"Well," he replied, "I have put work out of my mind this long, I suppose another half-hour will hardly matter."

They went up the walk to the house and were soon comfortably sharing tea in the back parlor.

"You look wonderful, you know," George said, replacing his teacup in its saucer.

She blushed prettily.

"You do say such nice things, sir," she said, smiling—thinking to herself, He is such a dear man.

"There is a question, though, that I must ask you. A bold question."

Sarah betrayed her tension by pursing her lips. After a few seconds of uncomfortable silence, George went on.

"Sarah, could it possibly be that you are expecting?"

She still remained silent, but he knew her well enough by now to wait. He had learned to give her the time she needed, whereas once he would have felt the need to fill the space with words. Now he spent the time observing her hands. She was wearing many rings today. Two opal rings on her right hand, the smaller one on her little finger was simply set, a large one on her index finger was surrounded by a circle of diamonds. On her left hand she wore a diamond and her wedding band. Her hands lay in her lap where she twisted a handkerchief nervously. Her beige raw silk shirt-waist with its mutton sleeves looked soft—so soft and full. Full enough to hide a fuller body, he had suspected earlier and, after the time in his room, was certain. His question was already answered in his own mind.

Sarah finally broke the silence. "Yes," she said. "But you must not make mention of it, for I have not told a single soul. I should have known, though, that you would notice. You always look at me so closely." She blushed again.

"Oh, Sarah," he sighed. She saw the lines across his brow deepen. "How pregnant are you, Sarah?" He asked it so softly that she had to lean forward to hear him.

She shook her head briefly, but gave no answer. I will not answer, she told herself. I knew he would ask me someday, but I am not ready yet to answer him. I might never be ready to give him the whole true answer.

"Sarah," George persisted, "the baby." She looked away. He took her chin in his hand and turned her face back toward him. "Could it be mine?"

When she still refused to answer, he jumped to his feet. For the moment, he seemed to have forgotten her presence. Then, abruptly, he sat back down beside her.

"Sarah," he said in a low, intense voice, "it *is* my baby! You are carrying my child and that is the real reason you haven't mentioned it to anyone, am I right?"

She absolutely refused to answer him, but her lips began to tremble.

"I wish you would leave now, George, and please do not ever ask me that question again!"

He felt a heaviness settle on his chest. It became hard to breathe.

"Before I go, Sarah, I must tell you that I wish you would come away with me."

She looked at him blankly.

"Away?"

"Leave Farrel," he explained. "Become my wife . . . my family. He does not need you the way I need you. He could not love you as much; of that I am positive. At last, I feel I have a claim that allows me to tell you what I feel. Come to me, my beloved, you were always meant to be mine!"

"God in heaven!" she exclaimed in a tortured voice. "What are you asking of me? Please. No more. I cannot bear it!" She bent her head to the antimacassar covering the sofa back. Ironed and starched as it was, it felt cool to her face. She remained tucked in that curled position until he had left. Then, cautiously, she lifted her head. The room was, indeed, empty. With George gone— perhaps forever, she thought—it felt emptier than it had ever been.

May 1, 1901

Dear Diary,

My life seems like a narrow bridge over an abyss, each step fraught with peril. Yet still I proceed, one foot in front of the other, although each step terrifies me and takes me into uncharted territory.

George's repeated urgings that I choose a different route altogether nag at my mind, although I do not dare to consider it seriously. The scandal! The shock that would reverberate through so many lives. No, I must not allow myself to think about it. And yet I do. And, the baby inside of me! No, put the thoughts away.

How many times have I forsworn my attachment to George! But upon the occasions when we can be alone together, twice more since I sent him from me, I cannot resist. The appeal of being close to him overpowers my weak resolutions.

307

Each coming together is ecstasy, only to be followed by my renewed vow never to let it happen again!

Then there is Farrel—the invisible Farrel who is still more absent than present. What are we to each other at this point in our lives? I ask myself. Held by society's chains but not by love. No, not love. That has had its day and has waned, perhaps forever.

"Children, be quiet!" Farrel snapped. "Can't you see that your father is trying to read his papers?" His loud voice made the children jump.

"Mr. Hurstwood," Sarah rebuked him in a sharp voice. "You have been gone more than you have been at home this entire year until the children hardly even know who you are! Then when you *are* at home, you are annoyed by everything."

The children, who were frightened by their parents' angry voices, stared at them in silence. When Sarah noticed their wide-eyed alarm, she moderated her tone.

"It is the day before my birthday, Farrel, after all. You were not even here with us for Christmas!" She had not meant to bring that up ever again, but the words slipped out. "Could you not put your work aside just this once? On such a lovely June day we could take the children on a picnic."

Sarah exhibited that radiant plump beauty common to women well along in pregnancy. Her charming looks were wasted on Farrel, though, since he refused to look at her.

"I only returned yesterday, my dear wife." Farrel's sarcastic tone cut Sarah. "Can you imagine the pileup of mail and magazines waiting for me at work? I must use this time to catch up. I should really be at the office, but I thought you would appreciate my working at home."

"I know all too well you only returned yesterday!" she answered angrily. "Your kindness at being with us would mean more if it were matched by kindness *to* us."

Turning her attention back to the children who had not moved, she forced a smile into place. "You children go out and play in the back yard," Sarah said. "Please, children. Clara will watch you. Go on."

Sarah herded Franklin, Jessica, and Lawrence out of the room, calling for Clara to come watch over them as she did so. Then, having at last begun to express her dissatisfactions, she continued to berate Farrel.

"Who do you think has kept this family functioning? *I* have, that is who. I have done it completely on my own. Then you come home grumpy, yelling at everyone, and want to be left alone so you can work. How much more of this must I put up with? How much more of it can I stand?"

Farrel folded his paper, still refusing to meet his wife's eyes. He glared straight ahead, his back stiff, while two red dots formed on his cheeks. He had sworn they would not repeat their pattern of fights, sworn he would never strike her again. Sarah fell silent. She fought against the tears that threatened to weaken her resolve. If Farrel refused to be a husband to her, by God she would leave him. She remained standing, her hands clasped before her. Farrel continued to sit. Someone entering the room might have imagined that the couple had been turned into stone except for the tension charging through the air like an invisible electric current.

Suddenly someone did enter the room, burst into the room. It was Clara with shouts of, "Come quick. It's Lawrence. He's hurt. Just lies there. Oh, God a'mighty, hurry!"

Instantly there was a rush of activity.

Sarah's hand leaped to her mouth. "Farrel," she whispered. Farrel jumped up from his chair and took Clara's arm, shaking her.

"Where?" He shouted as though at a deaf mute. "Where?"

The three of them crushed through the doorway and then, with Clara in the lead, raced along the corridor toward the back door. Outside, the warm air stifled them less than the horror of the scene before their eyes.

Lawrence, their first-born, lay unmoving at the base of a gigantic elm tree. He looked as though he might be asleep if it weren't for the bluish tinge to his skin and the crooked way his neck bent.

"Lawrence," Sarah screamed as she ran to the little seven-year-old boy and threw herself down beside him. "Oh God, Farrel." Her voice pleaded with him as he bent his ear down next to the boy's mouth.

"He's still alive," Farrel answered in a strained

voice. The other two children wailed in the background. "Clara, take those children indoors and run as fast as ever you can and call for the doctor. You hear me?" He screamed at her as she stood staring at him.

"Yessir, I hears," she answered and began shooing Jessica and Franklin before her toward the door that still hung open.

"Clara," Farrel called, stopping her before she disappeared inside, "what happened to him?"

"He fell, Mr. Hurstwood, sir. From the branch up there." Her voice was choked, but her words were clear enough. She pointed to a limb of the tree above Farrel's head. "He was just a'climbin' and then all of a sudden he lost his hold and falls."

"All right," Farrel answered. "Now, run!"

Sarah tugged on his arm. "Can you make him wake up? My poor baby." She brushed the curls off of his forehead. "Surely he is not too badly hurt, do you think? There is not a cut or a bruise on him. Tell me he will be all right."

"I don't know, Sarah. I just do not know. It does not look good, but he *is* still alive, thank God. We will know more when the doctor arrives."

"Can we pick him up and take him in the house? The ground is so hard and so dirty." Her voice sounded weak and vague. She seemed almost to be a child again herself, talking about a broken doll.

"I think we better leave him just where he is until Doc Lathrop sees him. You can cover him with your shawl, if you want."

Sarah bent over the boy and gently spread the knit shawl from her shoulders over the unconscious child. "Lawrence," she called, "Lawrence, baby. Mamma's here." She bit her lip against the sobs that shook her chest. It was all a dream—nightmare. She looked up at the tree spreading its broad branches across the sky and watched them spin into a blur.

"Sarah," she heard from far, far away. Then a sharp bitter smell made her twist her head away and cough. "Sarah." The voice sounded closer. She opened her eyes.

"What happened?" she asked.

"You fainted," Sam Lathrop answered. "Just sit awhile. You will be fine." He patted her hand.

"Lawrence," she cried, remembering. "Oh God, where is Lawrence?"

"We have moved him into the house," the doctor assured her. "Farrel's with him."

"Will he be all right?" she asked, dreading his answer.

"I must be honest with you; I just do not know. He has a skull fracture, but how severe it is, I am not sure. There's room for hope," he added, "but hope with caution."

He helped Sarah to her feet. With his arm around her, they made their way to the house. She insisted she wanted to sit beside Lawrence in case he awoke, although the doctor told her that was extremely unlikely and that she should really get some rest herself after the shock. "After all," he added, "you are about seven months pregnant." But she would hear none of it. So, reluctantly, they agreed to her plan and installed her in a rocker in the birth room where they had placed the hurt child.

"Farrel," the doctor whispered taking his arm, "I would like to speak with you." Farrel nodded, then turned to Sarah whose attention remained solely focused on the boy and said, "I will go and get us some tea; then I shall come right back."

She nodded half-heartedly, never removing her attention from Lawrence who lay lost to her in a distant silent world of his own.

If, if, if. The dreary refrain sang in Sarah's mind. If only I had gone outside with the children. If only I had not allowed myself to get involved in a fight with Farrel. Worst of all, because of its total illogicality, was the nagging notion that none of this would have happened if only . . . if only . . . if only she had never welcomed George Spencer into her heart. If only she had never allowed him to make love to her.

Doctor Lathrop and Farrel left the room and made their way down the stairs and into the back parlor.

"Bessie," Farrel called, and at once the old family helper appeared. "Please prepare a teapot and three cups for us to take upstairs."

"Yessir," she said; then added, "Will the little one be all right?"

"Hope and pray, Bessie. Hope and pray," Farrel answered.

Farrel turned to the doctor and asked, "What is it, Sam? Tell me the truth now. I need to know."

"It is bad. Very bad," Sam answered. "The eyes

are not responsive to light so there must be a terrible amount of pressure. We could try surgery to remove some of that pressure, but the chances are that we might leave him crippled or defective, if we didn't downright kill him!"

"God!" Farrel groaned. The two men sat in silence for a few moments. "What if we do nothing?" Farrel asked.

"He might come out of it, and he might not. If he does, he might be normal and he might be paralyzed or feeble-minded." Another pause. "You asked for the truth."

"I know."

"That tyke is mighty badly hurt. The prayers might help . . . if you believe in 'em. I am afraid that there is not much else that will."

"Sam, if it was your boy would you have the surgery?" Farrel asked, his thoughts and feelings a muddle.

"I don't think so. I don't think I would. If we only knew more about the brain. But we know so damned little. The anesthesia alone might kill him. If it were me, I would wait—"

"Doctor!" Sarah's scream startled them and they both rushed to the stairs. Farrel, the younger man by far, raced ahead. But Sam Lathrop, noting the hysterical sound to Sarah's voice, was not very far behind.

"What is it, Sarah?" Farrel asked reaching the top of the stairs where Sarah stood, wraithlike.

"He opened his eyes for a second, but then they rolled back in his head, and his color looks worse than ever!"

Doctor Lathrop brushed past her and hurried to the bedside. There he bent over his patient, checking his pulse, testing his reflexes, and watching helplessly as the color and tone of the skin became duskier and duskier.

Suddenly the air filled with the clatter of hoofs, the shouts of a man's voice. Sarah rushed to the window from which she could see down onto the courtyard beside the carriage house. There the roan pony they had bought so that Lawrence could learn to ride raced in mad circles, avoiding the groom's attempts at capture. Finally, though, it reared up on its hind legs, whinnied, shook its neck so that the long beautiful combed hair of its mane whipped out into the air, and stood still. As Bertie gentled him down with words and moved to get a firm hold on his mane, the small creature trembled and snorted, but made no further move to escape. Bertie led him back into the stall.

Sarah turned away from the drama at the window to confront the sorrowful eyes of the doctor that told her what she dreaded to hear. Before he could utter a word, she cried out, "No!" Then, as a bird will glide to the ground in one swift silent movement, she fell to the carpeted floor. She felt herself fall, but welcomed the dark escape into unconsciousness. The word 'no' formed itself into a howl in her mind as all other awareness fled from her.

Twenty

The next day a heated argument broke out between Farrel and Sarah's parents. They fought over the site for Lawrence's burial. The Seewalds, who had become increasingly overt in their Judaism, had helped to found the Conservative synagogue just a few years earlier. They felt that Lawrence was a Jewish boy whose body belonged in the Jewish cemetery. They also wanted Rabbi Dorfman, their rabbi, to officiate.

Farrel was unwilling to accommodate to this change of position. In his mind, Lawrence's christening made him a Christian and that was that. Moreover, as he pointed out, Lawrence had gone to church and to Sunday school classes. The minister, Mr. Archibald Lansford, knew Lawrence and viewed him as one of the congregation, whereas neither the rabbi nor the synagogue members knew Lawrence at all. He insisted that it would be a travesty.

Sarah, in a state of shock bordering on hysteria,

sat apart from the argument until, at last, she could stand it no more.

"Stop," she shrieked. "For the love of God, the child is dead! What are you all bickering about?" She broke into heartrending sobs. "My baby is dead," she went on, sobbing.

Shamefacedly, the others fell silent.

"Bubbele," Sarah's mother crooned, putting her arms around her daughter. "You are right, of course. We are all terribly upset. But we show it in different ways."

David touched Farrel's arm.

"Make the arrangements, Farrel," he said softly. "Go to your church and make whatever arrangements have to be made. Let us say no more about it."

It seemed to Sarah indecent the way the sun continued to shine down on the group of people gathered before the gaping hole. How could this happen? she asked constantly, how could this possibly happen? It was the most unnatural event in the world, she felt, that a child should die before his parents.

The minister spoke in gentle terms about the promise that Lawrence had held as a child, a bud that would never blossom on this earth. "Man that is born of woman," he said, "hath but a short time to live . . . He cometh up, and is cut down, like a flower; he fleeth as it were a shadow. . . ." Sarah only heard bits and snatches of his words. Handfuls of earth struck the tiny coffin. "We therefore commit his body to the ground . . . looking for the general Resurrection in the last day, and the life of the world to come, through our Lord Jesus Christ. The grace of our Lord Jesus Christ, and the love of God, and the fellowship of the Holy Ghost, be with us all evermore."

The words tore at Sarah's heart even as she winced for the extra pain her parents must be feeling as they heard the words that insisted on Lawrence's Christianity. Oh God, Sarah groaned, whatever and whoever you are, have pity on my baby . . . my poor baby.

Rabbi Saul Dorfman stood with the Seewalds, his head bowed. David and the rabbi and a few other mourners wore the little skullcaps, their *yarmulkes,* on their heads. Sarah glanced over at the rabbi and was touched by the grief she saw registered in his eyes when they met hers.

As they covered Lawrence's small coffin in the grave, she kept herself from screaming out by biting her lips until they bled. At least we shall have dignity, she told herself, at least that. But tears streamed down her cheeks beneath her black veil. Farrel supported her as she sagged heavily against him. He led her over to the waiting line of buggies for the mournful trip back.

Once home, Sarah's mother took charge of the guests. A few close friends of the family had returned from the cemetery with them.

Rabbi Dorfman took this opportunity to approach Sarah as she stood apart from the group.

"There are never adequate words, Mrs. Hurstwood, to express the heart's sorrow. It is the place where words lose their meaning."

"Yes." Sarah nodded. She had held the same thought, but had not formulated it before. "Thank you." She took his outstretched hand. He patted her hand as he held it.

"If you ever want simply to talk, or a place to be silent, the door to my study is always open to you. Please feel welcome." Sarah only nodded as the tears welled again in her eyes.

Rachel served the assembled mourners coffee and tea and a spread of food, which they ate in a muted and somber way—the atmosphere of grief. The men drank bourbon, throwing it back fast into their throats. Sarah, unable to cope with any more, excused herself as soon as she could and took to her bed.

When the guests felt they had lingered long enough for appearance's sake, they began to take their leave. Even those who generally found such gatherings a sort of comfort, most commonly the women who had been widowed during the previous year and could often use such an occasion to vent their grief, felt the double distress of this death. A child, after all, and not even through illness where there would be some warning, but a freak accident. With the mother so far along, too. It was more than pathetic, the mourners agreed. Some of them even held secret doubts, as did Sarah, about the wisdom and absolute goodness of God. These were hidden thoughts, though, not spoken aloud.

Soon almost everyone had left. Only George remained behind, to sit with Farrel. Rachel stayed, too, of course, to oversee the children and, especially, to be close in case Sarah needed her. Now she said, "I think I will just go up and check on Sarah, Farrel. She should eat a little something if I can convince her, but I will see what I can do."

Farrel looked up and nodded numbly. It was George who answered her. "Yes, Mrs. Seewald, that would be a good thing. She must make the effort to think beyond this tragedy, hard as that is to do. She must think of the new life to come, eh?"

"Exactly," Rachel Seewald agreed, and made her way to the kitchen where she could be heard arranging with Bessie for a tray to take to Sarah.

As Rachel waited in the kitchen, she thought about this George Spencer who spent so much time in Sarah's life. Oh, she knew about his partnership with Farrel and all that. But it was more than a business interest that kept him so close to this family, she felt sure.

She hoped that he had acted honorably toward her daughter. She felt confident, in fact, that Sarah would not stain her marriage promises. Most of the time she believed that. But she knew how easily a young and innocent person could be tempted. And she knew that Sarah was not truly happy in her marriage to Farrel. She tried to dismiss these thoughts, thinking instead what a lovely person this Mr. Spencer is, a *mensch,* as they say in Yiddish. Then the thought turned in her mind. It was precisely because he was such a man that Sarah might have fallen in love with him. He was a bachelor still. Why did he not choose to have a home of his own instead of invading this already established home? Oh, she was being unfair, she knew. Thank God for any kindness he had shown Sarah, her only daughter—her only child. If it was love that he offered . . . well, then, thank God for that as well.

Her thoughts shocked Rachel who had never before come so close to condoning adultery. Not in any form—not even in her thoughts. But poor Sarah, she thought, as she hurried toward her room, I want so much for her to be happy.

Although her knock went unanswered, Rachel opened the door and entered her daughter's room. At first, due to the darkness, she imagined it to be empty.

"Sarah?" she called.

"Yes, Mother," she heard a soft voice out of the darkness. "Here I am, sitting in the window seat."

"Sarah, why have you drawn the drapes?" Rachel, still carrying the tray, struggled to light the lamp with one hand. Having managed that so that she could see, she placed the tray down on the bed table and went over to her daughter. Sarah felt a hand stroke her head and for a moment she could forget everything and be her mother's little girl again.

"Oh, God, Mamma," she cried. "How am I to bear this?" Then she turned her face in to her mother's voluminous skirts and wept. Rachel said nothing, but continued to pat her daughter. Where no words would suffice, she believed, touches could still have a meaning. Standing there with her weeping daughter, Rachel was transported back to that terrible time in Odessa just before they left

321

forever. She herself was somewhere around Sarah's age then. She tried always not to remember, but now she could not help herself. It all came flooding back to her—the part of the Odessa pogrom she had never fully described to Sarah, the part she could never leave behind no matter how long she lived in America.

"Rachel, Rachel," she had heard the screams from down the street, down near the village water fountain. The Cossacks had just ridden through again, making a last circle to smash anything left unsmashed. As the dust settled, she had begun sweeping off the front steps which were littered with crockery fragments and torn branches. Then came the cries, and she began to run with all her might toward the square at the town center. Her neighbor, Frumme, came panting toward her, clutching her bosom. "Rachel," she cried in anguish.

"What is it?" Rachel screamed, shaking her by the arms. "Tell me quick!" She knew from the sound of the cries and from a strange smell of artichoke in her head that it was something terrible. That smell had always been a personal sign of sorrow, of evil.

"Your daughter, Zaydie," Frumme gasped. "The Cossacks." Each word struck like a mournful chime. Each vibrated in the air, then sank to silence. The silent pauses said more than the words. Loosing her hold on Frumme's arm, Rachel began to run again. Then she saw the crowd at the square, huddled around a figure on the ground. She came closer and knew. Zaydie! Her eldest child, Sarah's older sister. Max, another friend, saw her approach and hurried toward her.

"The pigs," he spat out. "The cursed swine; may they forever roast in *sheol!*"

"Tell me, Max." Her voice was cold, each word a frozen icicle. Feeling had left her. Her body as well as her heart had lost all senses. "Tell me."

"She is dead, Rachel. There can be no good way to say it. Please do not go and look! What they have done is too ugly. Let me clean her a little and then I will bring her to you."

Oh God, she thought at once, the thought plunging straight to her heart like a knife, they raped her. She was only eleven years old, but they raped her!

"Max," she asked, because she had to know for sure, "did they touch her?"

He nodded yes, and although she really knew already, when he confirmed her fears it was like a second blow to her.

"Oh God," she cried out, then fell like a stone, like a dead weight, onto the paving.

Sarah was only six then and had no real memory of her older sister, and they never talked of her death, not of her rape nor of her murder. Instead, the family left Russia and tried to put it out of their minds, and lives—the hatred they had experienced, been victims of, simply because they were Jews; the theft of their land and their personal goods, and most of all, the rape and murder of their oldest child. Impossible, of course, but they tried. And now this, the death of their only other child's oldest child. This brought it all back. No, there were no words. But where was God's mercy? Curse God and die, Job's wife had said. Perhaps she was right.

The two women, mother and daughter, wept for their losses together.

"Enough now," Rachel finally said, digging out the hankie she always kept buried in the bosom of her dress. She gave one to Sarah. Rachel then blew her nose noisily and sighed.

Sarah brushed at her eyes and cheeks. She knew her mother was right. It was time to pull herself together, at least enough to check on the children. How frightened they must be. She started to stand, but her mother's hand on her shoulder stopped her.

"Just sit another moment, darling," she said. "I have a little bite for us to eat together. Shared food, shared sorrow."

"Oh, I could no more eat," Sarah insisted, "than I could change the past!"

"You remember Sarah, your early training. After death, the Jews eat an egg. It represents God's promise of more life—a greater life to come. I brought us some zwieback toast and a little egg salad and a teapot. You can manage that!"

When Sarah continued to shake her head no, Rachel's voice grew firm.

"You must! There is not only yourself and your own private wishes to think about. There is a new baby inside you after all and the other two babies in the nursery, too. So no more foolishness! We

324

will have a little bit of food together, then I shall go home to your father, and you can check on your family."

Although each bite seemed to Sarah destined to choke her, she did as her mother bid. To her surprise, the food and the warmth of the camomile tea, did bring her a bit of ease.

"Thank God for you, Mamma," she said, in what was surely the most heartfelt compliment she had ever given to anyone.

Rachel smiled at her daughter, grateful that they should be such comfort to each other. But her heart continued to ache as she was sure Sarah's did.

By week's end the *Times-Dispatch* noted:

> *Death crept into the home of Mr. and Mrs. Farrel Hurstwood the afternoon of June 29, 1901. Through the sunlit rooms stole the Great Shadow, taking the Hurstwoods' eldest child, their darling son, Lawrence Seewald Hurstwood, into its cold arms.*
>
> *The child's body found its permanent home in the Hollywood Cemetery. The Reverend Archibald Lansford, rector of St. James's Church, offered prayers and what words of comfort he could to the bereaved parents and their accompanying group of mourners.*
>
> *May God welcome his new little angel!*

July passed in a slow and painful haze of heat and anguish. Sarah forced herself to be a part of the children's lives. The day would end, and she would gratefully succumb to the charms of Lethe.

Sleep seemed to offer the only possible escape from pain—sleep or death. At times her dreams were so unhappy that she felt only death would provide her with release. But then she would force herself again to get up and tend to the children. No, she could not bear to think of them motherless.

So July passed and most of August as well. She wrote nothing in her diary. She read nothing. She hardly noticed if Farrel was at home or away. She refused to see George. Then at the end of August, her will seemed to fail her entirely one morning.

The last dream she remembered was of little Lawrence hanging from a tree suspended over a cliff as she hurried up the hill to reach him.

"Wait," she screamed, but her words were whipped from her by an angry wind. "Hold on. Mamma's coming."

Thorns tore at her dress and at her hands as she began to crawl up the steepest part of the ledge. Then, just as she was about to reach out and save her boy, he fell. She shuddered awake.

Sarah struggled to open her eyes as she heard the household noises start up, but she could not seem to put enough caring into the process. She continued to lie in bed with her eyes closed, listening to the sounds. They will think I am asleep, she thought, and try to be quieter so as not to disturb me.

She drifted back into another uneasy dream. She was in a room with a glass wall, bigger than any window she had ever seen. She stood behind the glass, and she looked out on a city she had never visited. A steep cobblestone hill ran straight up from her room to a point out of sight, high above her line of vision. On the street were tracks—trolley tracks. And by the time she noticed them she could hear the clang of the trolley far up the hill. It began a mad descent, crazily clanging its bell. The trolley, out of control, headed straight for her behind her wall of glass. She searched wildly for a way to escape, but she could find none. In a moment glass shards would pierce her and the powerful metal car would crush her.

Then she woke. Farrel sat on the edge of the bed.

"Sarah," he said, "I'm sorry to wake you, but you called out so piteously I knew you must be having nightmares."

She nodded, trying to bring herself out of that other place, that dream place. Farrel opened the drapes to let some light in.

"Open the window, too," Sarah suggested. "We need the air. I can hardly breathe."

Farrel did as she asked without comment.

"Would you like me to have Clara bring you breakfast?" he asked.

The summer heat had not fully developed yet as it was still early morning, and so a soft breeze fluttered the lacy curtains. Morning birds still twittered occasionally. Sarah rested against the headboard, her eyes closed, taking in the morning without thought. Thinking, she told herself, is where the trouble always begins. The birds and beasts are luckier than we. I must avoid thought

327

and just look about me at the earth's beauties. Otherwise, I will absolutely not be able to go on at all.

"Sarah?" Her silence had begun to alarm Farrel, who felt all too clearly his incompetence in dealing with grief—either his own or Sarah's. He frowned. Sarah opened her eyes and looked at him. She saw the deep ridges creasing his face and realized for the first time that Farrel had aged a great deal. He was no longer the young man she had first seen at the streetcar site. My goodness, she reminded herself, that was almost fifteen years ago!

"Somehow I cannot seem to muster the energy to get myself up, though I know that I should. Perhaps you could help me." There was a question in her voice. Almost a note of pleading.

"Of course, dear," Farrel replied at once. "Shall I select some clothing? I am not sure that I will be terribly good at this." He laughed briefly and the idea of Farrel dressing her even forced a smile onto Sarah's face.

"You will do fine, I am certain. My rust-colored smock and that dark-brown gored skirt should do. There is no need for any more black in our household. It frightens the children and it cannot change a thing." She sighed and Farrel remained silent. Their eyes met in sorrow. He moved to the wardrobe and began searching for the clothes she had named.

"Are you sure you wouldn't rather have one of the servants help you?" he asked nervously. He had never invaded her shelves and drawers before.

"No," Sarah answered. "I would feel as though I

had to put on a performance of one sort or another for them. With you, I can be myself." As she said it, she realized it was true and that it was the nicest thing she had been able to say or think about her husband for a long, long time.

He sensed it, too. They were closer than he could remember them being. He found her clothing and helped her remove her satin gown. She began to dress using Farrel's arm to steady her. She was almost done when she doubled over in pain.

"Oh," Sarah gasped. "What—"

"What is it, sweetheart?"

"I don't know." She staggered back to the bed and sat down heavily.

"Here, Sarah, let me help you up. Maybe you're just weak. Let's move downstairs."

He lifted her part way up from the bed, then saw a sight that so alarmed him he froze. He gently lowered her back to the bed and said, "I think it would be better for you to stay here after all. I'm going to fetch the doctor to check on you."

Another pain hit her and she muffled a scream.

"What is it? Don't leave me. I'm afraid." Words rushed out of her mouth like a stream coursing down a mountain path.

He patted her shoulder. Struggling for control of his voice, he said, "You're bleeding. There's a puddle of blood on the bed beneath you. Please, darling, just lie still for a moment. I'll telephone the doctor and be right back. All right? All right?" He was frantic to leave, but he needed to feel that she would give him permission. At last, at her almost invisible nod, he raced from the room.

The baby born the next day struggled for each breath and between breaths lay like an exhausted swimmer who had lost a race. Sarah, too, lay exhausted and pale, looking as though she were deciding whether each breath were worth the effort it took.

Sam took Farrel and the Seewalds aside and told them to prepare for the worst. Two more burials, Farrel thought bitterly. Sam explained that he was doing his best, but the baby, a tiny girl, was not really ready for this world. The baby had arrived near the end of August, but was not due until the end of September. And Sarah, well, Sarah had lost a great deal of blood due to the hemorrhaging, but the worst part was that she didn't have the spirit to fight. The four people gathered together in a circle, sank into a silence which clearly expressed their distress.

"It's too much," Farrel muttered, which summed up everyone's feelings as well as any words could.

"Talk to her, Farrel," Rachel urged. "Tell her you need her. Take the children in to her. Let her see their faces."

Farrel agreed with his mother-in-law's plan. It was certainly better than standing here in misery not doing anything at all. At least it allowed him some room for action.

"Sam," Dave asked, "is there anything we can do to help the baby?"

"No," Sam answered. "It's all up to Sarah. If she

330

will nurse it, that would be its best chance. So far, she refuses even to look at it."

"Well, Farrel," Dave said, turning to his son-in-law, "it looks like you are the man in charge. It is all up to you, son. Go to her, and take her our prayers."

Farrel entered the dimly lit room with as little noise as possible. He stood a moment gazing at Sarah. She lay with her head half-buried in the pillow and what showed of her face was even paler than the white linen. Her hair's tangled curls spread across the pillow like tendrils from some plant. The air had the sickish sweet smell that seemed to accompany births, but which always had to Farrel the smell of death about it. He decidedly wished he were back in Europe, or in New York, or anywhere but here sent to do what he was least qualified to do—convince Sarah of how much he needed her.

How did my life become this messy thing? he asked himself, but just then Sarah stirred and he put away his concerns for himself.

"Sarah," he called to her. "Sweetheart, are you awake? Can you hear me?"

She struggled to turn part way toward him. Her eyes opened and he thought he had never seen a more ghastly look than the one she cast on him then. Hatred, he saw there, raw hatred and contempt—along with something else he could not name. Was it pity? he wondered.

"Yes, Farrel," she answered weakly, "I am always awake unfortunately. It is not as easy to die as I thought it would be. Just look!" She sat bolt upright then, spreading her arms wide. "Here I am still to confound you and continue on in my own misery." She began to laugh maniacally. The sound terrified Farrel who considered bolting from the room. Then just as fast as her laughter started, it stopped, or rather changed to hiccuping sobs. She fell back upon the pillows, and her eyes closed once more.

He moved to her side and knelt by her head. "Please, Sarah, do not punish me any more than I have already been punished." He stroked his mustache and tried to think of what to say. But the muddle of sensations pouring through his mind as little resembled thought as the goldfish in the nursery bowl resembled whales. "Perhaps you cannot possibly believe me because of my absences during past months and years, but I need you, Sarah. The children need you."

He pictured his life as a set of badly laid tracks. No engineer could find a way across them, no piece of machinery could survive on their surfaces.

"Did you bury the new baby next to Lawrence?" Sarah asked in a flat voice. Farrel thought she must be delirious. Her voice still had a hysterical edge to it.

"Sarah!" Farrel's voice revealed his shock. "The baby is alive. The baby is a girl, Sarah. A tiny, tiny baby girl. She needs you, too, Sarah. If you won't nurse her and care for her Sam says she *will* die."

"Alive," Sarah breathed. "Thank God. She was supposed to die, though, I know that. God told me she was going to die."

"No, Sarah," Farrel responded, placing his cool hand on her hot brow. "That was the sickness speaking within you. You have been very weak. Surely if there is a God he would never punish like that. It was not God's voice you heard. Just a dream." Then he added, "Why would God want to punish us anyway? What have we done but try our best? Try out best—" His voice trailed off.

Farrel took her hands in his and tried to rub his own energy into them. Sarah lay unmoving.

"I don't have any words, Sarah. I never did know the right words to say to you. You were always the one who was so good with words. I only have one thing to beg of you, but I mean it from my heart. Please do not die!"

Her eyes still held tightly closed, Sarah's weak voice answered, "I won't."

He didn't know if she meant it or if she only spoke to get rid of him.

"Sarah, would you like to talk to the minister?" He paused, then added, "Or your parents' rabbi?"

She weakly shook her head from side to side. Farrel, uncertain what to do next, let his head sink onto his chest. He closed his eyes; he gave up.

"Bring me the baby," Sarah said clearly. It was the first time her voice had sounded normal since Lawrence's death. She pushed herself up in the bed. "Wait," she said, stopping Farrel as he headed for the door. "Perhaps we should talk about a name first. Do you have a name in mind? I have forgotten the names we considered back when we first knew I was expecting." She remembered quite clearly the discussion she had

had with George about names, though. He had told her that if it was a girl he would love to have her named Maureen. If it were a boy, he said, he dreamed of naming it George, of course, although he knew that was quite impossible! But Sarah could not remember any of Farrel's suggestions.

"I don't remember our earlier choices either," he said, "but I thought maybe we might name her Laura. After Lawrence, you know."

"That is a lovely thought," she said. "But I hardly think that I could live with it easily—remembering, every time I called her name. It would be so painful."

"Yes," Farrel agreed, "I hadn't thought of it that way."

"Perhaps something similar, but not quite so close would do. Perhaps Maura," she suggested. "What do you think of that name?"

"Maura," Farrel repeated. "It is different. Pretty, too. Yes, I think that's what we should call her. Maura! Shall I go get Maura now? She refuses to take anything from the bottle. Spits it all up. If you nurse her, Sarah, the doctor says she has a chance."

"Yes, Farrel, go get her. I must try to nurse her. Go get our little Maura."

Farrel felt a lump fill his throat. It was going to be all right.

He had lost a son, but at least he was not going to lose everything. Thank God, he thought, as he walked toward the nursery to get the baby.

Twenty-one

God was frequently on George's mind, too, during these crucial days. God, he prayed, do not make Sarah or the baby pay for my sins. Keep them safe and well. Punish me, if you must. Then he paused midway through his prayers and thought, truly I am already punished severely by being separated from Sarah. Punished by being kept apart from the woman I love and from my only child, if this new baby is actually mine. Surely, he thought, separation from the thing you love is the most terrible punishment.

George seldom prayed. His parents had insisted on a ritual of daily prayer during his childhood, but George had simply gotten into the habit of calling prayer what others would have labeled daydreaming. His parents, Southern Baptists, had been active in the church, but George had never caught the fever. He could still remember the fierce struggle over the issue of whether or not the whites and the blacks should worship together.

335

When the church split into separate congregations in order to keep the two races apart, George decided that God—or at least his representatives in the churches on this earth—no longer interested him. Fortunately for family harmony, George left the country to continue his schooling abroad a short time later. So the issue of worship did not become the focus of family strife.

Having now caught himself in prayer, George reconsidered his attitude toward God. Really, he decided, his prayer for Sarah was a fervent wish—his old daydreaming habit again. He had no real belief in a caring God. No one in the universe responded with a compassionate heart to any individual's desires. No, no one responded to his words—no one even heard those words. He felt absolutely sure of that. If God was the name given to an all-good, all-powerful creature who took care of the beings of this earth, then he did not believe in God. I am an atheist, he decided. Maybe even something beyond an atheist because the only life force I see at work in this world is the blind groping of sheer instinct. Survival. Survival at any cost. What was the famous phrase of that Darwin fellow? Oh, yes, survival of the fittest—the fittest being the nastiest, meanest, most vulgar, and most vicious beings.

He sighed. The recent events had certainly darkened his mood, he realized. But just let Sarah and the baby be all right, he implored an uncaring universe, and I will reconsider my attitudes about everything.

*   *   *

The next day, as Farrel sat in his office, he addressed his thoughts not to a heavenly Father but to his departed earthly one.

"It is really most peculiar, Father," he thought, "but I feel closer to you since I became a father myself than I ever did when I was simply your son. Closer to you now, with you gone from me, than when we spoke together. You know, Mother always told me that I was just like you and, well, as a father, I am sorely afraid that she is absolutely right. Maybe neither you nor I was ever meant to sire children—or at least not to care for them. We have not the necessary loving nature. Perhaps each of us carried a sense of some other destiny closer to our hearts!"

He paced the length of the room and back again. It was such a customary routine that the pattern of the rug showed his tracks. Farrel stopped at his desk and picked up a hand-carved meerschaum pipe which he filled from a British tobacconist's jar. He lit up and puffed for a while until he was sure the tobacco had caught. Then he resumed his measured march and with it his thoughts.

"I do love the children in my own way, Father, and I love Sarah also. I suppose you would have said the same thing about me and Mother. I must admit that my deepest excitement still resides with electricity. My mind is always at play considering the range of miracles that can be brought about through its use. I wonder if you had any such feelings. Then we die, and what do we leave behind, eh? For my father-in-law it seems to be enough to know that he has lived a good life. For

337

George, too, life seems its own reward. But for me! No! I want to leave something behind. Something important. More important than a bunch of children who will carry on my name. Any beast can do as much!" Even as the thought crossed his mind, he knew it was a shameful thing to feel. Especially, less than a month after burying his eldest son! A fearful thought to hold at any time, but especially at this time. "God forgive me." He sighed as he collapsed into his leather swivel chair. He felt the ease of being in his office, his rightful place. Comfort almost immediately seeped into his bones whenever he was at work. "Why is everything else so complicated?" he wondered.

A knock at the door called him back to himself.

"Enter," he called, straightening in his chair.

"Farrel." George opened the door and poked his head inside. "I am so sorry to trouble you about trivia, but those new contracts on the interurbans that will run between here and Charlottesville really should get signed. Can you go over them with me today?"

"Come in, come in," Farrel said. "Trivia indeed! Those contracts took some connivance to arrange, I imagine, didn't they? That was quite a good job you did there. Bring them here and we can go over them line by line and then get them out by messenger before the day is over."

George felt pleased by Farrel's praise. He drew a chair up and sat next to him at the desk.

"Before we start," he said in a solemn voice, "I want you to know how damned heartbroken I am for you. Just that—and now we can go on. Oh, but

338

first tell me how Sarah and the baby are doing."

"They are better. Both of them. Sarah has started to nurse the baby so I think the crisis may have passed. We have even picked a name!"

"Yes?" George's spirits lifted just listening to Farrel sounding so much more hopeful than he had in this past while.

"Maura. The little girl will not be an *it* anymore. The baby's name is Maura. Sarah suggested it!"

George's hands, full of legal-size documents and yellow pads, began to tremble. Quickly, hoping that Farrel would not notice, George placed the papers on the desk. She has picked a name to please me, he thought. It is almost the name I suggested. It must be the answer to my question. Sarah has sent me a sign.

"I would like to see them, if I may," he said.

"Of course, my dear man, you must go by today. Stay to dinner. I believe that Sarah will be coming downstairs for the first time tonight! You are a member of the family, you know. I confess that I wonder if Sarah would have stood by me during all this travel, if it were not for your visits to keep her occupied!"

George could feel the flush crawl up his neck and cover his entire face. He bent his head over the papers and said brusquely, "Well, if we are planning to get these contracts out anytime today, we had best get to them right away, don't you think?"

Farrel, seeing George's embarrassment, interpreted it as the natural modesty of a simple man. George, he thought, you have been a good and true friend to me. Though George's conscience would have made him deny it just then, that was the truth of the matter.

Within two weeks of Maura's premature birth, the world heard the electrifying news that the President of the United States of America, President William McKinley, had been shot during a public reception at the Buffalo Exposition. As he lingered between life and death, Richmond citizens held prayer vigils for him as did other people throughout the nation. Nonetheless, the President succumbed on September 13, 1901. No one seemed to know much about the captured assassin except that his name was foreign-sounding with a lot of C's and Z's in it.

Suddenly, Teddy Roosevelt the hero of the Spanish-American War was the new President. George felt cheered by the fact that Roosevelt had founded one of the early wildlife-preservation groups. Well, he thought, at least this fellow will be strongly on the side of conservation.

Farrel felt cheered by the fact that Roosevelt was a man who believed in the American destiny to reach across the world and take charge of the development of other nations. With this new bold leader in the White House, he reasoned, George and I can begin to set up international alliances on a grander scale than ever before.

"I wish to preach," the new President announced, "not the doctrine of ignoble ease, but the doctrine of the strenuous life." Those were the words that set the tone for the times ahead.

A political change closer to home that was less pleasing to the two partners was the development of a strong antialcoholic movement. The Anti-Saloon League of Virginia began a campaign to make every county dry and were having good success at it. The issue soon divided the rural Virginians, who were mostly antidrink, from the urban Virginians, who felt the whole issue should remain a matter of personal preference and that no government rules should be involved. George and Farrel remained publicly neutral, but privately they contributed to the opposing group, the Virginia Local Self-Government League. As county after county went dry, they began to see they were on the losing side of this battle and quietly established ties to local bootleggers. Farrel went so far as to put money into the establishment of a speak-easy. He felt sure that no matter how people talked in public, no matter how people chose to vote, in fact, they would still crave the pleasures of drink.

The Blind Tiger, Farrel's speak-easy, was not to open until the first of the new year, but Farrel surprised himself by finding great pleasure in planning the red-and-black decor, the arrangement of the seats and the setup of the bar, the type of entertainment to offer. It was a world unlike any he had worked with and he found its somewhat shady ambience a secret delight.

October brought the surprising warmth of Indian summer. By then, both Sarah and the new baby had grown stronger. The sunny afternoon

341

lured Sarah into the yard where she lay on the chaise arranged for her comfort there. She felt her body and her spirit reviving.

Although she tried not to think about it, her inner life was still a torment of jumbled feelings and anxieties. She had begun to write in her journal again in the hope that the thoughts she could share with no person, she could share there. Perhaps, she thought, she could in that way free herself from them.

Maura was almost two months old, she realized; Lawrence four months in his grave. She moved the chaise longue a bit so it would be out of the sun's direct path. She enjoyed the shade of the huge weeping willow that dominated the yard. She had her diary with her today although it seldom left her room. In fact, she hid it in her bureau drawer when she was not writing in it. But today when she decided to bring her diary up to date, she wanted to feel the air and listen to the natural sounds around her. She told herself that that was a sure sign she was getting better. It was only recently that she had begun to notice the world around her again.

All to the good, she told herself. The half-life I have lived these past months is a poor way to be, as rotten as a wormy apple. The sun still shone; the birds warbled; Jessica and Franklin played their innocent games and filled the world with precious laughter.

Perhaps because she was feeling more positive, Sarah chose this day to reread some of her previous diary entries, entries made only intermittently since Lawrence's accident. That was how she thought about it now: The Accident! She could still not refer to her child's death more directly than that. Not even when she went to visit his grave.

She had planted autumn flowers there last week, hoping that their golden colors would somehow cheer his little spirit. She had planted rosemary there, too. Rosemary for remembrance. She knew it would probably not last through the winter, but it was something she had wanted to do. Being near his grave, feeling the loamy earth on her hands, had made Lawrence seem closer somehow, not lost to her forever as she knew he really was.

She opened the journal that lay on her lap. "Dear Diary," she read on a page that was dated July 4, 1901. "Independence Day! Would that I could gain independence from this bodily existence and leave this life today! That is my most fervent wish. I want to join my baby boy in a better place. Sometimes I dream that I am holding him on my lap and we are floating up and up and up.

"Sometimes, though, in my dreams a wicked demon laughs at me and says, 'Damned! Sarah Leah Seewald Hurstwood, you are damned forever and ever!'

"Then I fear dying more than I fear living. The best is never to have been born. I remember reading that in school, and I believe it is true."

Sarah skipped over to an entry dated October 15, 1901, only last week:

"In my secret heart, I have felt that my troubles

343

have been brought on because of my times with George. I was a wicked woman, I told myself and I even feared touching my baby, because I believed that Maura would then be cursed, too.

"Finally, shortly after my anniversary, fearing I was going mad, I decided to visit the rabbi and swear him to secrecy. It is a vow I believe he never would break.

"I had met him upon occasion, most memorably at Lawrence's funeral, but I really did not know him, nor he me. We sat in his study with the sun forming beautiful colors on his carpet as it streamed through the stained-glass windows.

"'Tell me,' he said quietly, and all at once I felt that I could."

Sarah closed the diary and remembered back to that day that had meant so much to her. That day last week when she had sat in the rabbi's study.

She had settled comfortably into a soft leather chair while he sat down behind his desk. He did not appear the least bit forbidding.

"Take your time," Rabbi Dorfman said in a soothing voice.

"I am a wicked woman," Sarah blurted out. The rabbi continued to regard her calmly, waiting for her to continue.

"A wicked woman," she went on, "and everything that has happened to my family is because of me. God is punishing me. It is a curse!"

"Just a moment now," the rabbi interrupted. "I need to know more about what wickedness it is that God is punishing you for."

"I can hardly bear to speak of it," Sarah said;

then she broke into tears.

"Oh, is it such a terrible sin that you alone have thought of it? Has no one else perhaps ever mentioned such a thing to me?"

"Others?" she asked raising her eyes to his. "I have never thought of others. For me, it is a terrible sin. Terrible enough, I am sure for me to be doomed to hell for eternity."

"Tch, tch," he clicked his tongue at her. "Sarah, I know it has been a long time since you studied your religion, but I cannot believe you have forgotten that there is no such concept as burning in hell in the Hebrew faith. Where did you pick up these notions with which you torment yourself?"

"I am an adulteress!" She spat the word at him sure that now he would curse her and send her away.

"Ah," he said, nodding his head slowly. "Adultery. Yes, that is a sorrow with which I am familiar. Is that the 'wickedness' you believe God is cursing you for?"

The miserable Sarah nodded, not daring to lift her eyes.

"Please, my dear woman," the rabbi said and Sarah heard kindness in his voice, "do not underestimate God's goodness. To my own mind, I might add, adultery, which is a matter of giving one's attentions and—yes, even one's love—to too many, seems much less wicked than giving no love at all to anyone. Too many people live that way, without sharing themselves at all. That seems so much worse to me. Doesn't that seem worse, to you?"

Sarah snuffled. The rabbi went on talking softly to her.

"Not to mention the terrible sins that rob the world of love: murder being the most frightful one. No, Sarah, God is not punishing you. Lawrence died. Who knows the reason behind such things? God's ways are beyond us. But to punish you? Ridiculous!"

"Wait!" Sarah cried out. "There is worse."

The rabbi eased himself back into his chair and waited. What new surprises did this mild-looking woman have in store for him? he wondered. He wanted so much to be a help to his people. He prayed silently that God would give him wisdom and the right words.

"When Lawrence fell from the tree—" Sarah paused and swallowed hard; what she was about to say, she had never uttered aloud before. "I was pregnant then." The rabbi nodded, encouraging her to go on. "It . . . the baby . . . the baby is not Farrel's child."

"I see," the rabbi said, needing time to find the words. The right words. "This other man, the father of the child, does he know?"

"No," Sarah said shaking her head firmly back and forth. "He guesses, but I have not told him. I have not told a single soul until you. Do you think I should?" Her voice was pleading. She wanted him to provide her with the answers she had been unable to find alone. "So often," she went on, "I have thought that if I just could tell everyone everything, then I would be at peace." She fell silent.

"No, Sarah, That would bring chaos, not peace. Then the torment would be a part of everyone's life. You spoke before about punishment, and that may very well be yours. To have to bear that knowledge and *not* tell anyone. That is the difficult thing you have to do."

They sat in silence awhile.

"This man," he went on, "what are your feelings for him?"

Sarah blushed. "I care about him deeply. Please do not ask me to stop seeing him"—she suddenly burst out with more animation than she had exhibited during the rest of the conversation—"because I do not think I can do that. I will not leave my husband, and I will be as good a wife as I can and as good a mother, but I cannot promise to give up this other person."

"I can see you care about him very much. If it is love, Sarah, then you must struggle along as best you can. Loving outside a marriage is both heaven and hell in itself. You need not worry about a punishment in the afterlife!"

They talked a little more before getting ready to say good-bye. Finally, he concluded, "I know you are sorely troubled, Sarah, and I hope you will view me as a friend. Come here anytime. Of course," he added, seeing her to the door, "whatever you say here is sacred. It will never be repeated."

"Rabbi," Sarah said, shaking his hand and smiling for the first time in a long time, "you have done more to bring me peace than I can ever tell you. God bless you."

"And you, Sarah," the rabbi answered, waving

347

at her as she walked down the curved cobblestone path toward the street.

Remembering that visit, Sarah felt gratitude flood through her again. She turned to the first fresh page in the diary and began to write:

October 20, 1901

Dear Diary,

Maura is beginning to look like a baby at last instead of like the scrawny monkey she resembled at first. She is hungry all the time, which makes sense, of course, since she has so much catching up to do. I nursed her for a while, but it seemed to take so much out of me that Dr. Sam found us a wet nurse to take over. Thank goodness, for it allows me to have my night's sleep when I am able to fall asleep. I feel exhausted much of the time, yet when I climb under the counterpane sleep eludes me. Mother says it is the leftover anxiety from the bad time still hanging on. She says it will pass, like all things, with time. I suppose that she is right.

Farrel has not begun to travel again the way he did before. I feel glad about that; yet I never seem to tell him so. Perhaps I am still carrying too much bitterness around. It is almost as though I do not want to tell him how glad I am to have him around evenings, because that would imply I had forgiven him for the many other times when he was not there. Oh, Sarah, if that is it, what a small person you are! Be it resolved, tonight I will express my gratitude to Farrel. (Unless he chooses to announce his plans for another trip!)

George visits occasionally; his eyes are sad. I have not told him of my visit to the rabbi, nor of his part in Maura's existence. He knows, I feel sure, but I have not spoken the words to him. I wonder if I ever shall.

A stir of activity over by the house drew Sarah's eyes up from her journal. She saw George being dragged along toward her by Jessica. Jessica loves him so much, Sarah thought, as she watched them approach. She closed her book and surreptitiously slid it beneath the fullness of her skirts.

"George," she exclaimed happily.

He beamed, glad she seemed pleased to see him. Her reaction is surely no match for my own, he thought, full of the joy he always felt when he was close to Sarah.

"Please do not move, Sarah. I want to gaze at you just as you are. A virtual odalisque."

"Why, George," Sarah responded in mock horror, "she has no clothes on, if I know the lady to whom you refer!"

George giggled and blushed and swept Jessica into his arms. He tickled and kissed her to cover the moment. Then he set her on her feet and said, "Now, Jessie, run along and play, please. I must talk to your mother alone. I have dark secrets to share with her and you must not listen." His spy act was one of Jessica's favorites, and she clapped her hands in appreciation. Then she ran back toward the house. George sat down in the chair near to Sarah.

"Sarah, Sarah," he sighed, "thank goodness I see a smile on your face again. I really can ill afford the time to visit, but—" He let his thought go unfinished. "So, since we have only moments you must tell me everything quickly."

"I have so little to tell, George. Maura is beginning to look like a real baby at last. That is my only news. Do you want to see her?"

"Need you ask?" George answered her. "Maura, what a lovely name!" He smiled knowingly and now it was Sarah's turn to blush. They had never before discussed the baby when no one else could hear them.

"Come," she said, jumping up in a gesture that reminded him of the earlier, happier Sarah. As she did so, the diary fell to the grass and George bent to retrieve it.

"Ah, your diary!" he said as he handed it back to her. "Someday I should like to learn the secrets contained in that volume."

"Yes, I must confess that your name appears there more than once," Sarah teased. "Perhaps someday you will know the secrets that I have written here. But not today!" Sarah stated emphatically as she took George's arm. They both felt exceedingly happy to be back to their old comfortable selves. Arm in arm, they walked toward the house to view Maura together.

Twenty-two

As winter closed in on Richmond, Sarah anticipated the seasonal holidays with mixed emotions. The addition of children had further complicated her feelings about the role of religion in her life. She had moments of surprising pain in regard to Lawrence's burial as a Christian. She wanted the other children to understand and love their Jewish heritage as well as their father's religion. She began to wonder why she had been so willing to erase that part of herself. She realized that when her parents had brought her to America, they had stressed how she must quickly learn to act like the other children. Even as a child, she knew that meant do not act foreign . . . do not act Jewish. How ironic, she thought, that now her parents had reclaimed their Jewishness, and she still spent her days acting non-Jewish.

After the early years, when she and Farrel had fought over her reluctance to accompany him to church, Sarah had abandoned any attempt to explain her confusion in this area. She could never seem to explain her feelings to her husband in any satisfactory way.

Now that she had three children who would never know about being Jewish at all unless she told them, it seemed worth another try. Sarah listed to herself ways in which being Jewish was special as she readied herself to confront Farrel.

There was the beauty of the Sabbath ritual—a day of rest dedicated to praising God for the beauties of the earth. And the lighting of the candles themselves, the prayer for everyone's safekeeping, and the soft circles of light throughout the evening as the tapers continued to burn. The idea of welcoming the spirit of God into the home every week.

There was the love of learning that her parents had always stressed as a particularly Jewish trait. There was the nonpunishing quality of the religion—no witch burnings or inquisitions in Jewish history—that, especially, Sarah treasured.

It was the beginning of December, and Hanukkah was to begin in a few days. But they had never celebrated Hanukkah before in the Hurstwood family. Christmas, however, received elaborate attention. Farrel directed the servants in a massive effort at transforming the house into a merry woods. Wreaths brightened every door, trails of leaves and berries crossed each mantel, mistletoe hung from doorframes, and a magnificent fir tree scraped the ceiling in the front parlor.

Sarah realized that Farrel probably did not even know what Hanukkah was, and that she herself knew little enough about it. Most of what she knew was blurred by the nostalgia with which people review their childhood holidays, but she could remember lighting the little orange candles which seemed always to bounce their light around the room in a jolly way. She remembered good food, especially potato *latkes* and sour cream, and a present of Hanukkah *gelt*—usually a bright copper coin—for the children. Yes, it was a memory that she would like her children to have in their hearts, as well.

So on the very day that Hanukkah was to start at sundown—the time when all Jewish holidays have their beginning—Sarah went to see Rabbi Dorfman.

"Sarah, welcome," he called to her from behind his desk as she stood at his study door. "How is the baby you were so worried about the last time you were here? Come in, come in."

"She is a lovely little bug who scoots around under everybody's feet." Sarah laughed.

"I really already knew that, I must admit. Come, sit down. Your mother never misses a chance to brag, you know. A proud grandmother!"

Sarah sat down in the chair beside the desk. She could hardly believe the pile of things that cluttered the desk's wooden surface: papers, letters, books of every description. "How do you ever manage to make room to work?"

"I just work right over it. Worse than that, though, my desk mirrors my mind. Too much clutter and too little sense of order. *Oi veh!*" He rolled his eyes up, shrugged, and lifted his hands up in a comical way as though it were out of his control.

"Rabbi, I need your help in a practical Jewish matter," Sarah began. She told him of her concern for the children's non-Jewishness, and how she wanted this year to mark a new beginning. She wanted to celebrate Hanukkah with them. "But I have no *things,"* she wailed, "and I really have only a muddled childhood memory of the ceremony to go by."

"The things—*oi,* such a term!—I can supply. Your mother could really do the rest."

"No," Sarah said firmly. "That might cause bad feeling in my husband. The issue is between my husband and me, after all, between us and our children. I would prefer to leave my parents out of it at present."

"Very well," the rabbi agreed. Then he began to recount the miraculous event which the Hanukkah celebration commemorated.

He outlined the miracle of the oil that the lighting of the candles recreates symbolically. He taught her the words to say as she lit the candles— one candle plus the leader candle the first day, two plus the leader the second day, and so on for the eight days of the holiday. Sarah listened studiously, almost like a little girl in class.

She purchased a menorah, the special candelabrum that held the nine narrow candles, and a box of forty-four candles, the needed number for the total number of nights. She also bought the children each a *dreidel,* the little spinning top that children played a good-luck game with at Hanukkah. Then, with her collection of goodies gathered in a string bag which she clutched in her hand, Sarah headed home to confront Farrel with the idea of celebrating Hanukkah this year.

"I just do not understand," he answered after having listened to her for a while, "why you suddenly have become so Jewish!" He paced before her, but she told herself not to let that make her nervous.

She smiled slightly at his words. "My dear husband, I assure you that I have always been one hundred percent Jewish, so I can hardly be becoming more so."

"By birth, of course," he acknowledged, "but it was never much of a reality in my mind. Nor, I had thought, in yours."

"You are quite right about that, but I regret it. I feel now that it was probably a mistake not to have retained more of my identification with my heritage. Now I want to be sure that at least the children have a bit of it."

"Mistake, eh? What if I told you that I believe it was a mistake that I did not insist on your converting to Christianity when you would have done so." He stopped before her. His glare, which once would have frightened her into silence, had lost a great deal of its power. In fact, Sarah thought, there is something infinitely sad about that attempt to control me with a look. Perhaps it no longer works because I am less acutely conscious of all that there is to lose. Life, her life and the lives of the children, that was really all she had; all she could ever lose.

"There have been many mistakes. We need not go into them," Sarah answered in a voice that had no trace of hysteria, no trace of fear in it. In both their minds the thought appeared, unbidden, that perhaps their marriage itself had been a terrible mistake, the worst mistake of all!

"Unless you forbid me, Mr. Hurstwood, I intend to celebrate the Hanukkah holiday with the children. I will tell them it is a Jewish holiday and that we are celebrating it because I am a Jewish woman—" Sarah stopped at the sound of her own words, amazed. She doubted that she had ever made such a statement before in her life. A Jewish woman. So to identify herself! That certainly is a statement the young girl she had been would never have made. Perhaps she had married Farrel under false conditions, she pondered. No, she had not been the person she was now. No, the earlier assumptions were correct for then, but she had changed. She was changing. Were you allowed to change, she wondered, in a marriage? Or when we promise to love forever are we really promising that we will never change?

"But they are not Jewish children. They are Christians. Oh, my God, I can hardly believe that we are having this argument, saying these words. Only our parents ever felt that this issue would ever have any importance to us. Yet here we are." He fell silent. "Celebrate if you wish. I will not be included, thank you. Do not push this issue too far, though, Sarah. Not too far!" Two circles of red appeared high on his cheeks. He felt a fury that made him yearn to pound his fist on surfaces, shout, shake this impassive woman before him; so well-known and yet so completely the stranger—his wife.

"They are half-Jewish, the children! I will explain it to them. If they have additional questions, they can ask your minister."

He felt she was pushing him beyond endurance. For the first time in a long time, he wished himself free of all this, free from encumbrance, free of the woman who caused him so much pain, who aroused in him so much fury.

She, on the other hand, felt she had just made an enormous concession. She had compromised so much that she even feared she had compromised herself. After all, they were more than half-Jewish, she thought, as she remembered that the rabbi had told her the Jewish law regarding inheritance. Any child born of a Jewish mother, he had said, was a Jewish child by Jewish law.

Throughout the afternoon she had brooded over that fact. Her children were Jews, really Jews—even little Lawrence, despite his christening as a baby. He had never chosen to become a Christian. Rabbi Dorfman had told her these things to reassure her in her concern over Lawrence.

Farrel continued towering above her during these moments when her mind drifted back to her talks with the rabbi. Farrel imagined that she was deciding what to say to him, how to placate him, but he could not have been further from the truth. Sarah had almost forgotten his presence. When she remained silent, Farrel mistakenly took it for

357

plain stubbornness.

Without a word but inwardly ranting, Farrel Hurstwood stormed out of the house. Sarah pursed her lips.

She would have to hurry. It was almost sundown, and she wanted to talk to the children before it was time to light the candles.

Soon she had them beside her. Jessica, being the oldest and almost six years old, took charge of the almost two-year-old Franklin as she always did, bossing him around. Sarah had left the baby in the nursery. Six months was too young for explanations and celebrations.

"Children," Sarah said to her son and daughter, "tonight we are going to have a special kind of party."

Sarah began by talking to the children about being Jewish herself. Then she told the story of the military victory and the desire of the people to thank God by rededicating the temple to Him. The Jews keep a flame going eternally, she explained, but they only found enough oil for one night. She spoke in a dramatic voice so the children would be entertained. She knew she was a good storyteller, and she had never before wanted so much for the children who were hearing her stories to listen carefully. It was a miracle, she said, but that little bit of oil burned for eight days. Long enough for the Jews to have found more oil to keep the flame alight. "So now," she concluded, "we light candles to remember the miracle. We call this time the Feast of Lights. And we can play games, too, and I even have a present for each of you!"

By now the little boy and girl were wiggling with excitement. A party! With presents! Sarah let them help her light the first candle and the leader, taught them how to play the *dreidel* game, gave them their little toys, and felt proud of herself for having begun their Jewish education in as painless a manner as possible.

By Christmas morning, Sarah was able to join in wholeheartedly with the family excitement. She felt a terrific sense of pleasure in her Hanukkah achievement. Farrel had ignored the nightly ceremony and now continued with his Christmas routine with the children as though this year were in no way different from any other.

After the present-opening, the children were sent off to play with their toys in the nursery, and George Spencer came to join the Hurstwoods for a Christmas brunch. Sarah had thought and thought about what gift to buy for George. Whatever she chose would be, of course, ostensibly from the Hurstwood family, but George would know that she had made the selection. She wanted it to be a gift that would somehow say to him what she had never been able to utter.

She finally decided she would give him a perfectly proper gift as the main offering. She chose a raw-silk cravat for that box. Then as her personal statement, she chose a photograph that George had taken of her with Maura on her lap and she had it framed in a beautiful cherry-wood frame. When George began to unwrap the box that contained the picture, Sarah became agitated.

What if Farrel realized the true significance? No, of course he could not, she reassured herself. But what if George betrayed himself in his surprised reaction? What if she leaped to her feet and shouted the truth? Was that what she really feared, she asked herself; was that what she really desired? To be free of her dreadful secret at last. To be free to start her life again with the man she so dearly loved. A man who would be the center of her life, and who would make her feel like the center of his. Oh God, yes. That was what she longed for, but that was what must forever be denied to her.

George thanked her warmly for both presents. Farrel seemed oblivious to any special meaning to the photograph.

"Well, I daresay that is one of George's better pictures. The subject matter probably made the photographer perform at his best, eh, George?"

"There can be no doubt about that," George agreed. "Your family provides me with my best models. Did you know, though," George added, sensing Sarah's discomfort and shifting the topic slightly in response, "that I have begun a series of photographs on the Negro servants in the Richmond area? The skin tones I find remarkable. Also, much of the suffering that they have experienced I find written large upon their features. It makes for damned fine pictures, let me tell you. But, as you say, Farrel, it is once again a case of the models improving the photographer's skills."

"You are far too modest. There is truly the touch of the artist about you."

"Sarah is right, George, about too much modesty. What fun is it to tease you, if you so quickly agree?"

The atmosphere in the room was warm and friendly. It had been too long a time since the three of them had shared such a good feeling. When Farrel left the room for a moment, George said, "More than words can say, Sarah! Thank you." She positively beamed at him, and he thought he would do almost anything to be the recipient of such gifts, such smiles.

That afternoon turned Sarah's thoughts toward the new year. She began to look forward to the approach of 1902 with at least some optimism, if not the absolute confidence she had once felt in the future. She would happily put 1901, the year that marked Lawrence's death, into the past. On New Year's Day, Sarah entered the new date in her journal with a flourish: January 1, 1902. Then she shuddered as she thought how the coldest days of winter lay in the two months ahead.

For heart's warmth, Sarah began to make plans for a Valentine's Day party which would be extra special because it would celebrate Franklin's second birthday. Sarah hardly needed much encouragement to design a party for mid-February. That time had always seemed to her the worst and grimmest section of the winter—the nadir of life, the time when it seemed hard to believe in the promise of spring.

So Sarah turned away from the windy out-of-doors and spent her days with the two oldest children. She showed them how to cut out fat red paper hearts, paste them on lace paper doilies and attach them to red satin ribbons which they would hang from the ceiling at various spots on the day of the party. With Clara's help, she showed them how to make and pull taffy. These preparations made with the children were the best part of the days in Sarah's mind. The party itself was a simple affair which gathered together just the family and a few close friends to share in birthday cake and champagne.

The day of the party the fireplaces blazed, and the crackle of the wood and the dancing flames added to the general merriment. Franklin, dressed in a blue velvet smock, long stockings, and a pair of high button shoes, looked like a big baby doll, but he tore open his presents with a manly energy that dispelled such an impression.

As everyone laughed and applauded his actions, Jessica leaned against her mother's hip. Sarah was saddened to see how much of Jessie's old playfulness had disappeared since her brother's death. The two children had been so close— almost like twins really. Jessica's moods now seemed divided mostly between a bossy arrogance toward Franklin and a whininess toward her mother. In company she turned shy and clung to her mother's skirts. Sarah took Jessica's hand and squeezed it, and the little girl looked up at her with bright eyes.

"I love you," Sarah whispered.

"I love you too, Mommy," Jessica answered.

Maura sat on her grandma's lap and contentedly sucked her thumb, oblivious to the party atmosphere. Sarah searched her baby face for telltale signs of paternity as she so often did. Once more she was reassured to see that the three children looked remarkably alike. In fact they all favored her.

Franklin was at work on his last present—a special gift from his father. It was a perfect model of a streetcar line in miniature. The car ran around a small circular track—electrically powered just like the real thing. Farrel had had it specially built for Franklin's birthday. It was a wonder, Sarah had to admit, and everyone admired its ingenuity. Unfortunately, Farrel never gave Franklin a chance to try it out. Well, tomorrow he would have it all to himself, Sarah reasoned.

When the presents lay in a clutter at the birthday boy's feet, Clara brought in the heart-shaped cake and Bessie and Sassafras watched from the doorway as their baby blew out the candles. Grandma Rachel transferred Maura to Sass's arms and took over the serving. She had Franklin carry the first piece over to his mother.

"Why thank you, son, and happy, happy birthday," Sarah said as she accepted the plate from Franklin's chubby little hands.

"I love you, Mommy," he said in his baby voice.

Sarah bent down and planted a kiss on his plump cheek, in part to hide the tears that had suddenly filled her eyes.

Twenty-three

Shortly after the party, Sarah received a letter from her friend Rose.

"Dear Sarah," Rose wrote from New York City, "I miss you, and I miss Richmond. Can you believe that I said I missed Richmond? I guess I have finally been long enough away to realize the charms it does possess. At times when I lie awake at night thinking through the day I have just spent in the crowded slums of this city, I can almost smell the spice-filled Richmond air. The spice factory was to me what the streetcars were to you, I think. Utter fascination. The smells of vanilla, of nutmeg, and of ginger come back to me now with a promise of enough space for every person to draw fresh breath. Am I making any sense?

"Yes, the city's teeming streets have begun to depress me. Particularly when the crisp snow has lain too long in the streets and turned into hills of black and sooty ice one must surmount in order to make one's way across the thoroughfare.

"There are, of course, compensations. I was right in believing that only the metropolis could offer me the chance to do meaningful work on a large scale. I am anxious to share with you the work I am doing—I mean in addition to my work on the newspaper. The feeling that I am making an important contribution balances the despair. At least most of the time it does.

"Lately, as I indicated, the despair has tipped the balance in its favor. Which brings me finally to the point of this discursive letter. I have some holiday time due me that I want to take soon. In March or in April at the latest. Whenever the first buds triumph over winter—ah, renewal—that is when I wish to be in Richmond. If it would be at all possible, I would like to stay with you, but if it would be too much trouble you must be a true friend and tell me so honestly.

"I had imagined myself staying at the grand new Jefferson Hotel. Oh what a vision I had of returning in triumph! The prodigal daughter returns and so forth. Then you sent me the account of the disastrous fire that burned it down. The clipping said that electrical wiring was at fault which made me shudder when I imagined that perhaps electricity would not be the savior we have made it out to be. Perhaps it would end up taking as many lives as the gas illumination it replaces! Well, I know I must not mention such issues within hearing of your husband, the electrical wizard.

"No, I promise to make no such comments. I

will be the perfect house guest: polite, humble, restrained, helpful. Oh God, I am becoming ill from this surfeit of virtue. Only when I am alone with you will I show my true, feisty, vulgar self.

"If I could not stay at the Jefferson, you see, the only place I could imagine feeling comfortable was with my dearest friend. I do hope you look forward to a reunion as much as I do."

Sarah wrote back at once:

> *Dear Rose,*
> *Come, come, come! The sooner, the better. How I welcome the possibility of a time with you to talk and talk to our hearts' content.*
> *We have an empty guest room which is yours for as long as you wish. I myself took charge of its decoration, and I am sad that the room has seldom seen cheerful use.*
> *Write me at once and tell me the date of your arrival. Make it, please, the earliest possible date. I will eagerly await seeing you, my dearest Rose.*
> *Your devoted,*
> *Sarah*

Meanwhile, Farrel had finally opened his speak-easy, the Blind Tiger. Sarah frowned on the idea of his involving himself in the alcohol issue. She had no objection to drink on theological grounds, but she did believe that a drunk was an obnoxious human being. And she could not help but think that Farrel's close association with a bar would mean he would begin his heavy drinking again. She said nothing, however, because she had no desire to renew their old daily arguments. She began to retire early, and Farrel began to return from the speak-easy late. Often he did, in fact, stumble from drink on his way up the stairs. Then he had an electrifying experience which made him swear off demon drink once more.

The event was his recognition one night, after a few too many drinks for reflection to calm his actions, that the woman who approached him at the bar was the same woman who had taken all his money that night in Chicago, Estelle!

"Hey, handsome," she began, "how about buying a poor working girl a drink."

"Sure, baby," Farrel answered. "Hop up here beside me." He reached over as though he were going to help her up on the stool beside him, but instead he grasped her arm tightly and pulled her close. He slid off his stool and said, "How have you been, Estelle?"

"Hey, mate. Let go. My name ain't Estelle either, so you got the wrong girl entirely."

Farrel could see the fear flicker in her eyes. She was the same girl. He was sure of that. She even carried the same black beaded bag. Farrel began to drag the unwilling woman along with him toward his office in the rear of the building.

"Make no sound," he warned. "I am the owner, you see. The owner."

He could feel her struggle against his hold on her, weak and ineffectual as the flutter of a bird with a broken wing. To his surprise, her terror excited him.

"Take what money I got," she said. She thrust her bag toward him. "I don't want no trouble."

He opened the door to his dark office and dragged her after him. He turned on the desk light which cast but dim illumination. He had planned it that way when he had set the office up. This room, after all, was hardly his place for serious work. Rather, he had expected it to be a place of escape; and that is what it had been for him. He had covered three of the walls with dark wood paneling; the fourth wall he had draped in red velvet as though it were a wall of windows, but there were no windows. For Estelle, he thought, this room offered no escape.

"Sit down," he ordered the woman as he locked the door. He released her arm and pushed her in the direction of the ottoman against the far wall. Although she trembled, she refused to behave as he demanded.

"You gonna call the cops?" Her voice had regained its tough tone, and she thrust her hip at him provocatively as she spoke.

Farrel watched her chest heave with each breath. The crescent of full creamy flesh at the top of her bosom grew as each inhalation pushed her body against the tight satin fabric of her gown. He could see she was growing increasingly afraid, and he liked the feeling it gave him.

"Perhaps that is exactly what I should do. Perhaps, in fact, that is what I shall do."

"Yeah, well if you try that, Buster, I can tell them plenty about you; remember that." She gave a nervous laugh that sounded like the whinny of a horse trying to pull out of the braces.

"You fool," Farrel spat at her, "can you imagine

that anything you would say would be given credence? A woman such as you? Absurd. This is my town. What I say will be the truth in official eyes." He wondered why he was belaboring the point. It must be the alcohol talking. He usually felt no need to tell people how important he was. "The police chief would love to do me a favor," he went on, but continued to stand rooted, not taking a single step toward her or toward the telephone. He had certainly drunk too much, he knew; he could feel the blurred sensation in his eyes; that was a sure sign. A dangerous excitement began to build within him. He told himself that he should unlock the door; he should insist that she leave and never show up in the Blind Tiger again. He should just throw her out and warn her that she had better leave town.

He was about to follow his own advice when Estelle chose that same moment to move toward him.

"Listen, honey," she said, her tongue flicking against her red lips, "I remember what you like." She ran her tongue around the circle of her scarlet-painted lips. He stared, fascinated, as the moist pink flesh of her tongue brought back the memory of that night. His body, that traitor, began to become aroused. She came up to where Farrel stood, his back to the door, and pressed her body against his. Her hand moved down between his legs, and she cupped his manhood in her palm. She stretched up toward his ear and whispered wetly, "I could take you in my mouth again." She glued her lips to his.

He thrust her from him with greater force than necessary, and she fell backward crashing back against the desk. Even the slightest trace of doubt which Farrel had harbored disappeared at her words. He advanced on her where she leaned against the desk.

"I could make you feel so good," she said in a placating voice, "just like the last time—"

A roar burst from Farrel, and his hand shot into the air seemingly without volition. A red stripe appeared across the woman's face. He had slapped her with his open palm. He swung his arm back in the other direction and caught her chin with the force of his knuckles. The signet ring he had taken to wearing on his little finger gashed a small wedge from her skin.

"Jesus," she said, her eyes wide, but she made no move to defend herself. Her arms remained hanging loosely at her sides as though she had decided fighting would do her no good. She accepted this treatment as one of the liabilities of her profession, but the reaction of her passivity on Farrel was to further enrage him. He demanded a response. She must not ignore him. He demanded more; he was an important man. He looked at this gaudily dressed, brightly made-up woman who stood before him with closed eyes and suddenly saw his mother's face—the look of contempt with which she so often had met his ideas. He raised his fist and smashed it across her head catching the entire left side of her face with the blow. For one instant her eyes flew open as her head snapped to the side, but then they sank closed, and she collapsed in an unconscious heap on the floor. Farrel was about to kick the inert body—he was still furious—when for an instant his head cleared and he was able to see what he was doing, what he had already done. . . . He ran his hand across his forehead. He walked around behind the huge desk and slumped into his chair. Christ, what have I done? he asked himself. The speak-easy world was at home with vice and gambling and crime and violence. It seemed that he was becoming a true citizen of this new world. Well then, there were advantages to that. Farrel reached for the telephone, and he put in a call to the police chief. The Blind Tiger had made payments under one guise or another for the law to look the other way in terms of its operations. Now they were going to have to do some work for their money. He wanted this woman out of his office and out of town, and he wanted no notice of this incident given by the police or the newspapers or any of the other local busybodies. The woman on the floor had not moved, but Farrel could tell by the rise and fall of her chest that she was still alive. He placed his call; then he went out into the back alley to wait for the police to arrive.

Twenty-four

Sarah never learned of the beaten woman. She could not avoid noticing the increase of a certain coarseness in his behavior as he became more involved with the saloon. However, after that night—the details of which Sarah was never to learn—Farrel went through a reversal back to the more cautious, more humane person he had been. He started to come home at an earlier hour and in a more sober manner. But her heart had so hardened against him during these postholiday months that she hardly cared how he came home or even if he came home or not.

Sarah did care very much, though, about the fact that her marriage had so quickly reverted to such an unhappy pattern. Perhaps that is the bond that holds us together, she reasoned, misery. But she had grown so accustomed to these feelings that they caused only a dull ache rather than a sharp pain. She was able to put it aside as she once would not have. Now she focused her attention on the upcoming visit of her friend Rose.

She sat down with her mother to plan a small gathering to celebrate Rose's arrival.

"She's such a big-city lady, Mamma. I want to invite people who will blend well together, who will be scintillating, so she won't be bored."

"Sarah, suddenly Richmond shames you? You were never so snobbish before."

"But she lives in New York City," Sarah wailed.

"She's your friend, Sarah. So start from that point. George Spencer is another friend."

"Yes, of course, we must include George." Sarah hoped she was not blushing. "That new reporter on the paper. We should invite him, too, along with his wife. I think Farrel knows him quite well."

The plans went on during that afternoon and the afternoons that followed. They included writing out the invitations, planning the menu, and freshening up the room where Rose would stay during her time in Richmond. Sarah wanted the rooms for Rose to be beautiful and warm and full of the feelings of love she felt for her best friend.

Then the days had passed, and as Rose stepped off the train Sarah rushed to her and took her surprised friend into her arms in a wonderful rush of hugs and kisses. Each saw in the other the distant shadow shapes of the younger women they had been, but they both protested how they could hardly believe how little change there had been in the other . . . how they looked wholly the same, exactly the same.

*   *   *

Back at the house, they sat together trying to find the path to their old comfortable selves. Time apart seems to shape new edges, Rose thought; time together sands the corners smooth again.

"Tell me about the places," Sarah urged. "Tell me everything: how the cities looked and smelled, how the food tasted. Oh, Rose, you have been around the world and I have been around the corner!" Sarah's face looked suddenly so pale and old that Rose felt a shock run through her.

"Every place is the same place in some ways, my friend. Lonely shadows, empty beds, unhappy people."

"Stop!" Sarah cried. "Please don't tell me of those things. There *must* be streets where lights blaze and people laugh and love each other more than life itself."

"Yes. There are such streets. Such moments. Perhaps there are even such lives—whole lives. But not your life or mine, I see. Not such happiness in our lives. What events have we lived through that were so unlike our dreams? I wonder. To make us so sad. No, say nothing! It must just be the afternoon's mood. Come let us walk through downtown Richmond, and you can point out to me the wonders of the city's changing face."

Sarah bent her head a moment. Grief tore at her heart. Oh, to be so far from George. To be apart from the man she so dearly loved. She seldom allowed herself to feel so fully her sorrow, but today it seemed to flood in upon her. Then she straightened and answered her friend.

"Wear a shawl. The weather is still a bit cruel."
She paused, then added, "What an odd word to
choose. Cruel. No, what I meant was there might
be a chill in the air."

Rose felt a new openness in Sarah along with
the increase in sadness. She looked forward at last
to being able to share everything with her. The
number of children that Sarah had had showed in
her body, Rose thought. There was a new
heaviness which somehow added a rich luxurious-
ness to the flesh of Sarah's arms. Even her slightly
thickened waist seemed to be profoundly femi-
nine. Rose wondered, as she so often did, if she
had made a mistake in not having had children.
No, she assured herself. That was simply an
animal function. She was living the life of the mind
which she truly believed to be infinitely superior—
except for moments like these when she saw the
fondness between a mother and her children.
Sarah was kissing the children good-bye. Rose
turned away and moved toward the door.

As they walked together, she began to ask Sarah
as gently as she could about her life with her
husband. Rose had always felt the gravest reservations about Farrel Hurstwood who seemed too
overbearing to her; too handsome as well. She had
always mistrusted men who lured women with
their looks. Granted, the few times that she had
met Sarah's husband, he did not seem to play that
particular game, but she still had her doubts. The
unhappiness she so often sensed from Sarah was
another reason for her concern.

She began the conversation by talking about an

article she was doing on the rise in divorce rates.

"Many people believe that marriage is no longer a wise way to live," she said.

"But what of children? They surely need a mother and a father both."

"Children, yes. That seems to be what it comes down to, does it not? Whatever happened to the notion of romance and a friend for life?" As she spoke, Rose glanced over at her friend's face. Rose watched for Sarah's telltale blushes. They had always revealed her true feelings. Sure enough, Sarah's cheeks began to flush.

"Sarah," Rose said, "you can talk to me. I am truly your friend. We've chosen such different paths, but perhaps we can share some of our feelings about our choices."

"Yes, I'd like to do that. I have often wondered how your life feels to you without marriage and children. It would be a real trade—fair deal, and all that—to exchange views. As for me, I should have liked to be a more adventuresome person who could go off and experience new things without fear. But I have decided that I am, after all, more timid than I had imagined, and my marriage provided me with a safe place to hide. Mind you, I never thought these things when Mr. Hurstwood first proposed to me. Oh no. In fact, I thought he would be so adventuresome that I would have my adventurous life along with him. I did not imagine then the vastly separated lives of men and women—even men and women who live together as man and wife!"

"I would say particularly those men and

women. Marriage has always seemed to me to be the ultimate unequal relationship, as you know."

"But then what of you? Do you not miss love and a home of your own and children?" Sarah felt very bold. She had never questioned Rose so directly. She had never teetered on the brink of revealing to Rose her true unhappiness with Farrel either. It felt as refreshing as the wind that blew against their faces to speak together so.

"Only when I see you with your children do I feel regret."

"But it is surely not too late?"

"For me, it is. I have chosen another route. I will never have a child, but I am perfectly willing to have love in my life. I have had lovers, Sarah, and I hope that does not shock you too much."

"Is it so impossible for you to imagine that I might also have had lovers? But no, give me no answer to that foolish question. At least, not yet. Tell me instead of your life now. Is there one person whom you love? One person who is to you more than bread or wine or life itself? No, let me better say, knowing the ways of you people in love with your work, is there no man in your life for whom you would give up your profession? Do you know such love?"

"No," the answer came at once. "I cannot give up one part of my life for another. There is a man I love, a married man who will never give up his family status. We have what we have—stolen moments and an occasional trip somewhere. In feeling, though, I think I have more than many married people." Rose's last words were spoken defensively, and she thrust her chin out as though to challenge a response.

"You do have that, I am sure," Sarah answered promptly. She and Rose exchanged a sharp look.

"You, Sarah? What is your marriage like for you? Are you happy?"

Sarah looked down at the street they walked along. They remained in silence as they went on walking.

Rose, who decided that the question must be too painful, changed the subject, mentioning the lovely smell of the spring air, filled as it was with a mixture of tobacco and spices. It was one of the sensations she had yearned to reexperience.

"I want to answer your question," Sarah interrupted. "I just have so much trouble even figuring it out for myself. Why do our lives become so uncomfortable? Well, that is hardly the point either. Come back home with me now and we can try to talk about it there surrounded with the atmosphere in which it exists. Do you like the way I fixed your rooms?" Sarah looped her arm through Rose's and they turned their steps homeward.

Their conversation turned, too, at that point to the mundane aspects of their lives: the articles that Rose was writing and her desire to get more involved with political exposés, Sarah's concern with the children's educations and her willingness to spend endless hours reading to them so that they would know more of the world around them than they might learn in school.

"You know, Sarah, you have had a lot of

children since we first met. Do you plan to have any more? Perhaps it is rude of me to ask. Many women are becoming involved with the movement toward limiting family size. I have begun to write a series on the possible ways to accomplish this control. The women should have the control!" The voice Rose now spoke in was the same impassioned one Sarah remembered from their days together in the school. It made her smile and hug her friend's arm close.

"I know so little about the whole subject, Rose. I can hardly say I planned anything in my life, let alone my children. But I feel sure somehow that I will know a great deal more about this topic before you leave Richmond." The two women laughed together and felt the comfort of their old selves settle upon them.

Back at the house they settled into comfortable chairs and drank cups of hot chocolate as they continued their conversation.

"This house is so fabulously comfortable, Sarah," Rose said. "How did you change it from the magnificent mausoleum it was when you first moved in?" Rose giggled knowing she was being shocking and that she could allow herself that excess with her friend.

"I know you are just teasing me, Rose," Sarah answered, "but I feel the same way about it. The house was my adversary for a long time. I hated its newness and everything Farrel installed in the way of gadgets. But I need not have worried. One thing one can always be sure of in terms of new things is that they will get old."

"The same can be said of people, I might add," Rose said.

"Yes, of people and of love."

Rose sat up straighter in her chair, untucking her left leg from where she had curled it beneath her. Was Sarah finally going to reveal herself in this setting? Rose had so long sorrowed for the certain sadness she sensed in Sarah.

"Love especially," Sarah went on. "It ages and changes, but it does not always achieve the rich patina of mahogany. At times it just becomes cranky and ugly and wrinkled. Or like an old gown, out of style, no longer fitting, and torn at the seams."

"My goodness, but you speak poetically."

Sarah gave a laugh that sounded more like a cough. "You may regret having asked the question at all. It is a topic I seem to myself to be quite bitter about."

"For as long as we have known each other, I have felt there was a gaiety in you that perhaps masked a less than perfect happiness. I want to be your friend and share in your sorrows as well as your joys. I will not regret having asked." Rose leaned over and touched Sarah's hand.

"The problems are of my making as much as of Farrel's, I am sure. He is a magnificent man in his work. At home, however, I see his clay feet probably too clearly. A better wife would hardly notice. Whoever said, 'man's love is of his life apart,' certainly said it truly in terms of my husband. But so what? I have my life at home. Money enough to do what I want. Why must I yearn always for something more?"

"Have you found something more?" Rose was unsure why she had asked that question, but she felt it probably was the direct response that Sarah had had on their walk to her statement about lovers. In any case, she felt it held the key to Sarah's life.

"Yes." The word hung between them like a shimmering ghost. It awed them both back into silence for the moment.

"Yes, I have found something . . . rather, some*one* else. But it changes no pattern in my ongoing life. It only offers me the tortured vision of possible love. No, it offers me more than that— moments of sheer bliss; moments of sheer torment."

"This man loves you?"

"Oh, God." Sarah began to weep silently. "Yes, he asks me to go away with him and start a new life—or he used to ask me. Now we have stopped talking about the possibility. There is no possibility. We still see each other. Frequently on a social basis for you see"—she hesitated a moment before committing the final folly of revealing George's identity—"he is Farrel's partner!"

Rose had to admit that her friend had finally managed to turn the tables on her and shock her. Always before it had been Rose's role to be the shocking one. Her husband's partner as her lover! Well, that was certainly a different view of Sarah,

Rose had to admit.

"Have you thought about leaving your husband?"

"Of course. I only seldom allow myself that indulgence though. After all, it is the life I have chosen. I have children to consider, and I am not insensitive to my position in society. What a scandal it would be in Richmond. I would hurt my parents and Farrel and Farrel's business, which is his life, and my children—for what? My personal happiness, which might, after all, fade away as my happiness with Farrel has done. No, the cost is too high."

"You see!" Rose said. "You are the same as I. You ask whether I would give up all for love and seem to disapprove that I would not, but you are not willing to give up all for love either."

"I suppose you are right. In our hearts, though, what have we given up there?"

"Am I to meet this man, Sarah, my dear? I would like very much to meet the man who provides you with a dream of love."

Sarah was uncertain whether her friend was being serious or sarcastic, but she answered seriously.

"I have planned a party for the weekend. You will have the chance to meet some of the luminaries of Richmond—new and old. Among them will be a Mr. George Spencer. A funny-looking man with the kindest heart in the whole world. It is he."

Sarah looked forward to the guests' arrival the

following Saturday night. The nervousness she had felt about entertaining during the first days of her marriage had dissolved eventually until she now felt completely comfortable in the role of hostess. Tonight, of course, there was a special little edge to her feelings in that Rose, who knew George's actual importance to her life, would be meeting him for the first time. Still, Sarah felt more eager than afraid, and when everyone gathered around the beautifully laid table together she felt happy that she had so many dear friends with her.

During the rounds of talks between groups of constantly changing twos and threes, Sarah found herself at last beside George.

"How I have wanted to find this moment," she began. "I hoped we might have a chance to speak alone."

"You are radiant tonight, my dear," he said. They clinked their glasses together in a toast. *To love,* it always meant in their secret world of symbols.

"It's spring, George, the season of our annual picnic." Sarah laughed like the tinkle of bells. She felt so light and free suddenly to be beside George. "Or at least we should have made it an annual event. I am eager for us to get back together; that much is clear, I hope." Then she smiled at him and waltzed away toward the spot where Rose stood between Sarah's parents.

George was left wondering at the flirtatious manner in which Sarah had acted. There was no doubt of her meaning. Yet it had been so long since

Sarah had allowed any intimacy between them that George hesitated to accept the validity of his interpretation. He knew she was not speaking of immediate plans because her friend would be staying for an indeterminate time. He was willing to wait. The prospect of being together with Sarah again would be enough to sustain him. Also, he was glad to see the cheery change in Sarah that Rose's visit had effected. There had been far too many periods of sadness, he felt, and he was delighted that they seemed to be emerging into a period of light and brightness.

It did not escape him that Rose was friendly to him in a special, almost conspiratorial, way. Had Sarah shared the secret of their love? he wondered. He hoped that she had, because it would somehow substantiate the cobweb of their romance. He knew that Sarah really loved him, but she would never tell him so in words. Well, he would have to live with that. He looked across at her now where she stood laughing with her friend, and warmth suffused him. She was his love.

The visit between the two friends extended beyond their first plans as neither was willing to end the delight of their close time together. Rose had not taken a vacation for any length of time since the day she had begun work in New York, so she felt it was only fair that she be allowed this self-indulgence. Together the two friends, sometimes alone, sometimes with the children, visited the neighborhoods of Richmond and even drove out into the surrounding environs. Sarah bragged about the increased distances that people could travel by streetcar or interurban and Rose teased her about being involved with too many streetcar men.

Finally, though, duty tugged at Rose, and she began to feel a restlessness to be back at work.

"Don't you miss it?" she asked Sarah. "Would you not like to be an adventurer each morning in search of the perfect story? I always hope for the award-winning scoop. I may never have it, but I thrill to the possibility!"

"Yes, I dream of such a life. But I fear it is not mine. The only way such greatness could come within my grasp, I fear, would be if it were somehow thrust upon me. I long for it, and I pray 'God forbid' at the same time. It feels as though it would be a destiny that would have tragic implications for me. Sometimes I dread the possibility and feel a suspicion that it may yet be!"

It was their last serious conversation in private. After that, Rose's time was spent saying good-bye to people and packing. Somehow the small amount that Rose had brought with her had multiplied into a vast amount. It had grown through her own purchases and through the number of gifts that Sarah had forced upon her. To be able to provide her friend with things she might need felt like a blessing to Sarah, and she was grateful all over again that her husband was such a wealthy man as to allow her such a delight—the delight in giving to others. That was a talent that Sarah had always had. Even when she was a child and the giving had cost her some small treasure of her own. Now it was many times greater in the amount that she could give, but her sensation of joy in giving remained a constant.

When at last Rose climbed aboard the train and headed for New York again, Sarah realized that most of the spring had passed. The air had the feel of moist heat by mid-afternoon. Summer was almost upon the scene. She knew that her conversation with George had stayed in his mind as it had in hers. She knew this summer would mark a new beginning for them. Still she hesitated to make the move that would turn the thought into an actuality.

Twenty-five

Finally, though, in midsummer George telephoned her. At first they made idle chitchat, but then George broached the subject of their meeting.

"Farrel will be going to Atlanta, Georgia, next week for a lengthy meeting," he said. "Most of August will be consumed between meetings and travel. I would like us to use some of that time to be together. It has been so very long. Would you please think about it?"

"What do you mean by a time together? Surely we can have some afternoons, but I sense that you mean more than that."

"Yes, I do, Sarah. I mean a trip together. Perhaps for a week. Could you invent a reason to be away, a place to go? I could take the time. We would tell people we were going different places and then meet. I have dreamed of this for so long that I have the plans complete in my mind. I could take care of everything, if you were just willing."

"There is a risk, of course," Sarah paused. "I will

have to think of a place to go. Something that would seem reasonable. The children are out of school, so that would be no problem. Besides, they have so much other attention I sometimes imagine they really hardly know their mother is around."

"You sound as though you might agree to my idea," George exclaimed. "It was my fondest hope that you would, but I hardly dared imagine it as a possibility. Sarah, please allow us this small time. It would be our eternity."

"I must think a bit about it, George, but if I can think of a way, then my heart already says yes. My heart that is so often with you anyway. But I must go now. Come by for tea tomorrow and we shall discuss it again."

Sarah hung up with her heart pounding. She had been bold in her speech, and she had been bold in promising to make every effort to have a vacation alone with George. Imagine a time alone with George for days! Yes, she knew that was what she wanted more than anything else. It would be the romance she longed for. It would be the peace she sought after. It would be her heart's fulfillment of her dreams. Rose's visit emboldened her to try to reach out for some of her dreams. She must think of a place to go—rather, to say that she was going. Perhaps she could tell her parents, they would really be the only ones to question her. Farrel seemed mostly unconscious of her movements anyway. With Rose's name in her mind, Sarah began to wonder if she might make a feasible case for a return visit to her friend in New York as an excuse for her trip with George. It would seem very soon, but she could justify it on the basis of their warm time together. Most important of all, Rose was the one person who would gladly provide her with the needed excuse. She would understand completely as soon as Sarah mentioned the idea to her. Yes, that would be the plan. When George came the next day she would tell him that she would accompany him.

It seemed an eternity until the next afternoon arrived and with it George, but at last they sat together in the little side garden that had provided them with so many hours of pleasure.

"George, have some more mint lemonade," Sarah urged.

"You know you're tormenting me by avoiding the primary subject of this meeting, don't you?" he asked. "I have admired your herb garden. I've drunk your lemonade. Now, for pity's sake, speak to me of my plan!"

Sarah was forced to laugh at George's melodramatic appeal. He smiled shyly as he always did when he made her laugh.

"Come closer, George." Sarah beckoned. "I want to whisper the answer in your ear."

Obediently, George leaned over until his head was almost touching Sarah's lips.

"The answer," she whispered, "is that the lady wishes to be at your side when you take your trip."

The rush of air from Sarah's lips caused a shiver to travel the length of George's body. Even his ankles felt the tingle. The power of her words added yet another dimension to his response. He leaned back in his chair. He could hardly believe that she had agreed. He had not yet brought out all of his rhetorical powers of pleading. She had agreed out of her own desire. That was the most thrilling part of all for him. In all of his planning he had never dared to let himself really accept the fact that she might say yes. Of course, he had also never accepted the fact that she might say no. It had all been a dream. And now the reality was upon him. The dream would become a living dream.

"Where shall we go, my love?" he asked. "Would you like to visit a great city or would you rather go to the country?"

"You know that I speak truthfully, George, when I tell you that all I want is for us to be alone somewhere. A place where we do not have to be careful of our actions and where we can remain anonymous."

"Splendid. That is exactly what I desire also. I think I can find us the perfect place. An old inn where the elite used to go in my parents' day, but which has fallen out of favor of late. It should be the perfect spot."

"When shall we go?"

"How about in two weeks' time? Farrel will already have left and we can spend a week—" He hesitated as he saw a frown appear on her face. "Can you manage an entire week?"

"Perhaps. I'll try."

"Good, then it's settled. Shall we seal the pact with a kiss?"

Before Sarah could answer, George leaned over and placed his lips gently against hers. He moved away again almost as quickly, leaving Sarah with the impression that a butterfly had landed on her face and immediately taken flight again. The impression was delicate and sensual at the same time, and Sarah sighed and closed her eyes to enjoy the sensation completely.

"I love you, my life," George whispered.

It was the perfect moment and it held. By the time they parted, the lovers had made plans enough to carry them through the busy days before they would be able to leave.

Farrel, during the days ahead, was concerned primarily with the business arrangements he had made to keep things moving along as he desired while he was gone. His actual travel arrangements, the packing and so forth, were taken care of for him by the servants in a long-established pattern that worked as smoothly as the oiled springs of the streetcars. In some part of his mind he heard Sarah tell him that she would be away part of the time that he was away, but he hardly paid it any attention. Sarah had become in his life one of the comforts that would always be there, but which required little attention, similar to the many other people who served his needs. If anything, she stood apart only in that she was more often an annoyance, and he could not count on her automatic agreement with his ideas. Well, he was too busy just now to worry much about his home life. If Sarah had found a way to amuse herself that would be a relief. He went on with his plans and was soon on his way to Atlanta.

Sarah too was busy with plans. She counted out outfits and decided, then undecided, then redecided among them. No, one was too demure. No, another was too maternal. Oh, dear, she at last despaired, there are no outfits that will do. Then she remembered as if by inspiration the oldest clothes she owned, the clothes from her schoolgirl days. She had never been able to part with them and had stored them away. She wondered if they might be made to fit her now. The symbol would be a happy one. She could imagine herself as the girl she had been, starting over. Yes, she would check on them at once.

And so it was that on the day that Sarah left, ostensibly to visit Rose but in actuality to meet with George at the first train stop north of Richmond, she wore a red- and white-striped shirtwaist and a full black skirt. The outfit had a quaintness to it and a youthfulness as well, both of which pleased Sarah enormously when she surveyed herself in the looking glass before she left the house. She placed a new red cloche on her head, careful not to mess her perfectly arranged curls. The hat was the one new purchase she had allowed herself. Now she stood back to gain the overall effect.

Yes, she had to admit, the years had been kind to her. She had just turned thirty-one at the beginning of the summer, and although she knew that made her a matron, she sometimes felt younger than her oldest child. Thinking of her children reminded her that Maura would be two years old at the end of August. But Sarah and

Farrel would be back home by then from their various jaunts. The child would have a festive celebration. It amazed Sarah that she could so calmly evaluate the situation of her departure. That in itself was enough to make her feel guilty— that she felt so little guilt. Oh well, she sighed, I had best give my good-bye kisses and be on my way.

The next few hours passed in a blur. The ride to the station, the roar and hiss of the train's approach, the rushed passage of houses before her window as the train left Richmond behind . . . and then she was climbing down to the platform, and she could see George waiting a few feet away. Their kiss of greeting would have gone unnoticed by passers-by. It was the way a reunited couple might welcome each other. But to Sarah and George it spoke of the mysteries of love. Only they knew the barely restrained passion with which they smiled into each other's eyes.

"Come, darling, I have a carriage waiting for us. The inn is a long and lonely drive into the country from here. Would you like to stop for coffee before we begin?"

"Yes, I believe I would. I was too nervous to eat this morning, and the train ride has left me jittery. A bit of breakfast before we start off would be welcome. As being with you is welcome, George," she added, and smiled shyly over at him.

George's looks had hardly changed at all since the first day they met. It was an odd fact that the less handsome people of the world seemed to fare better with the passage of time than those who had

393

too much enjoyed the admiring glances of others. He must be approaching fifty, Sarah reasoned, but each passing year seemed to allow him to grow more comfortably into the looks and body he already had. She took his arm and allowed him to lead her across the thoroughfare to a small café that stood just opposite the train station.

Over their small repast, they both relaxed and began to talk about the days that lay ahead of them.

"We can walk, Sarah, for as long as we wish and see nature undisturbed by man's improving hand. The area is still quite virgin; primitive, others might call it. Oh, how I look forward to time with you without concern for propriety!"

"Only so we can take long walks?" Sarah teased.

"Young lady! Can this be the girl who blushed at the mere mention of ladies of the night such a short time ago? No, I can answer that question for myself. You are no girl now, Sarah, and instead you have become a most wonderful woman—the woman I love." George's eyes gleamed as he spoke. She always brought him to the verge of tears. There was a spot in his heart that no one but Sarah could ever touch; a place within him which was hers exclusively.

"Shall I pour us a bit more coffee before we leave?" he asked, and Sarah nodded yes. It was so comfortable to be with her friend again, this man who meant so much to her. She hated for any one moment to end even though she knew it would usher in yet another special moment. So they sat on for a few minutes over their cups of steamy coffee. They spoke of nothing, but their silences spoke of everything that mattered.

Soon they were riding out into the country which, though less than a half-day away from Richmond, could have been on the moon, so far did they feel from all that was ordinary in their lives. George himself held the horses in check, and Sarah held George's free hand.

"It is a dream come true," George murmured.

Most of the ride was made in silence. They breathed in the air which held the smells of late summer—wisteria, magnolia—and heard the sounds of birds and a blend of other creatures that formed an orchestral background to their journey deeper into the countryside. Sarah wondered if living in a big city had dulled her senses to the riot of sights and sounds and smells or whether she was simply so doubly sensitive today because she was running off in this unlikely way with her lover. She sighed, closed her eyes, and allowed herself to drift into a reverie. This was surely paradise. She thought that even if she died this very moment it would be worth it. She would give everything for this moment. That must surely be the definition of happiness.

George, who seemed to pick up on Sarah's thoughts whenever they were together, now put her very deepest thought into words.

"'*Verweile doch, du bist so schön!*' I feel like shouting out with Faust."

"What does that mean, George?" Sarah asked.

"Those are the words that Faust cries out when he has at last found bliss. 'Linger awhile, you are so fair!' To me it has always meant that he found the one instant when life perfected itself. That is what I have found with you, Sarah."

"You plucked that thought directly out of my brain, George. Sometimes I wonder if you are not a witch."

"A warlock, you mean—a male witch."

Any answer she might have given was put aside by the fact that they had arrived at the gracious circular driveway of the inn that was their destination. A porter hurried over to greet them. He held the carriage as George dismounted and helped Sarah down.

"Have the bags delivered to our rooms, please."

George continued to hold Sarah's hand even after she was safely down from the carriage. He squeezed her fingers affectionately.

"Shall we check on our rooms before we go for our walk, dear?" he asked.

It was the kind of make-believe they often fell into when they were alone together. By his words, spoken in the most casual of tones, she knew he desired her. She wanted a time alone with him also. The need to feel his body against hers, to have his arms defining her shape, was so powerful that it made her stomach tighten. She could feel her pulse flutter in her throat.

"Yes," she answered as calmly as she could manage, "I might change out of my travel outfit."

These little word duets excited them both still further. They arrived at their room ready to tear off their clothes and fling themselves on the bed. But decorum prevailed. The boy put their bags on the floor of the hall closet and showed George how to operate the drapes and the location of the bathroom and the bedroom in their suite. He accepted George's generous tip with a smile and backed out of the room.

"I thought he would never leave," Sarah whispered, moving closer to George.

Without answering her, George took her in his arms. He bent to her lips and pressed upon them a kiss that went on and on. The variations within that kiss were like a musical composition with a theme and counterpoint. Both of the lovers allowed the moment to take them over, to sweep them into a state of ecstasy in which all they knew of reality was the point of space that connected them. When at last the kiss ended, it would have been impossible to say who moved away first. The coming together had been so full and perfect that it lasted what seemed a destined time and ended in the same way.

Sarah continued to lean on George's chest. He continued to hold her against him. In the silence they managed to tell each other everything necessary about the long dreary time apart from each other.

George kissed the curl beside Sarah's ear as he whispered, "I love you."

She pulled back slightly so she could gaze into his eyes. She smiled up at him.

"I am so glad we are here together," she answered.

"That idea about changing your clothes," George said. "What a perfectly splendid idea.

Come with me and I will show you to the bedroom, madam."

"Oh, George, I thought I was the shameless one, and all the time it turns out that it was you."

Their teasing had the comfort about it of old friends, but retained the excitement of new lovers. Sarah sometimes wondered if they had not managed to stumble upon the secret of eternal love with their intermittent trysts.

George led the way to the bedroom. There he settled himself into a green velvet armchair to watch Sarah undress.

"It has been so long," she said shyly, "that I feel embarrassed."

"No, my dear, you must not. It is such a joy to watch you move. You are all women to me. It is not only that you arouse me, but that you help me understand what a woman really is. Just to watch the way you dress or undress teaches me to know you better, and I want to know everything about you." He nodded his head in encouragement, and Sarah began to unbutton her blouse.

She found that, with George's eyes on her, her movements became slower and more deliberate, and that the consciousness about her actions lent a sensuousness to each gesture that was unique.

She had long ago abandoned the elaborate corsetry that required assistance in order to dress and undress. Now, with her blouse and skirt removed, she stood before George in a pair of ankle-length ruffled bloomers and a delicately embroidered camisole. She paused.

"You must not sit there fully clothed. Come join

me." She spread her arms wide to invite George into them. He stood at once, removed his jacket and cravat, and moved toward Sarah, who seemed to shimmer before his eyes. He put his arm around her waist and led her toward the bed. They lay across its length and intertwined their arms and legs until they felt themselves to be one creature of some special shape previously unknown on earth. They kissed and kissed, allowing their mouths to touch and explore every part of each other's faces.

George's hand stole under Sarah's camisole where there was nothing to prevent his feeling the soft skin of her breasts. He stroked her silky breasts until he could tell by her tautened nipples that she was as aroused as he. Almost as though by a signal, so closely attuned had they become, both George and Sarah began to remove the remaining layers of clothing that separated them from each other. Within moments they were naked beside each other, and then, magically, George was in her, and they rocked together in the wonderful rhythm of love which quickened and slowed as they tried to prolong their pleasure.

At last George had to give in to the pressure that had been building and building within him. As he felt himself about to reach his climax, he buried his head in the curve where Sarah's neck joined her shoulder. His lips found a spot there where he sucked and bit a circular bruise as he pulsed in her. Never before had he allowed himself to put any mark on Sarah's body. Today, though, with the luxury of a week before them, it seemed right.

The unexpected rush of sensation, the strange

new blending of pain and pleasure, brought Sarah to a point of passion so sudden that she too found herself caught up in a searing ecstasy. As the pulsations subsided, they both sank into a somnolent state resembling sleep but perhaps better described as a deep daydream. They remained locked together in their sweet twilight world for the remainder of that first afternoon.

The days that followed provided them with the comfort of love and the excitement of passion. Leisurely breakfasts followed leisurely awakenings filled with hugs and kisses and gentle lovemaking. Their limbs learned ways to shape themselves to each other until they intertwined so easily that they felt like one creature, one composite body of love. Afternoons they took long walks. Evenings they lingered over afterdinner drinks before the fountain in the inn's lounge, teasing themselves to a point of desire where they could no longer resist the yearning to return to the privacy of their rooms.

Their last afternoon found them in similarly somber moods. The source of their sadness, though, was very dissimilar. Sarah, having accepted the fact that she and George would truly be lovers forever, had started worrying about her children. During her days away, she had put them completely out of her mind, a feat which amazed her, but now with her return to the family imminent she began to feel guilty about her neglect. George, on the other hand, could not keep himself from brooding about his loss of Sarah.

These few days had simply intensified his already deep love for her. During these days she had been his completely; now he must give her up again. He felt morose. The fact that Sarah so easily seemed to accept their approaching separation upset him still further.

Nonetheless, they managed to have a romantic and tender lunch together and a cozy carriage ride to the depot before they had to say their farewells. There they were saved from a painful scene by the fact that they had misread the time schedule and the train they thought they were an hour early for was about to leave. There was only time for a hurried kiss and a wave of Sarah's hankie before they were parted. George was not to return to Richmond until the next day in hopes that such a plan might prevent gossip. He watched the train pull away with what was probably the deepest regret he had ever felt. This is despair, he told himself. Then he turned and made his way to a local saloon where he ordered a double Scotch.

Twenty=six

That was how the summer ended; the fall whistled into Richmond and people whose nerves had been strained by the debilitating heat felt themselves ready to begin another round of seasons. School began for the children and mornings were alive with their rushings about as they prepared for the day's adventures.

Farrel had finally allowed Sarah to convince him to send Jessica to school rather than having her tutored at home. She was six now and could already read simple stories quite well. She also knew some arithmetic and should have been a delight to her father who somehow remained as remote as ever from her accomplishments.

Sarah saw this with distress. The other two children were still babies, and Sarah could accept the fact that men had not much interest in babies. Now that Jessica was of school age and displaying evidence of real intelligence, Sarah had hoped that Farrel would show more interest in her. She had hoped that his interest would help Jessica feel important and also feel less acutely the loss of her brother, Lawrence. But that was to be. Farrel's attitude toward Jessica stayed as coolly distant as his response to the other children. The children were simply peripheral to his life. Sarah had to acknowledge that Jessica not only did not have a father who was warm and affectionate, but did not even have a father who felt true concern. Although Sarah tried to compensate for Farrel's lack of involvement by giving Jessica extra time and attention and praise, she realized she could never be to Jessica what her father might have been, if he had so chosen.

"Mr. Hurstwood," Clara announced, "on the telephone."

Sarah put down the copy of *Treasure Island* she was reading to Jessica, carefully marking her place with a felt bookmark. "Mamma will come right back to finish tonight's chapter in just a moment, dear," she said to the sturdy little girl who knelt at her feet clutching a rag doll. Sarah followed the maid to the hall phone. "I do hope he doesn't plan to be late; that hen will be ruined if it overcooks!"

"Hello," she said in the artificial voice she still assumed on the phone. "Hello."

"Sarah dear, I'm sorry, but you must have your dinner without me. Something has come up."

"Well, what is it? Is there something wrong?" Sarah asked, her voice immediately tense. It was February of 1903, a year and a half since Lawrence's death, but any slight shift in routine

403

still alarmed Sarah out of all proportion, although she tried to control it.

"I will discuss it with you later, Sarah," he answered peremptorily, "but please do not wait up. I have no idea when I might return. Good-bye, now."

Before Sarah could finish saying her good-bye, she heard the click of the other end which told her that Farrel had replaced his earpiece.

What now? she wondered. Please, God, do not let it be more trouble!

She went back to Jessica who had begun serving her dolly tea.

"Why, Jessica," Sarah said, "tea for dolly when it is so close to her dinner!"

"Oh, Mommy," Jessica laughed, "you know she's only make-believe!"

"Well, you are not make-believe, are you?" Sarah asked her oldest child. "So we'd better go talk to Bessie about *our* dinner! Daddy will not be able to come home just now, so I think I shall have dinner with you children in the nursery. Won't that be fun?"

"Oh goody." Jessica laughed. "Then we can all play Go Fish afterward."

Her daughter's pleasure made Sarah happy. This was what life was all about, she told herself. Simple moments of closeness during perfectly routine days, "I love you, Jess," she said.

Jessica flung herself at Sarah. "I love you, too, Mommy," she said, hugging her tight. Sarah hugged her back. Then she removed the little arms from around her neck and whispered, "Let's go see

404

Bessie. Maybe she will even give us a cookie before dinner!"

Jessica took Sarah's hand and began pulling her toward the kitchen. It reminded Sarah of the day she had gone to eat with her mother.

"Now, Jessica," her mother cautioned, "take your time, dear. Easy, now, easy." Their voices and laughter, a sound that made the whole household feel happier, could be heard by Bessie before they turned the corner and appeared at the doorway to her kitchen.

"Aunt Bessie," Jessica begged, "can Mommy eat with the children in the nursery tonight? She said it's all right, didn't you, Mommy? And can we have a cookie?" she chattered on, not waiting for an answer to her first question. She feels certain, thought Sarah, that all will be well for her. What a blessing. If only I can help her to keep that feeling for just a little while longer. God knows, no one can keep it for very long.

Twenty=seven

Sarah woke to a clattering in the hall. "Mr. Hurstwood," she called.

"Just a minute," he answered.

She closed her eyes and let the morning sounds lull her back to sleep.

"Good morning," Farrel announced from the foot of the bed. Her eyes sprang open guiltily. Lazy slugabed, she could hear her father's words come back to her from her childhood. She sat up, stretched her arms over her head and smiled at Farrel who was already fully dressed. He stood now struggling with his tie.

"What time did you get home?" she asked. "I tried to stay up, but I must have fallen asleep over my book. And what are you doing up and ready to go so early this morning?" She squinted at the clock and saw that it was only six thirty.

"There's some trouble that I have to deal with," he answered. "But I have time for coffee, if you want to join me."

Trouble?" Sarah repeated, as she climbed out of bed and went to the closet for her robe. She bent to pull her slippers onto her feet. Farrel was already on his way down the stairs. Sarah hurried after him, her heart pounding. Trouble, trouble, it seemed to beat.

"Morning, Bessie," Farrel called, sticking his head into the kitchen door. "Thank you for starting up the stove in the back room. We can use the heat this cold morning. Is there coffee ready, perhaps?"

"Of course, Mist' Hurstwood, and some spoon bread, too. You can't go off with no food in your stomach. Is it just you?"

"No. Mrs. Hurstwood is downstairs, too. The two of us, if you don't mind. We'll go into the back room, though, where it's so warm."

"Fine," Bessie answered with a smile. "I'll bring your food right along."

What a gem Bessie Bailerston has been, Farrel thought. She has been a big part of keeping this household on an even keel. At least as even a keel as could be expected considering the circumstances.

"Bessie is bringing the coffee," he said to his wife who had already seated herself close to the fire, curling her feet under her. "She is always so amazingly even-tempered, isn't she?"

"You mean not like me, I suppose?" Sarah snipped, wondering why she had said that. It must be because of the scare I got when Farrel said "trouble," she guessed.

"Sarah!"

"I am sorry, Farrel, I must still be asleep. You know I love Bessie. But what really concerns me is the trouble you mention."

At this moment Bessie interrupted their conversation by appearing with a tray full of steaming goodies. She set it down on the small end table and served the Hurstwoods their coffee the way she knew they liked it. Then she dipped them out scoops of the moist pale-yellow spoon bread which she topped with chunks of butter. Yellow rivulets streamed down the miniature mountains as the butter melted.

"I'll leave the extra coffee and the pot of spoon bread here, in case you wants any seconds," she said before leaving the room.

"Oh, yumm." Sarah began nibbling away at the spoon bread at once unwilling to wait for it to cool. "Trouble surely cannot seem as bad with a cup of coffee and a treat as tasty as this," she said.

"I'm afraid it is," Farrel said sternly.

Sarah's mood altered at once. She balanced her bowl on the arm of her chair, took a sip of her coffee, and turned to face Farrel expectantly.

"It's the damned outsiders doing it," he began. "Union, they call themselves. Trouble, I say. They've got the workers all roiled up over how unappreciated they are. They have a list of complaints. They want the company to deal with their agent. Well, we have to deal with the problem one way or another, that's clear."

"What are you going to do?" Sarah asked.

"I'd like to damned well fire the lot of them and hire different folks to run the cars."

'Fire all those men?"

"Well, no use talking about it anyway, because it's not up to just me. The entire board of directors has an emergency meeting today. We're going to try to decide if we should meet with the representative or not."

"What happens if you just ignore the whole thing, the way mother taught me to treat a breach in manners?"

"They say they'll strike. It wouldn't be the first ever, that's for sure. There've been strikes in other places around the country of late."

"A strike? I don't even know what that is. Should I?"

"No, I don't see any reason why you should. Troublemakers, like I said. That's what this whole union issue is."

"But what's a strike?"

"The men refuse to work unless we give 'em what they want. The streetcars just sit in the barn abandoned. The company loses money. That's a strike. They hope we'll meet their demands in order to avoid the possibility."

"That scares me, Farrel." Sarah's spoon bread sat unnoticed. Her coffee remained clutched in her hands, but was not raised to her lips.

"I admit it's scary. But don't get too upset about it. I can handle it. I'll know more by tonight, anyway." He scraped the last bit of spoon bread out of his dish, drank down his coffee, and stood. "I've got to go now. You stay and finish." Then he came over to Sarah, kissed the top of her head, and left.

Sarah sat awhile trying to sort out what she had just heard. Unions, strikes, workers' demands— these were all so new to her. She had a feeling that her education in these matters was about to take a sudden surge. No need to borrow trouble, she told herself, and went back to her spoon bread. It had cooled down just enough to be delicious. She had to warm up her coffee, though, which she did, and finished a second cup before she went back upstairs to see how the children were coming along with their preparations for the morning.

"I say let's not negotiate with troublemakers!" Farrel pounded his fist so hard on the conference table that the ashtrays shook.

"And I say, why not?" It was George. Ever the voice of reason, Farrel thought grimly. "Let's look at their demands. Can't we yield on some points and hold firm on others?"

"Well, now," Smythe, the banker drawled, talking around the huge cigar that filled half his mouth, "if we start that business, where's it ever going to end, I ask you? Seems to me the question is are we the bosses, or are the men on the streets?"

"Right, right, right!" Farrel jumped in with his agreement. "This namby-pamby approach to the workers is completely opposite to all the values we work for. Baby them and they'll just whine some more. Give an inch, they'll want the whole damned track!"

There were some snickers. Then Johnson, a reliable member of the board and one of the leading citizens of the town, spoke up.

"This talk is as foggy as this room! We don't even know exactly what it is that they want. Why don't we find that out first before we decide whether or not to give in to them?"

"Hell, Johnson," Farrel began, "we know what they really want—power, by God, they want power!"

George rose to his feet. "Let's just slow down. Bob's idea was sound. First, let's open the window a little to get rid of this smoke. Probably clouding our brains," he joked to ease the tension. "Then I'd like to tell you what I know of the demands. Anyone else can pitch in with additions. Then maybe we'll be ready for a vote."

The seven men at the table began moving around. Some stood, others shifted papers about in front of them, someone got up and left the room. Farrel, leaning on his fists, his face clouded, continued standing at the head of the table.

George buzzed for a secretary and gave instructions regarding the window, and the serving of coffee. Then he walked over to Farrel.

"So," Farrel said, watching him approach, "you're going to be my enemy on this, George."

"Never your enemy. But a difference of opinions between friends can happen. I think you're wrong, that's for sure. I'd like to talk to you privately for a minute."

They walked to George's office, Farrel holding his silence to him like a shield. Once inside, George closed the door and indicated a seat. Farrel threw himself into the chair.

"Well?" he asked.

"Farrel, this strike business could really hurt us. Other companies have been driven to the ground by it. I know, because I've been reading everything I could lay my hands on since this trouble seemed to be brewing. Even winning could still lead to bankruptcy. Now what kind of hollow victory is that?"

"No. The point is nonnegotiable. I won't deal!"

"I don't understand this attitude, Farrel. Your bulling your way along without even considering the implications. It's not like you."

"Let's go back to the others," Farrel said; "there's no reason to continue with this discussion. Come along, man."

George, shaking his head in dismay and disbelief, followed Farrel's retreating back down the hall.

"Gentlemen," Farrel announced in a voice intended to get attention, "let us get this meeting back to order." The men, scattered around the room, moved back toward the table and took their seats. A tray of pastries lay in the center of the table and a coffee service beside it. Damn, Farrel thought, that's George for you. Babying the board just as he wants to baby the workers! Well, let them have their coffee and sweets. I intend to have the vote!

"To my mind, the point is not what do the workers want, it is do the workers come to us and *make demands?* And I say *no. Hell no!*"

"Right," Smythe broke in. "Why should we have to meet with them in any case? They are our workers. They don't like something, let 'em quit."

The momentum seemed to build and a new voice entered with, "Besides, it's not even *our* workers who want to talk to us. It's some damned foreigners what's saying they speak *for* the workers. What with the workers too chicken-ass to speak up for theirselves."

"Now wait a minute," George said, trying to interject a note of reason.

"Never mind, George," Farrel blocked his attempt, "we all know you have a good heart and are sympathetic to everyone. But business is business!"

"Right." "Right," came a chorus of voices, and George knew he had lost them. That the streetcar's future might be lost, too, was what he feared.

"Are we all agreed, then?" Farrel shouted. *"No deals!"*

The hubbub indicated overwhelming assent. Farrel beamed and George let his head fall on his breast. He closed his eyes. God, he prayed, we sin in different ways, it is true, but we are all sinners.

The men stood about complimenting themselves on their perspicacity. When trouble begins, they reassured one another, that is the perfect time to stop it—right at the very start. Suddenly Farrel felt hungry and reached for a sweet roll. Others joined him, until soon both the tray and the coffee pot were empty and the room was, once again, full of the smoke George had objected to earlier. George, though, had slipped from the room and no one else seemed to mind.

George, alone in his office, knew it would be his job to tell the union representative the decision. It was a grievous chore, particularly when he so strongly disagreed with the decision he had to report. He could put it off for a while, he soothed himself. At day's end would be soon enough. He felt such a restlessness, though, that he knew he would get nothing done until he had gotten rid of this burden. He took his hat from the rack, slipped on his overcoat and left the office.

It was nearly teatime, he surmised, as he waited for Clara to open the door.

"Good day, Mist' George," she said.

He entered the vestibule and she locked the door behind him.

"Is Miz Sarah expecting you?"

"No, I'm afraid not. I was not even sure she would be at home. Would you see if she is free?"

"Surely I will," she said, scurrying past him into the parlor.

Almost at once the door opened again, and Sarah herself appeared.

"How nice! It has been a dull day, what with the cold weather and all, but it is cheered appreciably by your surprise appearance." Sarah took his arm and led him back toward the comforts of her parlor. It was so warm, he noted with pleasure. He could almost forget the morning's meeting. They sat close together on the sofa, and Sarah saw how pale George looked.

"Are you ill, dear?" she asked.

"No, Sarah. Not ill. Just very tired. And very unhappy!"

"Shall I get us something to eat? Have you eaten

yet? No? I'll get Bessie to set us a table. Just potluck, as they say, is what you must tolerate today."

The moment she left he noticed how much colder the room became. What was he to do? he asked himself. He had really already come to his decision, but the move he was about to make caused him pain to contemplate. To leave his darling Sarah; to be far from Maura who might be, who probably was, his daughter—probably the only child he would ever have. To leave Richmond, his home, and the streetcars which he loved dearly too. Tears blurred his vision. The fire before him leaped in strange wavy lines. Then Sarah returned.

"She promises to have it ready in a few minutes," she said, taking her place beside him. "But, George," she asked, when she saw how upset he was, "whatever is the matter?"

"Sarah," he said with tears in his voice, "I have come to tell you good-bye, because I am going to leave Richmond."

"God in heaven, no," Sarah said. She clutched his hands in hers. "George, George," she cried, as though he had fainted and she were trying to rouse him. "What are you talking about?"

"There is big trouble brewing at the company. Has Farrel mentioned anything?"

"You mean the unions. Yes, he talked a bit this morning. I cannot say I understand too much. What has that got to do with you?"

"It's the way Farrel's going about it. He won't even talk to them. Playing the tyrant. 'No' and that is it! I don't accept it and I won't take it." He stared down at her small hands resting on his. Her precious touch, he thought, must I give that up, too? "I think it will be better all around if I just get out of both your lives."

Sarah felt shocked. She could think of nothing to say. Food seemed the perfect delaying tactic. It was neutral and soothing.

"George, come and let us eat. You look half-dead which is a bad time to make big decisions. While we eat we can talk some more. Come now, dear." She urged him up. When he was standing beside her, she took his hand and led him into the dining room. The cherry-wood table was polished to a high shine. The circles made by their two white plates were a bold contrast. Just a snack, really, Sarah had told Bessie, no need to put out a cloth. A steaming tureen stood on the sideboard.

"Sit close by me, dear. I want so much to help you, if I can. You have been so constant a comfort to me."

"Bless you, Sarah," George said, as he sat where she indicated.

Sarah herself served out the bowls of corn chowder. Then she brought over a basket of hot rolls and a little crock of butter. She was pleased to notice that Bessie had also set out a tray of Smithfield ham slices and Cheddar cheese. How typical of her, Sarah thought. She knows a man needs more than a bowl of soup to satisfy him. She wondered once again, as she had so many times before, just how much Bessie knew. Probably everything, she figured, but there could be no safer repository for family secrets than Bessie!

Once she had piled their plates with ham and cheese, brought over the sharp brown mustard that she knew George loved, placed the bowls of chowder before their places, she sat down as close to him as propriety allowed—maybe even a little closer. Her hand stole across and rested on his thigh. He leaned over until his head rested against hers, and he closed his eyes. Like this, sitting with the woman he loved, nothing else seemed to matter.

They jumped apart at a noise from the door, but it was nothing. Guiltily, they began to eat. The chowder was rich and creamy. Bessie made it so that it seemed to coat your throat with the warmth of melted butter as it went down.

"That woman's a genius!" George exclaimed. He took several more spoonfuls before he glanced over at Sarah, smiling. "Food can be heaven, can't it, Sarah?"

"Yes," she agreed, but they were both remembering other heavenly experiences they had shared. Was it the way he said things, she wondered, that always had her imagination carrying her back to his bed? Whatever it was, she blushed now, and knew he knew she was blushing.

"George, you are a terrible tease," she laughed. "And I don't even know how you do it."

"Me?" he asked innocently. "Sarah, it was this lovely lunch I was referring to. Every bit is a delight. Every morsel—"

He grew serious; his face suddenly returned to its tired expression.

"But I must leave you, Sarah. You must help me to have the strength to leave you!"

She left her spoon in her bowl and turned to him in agony.

"No," she whispered, but that whisper contained a cry. "I cannot help you to do that! I have learned something over the past year that makes it impossible for me to be any help in that endeavor."

"What do you mean, Sarah? What have you learned?" George became immediately fearful that something was wrong with Sarah. He felt so alarmed that he failed to think of the paternity issue regarding Maura, although that was a topic that would at any other time have been in the front of his mind.

Sarah leaned so close that her lips brushed against George's ear.

She could hardly speak. Her throat felt dry and tight, her hands trembled in her lap. "I love you," she whispered.

George stared at her. "How I have longed to hear you say that . . . but I had given up. Can it be true?"

"Oh yes, it is so very true. Only my shyness . . . no, let me speak more honestly, my cowardice has kept me from telling you before this. Please do not leave me."

"Sarah," George began to speak, but then fell silent. His face showed the strain he was under. He remembered the meeting he had attended just a few hours earlier. Farrel's attitude. The impending strike, which would become a reality as soon as he

418

delivered the board's decision. He looked at Sarah. Her lovely, trusting face gazed at him and he could not doubt that the expression he saw there was one of love. She loved him. She had at last confessed it. What a wonder, he reflected, because he had loved her so long, loved her so desperately.

"I love you, Sarah, with all my heart and I would never willingly do anything to hurt you. I will stay on despite the trouble. I will not leave."

Sarah, throwing caution away, wrapped her arms around his neck and kissed him tenderly. "Thank you, my darling," she breathed.

"God help us all, Sarah, there is big trouble coming for Richmond and the streetcars." Then he kissed her back even more fervently than she had kissed him.

After a number of kisses, they both realized the foolhardiness of their behavior and pulled apart. Sarah dabbed at her eyes. George straightened his cravat self-consciously. Then he laughed at himself, and Sarah joined him.

"The soup has grown cold," she said.

"Not mine! Mine is done, slowpoke."

They felt the comfort of closeness.

"Would you rather I make you a sandwich, George?" Sarah asked.

"No, thanks," he answered, breaking a biscuit in half and slathering it with mustard. "I will just make myself some miniatures with these tender biscuits." He loaded the biscuit up with ham and a slab of cheese, then topped it with the crumbly other half of the biscuit. "Yummm," he said rolling his eyes, "Looove those tender biscuits!"

His antics made Sarah blush again. But seeing him acting foolish also made her happy. She took some ham and cheese onto her plate and had a biscuit on the side. For a while they did not talk as they busied themselves about their food. But then George wiped the mustard off his mustache and said, "Sarah, I wish you would try to talk some sense into Farrel."

"He has never come to me for advice, you know," she responded. "Not like you, George. I feel more a part of your life, if you know what I mean. Mind you, I am not criticizing. He is just so different." She sometimes felt caught in such painful tests of loyalty between these two men. "You know I really do care for Farrel. I never mean to be disloyal to him. Oh, it is all so crazy. How can I be saying that to my lover? But do you understand? I think somehow that perhaps you could."

He nodded, cleared his throat, and said, "I think so. I think the problem is you love us both."

"Yes," she responded excitedly, "that really is it. I do not understand how it can be, but I love you both. I love two men! Nobody ever taught us that such a thing could be. I think that is the main reason that I have felt such anguish! But finally I am making some sort of peace with it. I do love you, George, and I will not deny it. You know now that I will never stop loving you until I die."

George shuddered. What a strange reaction,

he thought.

"No talk of death, Sarah," he pleaded. "We have had enough death. Now we have our life. Let us think about that instead. I promise to love you for all my life!"

They heard Bessie approaching and both turned back to their plates.

"Why, child," Bessie said as she entered the room, "why didn't you holler? I'd have been glad to serve you all. And look at this! You don't even have a thing in this world to drink; why you must be as dry as that spider plant you forgot to water."

"Bessie," Sarah exclaimed, "you are awful! You must not tell my secrets. Besides, I did, too, water that plant, it just did not choose to stay healthy!"

"Uh-huh," Bessie mumbled. "So you tole me. Well, now, what do you all want to drink? Lemonade, milk, beer, or coffee?"

"Lemonade," George said at once. "Your lemonade sounds good both winter and summer."

"Me, too," Sarah joined in. "Two lemonades, please."

"I'll be right back with them," Bessie said. She removed the soup tureen and walked toward the kitchen. Her voice trailed back to them, "I have a cobbler that will be out of the oven in two more minutes. Bring it along, too."

"Well," George said with a sigh, "when I leave here, I must go to the union and tell them no. I do not look foward to it one bit. In fact, I dread it. But at least I won't go on an empty stomach. And I have other sustenance to take along with me, as

421

well, thanks to your sweet confession." He raised Sarah's hand to his lips and kissed it softly.

What will happen to this household and to all of our lives, he asked himself, if those workers go out on strike? And I fear they will, he admitted privately; I strongly fear they will!

Twenty-eight

Farrel sat alone in his office after the meeting finally broke up. He knew he had committed the company to a tough policy. He remembered back to the time when his father had allowed the employees to tell him what to do on a company issue. After that, he said he had never felt the same sense of being in control. He began to think the workers were always eying him for signs of weakness. It had happened shortly before his father's death, and Farrel remembered his father's statements about the situation more vividly than anything else his father had ever said.

It will never happen here, Dad, he promised his father's ghost. I am the man in charge, and I intend to remain the man in charge. He viewed workers as interchangeable nuts and bolts in a great piece of machinery—no more than that. If these fellows quit, well, then he would hire himself some others. He felt adamant on this point. He would not let the workers take over the management of his company.

George was just one of those soft-hearted fellows who took on everybody else's problems. In this case, Farrel decided, George would have to be the one to yield.

"Damn it, Farrel, you are a bull!"

"Call me what you will, George, there's no shaking my resolve!"

The two men were alone in the office and the lit lamps kept the shadows at bay, but night had long since fallen. Farrel puffed on his cigar, his brow heavily creased with worry lines that revealed a concern he denied.

"This is your last chance, you know?" George asked, placing both hands firmly on the desk so that he faced Farrel head-on. "If they do not hear from us before midnight, they go out on strike."

Farrel stared up at the spiraling smoke and refused to answer.

"It will be a disaster. It is the middle of the winter. People need the streetcars. Also, the townspeople will feel a lot of sympathy for the poor men picketing in the cold."

Farrel didn't stir.

"All right, then," George exclaimed, turning from Farrel, "that's it! Strike it is and the devil to pay!"

"Don't worry so much, George. We'll win. They need their jobs more than we need them." He checked his watch and discovered it was after ten. "By golly, it is late! I for one am going home." Farrel stood. He got his coat from the stand and wound a muffler around his neck. "Coming, George?" he asked.

"Yes, I suppose there's no point in staying around here." George went into his own office, the room adjoining Farrel's. From there he heard Farrel shout, "Do you want to stop for a nightcap at the club?"

"That's a good idea," George responded. "I won't be able to sleep tonight."

"Nor will I," said Farrel. "I won't sleep until I see the clock's hands slice the night in half and know the die is truly cast. We might just as well spend the time together having a drink or two."

Some of the men milled around while others clustered together in small groups. The warehouse they were using for their meetings was cold and bare. A few crouched on their haunches, others leaned against barrels. In the center of the floor space, someone had built a fire in a large metal wastebasket, which supplied a modicum of heat to those nearby.

A burly man in a fur coat seemed to be the focus of attention and the men kept an eye on him from every part of the warehouse. He moved from group to group, glancing at a watch he pulled from his pocket now and again. The glitter from the gold watch, heavy and impressive as it hung on its gold chain, seemed to promise security, better working conditions, more pay—the fulfillment of the workers' demands.

"Hey, Mike," one of the men huddled over the fire called, "what time d'ya make it to be?"

Mr. Michael Claridge glanced up to see who was calling. Noting the fellow, one of the conductors as he recalled, Michael Claridge walked toward him saying, "Not much longer now. It's past eleven-thirty." His voice rose in volume as he spoke until he had gathered in everyone's attention. "I don't guess they'll be sending any last-minute messages, fellows. So now it's up to us."

"What do we do?" someone asked. Another voice muttered, "Oh, Lord."

Claridge ignored the rustling, the noise, and the movement. He climbed up on one of the cartons and held out his hands for silence.

"This is it," he said in a strong, dramatic voice. It was the quality of his voice as much as his ability with workers that had moved him up in the union until he was always the person sent out to the frontiers to organize new locals.

"We have come to the hard place. They won't listen to you. They won't help you. They won't give you more money to feed your kids! Yet they tell you the union is outsiders and they themselves is your friends! Is that how friends act, turning their backs on you when you come to them for help?"

"No," came responses shouted from various points around the crowd.

"So what are you going to do about it?" Claridge could feel that the moment was ripe for action. If they were going to declare their allegiance to the union, it would have to be by going out on strike now.

"Strike," called the conductor who had asked

Claridge for the time.

"Wait a minute, John," one of his buddies said, tugging at his arm. "If we go out on strike, we get *no* money. How can that be better than the poor wages we get now? My family needs me working, you know."

"Ah, you know they—them bosses, I mean—can't let the cars sit idle long. They'll have us back in no time. And with more money in our paychecks, too."

"What if they don't?" a new voice asked. "What if they fire us for good?"

"Smitty," John answered him, "you always was a coward! We gotta go for it. We gotta make a try for a better life. I for one think the union is our only hope. Anyone agree with me?"

There was a chorus of "ayes." Here and there a "bravo" rang out. Michael Claridge waited out the uproar and then took over the meeting again.

"I know it's not an easy decision, men," he said. "But if you need help, National will help. We'll give compensation money. We'll help by organizing a campaign to win public sympathy, too. It's not right that the owners make the profits and the workers suffer. It's not right, is it?"

The men were angry. It was cold and late. They'd been waiting and waiting for the bosses to send them a message. To say they would discuss the workers' needs. Now they were ready to shift their loyalty from the Richmond Street Railway Company to the Federated Railway Workers Union. "Hell, no," they shouted, "it's not right." "Strike," they shouted. "Strike!" "Strike!" The echoes bounded back at them off the bare walls making their small number sound mighty. They looked at each other and gained strength. They looked at Mr. Michael Claridge the union's representative, who wore his prosperity like a badge, and knew that no evil could befall them if he was on their side. "Strike!" came the shouts over and over again.

"All in favor," Claridge shouted raising his fist high in the air. The roar was louder than ever. "Opposed?" he asked, confident that no one would reply. Even those who might be opposed would not be able to rise against this wall of solidarity, this flaming emotion. Claridge had counted on that. After all, that is how crowds always worked. He had been in this business long enough to know. "As of this moment, then, the streetcars of Richmond are on strike!"

Claridge sat alone in his room at the Old White Hotel. Well, he had made it this far. The streetcars would not be on the streets tomorrow morning. He knew he ought to call in the results to the Chicago headquarters, but he had some planning to complete first. He had to get flyers printed for the strikers to hand out. Yes, he would tend to that first thing in the morning. The placards for the pickets were already done. He had made assignments to the first shift of picketers. He knew they were ready to be on the street corners in the morning, but he had to make out the revolving sheets to guarantee covering every time slot. He had a strange feeling, like a chill between his collarbones, that made him think this was going to be a long one. When he made that call, he had better ask for some help.

After his drink with George, Farrel had returned to his office. He had fallen asleep at his desk and spent the entire night in his office. It was the first time that had ever happened. He had been working out the details for a new motor. A synchronized motor that could be operated by remote control. It was a great idea, he knew. An idea for the future. But he could not keep his mind off this damned strike business. He knew he was right not to give in. He had made himself into a success, let them go out and do the same thing if they were so dissatisfied with the work they were doing!

The clock caught his eye. It was almost seven in the morning. He would like just to get back to work, but he felt his chin and knew he needed a shave; he wished he had never shaved off his beard. Anyway, he knew his absence would have Sarah worried. Seeing that he was all right would reassure her. A phone call would certainly not have the same effect.

So he stood up and stretched, put on his coat, and went out the side door. The morning was brisk, but not fiercely cold, so Farrel decided he would walk a ways; then, if a streetcar came along, he would ride the rest of the way. He noticed people gathered at some of the stops. Well, this would be the time some people left for work, he figured, but it did seem to be too many people for this early. Then he noticed two men talking heatedly to one group. The pair looked familiar. Why yes, they were two of his employees. What were they doing at the car stop? They had some kind of white signs on, Farrel noticed, as he drew closer. Then he came close enough to read what they said. I do not believe my eyes, he thought. Christ almighty! They have really gone and done it. They have gone out on strike! Until this very moment he had denied the possibility to himself.

Farrel dashed back to the office. He tore through the outer rooms to reach the phone on his desk. He called out the familiar number to an operator and tapped his nails on the desk impatiently while he waited for a voice to answer.

"George?" he bellowed, in reply to the sleepy "Hello." "George, they have actually done it! The ungrateful bastards have gone and done it. They are out on strike! Get your ass over here. *Now!*" He hung up before George could answer.

George held the dead receiver in his hand. It doesn't matter anyway, George thought. Nothing I could say would change anything. It is too late for words. Besides, Farrel refused to listen to the words I offered before. Why should he start now?

George climbed out of bed. He brushed his teeth, washed the sleep from his eyes, and began to dress. He would be there within ten minutes, he knew, but if he judged the frantic tone of voice correctly it still would not be fast enough for Farrel!

Meanwhile, Farrel called Sarah and spoke to her briefly, assuring her that he could not come home, but that everything was under control. He was lying, he told himself, but what purpose would be served if she became alarmed? No, it was his job to protect her.

He hung up the phone from that call and made another. By the time George appeared, Farrel had notified the entire board and several steadfast employees. He had just about decided to notify his staunchest conductors that he expected them to take the cars out on the streets when George walked through the door.

"Slow down," George said in greeting. "Tell me what you have already done and what you are doing."

"Just hearing your voice is like music," Farrel said. "Soothing to the soul and all that. We can go get some coffee and I will tell you what I have done so far."

Only two or three men stayed on the job. The others formed a solid wall against the company. Farrel and George took out cars themselves for the afternoon and, along with the two or three loyal workers, they got through the slow midday hours. But the rush was coming and they knew there was no way they could handle that with only the handful of them. Also, the strikers stopped the cars whenever they could, shouting and waving fists and sticks. The atmosphere was charged with anger. Reluctantly, Farrel closed the Richmond Street Railway down for the day.

"I want notices out in all the surrounding areas," Farrel said as they sat at dinner. They had gone to the Hurstwood home so that Farrel could shave. Besides, they needed the privacy in order to map out their strategy. "Anyone who can manage to drive a streetcar has a job. And if they make out well, we will keep them on. The hell with the old workers. They have just left the company for good!"

"Wait just a minute before you go off getting steamed up again. There are some new laws covering this area of labor unions that might help us. Give me a chance to check it out. But meanwhile bring in the other workers."

Sarah watched the two men in silence. They were supposedly eating Chicken Divan with dumplings, green beans with salt pork, and corn bread, but mostly they were just pushing their food around their plates concentrating on the subject of the streetcar strike.

"Unless," George added, "you want to reconsider sitting down to bargain with the men. Personally, I still think that is the best route."

"No. No. No! And don't let me hear you raise the idea one more time!" Farrel scooped up the gravy on his corn bread and bent over his plate. Sarah and George glanced at each other. They knew it was anger, not hunger, that drove Farrel.

"If you hire other people to run the streetcars," Sarah asked, as much to break the tension as to gain information, "does that end the problem? What happens to the people who have been working for you?"

"Yes, that ends the problem. As far as I'm concerned, that is. George is afraid that will only

432

make the problem worse, aren't you, George?"

"There have been other strikes. There has been violence. I want to avoid that possibility; that's the point I am making, Farrel. Or trying to make when I can get any point at all through your thick head!" George reached over and pounded Farrel's shoulder. He hoped the conversation, the feel of someone else's hand, might rid Farrel of his feeling of isolation. Farrel raised his head and met George's look. Yes, George reflected, the friendship was still firm, despite their differences.

"Where?" Sarah asked. "Where else was there a strike? What happened? Why don't we ever hear of these things that go on?"

"The one I know the most about, I guess," George answered, "was up in Homestead, Pennsylvania. A division of Carnegie Steel. They had bad trouble there. People hurt, even killed."

Sarah gasped, raising her hand to her lips involuntarily.

"But the company won, Sarah. That's the thing to remember," Farrel interjected.

"Sometimes," George said in a gloomy tone, "winning isn't worth it."

"Nonsense!" Farrel burst out. "We don't have time for this philosophizing. Winning is always worth it. Eat up, George, we have lots more work to get done today. Notices in the paper, advertisements of employment, a statement to the public explaining our position. If trouble comes, we'll call out the militia. But for now we have other things to think about. So eat up, man."

*   *   *

433

By the end of the week the battle lines were clearly drawn. The lines of people coming in from out of town for jobs were met and diminished in number by the strikers. Sometimes they talked the people out of taking away their jobs. Other times they used more physical methods to dissuade them from entering Richmond. Still, though, a large enough number got through to get the streetcars back on the streets. "Scabs," the pickets shouted at the drivers as the streetcars rattled past. Globs of mud were hurled at the windows until the streetcars began to look like moving hills. Occasionally, instead of mud, the strikers would throw rocks which would clatter against the streetcar alarming the riders but doing no significant damage. One rock, though, did break through a window and knock a seated man to the floor. He was not badly hurt, but everyone was feeling jumpy.

Many townspeople had returned to traveling on foot or by carriage. The flyers that the strikers spread everywhere explained their cause and urged this boycott. It won great sympathy from workers in other jobs.

Claridge's steel hand was the force behind the scenes. He or his ideas spread everywhere. It was on his orders that small carriages, run by the strikers, began to make the rounds of the streetcar stops picking up passengers who wanted to ride, but who did not want to support the trolleys. These small carriages, "jitneys," seemed to be the most potent weapon the strikers had. Through their use, they not only decreased the profitability of the trolleys, but they earned some money toward their own survival. Townspeople were urged to contribute to the strikers' cause more directly too. And the money that was collected in that way was distributed to the strikers' families. Money came in from the union to help supplement these amounts, and so by scraping and patching the workers were able to make do and were ready to withstand a long period of unemployment.

George, standing on the sidelines one afternoon, spotted the labor organizer across the street. What was the man's name? he asked himself. Oh, yes, Claridge. He made his way past the cluster of strikers, ducking his head into his collar in the hopes that he could get by unnoticed. Whether noticed or not, he was able to make his way across the street without being accosted.

"How-do, Mr. Claridge," he addressed the man, who, like himself, seemed to be merely an observer of the scene.

'Why, Mr. Spencer, I believe it is. I thought that might be you over yonder. Well, and could it be possible that you are seeking me out with an offer of conciliation?" He waited no more than a second before continuing, "No, I can see by the look on your face that that isn't the reason."

"No, sir, it is not. In fact, I have no reason. Except that I cannot bear the ever-widening breach that is developing in this situation. I fear it, Mr. Claridge, I tell you in confidence. I speak to you now man to man, not as a representative of the company."

Claridge, his arms wrapped around himself,

pounded on his sides. He stamped his feet, too. The long days and nights of cold were making him miserable. This Spencer fellow seemed a sincere sort, he thought, but you have to be so cautious with these company types. Two-faced they were more often than not. After all, they knew which side their bread was buttered on, didn't they?

"It's a bad scene, for sure. We were ready to talk, you know, all along. Still are. But we won't give in! You can carry that back to your boss."

That griped, George had to admit. After all, Farrel was not his boss! He was his partner. Yet many people made that error. And in order to correct them he would come off sounding so damned pompous! What difference did it make? he wondered, but he knew it did. In the depth of his heart, it did make a difference.

"Well," he said now to Claridge, "I will certainly pass the word on to my partner, but the board is a stubborn group, too. I doubt they will deal." He began to turn away, but turned back hoping to transform this short encounter into something a little more personal. "You have been a long time away from your home. It must be mighty lonely living in the hotel, I don't wonder."

"Yes." Claridge bit at his lower lip. He was touched by Spencer's concern. Hardly anyone ever took time to notice he was a real live person, not just a cardboard emblem of the union. "Yes, I hardly have any other home than hotel rooms. I guess the union and organizing work has become my home, my life."

"Have you no wife, then, waiting up for you

436

somewhere?" George asked. He immediately followed his question with an apology. "Forgive me, Mr. Claridge, it is none of my business."

"Quite all right," Claridge hastened to answer. "I appreciate the question, and I will gladly answer it, too. No, the wife couldn't take this life anymore. She picked up with the kid and left when I was out with the last group of strikers. Now I have no need to hurry home, you see. I can stay where I am for as long as I am needed!"

Though the ironic tone was not wasted on George, he chose not to respond to it and said only, "Well, I am in many ways the same." Embarrassed, he added, "I guess I should be going now." They nodded at each other and George walked off down the street. There is a chap I could enjoy sharing a supper with, was the thought in each man's mind. But of course to share a meal with the enemy was unthinkable at this point in the war!

Twenty-nine

Sarah had called George and asked him to come over. Now she waited by the front door. Farrel would be away at another of his interminable meetings, she knew, and that was what prompted her to make the call to George. She paced the hall waiting for him. Still, his knock made her jump.

"I will get it, Clara," she called. She opened the door, and a smile of welcome crossed her lips. It was always so good to be close to George. "Come in. Come in. Thank you for coming right over.

"Are you starved? Did I catch you before dinner?"

"No, Sarah. You always want to feed me, but I have eaten, I feel fine, and I am delighted you called! I hope it is no new problem that is the cause, though, because I swear I do not know if I can handle many more crises!"

"Come, dear," she urged, leading him toward the back parlor, their favorite spot. "It is no new problem, but the same old big problem I called about: the strike."

They arranged themselves close together, hands clasped one over the other. She knew that their constant closeness, their touching, the proximity of their heads would lead not only to disastrous yet delightful moments of love-making, but to possible discovery and exposure by Farrel. Yet she went on with the meagerest of precautions. Ah well, she sighed to herself, not having thought of any resolution to that dilemma.

"Sarah, you have enough on your mind with the three children. The strike situation will work itself out somehow. I hope," he added under his breath.

"George, do not condescend to me like that, please. You sound like Farrel. 'Don't trouble your pretty little head.' Nonsense! You know I am an intelligent woman and I want you to explain this whole business to me. What is a union? A union of what? What do the workers want? What does Farrel want?" She had spoken in a rush, the words pouring from her. She noticed the dismayed look on George's face and stopped. "What's the matter, George?" she teased, leaning over and kissing his ear, then his cheek, and finally his lips.

He responded to this rare spontaneous display, by whispering, "God, I love you, my beautiful Sarah." They kissed again.

When they parted, Sarah began again. "George, it makes me feel stupid. You and Farrel talk and talk of this strike business; yet I really do not know the first thing about what is going on."

"I see your point," George said. "I never meant to imply you were not smart enough for the subject, believe me. It is just . . . Farrel and I are at odds over this and I didn't know how to be fair in discussing it. I don't want to slur Farrel to you. I suppose, though, I can explain the basics without delving too deeply into our differences.

"The workers—many different kinds of workers around the country, I mean," he began, "have discovered that each one of them alone is powerless. You know, if Jack Jones were to say he wants more pay, his boss would fire him and that would be the end of that. So Jack Jones is afraid to ask for more pay, because if he gets fired, where will he get another job? Well, that's one part of it."

Sarah sat back in her chair like the young matron she was and listened intently. She folded her hands demurely in her lap.

"But if all the workers get together and say to the boss, 'We want a raise,' well, he might not be so quick to fire all his workers at once. So when the workers do that—when they get together to tell the bosses what they want—they form what they call a union. There are lots of different unions. The Knights of Labor, the Federated Steelworkers, and the one that has organized the strike against the streetcars here."

"You mean the workers here want more money?"

"Yes, more money and shorter hours. But I think the thing they want the most is for the union to be recognized as their bargaining agent."

"How much money?"

George began to feel cross-examined. It must just be my discomfort about the whole business, he figured. Sarah was always acutely curious.

"They want a wage hike of three and one-half cents an hour. If we give it to them, they'll be getting twenty-two cents an hour."

"But isn't Farrel paying more than that to the people who have come in from out of town to run the trolleys?"

George nodded. It made no more sense to him than it seemed to make to her. He could not defend Farrel in these actions that he personally found so indefensible!

"Look at this. Have you seen this?" Sarah jumped up, walked to the table and came back with some papers. "Tonight's paper. Or this." She had another paper underneath the first one.

"What *is* that?" George asked, pointing at the second paper. *"The Opinion?"*

"Yes, the strikers have brought out a paper. I got hold of it today when I went out for a walk, but I have not shown it to Farrel."

"But you have read it, have you?" George asked, amazed. Sarah had managed to stay abreast of what was happening, he realized, despite her pretense of innocence. Perhaps pretense was the wrong word, he decided. Her sophistication was piecemeal. She was innocent in one area and knowledgeable in another.

"Shame, Sarah! Pretending you needed me to explain it to you."

"But I did, George," Sarah replied earnestly. "I knew the strikers' own paper would be biased in their favor, but I knew you would be fair, even though you are one of the concerned parties. And

441

you have been. Fair, I mean."

"Well, let us have a look at this. The daily paper, I imagine, divided their coverage between 'us' and 'them.' Right?"

He began to scan the workers' tabloid. "Yes," he muttered, "that's a good ploy. Forget about issues and make a pitch for sympathy. Poor families at home et cetera." He was mumbling into his mustache, but Sarah caught his words.

"But it *is* true, too, isn't it?"

"Yes, I suppose it is true enough, but business is business, Sarah. If we just gave away money out of sympathy, we would all be poor and in need of sympathy ourselves."

"But, George, if all the money in America were divided up fairly somehow, we would none of us be rich, I know, but everybody would have enough. Isn't that right? And no one would starve or lie desperate and alone in the poorhouse."

"Hush, Sarah," said George, glancing around the room as though someone might have been listening and would drag her off. "That's Communist talk. Don't let anyone else hear you talk that way. Especially not Farrel!"

A hubbub in the hall caused them to turn toward the doorway just as the children, dressed in their night clothes, rushed in calling out, "Mutti," "Mamma," "Ma," in their childish voices. Baby Maura, held in Sassafras' arms, waved her arms about shouting, "Ma, Ma." George and Sarah burst into laughter.

"Put her down, Mammy Sas. Just wait till you

see what she can do, George," Sarah said excitedly.

Sassafras, a tall woman, bent over and placed the tiny child on its feet. Because Maura was so small, she looked younger than her nine months and it seemed impossible that she could be standing. True, she wavered back and forth precariously, but she was standing.

"Good girl!" George shouted. Surprised by the noise, Maura lost her balance and plopped to the floor on her well-padded bottom. Her fall brought another round of laughter. The older children, Jessica and Franklin, joined in and so did Sassafras, who covered her mouth with her graceful hand as she laughed. Then she knelt beside the child, who looked about with a sweet smile on her face.

"Lamby," Sassafras said, "tell Mamma good night and we go up to the nursery and hear us a story. Say good night now, y'all." She picked Maura up while the older boy and girl gave their mother hugs and kisses. Franklin turned and shook George's hand rather formally before joining Sassafras at the door.

"Good night, my darlings," Sarah called after them. "Pleasant dreams."

"Franklin is certainly growing up fast, isn't he?" George asked after they had gone.

"Yes, Farrel is having him tutored now. He doesn't think there is a school around that is good enough for him. For Jessica, yes, but not for his son. I will not allow him to be sent away. Did you

443

know Farrel wanted to send him to boarding school? Oh, dear, let's not get on that topic. Just one problem after another, isn't it? Tell me more about the strike."

Plankton Detective Agency
March 1, 1903

Dear Mr. Hurstwood:

It has come to my attention that you are having troubles because of rebellious workers. Similar experiences around the country have taught us that the workers' discontent is brought about by outside instigators who are no better than common criminals and should be dealt with as such. We have seen repeatedly that if you can keep the work ongoing despite their efforts, if you can carry on, that is, they are soon brought to their knees. At that point, life can resume its normal pattern.

The Plankton Detective Agency can supply you with substitute workers to keep your business functioning until the strikers abandon their effort. Our terms are the following: protection of our men from the strikers, sleep facilities in some central location, and food on the premises. Your newspaper advertisement, which reached my desk, named two dollars per day as the offered wage, which is acceptable. You will send those wages to this office, of course, where the men can pick them up, less the ten percent agency fee, when their work for you has been satisfactorily completed.

The Plankton Detective Agency can provide you with a hundred men tomorrow!

Sincerely yours,
Jefferson Plankton
President

Farrel read the letter for the third time. Yes, it was the answer, he knew. Then why, he wondered, did he feel increasingly uneasy about the whole issue? It must be George and Sarah, united in their disapproval, who were working on his nerves. But there was no stopping now. He reached for the telephone and placed the call to Mr. Jefferson Plankton. This would be the decisive step. The workers would buckle. They would see that the company could hold out longer than they could. Farrel would prove himself right; Sarah and George would see, after all.

He could hear the phone ringing distantly in his ear. Imagine, a Boston firm devoted to breaking strikes! He had had them researched after the letter arrived, of course, to discover that bit of information.

"Plankton Detective Agency," a nasal voice answered.

"Mr. Plankton, please," the Richmond operator responded, "long distance calling."

The Plankton men began arriving by the end of the week. Farrel had cots set up for them in the carbarn. There was lots of room there. He set up some temporary heaters to keep the chill out of the air, but it was probably still too cold for comfort. He would have their meals served there, too. It was an efficient way to treat workers, he had to admit, although a bit inhuman, almost animalistic, like cows in a barn. But he could not back down now;

445

he could not and he would not! He would look a perfect fool. There was no way Farrel Hurstwood was going to play the fool to the townspeople, to the board of directors, to Sarah. No, especially not to Sarah. No, no, no. He had to win—at any cost.

The train carrying the first group of Plankton men was bombarded with sticks and rocks hurled from the sidelines.

"Scabs," the frustrated strikers screamed.

"You need work just like us," they shouted. "Don't fight against us. You're the same as us." "We're all dirt to the bosses!" "Scabs!"

Although some of the workers agreed with the strikers' sentiments, they averted their eyes. They themselves had been out of work too long to let sympathy affect them. After all, two bucks a day was hard to come by. The train chugged past the crowd and drew into the station.

"Come in, Charlie," Farrel said, ushering the mayor and two of his aides into the spacious conference room. "Isn't this a day and a half? Why it is almost enough to make you believe in spring. Even though winter may return tomorrow."

"Probably will," Mayor Bleystock said. The mayor's aides stood stiffly at his side. Farrel surveyed the stances of the men before him and assumed there was an ominous reason for the visit. He folded his arms across his chest.

"Let me come right to the point," the mayor said. "The business community has come to me and asked me to represent them. They want the strike to end! This damned strike is hurting the town's image. I am sure I do not have to tell you that it is bad for business. You know it, I'm sure. But what I do have to tell you is that you are arousing bad feelings against you by your unwillingness to sit down and negotiate."

Farrel assumed an air of casual nonchalance as he sat.

"Charlie," he began, spreading his arms out on the table, "my workers had no reason to strike. They had it pretty good."

The mayor cut him off. "That no longer matters and I do not want to hear about it. The issues involved are not my business, the city's future *is!*"

"So, what are you saying?" Farrel asked. He was beginning to feel trapped and it was making him miserable. Was everyone going to turn against him? Did no one in this whole town understand about ownership and free enterprise and not backing down?

"It has gone on for more than a month now. The workers' moods are becoming darker and darker. I say do something now before an incident occurs. If there is violence, it will be hard for Richmond to live down. Violence, you hear me? I see it as a real possibility." The air crackled with tension. The mayor lowered his voice. "If there is violence, it will be on your head!"

The words stunned Farrel. His friend Charlie Bleystock—the easygoing Charlie—threatening him! For, after all, wasn't that what this was? The mayor, who had remained standing, said to the still-seated Farrel, "I can find my own way out." The two aides, neither of whom had uttered a word, followed him out.

Farrel's fury came upon him in a rush and grew and grew until he could no longer sit still. He leaped up and strode into his office, slamming the door behind him. He buzzed for the secretary and when she appeared he ordered her to get the governor on the line. By God, he said to himself, you want me to do something? Well, I will do something all right, but I will not deal with those damned disloyal workers.

When he heard the buzz, Farrel lifted the phone and said, "Governor? Farrel Hurstwood here. I am calling you from Richmond, Virginia. Well, my workers, the workers from the Richmond Electric Street Railway have been on strike for more than a month now. There have been threats of violence, and I am getting worried. You know how heavily I contributed to your last campaign, Governor. I need to call in my chips. I want you to send me militia units to defend the peace."

He listened in silence a few moments, nodding his head slightly.

"Good," he finally said. "I can watch the events the next day or so and let you know. Meanwhile, you have your people do some mobilizing. Good. I would like to see some uniforms in this town. It would straighten things right out, I think."

He was silent again, then said, "Yes, I will be in touch tomorrow, and I appreciate your willing attitude."

He hung up the receiver just as George burst through the door calling, "Farrel, my God!"

"What is it?" Farrel asked, alarmed. George

never got upset for no reason, Farrel knew.

"All hell has broken loose. Somebody set up explosives. They stopped the car dead, women fainted, the strikers are doing a war dance around the stalled trolley. Come!"

Then he was gone, running through the rooms and down the street with Farrel close on his heels. By the time they arrived, the scene had changed. Police had arrived and routed the strikers. Officers were leading away one or two when Farrel caught up with George. Others were scattering in a dozen directions.

Farrel passed George by and bounded into the trolley.

"What happened?" he asked the shaken scab conductor, who only shrugged in reply.

Farrel's glance took in the alarmed men and women.

"Nothing to worry about folks. This outrageous situation is almost over. The governor will send the militia here tomorrow."

George said, "What are you talking about?" in a hushed voice.

The passengers seemed to have recovered, even the women who had fainted after the explosion. Farrel felt he should try to get the car on the move again in order to win their confidence.

"I think we can get you on your way home in just a second," he announced to the group at large. "George, come take a look at the undersides with me," he suggested. "You know, George," he said as they climbed down and knelt by their streetcar, "I didn't see any real damage as we came running up.

I bet it was just a noisemaker in the first place."

"Farrel," George said, stunned, "have you really called on the governor? The militia?"

"Ha! I was right," Farrel exclaimed. "Look here." He pointed to the burned spot on the rails. "It was just an explosive cap. Troublemakers, but only out for mischief. Still they may have served our purpose very well. Once we get troops in here, the workers will stop this nonsense, you can be sure!"

"You have gone overboard, Farrel. Taken this strike personally in some crazy way." George spoke to Farrel's knees, for Farrel had already stood up and was reentering the car. George followed him awkwardly. The conductor handed over his cap to Farrel.

"I ain't stayin'," he said. "No job's worth gettin' killed for." He climbed off the car and strode down the street toward the carbarn.

Farrel recovered fast.

"Well, folks," he said, to the edgy group in the center of the trolley, "he wasn't from Richmond, you know, so what can we expect from him but cowardly behavior!"

After that, thought Farrel, nobody else would dare budge from the trolley, and he was right.

"Come on, George," Farrel directed, "you and I can get these good people home. What do you say?"

"I say yes, of course," said George, forced to admire Farrel's quick thinking.

Thirty

Farrel called the governor again the moment he had completed that run. Sarah, coming to greet him, overheard, and that is how she learned of the streetcar incident. She pursed her lips when Farrel asked for as many troops as could be mustered from around the state, but she knew there was nothing more she could say. This strike was driving a powerful wedge between them. She began to dream of running off with George, a fantasy she had not allowed herself since little Lawrence's death.

"Is dinner ready?" Farrel asked now, replacing the phone on its hook. There was a smug pinkness to his face that enraged her, but she managed to control herself.

"I am sure it is, Mr. Hurstwood. Shall I check with Bessie or do you wish to change clothes first?"

"I am ravenous," he answered. "I think I have finally settled these strikers' hash!" He walked over to her and roughly kissed her. The events of the day had aroused an animal passion in him and he grasped her to him. "Sarah," he said, "I changed my mind about dinner. It can wait."

Sarah, revolted at first, felt the vibrancy of Farrel's mood begin to work on her. His sheer magnetism had always aroused her. "Whatever you want," she answered almost against her will.

"Then let the dinner wait," he said. "I want you!"

Although she hated to acknowledge it, Sarah could feel her heart pound as Farrel pulled her toward the stairs.

Troops were on the streets the following afternoon. A sudden fierce wind blew up causing people to scuttle along clinging to the edges of buildings. The governor had sent sixteen militia units; uniformed men carrying rifles were everywhere.

"I thought the war was over," joked one merchant nervously as he closed up his shop for the lunch hour.

"Well, it looks like Farrel Hurstwood has started it up again," his neighbor answered. They walked off down the street together, talking about the terrible strike.

The streetcar irregulars kept the trolleys moving, though on a slowed schedule. The soldiers began to ease into their routine activities. Even the townspeople, sharply polarized between strike supporters and company supporters, nonetheless began to feel that this routine was normal. Then the disaster that had been in the air the entire length of the strike exploded.

It was night. The patrols were making their rounds. The last streetcar was creeping along the tracks toward the edge of town. Suddenly a fireball filled the still air. Shots rang out from behind a barricaded section of the street. The militia returned the fire. Flames continued to light up the sky, casting shadows that made the people rushing back and forth look like devilish fiends. More gunshots ripped through the night. George, whose lodging was close by, was awakened, roused himself, and hurried out of the house. His action took no heed of the danger he might be putting himself in. All he thought about was that now the worst had happened—his town, strife-ridden, his neighbors and friends in danger, possibly shot, possibly dead. No, damn Farrel's soul forever, this evil must not be. He approached a scene that looked like a war field. The barricade, lit up by the bonfire on the tracks, was a makeshift affair of oil drums and crates. George could see some of the strikers he knew huddled behind it looking scared. Across the street, militia men sprawled on the ground with their rifles at the ready aimed straight at the barricade. The bonfire, between the two groups, blocked the progress of the trolley which sat unmoving on the tracks, a useless symbol of the fight's purpose.

"Hsst," called a voice from the shadows. "Mistuh Spencuh. Ovuh heah, suh."

George peered into the darkness, but saw no one to attach to the voice. He crouched down and made his way toward the barricade. I certainly should not be here, he thought, but he continued to crawl along until he collapsed at last, relieved to be still alive, behind the barricade's safety.

"Who is there?" he whispered.

"Here!" came the response.

George crawled over to where a man crouched over another man's body.

"Is he hurt?" George asked. "Has he been shot?"

He leaned closer to the man on the ground. It was Claridge!

"Mr. Claridge," George said. "Good God, man. You are badly hurt! Let me help you." George pushed the striker away and took Claridge's head in his lap. "Are you in pain? Where does it hurt?" He watched the red stain spread across Michael Claridge's white shirt even as he said these words.

"It should have worked," Claridge whispered.

George had to bend his head close to the lips in order to make out the words. He pressed his linen handkerchief to Claridge's wound.

"Talking uses up your strength," he said to the weak man. "I must go to get you some help!"

Claridge clutched his hand. "Don't go," he said. "You are the closest thing to a friend I have here and I need a friend. I never wanted to die all alone."

"But," George began, then reconsidered. "Schmitt," he called to the man who had beckoned him over in the first place, "wave your handkerchief so the soldiers will let you through. Go to them. Tell them we need a doctor. They probably have wounded, too. Tell them the shooting is over! Everyone here," he called, "lay down your weapons right now. Guns will do you no good; surely you can see that."

Schmitt waved his makeshift white flag and left the protection of the barricades. No shots were fired. Thank God, George breathed.

"Spencer," Claridge wheezed, "why didn't this strike go right? What went wrong here?"

"Call me George," he answered. "My name is George, to my friends." He swallowed back tears as he saw the wounded man growing paler and weaker before his eyes.

"Mine's Mike. God, it hurts! I guess my wife was right to leave me when she did. There was no future in it. No future." He clutched George's hand, groaned, and sank into unconsciousness. George doubted that the doctor would arrive in time. He felt no shame at the tears that dripped onto Claridge's hand.

By morning, Claridge had died. He had never regained consciousness. The strikers, several of whom had been wounded in the fray, felt confused and scared. They came to Farrel and begged to come back to work on the trolleys with none of their demands met. Farrel agreed. Two months after it began, the strike ended. It had cost thousands of dollars, one precious life, a half-dozen injuries, and the pride of a town that had believed in civilization. Farrel, edgy and defensive, was probably the only person who did not feel that the cost had been too high.

Thirty-one

The town struggled to return to normal. Once again people complained about the weather—too hot, too cold, too wet—expected their trolleys to run on time, and began to patch up their belief in progress.

Farrel felt himself to be *persona non grata* and kept himself invisible in terms of public appearances or even purely social gatherings. Even that action, though, could not completely protect him from the debilitating effect of the feelings engendered by the strike. At work he had to continue to deal with George, who laid Claridge's death at his feet. At home, what is more, he could seldom manage to avoid Sarah's cold, unloving eyes which seemed to accuse him of inhumanity.

Farrel still felt that he had taken the right actions all along the line. But the universality of the reaction against him made him surly and defensive. For the first time since he had beaten up the woman in his saloon a year ago, he began to drink heavily. The worst part of that, he found, was that even getting drunk seemed hardly to help. He gave it up again.

He would not have thought that other people's opinions meant so much to him, but he began to sink deeper and deeper into depression. He was suddenly so tired that he could not face waking up in the mornings. By the end of the day, he had to drag himself home. He often fell asleep shortly after dinner.

This pattern went on for a time long enough so that even Farrel could not ignore its implications. He tried to rationalize it in a variety of ways. He had been working at a frantic rate for a number of years. I must just be exhausted, he told himself. Or, perhaps, he was about to fall victim to one of the periodic sicknesses that seemed to sweep through Richmond in early spring. That would explain why this strike business had affected him so strongly, he reasoned. He would not accept the fact that he might have made a terrible mistake and that was why he was depressed.

"I'm bone tired," he said to Sarah one evening a month of so after the Richmond Massacre, as the bloody night that ended the strike was called. "I'm bone tired and I need to get away. The Louisiana Purchase Exposition is about to open in St. Louis." He waved the magazine he had been reading, a copy of *Harper's Weekly*. "They call it the St. Louis World's Fair. It will be full of exciting machinery, inventions, amusements. I would like to go and put Richmond completely out of my mind. Would you care to take such a trip with me?"

Sarah, who had been doing some needlepoint, laid the handiwork in her lap. She looked across the room at her husband. His hair had turned gray at the temples, she noticed. He does look tired, she realized. His handsome face was getting lined. This year had taken its toll.

She felt a surprising surge of compassion for the man she saw across from her. Poor Farrel, she thought; life fulfills so few of its promises. "The children can get along without mamma," she said aloud. "I think we deserve a vacation. Yes, that is a good idea. Go ahead and make reservations for us."

He smiled at her, and she forced herself to smile back. Then they returned to their private thoughts.

The next day Sarah set about planning for the trip.

"Mother," she lamented over the telephone, "help me, I need a new wardrobe."

"Bravo! At last you begin to think of your looks again. You have neglected yourself too long. But an entire wardrobe?"

"Farrel wants us to take a holiday together, our first since our honeymoon. But my clothes are old and out of style. Surely I should not go away wearing them."

"Make a pot of tea, *tochter,* and I can come right over with some magazines for us to look through for ideas. When do you need the clothes?"

"Oh, my goodness, Mamma, I forgot to ask! Come over anyway, and we can start the planning. When Farrel comes home at midday, perhaps he can give us an idea of the date."

"I will be by you in less than an hour. So good-bye."

Sarah hung up the phone and sat there thinking of the trip. It was an exciting prospect to leave Richmond behind just now. Imagine, she thought, that we have not gone away together since that abbreviated honeymoon.

She had been away with George more often than with her husband. She also felt clearly, now that she had the memory of their week together last summer and since the horrible experience of the streetcar strike, that she loved George more than she loved Farrel—more than she had ever loved Farrel. By what invisible strands, then, did Farrel continue to hold her? Custom, as much as anything, she reasoned. Well, she must put these thoughts aside.

She felt something for Farrel, and that was what she must think about now. Whether it was pity or love, at least it would allow her to go away with him. She could offer him her companionship during this time which was such a troubled time for him, and perhaps they would each benefit. Certainly anything that would serve to remove some of the bitterness and anger from her heart would be something she would welcome. This trip to St. Louis might be just the thing. She would have to read the article Farrel had been reading and see if she could learn something about the city she would be visiting and about the celebration Farrel had mentioned.

But for now she must have Bessie prepare some

goodies for her mother's arrival. What fun it was going to be once again to plan a vacation wardrobe. She would think of it as a second honeymoon. She hoped its outcome would be more favorable than that of the first one, when they were called back to Richmond due to the streetcar accident.

It was ironic that their first trip ended because of a streetcar disaster and this one would begin because of one. The Hurstwood name was anathema in Richmond since the strike's end, and Sarah knew that must be hard for Farrel to take. He so much defined himself in terms of whether or not people viewed him as an important and powerful person. It was that aspect of his personality that made him act boastful and pompous on occasion, the part of him she liked least.

The only people who seemed to really mean something to Farrel were George and herself, and now even they regarded him in a strongly negative light. Yes, these must be very bleak times for her husband.

As for her own situation, some people turned away from her as well, since she bore the Hurstwood name. They no doubt assumed that she could have influenced Farrel if she had so chosen. Sarah accepted this rejection philosophically. Her true friends—especially George and Rose and the rabbi—and her family, of course, knew her as she truly was, not simply as the bearer of a name. It was their opinion which she valued. The superficial world was ever fickle. Women

460

generally realize this more easily than men. Perhaps because we are the ones who bear the children, she thought. In a way, she felt sorry for Farrel and for so many men who tried to rule the world, but who had so little reality in their lives—so little true friendship, so little true love. Such a trivial understanding of what had worth, she thought.

As these thoughts developed in Sarah's mind, she realized that they reflected a change that had gradually been taking place in her. When she had first married and for a long time after that, being a rich lady and having people think highly of the poor little immigrant girl—which was how she saw herself then—was of great importance. Gradually, though, she had begun to recognize how empty the regard of people who neither knew nor loved you could be. Was it Lawrence's death, she asked herself, that precipitated the change? That might have been the initial catalyst—that and Maxine's suicide which was a desperate attempt to forestall the world's negative judgment, Sarah now thought. But she felt that most of her change had actually taken place more recently than that. It seemed to have something to do with the close bonds she had established over the last year with Rose and with George—the real love that she felt with them. Her sense that she could be herself with them, and still be accepted, seemed to have rearranged her priorities.

When her mother arrived, Sarah tried to tell her what she had been thinking, but the words she found seemed too weak to convey the power of her feelings. She gave up on the attempt and turned her attention to the current fashions. It would still be fun to play the game of looking fashionable, even though she realized it was a game. Also, it would please Farrel and that was to a great extent the reason for this trip: to help Farrel.

The following week was frantic for Sarah with supervision of the sewing and with fittings and with packing. Farrel took charge of the actual travel plans, of course, and Sarah was grateful for that. Then in a flurry of hats and bags and boxes and gloves, they were on their way—on their way to St. Louis, Missouri.

Sarah had never been so far inland. It amazed her as they traveled south and west how vast a country America was. Farrel assured her that St. Louis was less than halfway across its breadth. When they arrived, the weather was considerably warmer than it had been in Richmond, and the air was full of music. Everywhere one heard the virtual theme song of the fair, "Meet Me in St. Louis, Louis." Soon Sarah was humming along:

> *"Meet me in St. Louis, Louis,*
> *Meet me at the fair.*
> *Don't tell me the lights are shining*
> *Anywhere but there!"*

Sarah had read a great deal about the fair, but none of the facts had prepared her for the overwhelming reality. She had even memorized specific information so that she could impress

Farrel with her knowledge. For example, she knew that they had established a new channel way for the local river, the River Des Peres. By means of this diversion of the water, they had created a canal the entire length and breadth of the fairgrounds. People could ride through the fair in Italian gondolas along this man-made waterway.

Sarah knew this because she had read an article in *Harper's Weekly* which described the engineering feat involved. The writer had also stated that the fair covered one thousand two hundred and forty acres. That number stayed in Sarah's mind, one thousand two hundred and forty. Of course, she was not exactly sure how large an area one thousand two hundred and forty acres was, but she knew it was an awful lot of land. She also knew that when she mentioned the number to her husband, the exact number, it would impress him. He was so fond of facts, and she had always been so disregarding of them.

Other reading had taught Sarah that the Olympic Games would be held at the fair, the first time ever that they would occur in America. The ancient system of Olympic Games had just begun again eight years earlier, in 1896. Naturally enough, those games took place in Athens. Then in 1900, the games moved to Paris. And now, in 1904, Sarah Hurstwood along with hundreds of thousands of others would get to watch this athletic spectacle in America. She could hardly wait.

She had tried to remember the many different exhibits listed in *Cosmopolitan* magazine's article.

463

She had read it twice, but there were just too many of them. There were, after all, almost two thousand different buildings on the fairgrounds. The number stuck in her head the same way the one thousand two hundred and forty acres did. She knew there was a Department of Education and a Department of Fine Arts and a Department of Manufacture and a Department of Agriculture. She knew as well that there was a Department of Electricity and a Department of Transportation and that Farrel had been involved with them in some way during the planning.

Still, when she rode along the canal with her husband that first night, she could hardly believe she was in a real place. She almost felt that she had imagined it all, and that she was caught up in a sort of magic dream.

When she was a little girl, her parents had taken her to the opera where she had seen a beautiful lady lazing in a long boat as she sang of love. Sarah began to feel that she had somehow transported herself back to that time and that she had become that lady. She was the lovely lady who lazed the length of the boat as thoughts of love flooded her being.

There was music in the air. The song was one of love, in fact. But it was not Sarah who was singing. She was no child now, and she was not a part of the audience in the theater hall. No, she was a grown woman in a special place with the man who had been her husband for so many years that she could sometimes not remember a time when he was not a part of her life.

Sarah listened to the water lap the sides of the yellow-and-red gondola. The gentle sound accompanied the gondolier's deep voice. "Santa Lucia" he sang as he poled them along the lagoon past the lighted banks and illuminated fountains. It was their first night at the St. Louis World's Fair. Farrel touched Sarah's arm, pointing to the cascades, the terraced waterfalls flowing down to the lagoon from the Palace of Art high above them as the Venetian boat continued on its way. It glided under an arched bridge and then out again into the starlit night. With a graceful sweep the gondolier slipped his oar into the water which moved lazily by them.

Farrel's profile, outlined against a splashy backdrop of water-blurred lights, looked unfamiliar. Sarah could almost imagine she was with a stranger. It would be nice, she thought, to be able to leave behind their years together for a while and pretend she was with a handsome stranger.

Farrel noticed how seriously she gazed at him, and he saw that his child bride had grown up. She had become a mature woman, this lovely companion who sat across from him in the gondola. He lifted her hand to his mouth and began to kiss the fingertips one after the other. He felt a response flow from her and felt encouraged to continue with his attentions.

As for Sarah, her heart had begun to pound in the old slow way she had almost forgotten. She rested her free hand on Farrel's thigh, allowing the night to mask her boldness. A sigh fluttered at her lips. Farrel slid his arm around her waist. His

465

fingers caressed her through her crushed velvet cummerbund. In the daylight it had been a brilliant turquoise, a bold contrast to her navy skirt and pink blouse. In the dark it had no color, only a soft feel almost like flesh. A tightness began inside of Farrel. Perhaps, he told himself, they would skip the sightseeing tonight.

The gondola pulled in to the landing, and Farrel helped Sarah out. Their rooms were just a short walk away. He had chosen the poshest place for them, the Inside Inn, which was the only accommodation within the fairgrounds themselves.

"Sarah," he whispered in the voice that sounded to her like a stranger's voice, "Sarah come to the room with me. We will have other times to sightsee."

"Yes," she agreed softly, not wanting to break the spell.

Within minutes he slid his key into the door of Room 242. As he held the door open, she slipped past him like some secret paramour, still maintaining the pretense of anonymity which she found so exciting. Farrel closed the door. They stood inches apart in the encompassing darkness.

"It is so dark that I cannot see anything," Sarah breathed.

Farrel pulled her roughly to him. "There is no need to see," he muttered; "we can feel, can't we?"

His mouth sought hers ending the need for words. This ardent lover thrilled Sarah. It resembled no one she had ever known. The electricity that did not light the room pulsed through her body. The darkness allowed them to abandon restraint, ignore respectability. Fingers fumbled with cloth, with fastenings, until flesh found flesh. Hands and lips reached and touched. Soon they were lying across the bed over and under each other. Sarah cried out; Farrel moaned. They were invisible to each other. There were no judging eyes. Alone together in a strange room in an unknown city's exotic setting, fantasies set their juices flowing. Reality proved no disappointment. When they finally fell into sleep they were not strangers, but husband and wife. Sarah's last thought before she drifted into dreams was that this must be the true basis of marriage—this and the survival of children.

The fair was a catalog of miracles. Hundreds of thousands of visitors experienced ice cream and waffles for the first time, saw radium-lit watches and submarines, watched demonstrations of wireless telegraphy, moving pictures, automatic telephone service, and more and more and more. The Hurstwoods spent the mornings together wandering from exhibit to exhibit spread across the seemingly endless acres of the fairgrounds. By lunchtime, Sarah was in need of some quiet time alone. She returned to their rooms with her head spinning, full of sights, noises, and new ideas. She spent the afternoons either napping or writing voluminous letters to her mother, to the children, and to George.

"Dear George," she wrote in one of these letters, "I can express to you what I dare not speak about to my husband and that is my sense of the terrible wastefulness of this exposition. Surely any thoughtful visitor must feel the same way. The first thing which seems to me despicable is the great cost involved. Imagine, the cost of this spectacle is nearly forty million dollars! Even more horrifying than that, though, is the dreadful waste involved in the destruction of these incredibly beautiful buildings after the fair is over.

"Everywhere, my dear friend, everywhere there is the evidence that the planners have sought to produce bigness at the expense of harmony.

"Enough of my gloomy thoughts though. There are so many fascinating aspects to this Louisiana Purchase Exposition that I believe I could fill page after page with lists of modern miracles that I have seen with my own eyes. Just yesterday, for example, I saw a demonstration of a central vacuum-cleaner system to make the cleaning of dust from a house a simple matter. One person could easily handle the work, it seemed, no matter how large the house was. There was also an electric machine to wash dishes. Can you believe that? And an electric pot in which to make coffee. Soon all the work within the house as well as that outside the house will be performed by electrical servants! Whatever shall we do with the hours of extra leisure? I wonder."

To her mother, Sarah kept her tone lighter. She stressed the toys and fun of the fair. She tried to describe the look and feel of the fair.

"There is a section of the fairgrounds, Mamma," she wrote, "called the Pike where one can view wondrous amusements. I saw a team of oriental jugglers there who could balance a half-dozen items in the air. There were tightrope dancers, also, who stepped out upon a gossamer thread so high above me that I had to strain to see. The spotlight caught the glitter of the costumes, and I could imagine the gyrations taking place over my head to be the antics of some marvelous insect. When I allowed myself to realize that these were actually human beings, I shuddered at the thought that one slight movement out of equilibrium and they would plunge to their deaths before our eyes.

"Most amazing of all the activities on the Pike, I thought, was the display of the new entertainment form, the moving picture. I must remember to tell George Spencer about them when I return. You know of his great interest in photography. Well, this moving-picture idea carries photography into a new realm. The pictures tell the story in action. It is quite as though one of my novels had come to life. I saw an amusing bit of nonsense with cops chasing some foolish louts who were not really wicked but seemed to go from one bad situation to another. No matter how hard they tried, they remained in trouble with the law. It was highly comic although I am sure many lives are just like that and to those people it is not amusing at all.

"Another moving picture was a romance, and I saw how easy it would be to drift into the delight of make-believe happiness. When these moving-picture palaces are in every city in America, they may prove to be dispensers of a very powerful opiate, a drug to keep the unhappy people of the world from action. I think the name of the drug could well be *dreams!*

"This morning we visited the exhibit of the Department of State. It took place in the U.S. Government building which was a huge building with numerous Doric columns outside. Inside, however, it was strangely bare and felt a bit like a huge barn—quite unlike the rich plushness of the Brazilian Pavilion. It made me quite sad to think that we could not have presented ourselves better in our own country. Nonetheless, it was interesting to see the treaties and medals that have been so important a part of our history. I saw a Wedgewood bust of George Washington as well as his quaint little eyeglasses. There was also a brick from the Great Wall of China! I heard a speech by Mr. John Hay, the Secretary of State, who had come down from the capital for the occasion. He exhorted us to remember that America was the greatest country in the world and the message was well received even by the many foreign visitors in the audience.

"There are so many buildings that I cannot possibly see them all so each day I must decide for that moment. In the mornings, I frequently plan to accomplish twice as much as I actually do. The time going from place to place is always longer than sightseeing; also a very wearying experience, so that by midday I feel quite exhausted and must return to the rooms to rest.

"Tomorrow, though, is our last day, and I intend to visit the Department of Fine Arts where they have many famous paintings on display including Calixto's 'Wood Chopper.' Also, Farrel has mentioned something about taking me through the Department of Transportation so it will be a busy day. I wondered that he had not taken me there at once. Surely his streetcar is on display. It is unlike him to be so modest.

"Soon I return home, and we can talk at greater length together about this wonderful trip. Let me only state once again how close it has made me feel toward Farrel. Perhaps that is really the greatest miracle of the fair. My husband and I have been happy together during our days here."

Farrel used the time during which Sarah wrote letters to explore the work being exhibited on motors, to talk to others involved as he was in their development and refinement. He was proud of the fact that two of his latest ideas were on display. He had not mentioned it to Sarah. He was saving that for their last day. He thought it strange how shy he felt about showing off for Sarah—afraid she would either not understand or not care. Embarrassed in a way he could hardly figure out himself, he thought about waiting with his breath held for Sarah's praise.

The first of Hurstwood's inventions on display at the 1904 World's Fair was a streetcar motor which could use alternating current. Previous street railways had needed expensive substations to convert alternating current to the direct current the cars required. This development marked a tremendous advance in streetcar operation, making them more economical than anyone had ever dared dream.

The second of his inventions was the safety-clutch handle. A knob on the controller which the conductor must press continuously for the car to remain in motion. If an emergency occurred, if the conductor had a heart attack, say, his hand would automatically release its pressure on the button thereby activating the brakes. The car would come quickly and safely to a stop instead of hurtling madly along out of control. Its popular moniker was the "dead man's switch," and Farrel felt sure it would prevent many accidents in the years to come.

When Farrel finally did lead Sarah through the Transportation building her reaction did not disappoint him. She thrilled to his importance, to his streetcar model elevated on a revolving platform so people could inspect its undersides, to the mysterious workings of his mysterious mind.

"You are truly a wonder," she said. She spoke fervently. He could not doubt her sincerity. "I am married to an amazing and brilliant person." She pressed his arm. They were able now to communicate more easily by subtle touches than through words. During the five days they had been in St. Louis they had made love every night, some mornings, and had shared kisses and hugs at other times throughout the day. Such an abundance of romance, such fervor, had never been part of their lives together. It was another of the fair's miracles, perhaps. They each put aside bitter memories. On this afternoon, as they stood arm in arm before the spinning model of the magic machine that had brought them together, Farrel's streetcar, they were closer than they had ever been.

"Soon we must leave for the train, you know," he said softly.

"What a shame," Sarah answered, expressing both of their feelings. They shared a smile.

"I hired a special car to take us to the station. The Expo's car, in fact. Pulled a few wires, as they say." He was the old boastful Farrel again. Sarah laughed. "We can grab a bite to eat before we leave," he suggested.

Together they made their way through crowds of couples clinging and staring, laughing and touching, just like themselves. But after lunch they sat in a special car and sped away from the fair at forty miles per hour, not at all as the others would do.

The automobile they were in had plate-glass windows covered with silken curtains. They sat in plush individual armchairs. The driver sat in his own compartment, separated from them by a glass partition. There was a phone; they could contact him with it if they wished.

"My God," Sarah exclaimed, "what does a car like this cost? What an incredible luxury. And so fast!"

"The sign on the exhibit listed it at eighteen thousand dollars." Farrel laughed at the expression of shock on Sarah's face, but privately he agreed that such an outrageous expenditure for a single family to make in order to own a motorcar was a disgrace.

Thirty-two

It was a blessing to Sarah to be able to return to Richmond with a feeling of closeness to Farrel. In order to maintain it, she allowed herself to forget the pain left in the wake of the strike, and the ongoing anguish felt by the families of the strikers; tried even to ignore the stricken look that remained on George Spencer's face. They seldom saw each other.

"George," she said into the phone receiver several months after her return from St. Louis, "this time I refuse to take no for an answer. You have refused every invitation to step foot into this house for too long. Enough is enough. I expect you at five!"

"Sarah—" he began.

"Not another word, my love. Bye." Sarah hung up before George could answer. She sat with her trembling hand on the receiver. The call, carefully planned and rehearsed, had cost her more effort than its casual tone implied. She could not bear

474

the hostility that continued to flame between George and Farrel. She had determined to do everything in her power to ease it. This dinner was to be a big step in that direction. It would be just the three of them as it had been so many, many times over the years. So many dinners in happier times. She hoped the echoes of those times would reverberate through tonight's meal.

Sarah pressed a button beside the phone; one of Farrel's wonderful inventions, a buzzer to call the servants. Every room had such a button and each button lit up a special square in the butler's pantry. Then one of the servants would know at a glance where he or she was wanted.

"Yes'm," Clara spoke from the doorway. Clara had stayed with the Hurstwoods through the years. Sarah, looking across at her now, saw her own increasing age mirrored darkly.

"Clara, how is Bessie?"

Bessie, the mainstay of the household for so long, had fallen ill over the summer with some mysteriously undiagnosable disease. The best the doctor had been able to offer was laudanum, a painkiller which had only a brief period of effectiveness. Recently, Bessie's legs could not manage to support her weight. She had had a bad fall in the kitchen a week ago and had remained in bed since then. Clara had taken over the cooking and did a pretty good job of it, too, Sarah thought.

"She's awful weak. Weaker every day it seems."

"Oh, Lord," Sarah sighed. "I must call the doctor again. Maybe I had better have a visit with her today, too."

"Yes'm," the servant answered and turned to leave the room.

"Wait," Sarah called. "I rang for another reason, too, Clara. Mr. Spencer is coming for dinner. Can you make something nice? I know it is short notice for you."

Sarah had remained seated during this conversation. Now she rose and walked toward her servant as Clara answered, "Of course I can. Don't you worry none about me."

Sarah reached out and held on to her old friend's arm. They stood that way for a time.

"We are in our thirties, Clara, imagine! Practically old women! My God, where does the time go?"

Clara whistled softly through her teeth and closed her eyes. Opening them again she shook her head.

"Our little ones are the same good friends as we was when we was little. Sometimes I looks at them and I don' know how it all happened. These years roll by and roll by."

Sarah felt her throat tighten. She could hardly swallow. Her hand dropped to her side. What was she crying over? she asked herself. Bessie, or Clara, her parents growing older, or herself. Aging, aging, and then death.

"Thank you, Clara," she said. "It will be just the three of us. Have the children fed early."

"I'll take care of it, don't you fret."

Later, Sarah stood nervously outside Bessie's room. She never felt comfortable talking to sick people. Illness scared her; she could never hide it. She forced herself to raise her hand and knock. There was a scuttling from inside the room. Then Hector, Sarah's driver and the father of Clara's children opened the door.

"G'day, missy," he greeted her with a wide grin. "Clara told me you'd be comin'." He bowed her into the dark room. "I'll leave you two alone awhile." He ducked out the door and pulled it shut behind him.

There was so little light Sarah could hardly make out Bessie propped up on her bed in the corner. Gradually, though, Sarah's eyes adjusted to the dark.

"Bessie dear, it's Sarah. Would you like me to open the window and let in the light?"

"Is it sunning out?" Bessie's weak voice asked.

"Yes, it's a glorious day."

"Then open it up, darlin' and let God's smile in." As though even these few words exhausted her, Bessie fell into a fit of coughing. Sarah pulled aside the dusty drapes, flung up the window and hurried to Bessie's side.

"Bessie, Bessie, what can I do to help?"

Sarah leaned over the coughing figure. She patted her shoulder helplessly. In horror she felt how skeletal the sick woman had become. Her once-hefty body was gaunt. Her eyes still gleamed, but they seemed to be the last repository of her vital energies.

"Help me die is all."

"Oh no," Sarah cried out, tears stinging her eyes. "No more dying. Don't even talk of it!"

"Child," Bessie began, pulling Sarah down to a place beside her on the bed, "there's lots worse than death when your time is up. I'm old and tired, lambie. I don't mind the idea of rest with no more pain. Not one bit."

"The doctor's coming again. He'll be here soon, and he can make you better," Sarah insisted despite the contrary evidence in Bessie's face.

"Just pray with me. I never get tired of Psalms." Bessie lay back against the pillows. Sarah picked up the worn Bible in her outstretched hand. She flipped through a few pages before deciding on the psalm she knew best, the one which she could recite by heart.

"The Lord is my shepherd," she began, "I shall not want."

A lovely smile covered Bessie's face as she heard the familiar lines. There was a knock on the door and Hector stuck his head in. "Doctor's here."

"Tell him just a minute," Sarah answered and continued the prayer down to the Amen which Bessie echoed. "Bring the doctor in now," Sarah called. She leaned over, kissed Bessie's forehead, and whispered, "Bless you."

"Good-bye my darlin'. Tell the babies Bessie said good-bye."

"Oh, Bessie," Sarah began, but the doctor took her by the arm and led her to the door.

"Will she be all right?"

"God knows. Now go back to your family."

The door closed and Sarah was back in the hall. Somehow she knew that Bessie's instinct was sound. She would die soon. Another death in the household. Sarah leaned back against the wall allowing the coolness to ease its way along her back.

Over sherry that evening, before Farrel's arrival, Sarah confronted George.

"You have been avoiding me since my return from St. Louis, George, and I want to know why. Have I done something to offend you?"

George regarded the woman sitting across from him. She had a new self-assurance that made her, as the French say, *formidable*. He noticed for the first time strands of gray in her hair, which she now wore parted in the middle and pulled tightly back in a bun on the nape of her neck. A proper matron, he thought, but knew as he thought it that it was an inappropriate phrase. There was a force that shone from Sarah which transcended the customs of the moment. She was Woman, pure and simple, with all the power that implied.

In many ways her appearance had changed little since he had first met her and yet he realized with a shock that she had passed the thirty-year mark, had turned thirty-one on her last birthday. She was a plump morsel, as she had always been . . . her soft, round arms seeming to invite his caress . . . her full bosom the place he most wanted to rest his head. It had been so long since they had been together.

"Sarah," he whispered hoarsely, his voice affected by the direction his thoughts were taking, "I have stayed away because of the trouble over the strike." He paused, hesitant as to whether he should bring up the rest of it.

"Is that the real reason? The only one?"

He shook his head. Clearing his throat, he said, "You and Farrel seemed to be doing some making up. I knew that my being around would not be any help."

Sarah frowned, pursing her lips into a little O. She sipped her drink.

"Your feelings are right," she admitted. "Your presence does make me painfully aware of Farrel's shortcomings. Also of the alternative which you offer. But I must put that out of my thoughts and so must you. I need your friendship, George. I treasure it. Let us step aside from the other aspects and return to the true basis of our friendship."

His heart felt like a heavy stone. He realized the significance of what she was saying. She was setting down her terms, and her terms meant no more languorous times lying stretched out beside her sweet soft body.

"Never," he exclaimed, horrified, his tone somewhere between a question and a despairing cry.

A bustle in the hall signaled Farrel's imminent arrival.

"For now," Sarah relented, placing her hand on his for a moment. She had indeed meant never, but could not bear the pain she saw reflected on her dear friend's face. She stood up and called to her husband.

"Mr. Hurstwood, we are here in the parlor awaiting you." More and more often she called Farrel by his first name both in public and private, but she felt awkward doing so just now before George, as though somehow it would carry more meaning than she intended.

In a moment Farrel stood before them, filling the doorway. The three of them formed a tableau held poised in a dynamic balance. Each of us, Sarah thought, is a magnet drawing the other two close. A strange triad.

"Here we are at last back together as we should be."

Her words marked the start of a pleasant evening which did indeed begin the healing process between the two partners, just as Sarah had hoped.

Thirty-three

As the year ran down and 1904 aged to 1905, Richmond, too, allowed the bitter memories of the streetcar strike to slide into the darkness of the past which included other such sorrows as the financial panic of 1893 and before that the dreadful defeat of the Confederacy. People continued to believe in the power of the future, and after all, it was still early in the new century. Richmonders could read their news in either the morning *Times-Dispatch* or the afternoon *News Leader*. The news they read in either paper was of growth: the railroads were expanding and Richmond was going to be an important train center. Granite quarrying was going to be an important new industry. The local quarry was going to provide more jobs, more wealth. Between the lines of the papers the people read the essential message of the twentieth century, that the future looked bright, brighter than anything they had even dreamed.

By the spring of 1905, Sarah could invite George over for the evening when Farrel was out of town and they would talk together or play with the children without any secret looks or touches. And Sarah spent her days so involved with the children that she hardly missed the old days. Someday, though, she thought, when the children are older I would like to go back to my teaching.

When the lazy days of summer arrived, Sarah discovered she was pregnant again. Farrel felt delighted. He thought it marked the bond of their new closeness, the rededication of their marriage that had taken place during their St. Louis trip. Sarah shared his delight and felt an added relief that she had not been with George in that way. In her secret heart she believed this new baby would replace the baby she had deprived Farrel of—her daughter, Maura—George's baby. As far as she knew, he suspected nothing, but still this new baby would be important—her special gift to her husband. The apology she must never state in words—for all their sakes.

When George heard the news from Farrel, he offered his congratulations sincerely. He felt a pang of loss, though, which he experienced most strongly when he was back in his room alone. He mulled the situation over in his mind many times. It seemed like the final barrier that would prevent him from ever truly winning Sarah. No, he realized, it was never to be. She would never run off with him to be his alone. He must learn to live with the situation as it was or go off by himself and try to find a different life. Even as he thought it, he knew he could never leave. Sarah was the love of his life. He must remain close to her however he could.

He threw himself into his work on the continuing expansion of the streetcar and interurban lines while Farrel went on inventing still further refinements in the already existing system. They worked together well. Time passed as it does whether we wish it or not. Soon they were celebrating another new year, 1906. With such holidays as Christmas and New Year's Day added on to everybody's birthdays, which Sarah insisted on making a fuss about, there seemed always to be a celebration these days at the Hurstwoods'. An extra special one was being planned for the middle of February to celebrate George's fiftieth birthday. Sarah had secretly designed a surprise party that would include a large chunk of the local populace, but George had somehow gotten wind of it and pleaded with Sarah fervently to settle for a small party. That would please him, he insisted, infinitely better. Just his co-workers, Sarah's parents, and a few of his friends whose names he provided to her. Reluctantly, she relented and did as he wished.

She was large with child and due before March so it was really most improper for her to be doing any entertaining. "But a fiftieth birthday," she exclaimed to Farrel when he asked her to reconsider. "It is too important an occasion to let propriety stand in the way." So she went on with her plans. I can always establish myself on the sofa, she reasoned, and be the *grande dame*. Just a little gathering, she added, not the big surprise party I had in mind.

The party night, though, held surprises of its own. More than enough surprises, as it turned out. The guests gathered, the champagne punch was having its salubrious effect, the candles glittered with that wonderful soft light that made people look prettier than they were, and Sarah signaled for the cake's arrival when she felt the first unmistakably powerful labor contraction. She had been ignoring twinges most of the afternoon, but this pain was too powerful to ignore. She turned to watch George's face as the butler carried the huge cake, blazing with candles, slowly, slowly like a ship of state toward him. His eyes, though, turned out to be fastened on her and she felt herself flush. Then a terrific contraction rolled her body over into a ball of pain. George rushed to her side. Since he was the birthday boy and as such the center of attention at the moment, everyone was suddenly surrounding Sarah who sincerely wished she could simply disappear.

"Please, Mr. Spencer, please," she insisted, "blow out your candles and make a wish. I will be just fine, really. Here, let me give you your birthday kiss!" As she leaned forward brushing his cheek with her lips, she whispered, "Don't make a fuss, George. Please."

With effort he turned from her. He walked to the cake which Samson had placed in the center of the table.

"Hurry up, George," a man's voice called. Was it Farrel? "You're melting the icing." He blew at the mass of candles. Then he blew again. And yet again. Finally all the candles were out. The guests laughed and clapped. Sarah's mother said, "Well, maybe your wish will come true anyway," as she helped him begin the cutting.

"No, Mrs. Seewald," he answered, smiling at her, "I don't think so."

His voice was so sad she could not resist giving him a hug. But she also could not help wondering if somehow Sarah was responsible for this man's unhappiness. He never seemed to bring any women friends around and he seemed always to be with the Hurstwoods—almost a member of the family.

It was not until the cake was served and people were standing around drinking cups of coffee that George had the leisure to try to seek out Sarah. Then he noticed that she was gone, as was Farrel, and the doctor. So, he thought to himself, I was right. Sarah is about to have her baby. Then it struck him that this baby was going to be born on his birthday. If it had been possible to believe, he would have believed that Sarah had planned it this way as his birthday present. Then there was no more time for such thoughts, for his friends drew him back into the mood of the party. They insisted he be jolly. They toasted him and clapped him on the back. There were presents to open. Through it all he remained painfully conscious of the drama that must be going on above his head. When he noticed Farrel had rejoined the party group, George signaled him to the side.

"Is it true, Farrel?" he asked. "Is she all right?"

"Yes, yes," Farrel assured him, putting his arm around his old friend's shoulder. "Sam says it will be within the hour. Well, partner, we'll be able to celebrate another baby together."

As they looked into each other's eyes George asked himself as he had many times before just how much Farrel knew or suspected of his love for Sarah. It was a futile question, he knew, and he abandoned it. Farrel called for attention.

"One last toast," he announced. "To George, the best partner anyone ever had. And my best friend."

"To George" echoed around the room. It was the last burst of party spirit. Soon everyone was realizing how late it was and that they ought to be getting home. Not too much later, George and Farrel were left alone to wait out the arrival of another Hurstwood baby. Sure enough, just at the outer edge of the hour Sam Lathrop had predicted, he came down the stairs to announce the birth of a big bouncing baby boy.

"A boy," Farrel repeated after him.

"How is Sarah?" George asked.

"Fine," Sam assured them. "She's asleep now after her hard work."

"If it was a boy," Farrel went on, "we had decided to name him Powell. But arriving on your birthday like this, George, must be a sign. I am sure Sarah would have no objections to his being named Powell George. What do you think of that, old friend?"

George felt stunned. But after a few moments he recovered enough to answer, "I am deeply honored."

"Well, that's it then. Let's drink to the baby's health."

Farrel poured out brandy for the three men and they shared the absolutely last toast of the night, a wish for baby Powell George Hurstwood's good health.

Thirty-four

In the days that followed, the baby's health did prosper. Sarah, though, had a hard time recovering from the baby's birth, harder than from any of the others. Her spirits were good, but she just could not seem to get her strength back. Dr. Lathrop, though semiretired and taking on no new patients, came every day to check on her. He painfully dragged himself up the stairs to her bedroom.

"Young lady," he announced finally when Powell was almost two months old, "I am too old to climb these steps, and you are too young to take permanently to your bed. It is time to get you up on your feet."

"But I do try! I have made it downstairs a number of times, but I get so weak and tired I need help to make it back to my bed. What's wrong with me?"

"I'm not really sure."

Sarah was dressed in a chintz dressing gown.

She sat in the cushioned rocker near the window. There were roses in her cheeks. Sam thought she looked as handsome as he had ever seen her. What then could her problem be due to? He asked himself that over and over.

"I seem to have trouble catching my breath. My chest hurts just about all the time."

Her words sent a chill of fear through him. Perhaps she had contracted a lung disease of some kind.

"Why don't we see about moving you downstairs for a while? That way you can be more a part of the family without the strain of going up and down the stairs."

"Oh, I would *love* to be downstairs."

"Come on then. We can help each other make it down. It will do the entire family good to see you in their midst."

He put his arm around Sarah's waist and lifted her to her feet. Together they made slow progress along the hall and down the steep and long flight of stairs. Placing Sarah in a comfortable chair, the doctor called to Samson to make preparations for Sarah's removal to the back parlor. Sarah could hear him off in the other room giving orders, but she felt so weak she did not even bother to listen. It was dizzying enough just to be downstairs in her own parlor at last. She could not take in much more than that at one time.

The sun made playful shapes on the parquet floor. Sarah watched them. She tried to relax and breathe easily. She may have dozed off, she was not at all sure, but suddenly amidst a flurry of activity she felt herself being half-carried into the back parlor. Like a china doll, she was laid delicately on the sofa that had been transformed into a day bed. Sarah looked around her like a queen surveying her realm.

"Oh, what a splendid idea. But someone will have to bring me Powell at his mealtimes."

"No, honey," Dr. Lathrop said in a kind voice as he sat beside her. "You'd better leave off nursing. I do not want you tired out any more than need be. Maybe so many babies have drained your system."

Sarah took his hand. "Can you remember how long a time I thought I would never have babies? Now here I am with Powell and Maura and Franklin and Jessica. My goodness, I have almost enough children to start a classroom of my own."

Sarah began to laugh, but then the laugh froze in her throat as she gasped for breath.

Sam leaned over her, loosening her gown at the neck and waist, helping her bend forward so she could catch her breath. When at last she was breathing easily again, the doctor ordered her some tea and left, promising to look in on her regularly.

"Remember," he chided her, "dress every morning you can and set up camp down here for the day. After dinner you can return to your bed. I think this regimen may help. Warmer days will be here soon. We will all watch you frolic then!"

During that afternoon and those that followed, Sarah gave in to the pleasure of lying about. She read a bit, had visits from the children, and often simply watched the sky change colors and shapes.

By summer she was well enough to care for the children and move freely about the house and grounds. She felt her life had been given back to her. It was a good life. She stopped questioning its purpose. Powell was a beautiful sunny baby and just watching his little six-month-old body squirm brought her joy. Her birthday passed and then her anniversary, those dates she once had believed held the essential clue to her understanding of life. Just days, she thought now, with cause for celebration. But every day was cause enough.

Farrel and George were still away more than they were around, but she did not seem to mind that too much anymore either. She was happy with her children, the men could play their industrial games. They were busy building a nation's machinery. This new attitude, Sarah decided, must be a sign of middle age. I would never have imagined it could be so peaceful.

Farrel and George were both gladdened by Sarah's recovery, for itself and because it allowed them to rededicate themselves to the expansion of the interurban. They were busy everywhere, pushing, touting, selling, building. Farrel continued to have periodic bouts of remorse about being away from his children. George had occasions when he longed for Sarah so badly he could not sleep. Then he would get drunk, buy a streetwalker's favors, hate himself the next day, and get back to work.

Time glided through the air like sand through the narrow tunnel dividing the top and bottom halves of an hourglass. The children grew taller and older. The streetcar empire spread its tracks across more and more miles of America. The calendar's sheets of days fell like leaves from a tree, and then it was the spring of 1910. Life seemed to be fulfilling at least some of its promises.

The three oldest Hurstwood children had established their own internal hierarchy from which baby Powell who had just turned four was for the moment exempt. Jessica, burdened with being the oldest, acted the role of general over her younger brother and sister. Franklin and Maura, in response to her attitude, became the rebellious privates in this family army. They disregarded her orders whenever they could get away with it. They had secret jokes, almost a separate language, and their own ways of undermining Jessica's rules. Maura was now an eight-year-old dumpling of a girl who totally adored her ten-year-old brother. Franklin, highly conscious of his role as the oldest male, resented Jessica's attempts at control. He accepted Maura's worship as his due. He used the natural power her love gave him over her to help him undermine Jessica's authority as often as possible. So it is in many families that constant skirmishes for power delineate the unending wars of childhood.

Jessica herself, now almost fourteen, was caught in the confusing process of becoming a woman. Her body was beginning to change shape, assuming the round proportions that would mark her transformation. She found herself the victim of mood changes so drastic that at one moment she would be laughing at some silly tease by one of the boys at school but in the next she would be caught up in tears and have to flee to the cloakroom. She had never felt very close to her mother, but now the tension between them was exacerbated both by Jessica's new nervousness and by her greater-than-ever need for a mother's guidance.

Unlike her mother, Jessica did not have an easy time making friends in school. She was good in her studies, but she spent most of her days alone—except for her time at home, when she felt she never got any chance to be alone. There were always those two bratty kids to be taken care of.

Jessica envied Franklin and Maura. They always seemed so close to each other. She sometimes imagined a world where she and her father could be that close, a world where they might laugh together and play silly games. At night when she lay awake in her bed longing for sleep, Jessica pretended her father would come to her room and talk to her. He would ask her about school and tell her how proud he was of her. She always struggled to get top grades so that he would be proud of her. In her favorite fantasy, her father came and sat on her bed. He called her his baby and his darling. He took her hand and drew her to him. She was sitting on his lap, and she was stroking his head. Then he would lean toward her—in her imagination she could feel his breath on her cheek—and he would kiss her. She always stopped herself from going any further when she imagined them kissing. She knew such thoughts must be very wicked. He was her father, after all. But when she lay wide awake in bed such thoughts came unbidden into her mind.

Sarah felt an awkwardness with Jessica that she could not seem to overcome. She knew her daughter wanted more from her than she could offer, but she never felt comfortable enough to reach out to Jessica. Jessie's eyes seemed always to judge her actions and always to find them unacceptable. If I could just take her in my arms, Sarah thought, just hug her and tell her that I love her, then it might be all right. If I could . . . Those eyes, though, Jessie's cold eyes, always seemed to dare her approach, and Sarah felt thwarted.

Sarah's thoughts often turned toward her daughter, her oldest child, and so it was on this night. Farrel was in New York trying to finance another venture. Sarah played with Powell distractedly as she listened to the rumbling approach of a storm. Jessica was out with the two younger children, and Sarah hoped they would hurry home. It was already dark. They should have been home before now. Where were they?

With a blast of wind that sent rain pounding against the windows, the storm struck. Powell clutched his mother around the neck and screamed in terror. Sarah heard the front door slam.

"Jessica?" she called.

"Yes, ma'am," her daughter answered. "It's me."

"Not 'it's me,' Jessica," her mother corrected; "you mean it is I. Come in, darling, by the fire. Were you caught in the storm?"

495

The fourteen-year-old, awkward but lovely, hair dangling in wet strands, came over to her mother and gave her a kiss.

In the last few months, Jessica had shot up several inches, so that now she was taller than her mother. Her hair was rust colored, and she had that almost transparent quality to her skin that marks some redheads. Her clear blue eyes, the most expressive features on her face, gazed at the world in a dazzle of beauty. Sarah looked at her daughter and realized that soon Jessica would be part of the mate-seeking world. It made her almost sad to realize that her daughter was about to enter, if she had not already, the lifelong dilemma of loving.

"Those two brats are out in the storm. If they had listened to me, we would all have been home ages ago."

Sarah felt a sense of alarm at Jessica's words.

"What do you mean, Jessica?"

"They absolutely refused to listen to me when I said a storm was coming. Brats! Powell, honey, give me a kiss."

The angular adolescent nuzzled her brother's neck until he giggled.

"Jessie, where are they? Did you bring the children home with you? Jessie, answer me!"

"I couldn't, I tell you. They refused to obey me. They ran off when I yelled at them so I came on home by myself."

"Oh, no." Sarah stood and involuntarily her hand went to her mouth.

"They'll be fine, Ma. Don't worry. They know

their way home. They'll be along soon."

"No! The thunder will scare them. What if they're lost, or hurt? I must go find them. Jessica, you stay with Powell."

Before Jessica could protest, Sarah rushed from the room. Jessie ran after her. She reached the foyer just in time to see her mother, a cape flung across her shoulders, disappear out the door.

"Ma," she called plaintively. Powell, scared by the tension in the air combined with the noise of the thunder, began to cry. His sister hurried back to the parlor and sprawled on the rug beside him.

"Don't cry, Powell, we can play a game." As if by magic, a smile replaced Powell's tears. Jessie was his favorite. She rummaged around until she found a deck of cards. They began to play Old Maid.

Meanwhile, Sarah raced along the dark streets pelted by rain and a surprise spattering of hail. She waded through puddles as she searched wildly under trees and down side streets, but she could not see her little girl and boy anywhere. She grew frantic wondering where they could be. Suddenly she realized that they must have gone to the pharmacy. Why had she been so alarmed? They loved their grandparents' shop. They could always cadge a dish of ice cream. The thought gave her a sense of relief. She hurried toward her parents' shop. The ferocity of the storm did not let up. When at last she burst through the door, she was exhausted and soaked to the skin. At her first sight of Franklin and Maura sitting at a little table, both of their faces smeared with ice cream, Sarah cried out, "Thank God!" The words escaped her before she thought about them. The children half-grinned, shamefaced. They knew they had been naughty not to listen to their sister. Before they could say a word, though, Sarah's mother took one look at her daughter and rushed away from them to her side.

"Sarah, what are you doing out on a terrible night like this?"

"I was worried about the children," she said, as she sagged against her mother, who helped her to a seat.

"Darling, surely you knew they would come here. Surely you knew that we would take good care of them. We were going to bring them home as soon as the storm let up."

"I could hardly think straight, Mamma. They were out in the storm, and I was afraid. It was foolish."

Sarah fell into a fit of coughing.

"Papa," Rachel called out. "Quick, come quick. Bring Sarah a glass of water—and some cough syrup, too. Hurry."

The children sat frozen in their seats while their grandparents rushed around caring for their mother. As soon as possible, they were all bundled together in the carriage on their way back to the Hurstwood household.

Their arrival there caused another commotion. Rachel took charge of keeping the children out of the way while Clara helped Sarah up the stairs to her room. David drove off to get the doctor.

Sarah was grateful for Clara's strong arms. She gladly accepted Clara's help out of her clothes and into her nightgown. Clara gently toweled Sarah's hair dry. Sarah lay back against the pillows letting her eyes close. She felt so chilled, so weak. By the time the doctor arrived, she was feverish and swept by bouts of coughing. The doctor checked her lungs and returned to the waiting parents with an ominous message.

"Get hold of Farrel at once. Wire him. Tell him to return as fast as possible. I am seriously worried about Sarah."

"What is it, you think?" Dave asked.

"It is her lungs that scare me. They never completely healed, you know. It is her weak point. This whole night didn't do her any good, of that I am sure. She is burning up with fever."

The three old-timers sat silently together awhile. Then the men set out for their homes, while Rachel went upstairs to sit beside Sarah's bed through the night.

The next morning Sarah was no better. By the time Farrel returned to Richmond three days later, she was seldom alert enough to speak.

"Sarah," he cried out when he first saw her pale blank face cushioned on its pile of pillows. He had just done days of riding coaches cross-country, had hardly slept or eaten, had dashed from the station and run up the steps to her room. When he came closer and noticed how far she seemed to have gone from him, his knees buckled. He sank heavily down on the edge of the bed. Farrel stretched his hand out to touch her lips, and

Sarah stirred.

"Sarah," he called again desolately. "Can you hear me?"

Her eyelids fluttered, then gradually her eyes opened and came into focus. "Darling," she whispered. Sarah raised her hand partway toward his face.

"How do you feel, Sarah? Sam says you've been mighty sick."

"I'm so weak—too weak—"

"No! Fight, Sarah. You must fight."

But she had already slipped back into that deathlike sleep and he could not rouse her. Awhile later, George joined him in his vigil.

Intermittently they dozed off. George woke with a start toward dawn and noticed Sarah's eyes were open. Farrel was slumped in his chair.

"Sarah?" he asked tentatively.

"You!" Her voice was a hoarse rattle. A slight smile turned the corners of her lips up. George leaned over her until his mouth touched the tendril of hair that lay over her ear.

"I love you so much. Don't be afraid."

"I'm not," she answered, her voice sounding stronger. "Truly. I feel so tired. I just want to sleep forever, but I feel no fear. But George," she slid her arm around his neck pulling him closer until their heads lay side by side, "I must tell you. . . . Maura . . . she is your daughter—" Her hand slipped back to the bed.

"Oh God, Sarah."

She smiled at him, then her eyes closed again. Her words, her weakness—he felt sure she was

500

dying—caused a terrible turmoil inside of George. He was glad Farrel still slept so he need not hold back the tears that rose to his eyes and coursed down his cheeks.

In the morning, Farrel and George awoke disheveled and distressed, having spent the night asleep fully dressed sitting up in their chairs.

"Farrel, it looks bad," George said.

"Don't say that!"

"But look at her. Listen to her breathing—"

"Shut up, George! I mean it." Farrel stomped to the bed. "Sarah," he hollered, "Sarah!" He knelt by the side of the bed and clutched her shoulders, shaking her. Her tongue moistened her cracked lips. She struggled to open her eyes, finally managing it.

"It hurts," she said.

"Fight, Sarah, damn it. Fight!"

Her eyes closed and for a moment Farrel thought she had slipped back into her new world, that world that resembled sleep but seemed so much more ominous. But then she spoke. Each word was followed by a pause.

"Husband . . . you were always . . . the fighter . . . in this family."

He waited for more words, for her to continue, but this time she had drifted back into her dreams.

After the doctor visited Sarah that afternoon, he beckoned the two hovering men out into the hall. "This is no good what you two are doing. Go get bathed. Take a nap. You are not helping her, and she doesn't know you are there now anyway."

"What are you saying? She will get better?"

Farrel's voice held nothing but questions.

Sam hesitated. "She is very sick. Miracles happen, but not often. Best to prepare yourself. I plan to call some people doing work on lungs in Europe. I can tell you more after I talk to them."

The three men's frowns mirrored each other. They shared an emptiness that no words could fill. "Now go get cleaned up," he commanded. "I will be back later."

The men parted company. George took the doctor home and then went home himself. Farrel called for his bath to be prepared. Within the hour he was clean and deep in a nightmare-tossed sleep. He saw Sarah sinking in high waves. She called to him in a piteous voice. He jumped awake. Though he heard nothing but silence, he hurried to Sarah's room. From the doorway he could see she was in distress. Her body was rigid. Sweat beaded her face. Her eyes were bulging as she gasped for breath. He rushed to her side.

"Sarah, you must not leave me."

Her frenzied eyes came into focus. They pierced him. She seemed to be making a desperate attempt to reach him; then she collapsed against his shoulder.

"Get the doctor," he screamed at the top of his voice, but even as he did so he was afraid that it might be too late. Sarah's skin, which had been flushed as she strained for air, paled rapidly. Even as he held her, unable to believe she might be gone from him for good, she seemed to shrink into a smaller shape. Farrel felt a dry tightness in his throat, but no tears. Later, when Rachel and the doctor and George arrived, they found Farrel still

502

numbly holding Sarah in his arms.

The doctor rushed to his patient, pushing Farrel out of the way. Sarah's parents felt certain that they had already lost their daughter or were just about to do so.

"Get out," Sam yelled at them. "Everybody get out now."

To Farrel it meant the end had come. He looked over at his in-laws.

Rachel rocked back and forth cuddling her grief and terror. She sobbed softly into her handkerchief, muffling the sound as best she could. David stood next to her, his hand on her shoulder.

Farrel could hardly bear the weight of the stone that had replaced his heart and was crushing his chest. He had to be alone. He had to lie down. He had to sleep so he would not think. He left the room. The doctor had left a sleeping draught which he drank down eagerly, hoping it would put him beyond the reach of memories, dreams, pain.

When he awoke many hours later, it was the morning of another day. He had expected Sam to wake him with news of Sarah's death, but the household, though hushed, seemed to be going about its routines in a fairly normal way. My God, he thought wildly, she must still be alive! He burst into her room. The doctor sat there beside the bed where Sarah lay still and pale.

"Sam, what is going on? Why didn't you get me up?"

"There was no need, and you could use the rest. A madman is no help to me here. There are decisions to be made. Can you make them now?"

"Decisions? What decisions?"

"How about breakfast? We can talk; she can sleep. Besides, an old man needs food! I mean you, of course. I carry my age as lightly as a feather! These night-long vigils are no strain on me."

Farrel gleaned some hope from Sam's manner. If it were the final word, the death sentence, that he had to deliver, surely he would be unable to make such light-hearted comments. The two men went down to the main floor.

"I consulted with a specialist by telephone last night," Sam said when the two men were seated over coffee. "He agreed to see her, but I have to decide if she is well enough to travel."

"Travel! Absurd! Have him come here. I can pay whatever he asks." Farrel pounded his fist on the table, and the cups clattered in their saucers.

"If you hired a car and a driver to bring him from New York and take him back, then I suppose that would be possible."

"Consider it done."

"But, Farrel, not so fast. There are other aspects to consider."

"Then tell me, for God's sake! Is Sarah all right alone up there?"

"Oh, yes. I think she will sleep a long while now, and that is as good as any medicine I have for what ails her."

"You know? You know what ails her? What is it, Sam? Will she live?"

"If I am right—the specialist will confirm that—she can live if she gets the right treatment, and if she has a little bit of luck, as they used to say in the old country."

"Well, what is it and what is the treatment?"

"I believe that your wife has consumption."

The word hung in the air between the two men the way the little silken parachutes from a puff of dandelion will stay afloat on any tiny lift of air. The word, the terror of that word, stunned Farrel Hurstwood. Images of blood and wracking coughing fits and death filled his mind. But he knew that Sam was right with a certainty that defied logic. No sooner had Sam uttered the dread diagnosis than Farrel felt certain that consumption—galloping consumption, some people called it because of the rapidity with which it seemed to devour its victims—was the disease from which Sarah suffered.

"What should be done?" Farrel asked in a grim voice that communicated to Sam the realization that Farrel had taken in the diagnosis and had accepted it.

"She should go away. Where the air is warm and dry. They do a lot of work with tuberculosis in special treatment hospitals in Switzerland. There is a sanatorium, the largest in the world, I think, in Davos. If the specialist in New York City confirms my suspicions, we should put Sarah on the boat right then and there. That is why I think we should see if she can travel, rather than bringing the doctor here, you see?"

"Yes, yes. As soon as possible. Will you go with her to Switzerland? Should I?"

"If you can, Farrel, by all means. It would cheer her to have you nearby, I feel sure. When she is aware of it, that is. But most important is to hire a nurse. I cannot go and, frankly, you need not.

Mostly Sarah will sleep or doze."

"Yes, a nurse. I really can ill afford the time unless you feel it is crucial."

Sam pondered over the fact that this was the same man who just yesterday was frantic with despair at the thought that his wife had died. It was a quick readjustment.

"The important thing is to get Sarah ready as soon as we can. You must have her clothes packed and make arrangements for our trip to New York—we should both accompany her that far. I will check her again and explain to her the moves we are making in her behalf. We should be ready to leave within the next day or two. I think speed is important. It will work to her benefit. The sooner she gets to purer air and to treatment, the better."

"Sam," Farrel said, stopping the doctor who had stood and was about to leave the room, "how long will this treatment take? How long will Sarah be away?"

Sam sighed. His eyes closed, and he shook his head slightly.

"It takes time. The lungs repair themselves so slowly. I think you should count on three months at least. At least three months."

Sam was playing the diplomat with this answer. The cases he had read of in the medical literature had taken a great deal longer than that. Of course, the cases that got written up tended to be the worst ones. Perhaps Sarah would be lucky. As a matter of fact, she already was one of the lucky ones to be alive at all. She was one of the most especially lucky ones to have someone with enough money to get her the best medical care available anywhere in the world.

The days after the storm remained storm-ridden to Sarah's feverish mind. She knew there were periodic rushes of activity around her, but she could not rouse herself to enough awareness to make sense out of them. The trip to New York was in Sarah's experience merely a protracted series of bumps and jolts and fits of coughing. Racking coughs shook her body so violently and frequently that her ribs ached and her head pounded continuously.

To Farrel and Sam the trip seemed merely tedious, tedious and much too long. Each of Sarah's bouts of coughing seemed to stress the length of time the journey was taking.

The specialist, of course, confirmed Sam's fears and made the arrangements for Sarah's admission to the Swiss tuberculosis clinic. With a nurse as her companion, Sarah was soon ensconced in a first-class suite on a luxury liner for the next portion of her journey to Switzerland. It seemed to Sarah that the boat pitched through mountainous waves. Her sense of herself was of a leaf spun around and around in a puddle in the gutter. There seemed to be a wind that rattled through her bones. The nurse, whom Sarah saw only as an unknown pale woman in white, roused her to eat small portions of simple food: broth, boiled meat. Sarah began to wonder if spices were considered poisonous, but she really found it only a mildly amusing thought. She really had no concern for the food one way or another, and its blandness hardly bothered her. The effort of eating overwhelmed her. Even when the nurse brought the food to her lips, Sarah had to struggle to chew, to swallow, to breathe. The coughing so exhausted her that she tried to bury her head in her pillow and tried to clamp her mouth and throat closed against the pressure that nonetheless built up and exploded from her.

The nurse spent most of her time reading or strolling the calm, sunny decks. The crossing was, in fact, a smooth one except in Sarah's tormented being. The nurse had cared for other consumption victims and regarded Sarah as no more or less than another sick person. She formed no attachment to her. She made no judgment on her chances of survival and recovery. Her job, and she viewed herself as a topnotch professional, was to get Mrs. Farrel Hurstwood to the Talhof Clinic in Davos, Switzerland while she was still alive. When they landed, she would have to make arrangements for their land travel. Then she would check her patient in to the clinic and be free for her return trip. Oh, she daydreamed about that journey. Perhaps on the ship ride back with no patient to care for, she might find romance. Meanwhile, though, she had her work to do. It was midafternoon, and she must gather up the tea things and try to coax Mrs. Hurstwood through another few mouthfuls in order to keep her strength up.

Sarah spent most of her time in a world of dreams during these days. She had dreams of terror where she was being pursued down a path that became increasingly narrow and increasingly steep. She had to struggle to breathe. She gasped for breath. Finally, unable to go on, she collapsed along the rocky path aware only that her unknown, unseen pursuer was about to plunge a knife into her back. Then she would shudder into wakefulness usually caught up in a terrible chatter of coughs.

Other dreams were more peaceful. She would be standing on a cliff looking down on the waves as they crashed below her when suddenly she would be flying high above them. Soaring, soaring, free from her earthbound body. Free from the pain of her sick and tortured body. In this dream, Sarah could remove herself from human concerns . . . from pettiness and vanity, from ego and anger. . . . Yes, even from the bondage of love. She could see children playing on the beach below her and realize that they too would follow the universal pattern of birth and growth and death. She had never felt so apart from humanity, or so much at one with the universe. When she awoke from these dreams, she would have a calm acceptance of the fact that she was dying. It seemed like a perfectly worthwhile activity.

By the time the ship pulled into port, Sarah had increasing moments of lucidity. The journey which followed interested her enormously when she could call her mind to attention. There were a variety of conveyances involved. There were regular trains and narrow-gauge trains; there were funiculars, those little aerial wagons that swung one into the sky along an overhead wire that paralleled the almost vertical slope of the mountain's face; and finally there was a horse and buggy that carried them along the last treacherously winding roads, rising ever higher into the magnificence of the Alps.

Occasionally Sarah roused herself enough to really see the countryside spread out around her: the black-green firs stolid against the brilliance of snow or the jagged peaks above her that seemed to scratch at the very sky itself. The air became cold and dry and bright; then colder and drier and brighter. The sun looked like a fat haloed disk pasted on the sky by some kindergarten artist. Sarah's breath became more shallow, but at the same time easier. She felt almost as though the fist that had been squeezing her ribs in its giant grasp had loosened a degree or two. But she still spent great periods of time in the semiconsciousness of the twilight world of her sleep.

At last she was jostled awake by the lurch of the cabriolet as it stopped before the doors of the famous Talhof Clinic, the Swiss tuberculosis sanatorium to which Sarah had been heading, it seemed, all of her life. At last, she sighed, I am here where I belong. Even she herself in her most secret heart could not have said what she meant by that statement. She only knew that as she was helped from the carriage and saw the short bearded doctor standing at the door ready to greet her, she felt she was on the brink of a new reality. When she passed within those doors, she somehow sensed, Sarah Hurstwood would die—the Sarah Hurstwood that the world had known, that is. The person who might emerge again at some later transformation would be an altogether new creature. Sarah thought of herself as a caterpillar about to enter her cocoon. She hoped that she would be able to become a butterfly.

Thirty-five

Back in Richmond, Farrel had suddenly become the only parent to his four children. He felt certain that Sarah would die far from him and in a foreign land, and the thought lent a crazed intensity to his sense of responsibility. He must work harder and faster; he must earn more and more money, because he must provide well for the children. In truth, he had already amassed a small fortune which would more than adequately care for the children for the rest of their lives, no matter how long they lived. What the children really needed at this moment when they felt abandoned by their mother was love and reassurance, but Farrel could offer them neither of those. Instead, he redoubled his efforts at work which meant he was virtually absent from the home altogether. Essentially, at this moment, the Hurstwood children had become orphans.

Their emotional needs were enormous. Jessica felt tormented by the guilty notion that her misjudgment in terms of her behavior that stormy night had caused her mother's desperate illness. In response, she became even more introverted, cutting herself off from the world almost entirely. She completed the school year, which was almost over anyhow, and then spent the days of summer locked away in her room.

Franklin and Maura also carried with them a residual sense of guilt regarding their mother's illness and their part in it. Unfortunately, no one thought to explain to these children that Sarah had been ill for a much longer time than they had realized, and that the experience with the storm only had accelerated the disease's progress without in any way altering its essential nature. These two children, however, responded differently from Jessica who carried her burden solitarily. They had each other, after all. They discovered at their tender ages the lesson that would stay with them throughout their lives: that a burden shared is only half a burden. They also learned that in all the world the one person each could always count on was the other. Their bond, formed during these early years, created a future passion that would alter their lives profoundly and forever.

Powell's response to his mother's absence was pristine. He felt nothing but despair. Why had his mother abandoned him? At four, he was too young to comprehend the cause of her absence. He began to cry out during the night with terrible nightmares, and it was this situation that drew Jessica back to the realm of life. She woke to the piteous howls and could not ignore them. When she took Powell into her bed, he would hush and return to sleep. No one else seemed able to placate him. To her surprise, Jessica began to find a comfort for herself in the snuggly little boy who turned to her more and more, as though she were his mother.

When Farrel did return at night, long after the children were in their beds, the darkness struck him like a mallet. In the mornings, the servants kept the children out of sight. Farrel did not seek them out. He could not seem to imagine a world of home and children now that Sarah was gone.

George felt Sarah's loss equally keenly but responded in a totally different manner. After all, he had lived through these many years holding his love to him, but at a physical remove. This was not so terribly different a situation. He began a correspondence which he hoped would cheer her. He insisted in each letter that she must will herself well, that she was not to worry about answering his letters, that she must hurry back to the world of Richmond which still held so much of her life. He hoped in this way to counterbalance the effect he had read about in sanatoriums where the ill formed their own society and had no desire ever to return to the world of the well.

George also noticed Farrel's lack of interest in the children. He tried at first to mention it lightly in passing. But when he saw that had no effect on Farrel, he began to belabor the point until Farrel insisted that if he cared so damned much, then why didn't he spend more time with the children? At that point, George backed off from direct confrontation. He did try to stop by and visit now and again, but he knew that his visits could never replace the presence of parents in their lives.

The grandparents did what they could. They were aware of the problem too. But parents hold such a special place in each child's life that it is hard for any other to replace them. No, Farrel's neglect could not be so easily remedied.

Despite attempts by the Seewalds and George Spencer to alert Farrel to the damage he was doing, the situation continued for months, through the remainder of the spring and into the summer. Then one hot August day Farrel received a call at the office from a hysterical Sassafras. Unable to understand her, he reluctantly agreed to return home in the middle of the day. Chaos greeted him.

Sassafras was pacing in the front hall with Powell trailing along behind her hanging on to her skirt and crying. Franklin and Maura were filthy and sat, hand in hand with their backs to the wall, on the floor in the front parlor. A picture taken in a madhouse, Farrel thought. It was the first time since Sarah's departure that he had actually looked at his children.

"What in the name of God is going on here?" he roared.

"It warn't my fault," Sassafras blubbered. "She was just gone awhile visiting friends I thought; then Clara found this note under her pillow."

Farrel snatched the note from her hand. Sassafras sank to her knees clutching Powell. The two of them filled the air with wails as Farrel read the note.

"Father," it said, "I am gone for good and ever. I know you blame me cause Mamma got so sick and went away. If she had not gone out that night, if I had brought the kids home, it would never have

514

happened. Maybe you are punishing me by pretending we are all dead, Mamma and us kids, too. I cannot take it anymore so good-bye forever. Jessica Hurstwood."

The signature was like a final slap in the face. Farrel could feel his face flame.

"Sassafras, stop that whimpering."

"Yes, sir," she snuffled. "We will find her, sir. I'll send Hector off right away."

"No, we will not go looking for her. She chose to leave."

"But she's just a child—"

"Enough," he broke in. "I do not want to hear her name ever again. Never again! Now go and tell the others while I talk to the children. Go!" he shouted when she hesitated at the door. He called the children to him when she had disappeared down the hall.

"We are all going upstairs to my room. Come with me." He picked up Powell in his arms and signaled the other two to get up. They followed along behind still holding hands. Slowly. They had none of them ever been allowed in their father's rooms before. They tried to be brave, but this strange harsh man, their father, scared them.

Farrel ushered them in and closed the door. He stripped off his jacket, loosened his tie and rolled up his shirt sleeves.

"You two big kids go in there and wash up; you look like pigs. I will scrub Powell."

They went obediently without a word. Powell sat still on the bed. Farrel got a cloth soaped up and scrubbed his face and hands. Within minutes the grubby group had been transformed into a semblance of the family Sarah had loved. Even Farrel, a slight smile on his lips as he looked at the three children lined up on his high bed, looked more like the Farrel Sarah had cared for over all those years.

"Children," he said, "until your mother gets well and comes home, we are the whole family. I have not been much of a father lately, but that is going to change."

He sank into the chair across from them and looked at his children. It struck him like a blow that Sarah would curse him to see her precious children so neglected. He covered his eyes. Maura slid off the bed and went over to him. Awkwardly she put her arm around his shoulders and kissed the side of his forehead.

"I love you, Daddy."

Tears leaked through Farrel's fingers. He felt the release of tears that had been denied him this long time since Sarah's departure. The boys joined Maura at their father's side. Powell crept into his father's lap. Farrel hugged the small boy to him. My children, he thought, my darling children. They are all that really matters right now. Everything else is emptiness. He remembered how the rabbi had answered his bitterness about the unfairness of Sarah's illness. She should be well by now, but she was as sick as ever, the doctors said. "Nothing is fair," the rabbi had said, "but the Talmud teaches that the true opposite of injustice isn't justice, it is love."

"I love you, children," Farrel managed to say. It was the first time in their lives that he had ever actually uttered the words.

516

Thirty-six

It was only a matter of days before most of Richmond had heard of Jessica's disappearance. George questioned Farrel about the steps he had taken to secure the child's return. When Farrel insisted that he had done nothing and would do nothing, George began to rage at him.

"Farrel Hurstwood, you are a goddamned stubborn man and a fool to boot. You let your stubborn pride stand in the way of your judgment during the streetcar strike, and I stood aside and watched you lead us to virtual destruction. This issue is even more crucial. We are talking about your daughter, your oldest child, your own flesh and blood. What does it take to make you see that you must not turn your back on her? That note she left! It's a plea for attention. She thinks it was her action that is responsible for the sickness that she thinks is killing her mother now. She needs you to tell her she is innocent. If you don't go after her, I was wrong about you all along. I thought that you

517

were a good man. I always thought that."

Upon those words, and not waiting for an answer from Farrel who stood at the window with his back to George, George stormed from the office slamming the door with an unnecessary forcefulness that felt surprisingly satisfying.

Although Farrel had stood seemingly unresponsive throughout this tirade, he was in fact deeply shaken by George's words and even more perhaps by his manner.

Maybe, he thought, just maybe I'd better rethink my stand. Jessica. He tried to bring his daughter's face to mind. Instead, what he saw was her face when she was a wee girl struggling to master the fine art of standing upright. How strange that he should still be able to recall that event so clearly. But the young woman Jessica was now, could he remember her? Really remember her? He closed his eyes and tried to see her. To his further amazement, the face that appeared was the face of the young Sarah, the girl he had first seen hanging around the streetcar tracks as they were put in. The face was the same! My God, Jessica looked just like the young Sarah. No wonder he always felt so uncomfortable when she tried to act cuddly and affectionate. It felt wrong. It felt positively unnatural.

But the fact that she happened to look so much like her mother, well, that was hardly her fault. Hardly a reason for him to reject her. He felt as though bandages had just been removed from his eyes, that he was seeing the world clearly for the first time in a long time. Of course, George was right. He must go and find Jessica and bring her home. And not send Hector either. No, he must go himself. She was his baby and she was out in the world alone. Who would she turn to? he wondered. She might be in danger. With a new sense of urgency, he turned from the window and rushed from his office.

That same night, Farrel Hurstwood started out in pursuit of his daughter. She had left fairly clear tracks, he learned as soon as he began to ask questions. She had spoken to friends about her decision to run away and named the small town down near the Norfolk area where she was going to go. Why this area appealed to her, Farrel had no idea. Actually it was the romance of the sea. Jessica had always carried with her a longing for the fairy-tale romances that included a handsome sailor lover. So it was that she headed for the nearest coastal area when she went out into the world.

Once Farrel began to make inquiries among Jessica's old schoolmates, he quickly discovered her intended destination. Then it was a simple matter to arrange to follow her. When he arrived in the town, he spent less than half a day checking through the boardinghouses before he located the landlady who admitted to having rented a room to a young girl fitting Jessica's description.

"But she's out just now," the puffy old woman told him querulously, "and I don't allow no strangers up in my boarders' rooms."

"Madam," Farrel assured her, "it is my daughter whom I seek. I shall gladly wait here in your parlor until she returns." With those words, he seated himself upon the horsehair settee. He was perfectly at ease in these somewhat seedy surroundings as he was perfectly at ease in any surroundings in which he found himself.

The landlady, after harrumphing around him for a while like a dog sniffing at a strange new mongrel in its territory, moved off to complete her chores, whatever they might have been. Farrel opened the newspaper which he had brought with him and settled in for a long wait. To his surprise, however, he had hardly finished reading the headlines—something about economic trouble brewing in Austria—when he heard the bell tinkle to announce the opening of the front door. He glanced up and was surprised to see Jessica just within the doorway. Needless to say, his surprise was more than matched by hers.

"Father!" she cried. "What are you doing here?"

"I might ask you the same question, Daughter."

They stared at each other in silence. Then Jessica began to cry. Sobs burst from her. Farrel moved to her side and took her in his arms.

"No need to cry, Jess," he said. "I've come to take you home with me. Back home."

"But, I'm not going back. I *can't* go back!" she insisted through her tears.

"Shush, now. First stop crying. Then I'll buy you lunch. Have you eaten?"

The miserable young woman shook her head no.

"Good. Neither have I, and I'm starved. Also, hate to eat by myself, so you must be my companion."

Jessica could hardly believe that she was awake. Could this really be her father saying these things to her? It was as though somehow the fantasies she had dreamed had turned into a reality. Perhaps it was the magic of the sea after all. Farrel took her arm and guided her back out the door through which she had so recently entered.

"Have you found an acceptable café?" he asked.

"Oh, I've seen one—a lovely inn. But it looked as though it cost too much money for me, so I didn't go there. It's just down at the end of this street."

"Fine. Together I think we may have just enough money to be able to afford a marvelous meal. What do you think?" He smiled over at his daughter and winked.

She squeezed his arm and ducked her head. She had never felt so completely happy in her entire life.

Over a lovely brunch of eggs Sardou and muffins, the father and daughter spoke of the issue central to Jessica's running away from home.

"There's no blame involved in terms of your mother's illness," Farrel insisted. "Dr. Sam has raised the hypothesis that, in fact, there may have been a weakness in Sarah's lungs—your mother's lungs," he corrected himself, "from her childhood. You knew that her upbringing in Russia was very harsh in some ways, didn't you?"

Jess nodded.

"I know I've neglected all of you children, and I'm sorry."

"No, Daddy," Jessica cried out, causing several other patrons to turn in her direction. "Please say no more." She could hardly bear to hear her father humbling himself. Although he spoke the same

521

words she had used to accuse him only a few days ago, she now wanted him to be his usual suave self.

"Finish your meal," Farrel said in a more usual tone. "Then we'll pack you up and head home. The other children miss you."

That was more like the father she was familiar with, Jessica thought. She smiled as she drank down the last of her glass of milk.

"You came to get me," she whispered as much to herself as to him. "You really did."

Farrel reached over and took her hand. "You are my oldest child," he said, remembering George's words of the day before, "my daughter, my flesh and blood."

There had never been a happier ending to any of Jessica's dreams than this real-life moment. She felt as though she could die then and there and her life would be complete. They had no further need of words.

When Farrel Hurstwood returned to Richmond with his daughter in tow, the household seemed to breathe a sigh of relief, and life returned to normal. In fact, life for the Hurstwood family became in many ways better than normal. At last the children had a real father, and Farrel Hurstwood felt himself an integral part of family life.

It was soon the beginning of another school year and the children turned from their personal misery over the loss of their mother to the excitement of seeing old friends and learning new things. The world of children is a world of rapid adjustments and it soon seemed that they had lived all their lives in this manner—with servants for care and a father as overseer and no mother at all. Oh, of course they wrote the weekly letters to their absent mother which Farrel required, but they soon wrote them to a memory that grew ever more vague in their minds.

In a strange way, their drift away from a true awareness of their mother mirrored the condition in Sarah's mind. She had by this time become so much a resident of the tubercular community which had its own culture, its own habits, even its own language patterns, that when the children's letters arrived they were like messages from another planet, another life.

Her existence now revolved around sputum tests—everyone carried a strangely beautiful blue glass bottle for sputum collection—and such terms as rales and moist spots on the lung. In this way the patients talked to each other about their conditions, and the doctors talked to the patients about their progress. The term was always progress, but seldom did the word "cure" occur. Only occasionally did the group have to adjust to the departure of one of their members. And it was as often to the graveyard as to the funicular station.

The sense of invalidism that became Sarah's comfortable existence led to a special sense of isolation from the world of normal healthy people. Even the doctors began to take on an intimidatingly energetic appearance as Sarah slipped into the ease of considering herself as frail. When drawing breath was an effort, then every activity became a monumental chore.

The primary therapy was something called "heliotherapy" which meant simply sitting in a bundled heap on a lounge chair on the little balcony outside of each room, and letting the sun and the thin, clear air work a naturopathic cure. Sarah spent long hours staring blankly at the varied terrain before her. She regarded the snowy peaks and the valleys dotted with mountain flowers as though they were paintings put on display exclusively for her benefit. Occasionally she thought about reading a novel or writing in her journal, but she remained instead staring steadily ahead of her.

Time passed in a mysterious way. She began to lose track of hours and of days, and only retained a larger pattern of time movement that was almost seasonal in scope. She realized with a shock when she read it in one of George's letters that she had been in Switzerland for an entire year. It was spring again and the year was 1911. Soon it would be summer. The lethargy that sat heavy upon her refused to lift.

Sarah wasn't sure exactly when she first became aware of the fragile young man who lay on the chaise longue to the right of her. It seemed, that moment of recognition, to be linked with the beginning of her own recovery. Perhaps he had always been there, and she had simply been too sick to notice. But once she took notice of him, she could hardly look away. She began to spend almost as much time gazing at his porcelain features as at the mountain view. Both seemed miracles of nature. She got in the habit of staring at him, quite forgetful of the good manners she had been carefully taught. After all, he seemed always to be asleep. It was almost as though he were a statue and she were enjoying admiring a work of art.

Just the look of him enchanted her. His skin was so pale it seemed almost translucent. Only the bright circles on his cheeks, a typical symptom of the feverish stage of their disease, revealed the fact that his sleep was unnatural. He had blond hair that lay in long strands along his cheeks and across his forehead. His painfully thin body seemed to belong to an eternal youth rather than to a man; it was not robust enough to arouse in Sarah any of the warning signals about keeping herself safe from harm. There seemed no possible harm here. And so, before she even met him, Sarah was half in love with Peter Wertmann.

During one of the sessions when she was admiring his beauty unself-consciously—the graceful way his hand lay along the arm of the chair at that particular moment—something drew her gaze upward toward his face. With a shock, Sarah saw that the man's eyes were open. Open and regarding her with an amused tolerance, it seemed. He had huge liquid eyes as pure as a doe's and of an equally dark-brown color. Sarah quickly looked away, focusing on the furthest point on the hilltop.

"My name is Peter," he said in a resonant voice. He pronounced it Pay-ter, in the German manner. Sarah could hardly breathe for a moment. It was as though a painting had suddenly come to life and demanded that it be acknowledged.

Slowly, slowly, she turned her head back

toward him. Their eyes met. For the first time she saw him smile, a gentle wistful smile. He had delicately carved lips and fine even teeth.

"Verzeihen Sie mir," Sarah apologized. "I should not have been staring at you. I am Sarah Hurstwood." She extended her hand toward him. He reached out to her. They touched. She reminded herself it was only a handshake as she felt her heart begin to pound. It had been so long since feeling had forced its way along her body that she could hardly distinguish it from some new symptom of her disease. Perhaps I am about to suffer from heart failure, she told herself. But no, memory told her that the strange sensations that sent chills down her spine had nothing to do with tuberculosis.

"Sarah," he said. "What a lovely name. It was my mother's name." Then he began to ask about her illness. It was the one topic that everyone returned to in this locked-away world, the self-absorbed world of symptoms. How long they had each been here they had both lost track of. The normal world with its emphasis on clocks and days full of important things to do simply had no reality. It was only after the nurses had come to return them to their rooms that Sarah realized her hand had lain in his throughout their talk. She could still feel the magic of that touch as she lay in her bed trying to sleep.

In her dreams, she was with a beautiful young man at the top of a mountain. They had skis on their feet. But she stood frozen by fear. She surely could not ski. Then she looked across at the man beside her and he smiled with his delicate lips and even teeth, and she believed that she could do anything. She pushed her poles into the snow and began to skim along the mountainside, down, down, down, in a rush toward the town below. Ecstatically, she felt the wind blow through her tresses, kiss her cheeks; she felt a shout of victory rise in her lungs—and then she awoke and lay still feeling the throb of energy and hope that followed after the dream. For the first time, Sarah believed that she was going to survive. She would not die here. She was going to get well.

Soon it would be morning. Soon it would be sun time. Soon she would see Peter again. Soon.

Life was good. She had a sense of the exotic pleasure of the body that seemed almost ethereal. As the ability to breathe became easier, Sarah found an almost sensual delight in the simplest things: sipping a cup of broth, gazing at a single delicate mountain flower. Edelweiss was the name of the Swiss national flower, and just the sound of that name gave Sarah a tingling pleasure. It was as though, having gone so close to the grave, her senses were brought back to life in a highly intensified way. Just feeling better seemed miracle enough. She refused to think about any other life. She refused to think about returning to the other world, the world of healthy people. She knew that someday she must; someday she would.

It was the autumn of the year when Sarah first met Peter. Suddenly her entire range of feeling seemed centered on him and she longed for the hours when they lay side by side in the sunlight. Along with the change in seasons, of course, came a change in the sun's intensity. It seemed only a pale imitation of the former days full of heat. Now the patients lay bundled up against the chill, and the sun gave them light enough, but not heat. It seemed a frightening omen to Sarah who thought that she could behold the same fading of intensity in Peter's bodily strength. Surely, she told herself, she was just imagining things. Or perhaps it was simply her reaction to her own increasing strength. Perhaps Peter was staying the same—not getting worse as she feared. Most of their time together was spent in silence. Usually he slept. Only occasionally would they have a conversation, yet Sarah felt that she knew him as well as anyone she had ever known. Was that, too, part of the madness of this place? she asked herself. But no, she really did share a closeness with him that she shared with no other. The very uniqueness of their shared illness guaranteed that.

She discovered during one of their talks—again they held hands as she listened—that he was a composer. He had been hard at work on a symphony—he believed it would be his greatest—when he began to cough up blood and was sent to Davos. He tried to describe the music, but how can tones be talked instead of heard? He spoke to her with a fervency she had not seen before, when he spoke of music. All he wanted in this world was time enough to finish this one symphony. By this one piece, he believed, he would live forever. People would play his music long after his death, he felt sure.

"But does that matter?" Sarah asked. "Does it really matter what happens after we are dead?" Death was a word seldom spoken at the clinic, so

Sarah whispered it to Peter leaning closer to him so that her lips were only inches from his ear.

"Yes!" Peter almost shouted. He struggled to sit upright and his efforts alarmed Sarah who tried to calm him.

"Peter, Peter, please," she cried, "do not alarm yourself."

"It matters," he said allowing himself to sink back against the chair. "Greatness. Immortality. That is what *does* matter. This life, these few years of transitory pleasure—they do not matter. Constantly I torment myself with the question of my greatness. If I am not great, there is no need for my music, you see. No need for more mediocre music."

He stopped talking. His eyes closed. Sarah had no answer to offer. She had never heard of anyone speak about greatness in this way. She had never given any thought to whether anything she did would live after her. In her case, she realized, nothing would. She had no talent. Then she thought of the children, her children. Of course, that was what would live after her and keep her memory alive. The children were her immortality.

She gazed at Peter's face which looked so terribly, terribly frail. How dear it was, how dear and delicate. When she looked at him, Sarah realized how precious life really was—precious and fragile. She leaned over and kissed him ever so gently upon the lips. His eyes remained closed. She was sure he was asleep and could not feel her kiss. That was fine with her. Her love for him was so pure that she wanted nothing but his life and health. She lay back in her chair. "Thank you, Sarah," Peter said in a voice so soft it imitated the softest sound of the wind. She looked over at him, but his eyes remained closed. He was smiling.

Soon Peter would awaken, Sarah thought, and they would have more chances to get to know each other better.

But for the meantime she looked at the brilliance of the sunlight on the landscape and thought about how it redefined her notion of light. In Richmond on a bright day everyone would rush into the streets to gaze at the beautiful patterns the sunlight would make on the buildings and trees. Sunlight was a treat. Here, though, where sunlight was a blazing daily reality, she almost sought out those spots where the terrain was cast in shadow in order to rest her eyes. The dark shadows defined the light—the shadows that seemed darker than any shadows she had ever seen because of their intense contrast to the bright light.

It all became poetry in her mind. The shadows under the rocks. The shadows on the x-rays of her lungs. The light of the sun and of God and of eternity.

So it went for some period of time. But the days no longer seemed without shape to Sarah who now counted off the time in terms of length of hours apart from her dear friend, Peter. She began to dream that she could inspire him back to health. She knew her idea had no scientific validity, but she let herself dream the possibility anyway.

During the occasions of their conversations, Sarah raised the topic of his symphony frequently and listened carefully as he tried to explain to her what it was he was attempting to do in the music. Although she could no longer avoid the recognition that his strength was failing him, she hoped against hope that his passion for his work would encourage him to fight against the encroachment of the disease within his lungs.

But as the fall drifted inevitably toward winter, as the seasons showed their change in colors leaning toward the monotonous gray and white of winter, as the clinic personnel tried futilely to inspire their patients with the excitement of the approach of the holiday season, Sarah learned that her efforts at inspiration were futile also. One day Peter was not in the lounge beside her. The immediate alarm that made Sarah's breath jump within her revealed a knowledge that she denied to herself. No, Peter could not be gone from her, she told herself. No, he must simply be feeling poorer than usual. She could not sit there helplessly waiting for word. Instead, she dragged herself up and began laboriously to walk toward the room she knew was Peter's. She had seen him wheeled there by the attendants at the end of their sun time.

Now she saw that the door was open. She paused in the doorway. The room was full of people, or that is how it seemed. She could not take in the reality of the scene before her. At first all she was able to see was blood—blood everywhere. The rooms were all the same so she knew the placement of each item—the desk, the bed, the table with its kerosene lamp. She saw none of these things except as they became part of the bloody picture. A desk covered with papers and blood. Pools of blood on the floor. And on the bed . . . Peter's body drenched in blood, his face a pale ghost of the Peter she knew.

"Oh, no," she cried and it was the first time that the people in the room, the doctors and nurses and attendants, became aware of Sarah's presence.

"Get her out of here," one of the doctors ordered.

"No, I won't leave," Sarah insisted. "Tell me what happened. Peter was my friend. You must tell me."

Sarah's favorite nurse came over to her, took her arm, and led her from the room whispering assurances that she would tell Sarah everything as soon as they got her back to her room. With that, Sarah allowed herself to be drawn away from the ghoulish sight. At the door, she paused just once to look back at the face she had spent so many hours staring at, so many hours loving. It was no longer Peter. How quickly the change takes place, she thought. The spark of life, they say, and the expression is true, very true. There was no spark left in this face. Her Peter was no longer there.

Sarah sank back into darkness the way a flower folds itself away at dusk. Once more the days lost themselves, and she lost herself within them. She learned that Peter had begun working on the symphony at night when he couldn't sleep. He had worked long hours, extending himself beyond the possibility of his strength. Suddenly, the best evidence indicated, he had had a massive hemorrhage and had died in the very instant of its happening. Sarah hoped that he had had a vision of the symphony's completion to comfort him.

Thirty-seven

As the year's end approached—it would soon be 1912—a new calamity struck. There had been a sensational murder in Peterboro that had attracted a great deal of attention. People turned out for the trial of the accused murderer as they always did for an important news event. This time, though, the biggest news to come out of the trial had nothing to do with the murderer's guilt or innocence.

The courtroom had been packed from early morning on with people milling about for the best vantage point. The overflow crowd had pushed onto the balcony overlooking the courtroom. Suddenly a cracking sound split the air followed rapidly by a groaning sound made by the breaking away of wood and plaster from their foundations. Then, while everyone remained motionless uncertain as to what was happening, the entire balcony swayed and collapsed carrying with it the people standing in the balcony and hurling them onto the people seated in the auditorium below.

Hysteria mounted as people scrambled to avoid the crush of walls and bodies. Shrieks filled the air. The judge, unharmed but stunned, sat motionless for moments that seemed endless, viewing what was surely a scene from hell. Before his eyes lay the wreckage of the courtroom and in the debris lay writhing bodies. He could not take it in as a reality. It seemed rather to be a nightmare vision or a terrible judgment upon him. He thought perhaps he had gone mad.

Although it seemed like an eternity, it was a matter of minutes before the commotion had drawn rescue attempts by the outside community. Fire trucks and other emergency vehicles wailed their way along the town's streets and people from everywhere rushed to the courthouse to help. The hospitals surrounding the town were soon crowded to capacity as was the local morgue. To the amazement of everyone who actually saw the extent of the damage when the balcony first collapsed, only fourteen people were actually killed, although the number of injuries was more than quadruple that number.

Among the people whose funerals were held during the first week of the new year was David Seewald, Sarah's father. Rachel, who had become somewhat morose since Sarah's illness, seemed at first able to handle the loss. She sobbed at the funeral, crying out, "You promised not to leave me. How could you leave me?" But within a few days, the crying had stopped. Unfortunately, her

534

life without the man who had been her companion for all her days seemed not worth much to Rachel. When Farrel tried to get her to move in with him, she demurred, insisting that the memory of David was closer to her in the rooms they had shared for so long.

Alone at night, though, she began to talk to David as though he were still alive and beside her. She often scolded him for having abandoned her. "I was the one who was supposed to go first," she insisted.

Together the family had decided that the news of her father's death should be kept from Sarah. She would be unable to attend the funeral in any case, and the bad news might hinder her own healing process. When, however, less than two months after her father's death, her mother succumbed in a matter of days to a case of influenza, the family held another conference on the subject. The family had become extended to include Dr. Sam and George, both of whom seemed to be as concerned as anyone could be.

"She just didn't care to fight it," Sam said as he had a dozen times before. "She was a strong woman and could have lived longer, but without Dave . . ." He let his words trail off into silence.

"But what shall we do about Sarah?" George insisted.

"Both parents in such a short time. I really don't know if she can take it," Farrel said.

Sam spoke up. "Why don't you wire the doctors and see what they have to say about Sarah's current condition? They're the ones who would best know whether or not she should be informed."

The idea was a good one and everyone also appreciated the fact that it allowed them to put off the final word for another few days. Farrel sent the wire at once.

The answer came within a matter of days.

The doctors insisted that Sarah still needed more treatment—there must be no talk of taking her out of the clinic—but she was responding well and they had every hope that her eventual recovery would be a complete one. As to telling Sarah about her parents, the doctors felt that perhaps that should be left to them. After all, they were professionals who could deal with emotional reactions adequately. But, they hastened to add, they would await further word before doing anything.

Farrel felt a sense of relief when he read this answer. Perhaps the decision would be taken out of his hands. Perhaps he would not have to deal with the emotional reaction that Sarah would naturally have in response to such a shocking bit of news—the death of both of her parents.

But to Farrel's surprise, George was furious when he read the wire.

"Let strangers be with her when she has need of friends?" he asked. "Let strangers tell her what should only be part of the shared sorrows of her life with us? I cannot imagine your even considering allowing it!"

"But George," Farrel remonstrated, "my schedule is so full for the next few weeks that the idea of a trip to Switzerland is unthinkable, man. Also, I have to admit, this emotional business is far from my forte."

"No matter," George insisted. "I can take the time, and I will tell Sarah. If that is acceptable to you, I mean," he amended.

"God, George, would you?" Farrel felt the same sense of relief that he had felt when he had received the wire. His friend would come to the rescue.

Thirty-eight

Had the news of the Seewalds' death not required George's visit to the Talhof Clinic, Sarah might have continued on as a patient for an indefinite time. So many people—especially wealthy patients, George thought—seemed never to show adequate health to be allowed to leave. The atmosphere invited one to linger, he had to admit. It was like the land of the lotus-eaters, the mythical place where the local fruit drugged one into a wondrous lethargy. No one even wanted to escape. It was a situation where the prisoners were held without restraints. The controls were inside of them. That was the situation George discovered when he arrived in Sarah's room.

He had arrived unannounced at the clinic and insisted upon being taken at once to Mrs. Hurstwood's room. When he entered the room, he was first dazzled by the scene from the window where a blaze of light filled the space and revealed the balcony and the countryside beyond with a crystal clarity. On the balcony sat a wrapped figure whom George approached after he dismissed the nurse who accompanied him.

"Sarah," he called softly from a short distance away.

The figure seemed to emerge from the shawl which blanketed her. It was Sarah. His own Sarah!

"George," she sighed, and a smile that rivaled the brilliance of the sunlight broke across her features.

"Surely my thoughts have created you here! Just now as I lingered over my camomile tea, I recalled our first night together so long ago when we had gone in search of a Christmas tree and were stranded by a storm."

"Blessed storm!" George said as he moved toward Sarah who rose to meet him. They came together in a kiss as passionate as any they had ever shared.

"My dearest love," Sarah murmured when at last their lips drew apart. "Have you come like Lochinvar to rescue me?"

At her words, George realized with a sudden certainty that that was exactly what he had come to do. She no longer belonged in this place, half a world away from her home in Richmond. It was time for Sarah to return.

"Yes, I believe that I have," he answered. "But the doctors here are like magicians, I think, and they may put up a resistance to your escape." He spoke melodramatically in the hope that he might turn into play what he thought of as a very real danger. "I will approach them slyly and ask only for a weekend release for you, my dear. Then we can plan our actions together. You would like a weekend with me, wouldn't you?" The question itself was only half in earnest as he could tell from her eager response to his kiss that Sarah was still his lover.

"Yes, George," she whispered and blushed sweetly.

He laughed aloud with a simple joy he had not felt in years.

"Good. Then you begin to gather up your things. Just enough for a weekend now. Everything else can be sent after you."

"Are we really going to run away then?" she asked.

"Yes, Sarah, I am going to steal you away. Remember though, to hurry. And not a word to anyone. I will go to the office and make the necessary arrangements. Just to take you for the weekend, I shall say."

"But, George, there are some people here, special people. I must say good-bye."

"Fine. Say good-bye but only for a weekend. That must be what you make them believe. You can write them later. To you, of course, the good-bye will be more poignant, I am sure. My tender-hearted woman!"

They kissed again, and then George hurried off to explain to Sarah's doctors how he needed a more private environment and more time in order to tell her about her parents. He knew that only a subterfuge would enable him to spirit Sarah away. He felt that the pathos of the news he brought with him might serve the purpose well, and indeed it did. The doctors agreed to allow Sarah to leave the clinic compound for the weekend. George felt he had won a major victory. Later he would come to feel that he had perhaps saved Sarah's life.

Within the hour, two figures could be seen entering a carriage, the frailer one leaning upon the other. It was George and Sarah about to embark on the journey back down the mountain.

At the bottom of the funicular line, instead of boarding a train that same day, George and Sarah stayed on in a small hostel. Sarah was now so unused to normal society that she shrank from the notion of having dinner with the other guests.

"Please, dear," she begged, "can we not eat alone together in one of our rooms?"

"Dress yourself up, my sweet, and prepare for a lovely candlelit dinner for two in the main dining room. A meal that includes something for you to use your knife and fork on, I might add. By God, Sarah, you look as though you have been subsisting on that damned broth you told me about on the way here. Your skin is as lovely as ever but almost transparent. Tonight we begin your new healthy existence!"

"It scares me," Sarah said, her voice full of misgivings.

"Yes, yes, I know. But that will be half the excitement. That and the fact that whether you realize it yet or not . . . I only reserved one room for us. Tonight, my love, we are Mr. and Mrs. George Spencer."

Sarah had to smile at the boastful way George was acting. "That scares me more than food I need to cut with a knife," she admitted. Her blush was the first sign of the old Sarah.

"Nonetheless we must start with food for the body. In your case that seems to have been long neglected."

"My dear," Sarah said, laying her hand on his arm, "so has every other form of sustenance."

At this frank statement, George laughed aloud. It felt as though these hours since he had joined Sarah were the first moments he was truly alive since the day she had left Richmond. Then, with a pang, he remembered that he was here to inform Sarah of her parents' deaths. Well, he thought, tonight we will get back in touch with each other. Then I will know better how to broach the painful subject which was my ostensible mission in coming to Switzerland. He no longer felt that telling Sarah the sad news was the most important reason for his trip. Now he felt that bringing Sarah back home was the real reason he had crossed the sea.

"I am unused to dressing and undressing myself these days," Sarah said. "You may be called upon to help me."

George thought that he noticed a flirtatious twinkle in Sarah's manner, but he could not be sure.

"Let me help," he said. "It is my pleasure as always."

Arm in arm they made their way down the long hall that led to their room. There, in the privacy of the luxuriously appointed room, George assisted Sarah in her preparations for dinner. Although he did no more than look on her body—he forbade himself even the hint of a suggestive touch—the intimacy between them was immediately reestablished. With a sense of pity, George noted how frail Sarah's body looked. If it is in my power, he vowed, she will soon be back to the lovely laughing young woman I first met when Farrel brought me home to meet his wife. We can spend a week or so here before we return to Virginia. That and the time on the ship should be enough to make a significant improvement. I can sense the will to live, strong within her. My love and care should help to reinforce that, I hope. Such tender thoughts as these filled George's head during the time Sarah prepared to go to dinner and during the time they waited at their small table for the waiter to appear.

"Perhaps I should order," he said, "since it has been an eternity since you have had the chore. Or would it seem a playful game to you?"

"No, today has already been more adventure than I have had during my two years here in Switzerland. It would be a kindness to me if you would do the honors. But do remember that I can hardly imagine eating a meat dish. Try for simple fare, my dear friend."

George grew suddenly concerned that he had indeed taxed Sarah beyond her capability. He would order a simple supper for them both, he thought, and then they would retire at once. Sarah need not fear any advances from him. No, all he wanted was to have his love beside him. That would be more than he had hoped for when he had arrived at the clinic this morning.

He ordered and within a short time they were served a lovely omelet with an assortment of crisp hard rolls on the side. George had also ordered a fine white wine in the hope that it would help Sarah brace up to the excitement of the day and the variety of adventures that lay before her.

To his delight, the wine worked marvelously, and he soon spotted two circles of color on Sarah's cheeks. There was also a light in her eyes that did not seem in any way the effect of fever. She was already beginning to look a bit more like her old self, he was sure—or he was almost sure. Then she leaned toward him and whispered, "George, I do believe you are right in thinking that you may have saved my life by coming to get me. Oh, and George, you know one thing has not changed during these two years—my love for you."

He felt, at these words, that his heart must burst for joy. Sarah not only loved him, but she told him so without his even asking her for reassurance. This mystery of love was always confounding him. No sooner did he feel that he had made peace with one state of affairs than it changed itself into a different situation entirely. His bewitching Sarah loved him—still loved him. He leaned toward her as well and their lips met softly in a brief kiss.

"You are my life," he whispered.

The food tasted so special that George was tempted to believe the Swiss had discovered a magic spice, and Sarah was sure that the way to discover the pure joy of food was to eat hospital food for a protracted period of time. In fact, the combination of their happiness at being together and the fresh mountain air worked its own spell to make the simple food—which was fresh and wholesome—seem extravagantly good.

At the end of the meal, though, Sarah could not

deny that she was extremely tired. The day had been a strain on her after all. She asked George if he would mind her returning to their room and he assured her that all he wanted was for her to feel rested and happy. He would happily return with her and read to her while she rested or simply sit beside her while she slept, if that was what she preferred. They rose from the table having finished their meal, and arm in arm they strolled toward their room.

Sarah, clothed in her night dress, lounged across the bed while George, still fully clothed, sat in the chair beside her. She sighed contentedly.

"I keep half-waiting for the nurses or the doctor to appear to test me. In a sense, I feel more relaxed and more alive than I did during my entire stay at the Talhof Clinic. I shall forever be grateful to you, darling. I believe you really may have saved my life by taking me away from that place."

George remained silent beside her. He was so happy for the chance to be close to her that there seemed no need of anything else—not words, not touches. After a moment, Sarah spoke again in a halting, drowsy voice.

"I read a poem once by Mr. Keats and a phrase stayed with me. It expresses the mood of the clinic, I think. My mood until now. Something about being half in love with easeful death. Yes, that was it. Easeful death."

Her voice trailed off. She was asleep.

During the relaxed days that followed, Sarah grew more and more like her old self. George stayed with her every moment, but never forced his attentions upon her. She seemed still too frail for love-making. He felt a tentativeness that reflected itself in inaction. If there were to be a fuller reunion between them, she would have to initiate it. And, on the last night before they were to start for home, she did.

Although for the longest time her body had seemed to her only a mechanical device which needed repairs, these last few days with George had reawakened a memory of another way for the body to respond. At one moment when his hand simply brushed against hers as he was passing her the cream for the coffee, she felt a prickle of sensation almost like a chill race along her arm and settle in a special spot in the middle of her back. Later that same day he tucked a stray tendril of her hair behind her ear, and she almost shuddered. Some place in her chest began to ache for him to hold her. Her lips wanted the hard pressure of his special kisses, the kisses he shared with her only in the heat of passion.

She had tried to indicate to him over the last several days her readiness for the renewal of their love-making, but he was so worried about her health that she could sense his reserve. The subtle signals he would normally have responded to were now simply ignored. Yet Sarah could hardly imagine herself being more direct. It was a situation she had never found herself in before. In itself, it added an exciting dimension to her responses. How was she to invite this lover to enjoy her body? She began to touch his hand whenever she found any excuse—and she soon found herself inventing excuses. She gazed into his eyes when he spoke to her, even if he was only describing the grasses indigenous to the Swiss Alps. At first, it was as though he refused to believe the knowledge of his senses. Then, over the course of the afternoon, she began to notice a gradual change taking place in George's awareness of her.

As they walked along the town's cobbled streets, he placed a hand protectively around her waist—as he had done a hundred times before, only this time with a difference. The fingers tightened around her body. She could feel her own new slimness through his touch. She leaned a bit more weight against his hand. He spoke softly in her ear; the heat of his breath shivered down her spine. "Sarah, my love, what are you doing to me? I feel newly bewitched."

Her laughter was the delicate sigh of tiny mountain flowers swaying in a soft rush of air. The provocative tilt of her chin lifted her breasts which had retained their fullness despite her loss of weight. The dress she wore today was cut low enough to reveal to George's appreciative eyes the cleavage between her breasts. How he longed to touch her breasts, to kiss them, to suck them. He could hardly believe that his tender feelings had been transformed to these passionate longings. He could hardly accept the fact that Sarah had caused the change. Yet he had to admit her behavior was unusually seductive. Her body curved toward his at every opportunity, and his ached for hers. When afternoon teatime approached, George asked her where she wanted to take her tea and held his breath for her answer. Afternoons had always been their most special times together.

A smile curved her lips. "In bed," she mouthed in what was surely less than a whisper. Yet the sound sang through George. He clutched her to him, oblivious of the people around them. They broke apart and luxuriated in the warmth of the look they shared. Then, wordlessly, they moved together back toward their inn, their room, their bed.

Their first coming together was so swift and direct it would have been hard to determine whether it was pleasure or pain, but it left an aftermath of joyful awareness of a love between them that neither time nor distance could erase. They were lovers in the true and grand sense of the word.

Then, after a brief respite during which they stroked each other's bodies and whispered sweet and foolish endearments, George once more reached for Sarah. This time they moved together in the beautiful harmony of a symphony with its layer upon layer of meaning and rhythm and theme. As with a symphony, there was a sense of moving toward completion in its own fullness of time. No hurry. At moments, George would stop the luscious plunging movements of his body into Sarah's. He would close his eyes and wait for the rise of passion to diminish slightly, just enough for him to be able to continue. He had no desire for this moment to end. The pleasure of the final moments could never replace the ongoing ecstasy of these feelings, the surge of sensation through every cell of his body, the new sense of the nerve endings along every centimeter of his skin. Sarah, oo, lay in a delirium of sensory delight. Each subtle move brought her waves of pleasure. When at last George reared above her, moaning, "Now, my love," she responded completely. It was like the loss of this world. She neither saw nor heard anything, so lost was she in the whirling vortex of feeling. It carried her to another plane of existence where she became a part of her lover and together they became a flaming light.

The next day they left for Richmond, Virginia, which seemed a universe away. When they were finally settled in their respective staterooms aboard ship, they settled back into their patterns as Mr. George Spencer and his partner's wife. The time the trip afforded them to reacclimate themselves to these roles was welcome. Midway through the trip, George told Sarah of her parents' deaths. He waited until she seemed calmer than she had been in Switzerland, calmer and stronger.

To his amazement, Sarah responded to the news as though it were no surprise to her.

"A while back, George," she explained, "I began to have terrible nightmares. At first, they were about my own death. I talked with the doctors about them, but they merely treated them as though they were a response to the notion of being in a medical place where people might at any time die and no one be surprised. They have no great faith in dreams there. But I felt sure that my dreams had some meaning other than that. So I prayed for understanding."

They walked up and down the deck as they talked. The sea breeze brought fresh tangy smells to them. Despite the solemn topic there was no morbidity to their words.

"Dreams of death. Oh, my dear," George said "I think I have not come a moment too soon!"

"There was a friend of mine . . . one of the patients here." Sarah found it difficult to talk about Peter even with her closest friend, George "He was a composer."

Once started, Sarah talked on about Peter Wertmann, experiencing the relief of shared confidence. She described the beauty of his face and his body, the delicacy of his constitution, the profundity of his mind. She spoke of his longing for greatness, of the unfinished symphony he had written up to the last moment of his life. And at last she spoke of his death, and felt the healing release of tears. She herself was unsure whether she cried more for Peter or for her parents.

"So did the dreams stop troubling you?" George asked hoping to cheer Sarah out of her tears by shifting back to the subject of her dreams.

"They changed," Sarah said wiping her eyes with the handkerchief George offered.

"Tell me, sweetheart."

"I had several dreams that were absolutely clear. Yes, clear. They revealed my parents' deaths. But more important even, they brought me a message of comfort from Mamma and Papa. They assured me they were together again and that all was well. It was God's world, and all was well."

They stopped walking. Sarah leaned against the railing. "That comfort has stayed with me," she said.

Thirty-nine

Farrel Hurstwood was at the dock hours before the boat was due to arrive. He was experiencing an amazing amount of anxiety about seeing his wife again. These past years he had begun to live like a widower. Now suddenly he must reassume the cloak of husbandhood. He had never felt that he was very good at being a husband anyhow. What would be required of him in this new phase of that experience? he wondered.

The huge sea liner appeared first as a dot on the horizon and then grew and grew until it surged toward the shore seeming to threaten the crowd gathered to watch it dock. Farrel searched among the faces pressed along the railings for Sarah. He finally spotted George. There, he thought, that woman beside him must be Sarah. She was almost unrecognizable. Would this person ever be his wife again? She smiled and waved. There was almost a wistfulness about her. He smiled back and waved his hat. Two strangers, he thought, with a history together. How bizarre.

By the time the unloading had been completed and the passengers and the greeters had gotten together, it was too late to consider traveling any farther that day. Farrel informed George and Sarah that he had arranged hotel rooms for them. Shortly after that, Sarah retired to her room and collapsed on the bed. God, the strain of the homecoming, she thought. What expectations did they both have? she wondered. What would their life be like now? Within minutes, despite her concerns, she was asleep, fully clothed, across her bed.

Farrel and George sat together in the bar and discussed Sarah. George described his feelings when he first saw Sarah in the clinic. He had wired Farrel that he was bringing her back home.

"They would have kept her forever, I feel quite sure," he said now.

"How did she take the news?" Farrel asked.

"She is a solid woman. Everything is going to be all right now that she is back home." George responded to what he felt Farrel was really asking rather than to the words.

"God knows I hope so," Farrel murmured.

They moved aside from this topic then, and they began to discuss changes in the business. The automobile was an ever-increasing threat to their business nationwide.

Farrel felt sure that the automobile manufacturers were sabotaging the streetcar industry by buying up small systems under false names, then claiming that they were not making a profit, and finally disbanding the companies and tearing up the tracks. That left the communities virtually bereft of transportation facilities with the exception of the automobile. Since the tearing up of the tracks was an expense that was unnecessary to a company, and since these companies were claiming that they had no money, Farrel felt his understanding of the underlying significance of the moves was correct. But what to do? He had begun to contact small streetcar lines to alert them to the danger. But when a good offer came in, it was hard to tell a businessman that he should turn it down in the interest of the continuing success of the industry.

George and Farrel discussed this issue long into the night, but without finding an acceptable solution to their dilemma. George suggested bringing court action, which seemed a possibility, but would be so slow a process that much of the harm would already be done before they could get any kind of judgment. Meanwhile, though, Farrel reminded him, the companies where they had invested most of their money would continue going strong. For the time being.

By the time they reached Richmond, Farrel and Sarah had begun to be a bit more comfortable with each other. Some of the politeness of two strangers talking had eased off. They had not yet shared a bed; they had not yet really shared a kiss—only the perfunctory grazing of lips that propriety demanded upon their reunion.

Sarah seemed to be more nervous about seeing

the children again than she had been about anything else. During the time in Switzerland, she had almost let them slip from her mind. It was the only way she could survive the lengthy separation. Then on shipboard, she had begun to yearn for them. Now she seemed, only minutes away from seeing them, to be almost terrified of their reaction to her. Would they kiss her? Would they love her? Would they think she had grown old and ugly and strange during this time? What were they like now? Jessica would be a grown-up lady, and even Franklin and Maura would have passed from the cuddly period of childhood. Only Powell might still be her baby, and he would hardly remember her.

Then she was in the midst of them. The children rushed around her to be the first with kisses, the first with hugs.

They were all marvelously changed, it was true. But they were still her children. They still rejoiced in the fact that their mother had returned to them. Sarah wept for joy. She was really home. She had abandoned any belief that this day would ever really come about.

Oh, she knew there would be troubles ahead: troubles with Farrel and troubles with the children as they all struggled along in this strange life. But they were united again, and they could work out whatever problems they had, as a family should solve their problems—together. It was a moment of peace and reconciliation that Sarah felt she had traveled many miles and many years to reach. She remembered the words her mother had spoken to her so often over those years, reminding her of the beauty life could hold and of the value of love and family and loyalty. Sarah looked around her now. The faces of the children were like flowers in a garden, her garden—the most beautiful garden in the world.

"My darlings," she said, "Mamma has come home for good."

Forty

As time passed and Sarah became once more the lady of the Hurstwood mansion, she occasionally thought back to that young and idealistic girl who had rushed through the streets at dawn to see the inception of that great technological miracle, the street railway.

More had changed than her own innocence, she realized, since those days and years of the 1880s. The entire world had lost its innocence along with her. She could see the change in the way Jessica looked to her role as a woman. She wanted to become a social worker; she had no desire to marry and have children. Sarah could see the change constantly, of course, in the way the people around her, and she herself, accepted machinery as part of the normal way to do things. If something took too long or cost too much money, then someone should invent a machine to do it better. Of course this had led to economic problems and unemployment. But surely those were only temporary problems.

Yes, there was an ease and comfort to life these days that seemed well worth any price the world had had to pay. The only worry that nagged at Sarah's mind beyond her circle of concerns regarding her little family, was inspired by mutterings she sometimes half-heard in the streets and by articles she read in the newspapers about the struggle overseas. War, a word Sarah dreaded more than any other, seemed to appear with increasing frequency. But that was another land and, besides, these were just rumors. Surely America would never get involved. America, the land of the free and the home of the brave, the greatest country on earth—could it be possible that America would go to war? No, certainly not, Sarah decided. Then she turned her attention back to the needs of her family.

Despite the changes she saw around her in the greater world, Sarah had come to realize that certain values remained constant. She loved her children with a tender protectiveness that could turn to ferocity should they ever be threatened. She felt the same intense love for the very idea of family. She knew now that she would never leave Farrel no matter what happened, because he was the father and she the mother. Now that her own parents were dead, she felt the importance of that relationship more acutely than ever. She was grateful to Farrel for the good life he had provided her, and his awareness of her feelings made him comfortable enough to be a good husband to her, a good father to the children.

She would always have a special feeling for George. They would always share a secret love. But it would never be allowed to threaten the stability of her home. She knew that George understood, and although at moments she felt a great sorrow that he was not to have the security and comfort of family in the way that she did, she knew it could not be any other way.

George would always be her lover, but Farrel Hurstwood would always be her life.

READ THESE MEDICAL BLOCKBUSTERS!

FICTION FOR TODAY'S WOMAN